The Quality of Mercy

Barry Unsworth was born in 1930 in Durham. He was the author of many novels, including *Pascali's Island*, which was shortlisted for the 1980 Booker Prize; *Stone Virgin* (1985); *Sacred Hunger*, which was joint winner of the 1992 Booker Prize; *Morality Play*, which was shortlisted for the 1995 Booker Prize; *Losing Nelson* (1999); *The Songs of the Kings* (2002); *The Ruby in Her Navel* (2006); *Land of Marvels* (2009); and *The Quality of Mercy* (2011), which was shortlisted for The Walter Scott Prize for historical fiction. Barry Unsworth died in 2012.

ALSO BY BARRY UNSWORTH

Praise for *The Quality of Mercy*

'Readers new to Unsworth need not hesitate about starting here. *The Quality of Mercy* stands alone as yet another example of the author's extraordinary ability to turn dry history into dramatic narrative ... It ought to be obvious who the villains and heroes are in this novel, but Unsworth takes great delight in wrong-footing the reader ... *The Quality of Mercy* is ultimately a novel about sympathy and compassion. With so much happening on the page that is dramatic and plot-based – the many different narrative threads eventually tie together in an entirely satisfying fashion – it could be easy to overlook the instances of quiet psychological transformation that give this novel its particular power.'
Christopher Potter, *Sunday Times Culture*

'What a treat to come upon that rare thing: a proper, old-fashioned, omniscient narrator. Barry Unsworth's new novel – a sequel to his 1992 Booker Prize-winner *Sacred Hunger* – is written with the luxurious assurance of a narrator who knows what's ahead, can sketch in the historical context and will tell you all you need to know about the landscape and the weather. It means that, whatever else you feel as you read *The Quality of Mercy*, you do feel in safe hands ... it is deeply sentimental, at times robustly comic ... This is a silkily written potboiler, wonderfully well-realised, entirely engrossing.'
Sam Leith, *Financial Times*

'*The Quality of Mercy* is the work of one who is both artist and craftsman. There is not a page without interest, not a sentence that rings false. It is gripping and moving, a novel about justice which is worthy of that theme. In short, it is a tremendous achievement, as good as anything this great novelist has written.'
Allan Massie, *The Scotsman*

'[Unsworth] is a historical novelist of a reliably old-fashioned sort: the writer who offers a plausible recreation of a bygone age and animates it with people whose motivations are consistent with the tenor of their time, while noting that the past is never neutral and that the behaviour of the men and women who wander about in it is there to be judged ... sequel to 1992's *Sacred Hunger*, has all these qualities in spades ... the fact that his characters never turn into moral ciphers is one of his greatest strengths.'
D. J. Taylor, *Independent on Sunday*

The Quality of Mercy

BARRY UNSWORTH

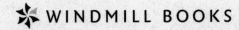
WINDMILL BOOKS

Published by Windmill Books 2012

2 4 6 8 10 9 7 5 3 1

First published in Great Britain in 2011 by Hutchinson

Windmill Books
The Random House Group Limited
20 Vauxhall Bridge Road, London SW1V 2SA

Addresses for companies within The Random House Group Limited can be
found at: www.randomhouse.co.uk/offices.htm

The Random House Group Limited Reg. No. 954009

www.randomhouse.co.uk

A CIP catalogue record for this book
is available from the British Library

ISBN 9780099538226

The Random House Group Limited supports The Forest Stewardship
Council (FSC®), the leading international forest certification organisation.
Our books carrying the FSC label are printed on FSC® certified paper.
FSC is the only forest certification scheme endorsed by the leading
environmental organisations, including Greenpeace.
Our paper procurement policy can be found at:
www.randomhouse.co.uk/environment

Typeset in ITC New Baskerville by Palimpsest Book Production Limited,
Falkirk, Stirlingshire

Printed and bound by CPI Group (UK) Ltd, Croydon, CR0 4YY

For Aira

Love to faults is always blind;
Always is to joy inclin'd,
Lawless, wing'd, and unconfin'd,
And breaks all chains from every mind.

William Blake

Spring and Summer 1767

1

On finding himself thus accidentally free, Sullivan's only thought was to get as far as he could from Newgate Prison while it was still dark. Fiddle and bow slung over his shoulder, he set off northwards, keeping the river at his back. In Holborn he lost an hour, wandering in a maze of courts. Then an old washerwoman, waiting outside a door in the first light of day, set him right for Gray's Inn Lane and the northern outskirts of the city.

Once sure of his way, he felt his spirits rise and he stepped out eagerly enough. Not that he had much, on the face of things, to be blithe about. These last days of March were bitterly cold and he had no coat, only the thin shirt and sleeveless waistcoat and cotton trousers issued to him on the ship returning from Florida. His shoes had been made for a man with feet of a different calibre; on him they contrived to be too loose at the heel and too tight across the toes. The weeks of prison food had weakened him. He was a fugitive, he was penniless, he was assailed by periodic shudders in this rawness of the early morning.

All the same, Sullivan counted his blessings as he walked along. He had his health still; there was nothing amiss with him that a bite to eat wouldn't put right. He would find shelter in Durham if he could get there. And there was a grace on him, he had been singled out. It was not given to many just to stroll out of prison like that. Strolling through the gates . . . His teeth chattered. 'Without so much as a kiss my arse,' he said aloud. In Florida he had developed a habit of talking to himself, as had most of the people of the settlement. No, he thought, it was a stroke of luck beyond the mortal; the Blessed Virgin had opened the gates to him. A sixpenny candle if I get through this. Best tallow . . . He thought of the holy flame of it and tried in his mind to make the flame warm him.

He did not think of the future otherwise, except as a hope of survival. There was an element missing from his nature that all wise persons are agreed is essential for the successful self-governance of the individual within society, and that is the ability to make provision, to plan ahead. This, however, is the doctrine of the privileged. The destitute and dispossessed are lucky if they can turn their thoughts from a future unlikely to offer them benefit. Sullivan knew in some part of his mind that evading recapture would put him at risk of death in this weather, with no money and no refuge. But he was at large, he was on the move, the threat of the noose was not so close. It was enough.

An hour's walking brought him to the rural edges of London, among the market gardens and brick kilns north of Gray's Inn Fields. And it was now that he had his second great stroke of luck. As he was making his way through narrow lanes with occasional low shacks on either side where the smallholders and cow keepers slept during the summer months, at a sudden turning he came upon a man lying full length on his back across the road.

He stopped at some paces off. It was a blind bend, and an early cart could come rounding it at any moment. 'This is not the place to stretch out,' he said. 'You will get your limbs destroyed.' But he did not go nearer for the moment because he had remembered a trick like that: you bend over in emulation of the Good Samaritan, and you get a crack on the head. 'I am not worth robbin',' he said.

A half-choked breath was the only answer. The man's face had a purplish, mottled look; his mouth hung open and his eyes were closed. Across the space of freezing air between them an effluvium of rum punch came to Sullivan's nostrils. 'I see well that you have been overtook by drink,' he said. 'The air is dancin' with the breath of it over your head. We will have to shift you off the road.'

He took the man under the armpits and half lifted, half dragged him round so that he was lying along the bank side, out of the way of the wheel ruts. While this was taking place, the man grunted twice, uttered some sounds of startlement and made a deep snoring noise. His body was heavy and inert, quite helpless either to assist or obstruct the process of his realignment.

'Well, my friend,' Sullivan said, 'you have taken a good tubful, you have.' The exertion had warmed him a little. He hesitated for a moment, then laid bow and fiddle against the bank side and sat down close to the recumbent man. From this vantage point he looked around him. A thin plume of smoke was rising from somewhere among the frosted fields beyond the shacks. There was no other sign of life anywhere, no human stirring. A faint sun swam among low clouds; there was no warmth in it, but the touch was enough to wake a bird to singing somewhere – he could hear it but not see it. 'There is stories everywhere, but we often get only the middle parts,' he said. The man was well dressed, in worsted trousers, stout leggings and boots, and a square-cut, bottle-green coat with brass buttons. 'Those are fine buttons,' Sullivan said. 'I wonder if you could make me iver a loan now? I am hard-pressed just at present, speakin' frankly, man to man.'

The man made no answer to this, but when Sullivan began to go through his pockets, he sighed and choked a little and made a motion with his left arm as if warding off some incubus. His purse contained eighteen shillings and ninepence – Sullivan had to count the money twice before he could believe it. Eight weeks' pay aboard ship! He extracted coins to the value of nine shillings and returned the purse to its pocket. 'I leave you the greater half,' he said.

Again, at this intimacy of touch, the man stirred, and this time his eyes opened briefly. They were bloodshot and vague and sad. He had lost his hat in the fall; it lay on the road beyond him. His goat's-hair wig had slipped sideways; it glistened with wet, and the sparse, gingerish wisps of his own hair curled out damply below it.

'I have nothin' to write with an' neither have you,' Sullivan said, 'an' we have niver a scrap of paper between us, or I would leave you a note of hand for the money.' He had never learned to write, but knew this for the proper form. 'Or yet again,' he said, 'if you were in a more volatile state you could furnish me with your place of residence. As things are we will just have to leave it unsatisfactory.'

The man's face had returned to sleep. Sullivan nodded at it in valediction and set off again along the lane. He had not gone far, however, when it came to him that he had been the saviour of this man and that nine shillings was hardly an adequate reward for such a service. To rate a man's life at only nine shillings was offensive and belittling to that man. Any human creature possessed of a minimum of self-respect would set a higher value on himself than that. Even he, Sullivan, who had no fixed abode and no coat to his back, would consider nine shillings too little. If this man's faculties were not so much ravaged and under the weather, he would be bound to agree that eighteen shillings met the case better.

Full of these thoughts, he retraced his steps. The man appeared to have made some brief struggle in the interval, though motionless again now. His wig had fallen off completely and lay bedraggled on the bank side like a bird's nest torn from the bare hedge and flung down there. His hair was thin; pinkish scalp showed through the flat crown. His breath made a slight bubbling sound.

'I do not want you to go through life feelin' convicted of ingratitude,' Sullivan said. 'You may take the view that death was problematical, but that I rescued you from the hazard of mutilation you are bound to agree on.' The purse was of good leather. Sullivan kept hold of it having first restored the ninepence to the man's waistcoat pocket. 'In takin' these shillin's I am doublin' your value,' he said. He was silent for some moments, listening intently. He thought he had heard the rattle of wheels. He went to the bend and surveyed the long curve of the road: no sign of anything. His eyes watered and he was again racked with cold. He clutched at himself and slapped his arms and sides in an effort to get some warmth into them. Still striking at himself, he returned to the victim of his kindness. 'I had a coat once with fine brass buttons on it,' he said. 'But the coat was stole off me back aboard ship on the false grounds that it was verminous, an' the bosun kept me buttons though they brought him no luck. One I found again after twelve years through a blessin' that was on me, but I gave that to a man who was dyin'. It is only justice that you should reinstate me buttons, havin' saved you from injury or worse. If I had a knife about me I could snip them off, but lookin' at it another way I am not the man to desecrate a fine coat . . . Here, hold steady.' Feeling the coat being eased off him, the man struggled up to a sitting position, glared before him for some moments, then fell back against the bank.

The coat was rather too big at the shoulders for Sullivan, a fact that surprised and puzzled him, conflicting with his sense that this encounter by the wayside was perfect in all its details of mutual benefit. 'You will be a local man,' he said. 'You will not have far to go. I am bound for the County of Durham, an' that is a tidy step.' He had been unlacing the boots as he spoke. Now he raised the man's legs to pull them off, first right, then left. The thick legs fell heavily to earth again when released. The man's eyes were open, but they were not looking at anything. The boots fitted Sullivan perfectly. He slipped his shoes on the other's feet. 'Each man will keep to his own trousers,' he said magnanimously. In fact, he had grown hasty in the lacing of his new boots, and was eager to be off. He straightened up, took his bow and fiddle, and moved away into the middle of the lane. 'The morning is not so cold now,' he said. 'I have been your benefactor and will remember you as mine.'

No sound at all came from the man. He had slumped back against the bank. His head had fallen forward and slightly sideways, towards his left shoulder. He had the look of total meekness that the hanged possess, and perhaps it was this that brought a sudden tightness to Sullivan's throat and made him delay some moments longer.

'At another time I would have saved your life free of charge,' he said. 'You are gettin' me off to a good start an' I am grateful.' Still he paused, however. He had no natural propensity to theft, and there was the important question of justice. Because of him this man's waking would be unhappy. He was owed some further explanation. 'I had a shipmate,' he said. 'A Durham man, name of Billy Blair. Him an' me were close. We were pressed aboard ship together in Liverpool. She was a slaver, bound for the Guinea Coast. We took the Negroes on but we niver got to Jamaica with them, we came to grief on the coast of Florida. Them that were left lived on there, black and white together. We had reasons for stayin' where we were, but I will not occupy your time with them, as bein' irrelevant to the point at issue. Billy sometimes talked about the place where he was born an' about his family. He ran away to sea when he was a lad of fourteen, to get away from minin' the coal, so he said. He was always intendin' to go back some day, but he niver did. An' now he niver will. I made a vow that if iver I got free of me chains an' had power over me own feet again I would find Billy's folks and tell them what befell him. An' now I am bound to it, d'ye see, I can't go back on it because me vow was heard, the gates were opened to me.'

The hat was still lying there. He picked it up and set it firmly on the man's lowered head. 'I have spoke to you in confidence, man to man,' he said. 'I am trustin' you not to promulgate me words to any third party. An' now I will bid you farewell.'

He walked for an hour or so in the sullen light of morning. Nothing passed him on the road and he met no one. At a junction of lanes there was a huddle of houses and a small inn. He was hungry but he did not dare to stop. One way led to Watford, the other to St Albans. He took a shilling from his new purse, and tossed it. It came down heads. St Albans then.

A mile further on he came up with a wagon setting off north with a load of shoring posts. A threepenny piece got him a place up beside the driver. As the wagon jolted along, he thought of his luck again and of poor Billy Blair and of the meekness of the hanged. After a while he slept.

2

Late in the afternoon of the day of that fortunate wayside encounter, a Durham coalminer named James Bordon, who was married to Billy Blair's sister Nan, was standing near the head of a steep-sided and thickly wooded ravine known locally as the Dene. He was looking in the direction of the sea, which at that distance was no more than a change in the quality of the light, a pale suffusion low in the sky. At his back, little more than half a mile away, was the colliery village of Thorpe, where he lived, though nothing of it could be seen from where he was standing; cottages and surrounding fields belonged to the upper world; here below, vagrant streams, over great spans of time, had gouged through the bolder clay and limestone to make a deep and narrow chasm.

Bordon had not attended any school, and he could not read or write. He was ignorant of this long scooping out of the rock, the millions of years that had gone into it. But he knew the Dene with a knowledge no study of geology could have given him. He had known it all his life; he had played here as a child, made tree houses with other children, fished for sticklebacks and newts in the beck that run through the gorge below him, slate grey in colour now, under this lowering sky. Childhood had ended for him at the age of seven, when his father, in accordance with the general habit, and as his own father had done, had taken him down to work in the mine. His father was gone now; he had died as a good number of miners did, his lungs choked up with all the years of inhaling flint dust.

Bordon had come here straight from the pit, as he sometimes

did – more often nowadays than before, as if from a need that was growing. He was black with coal dust; the acrid smell of it, together with the sweat of his labour, rose to him from the folds of his clothing, thick cotton shirt and trousers, leather waistcoat and apron and knee pads. For fourteen years now he had been a full pitman, a hewer, cutting out the coal from the face. He had worked for ten hours that day, starting at six in the morning, and he had done his stint – he was not paid by the hour but bound by contract to cut coal enough to fill six corves, thirty hundredweight, in one working shift, or suffer loss of wages if he came short of this. The condition met – and the judgement was his – he was free to leave the coal lying for the putters to load into the corves and drag to the pithead.

He stood still now, letting the peace and silence of the place settle around him, and the strange sense of a stronger existence that came with them. He could not easily have found words for this. He was unpractised in speaking about feelings, and there was no one, in any case, with whom he might have made the attempt, without fear of being thought soft-headed. But it was mainly the reason why he came to this place, the sense of intensi- fied life that visited him when he stood alone here. Partly he knew it, though confusedly, for the shelter afforded by the open sky, the removal of a roof too close, the fact that he could raise his head and shift his limbs freely, the steady light after the hours of kneeling with hammer and wedge at the narrow seam, in the close heat, by the variable flame of the candle.

But it was more than this, more than mere awareness of freedom; he felt a gathering of the heart and pulse of his exist- ence, stronger now for the faint sounds that came to him as he stood here, sounds of other existences blending with his own, voices of children from somewhere among the trees, the calling of curlews from the fields in that other world above, the distant hiss and clatter of the pump bringing up water from a flooded shaft somewhere among the mine workings.

The children's voices came to him again, too faint for him to know whether happy or angry. They were lower down, some- where close to the bank of the stream. Down there, further into the Dene, the ground levelled out and the beck made a turn southward, out of the path of the ice-laden winds that sometimes came in from the sea and tore through the long hollow of the glen. Here, in this sheltered loop of land, the climate was different, milder; there were zones of air that never felt the frost; willowherb grew here and wild daffodils, and a thick vegetation of ferns and flowering grasses covered the ground. Two acres, roughly speaking. Fertile, well-watered, level ground, screened from the worst of winter, designed by nature for a market garden . . .

It was a thought that came often to him, more a kind of vision than a thought. It had accompanied his life, or so it seemed – he could not remember when first this picture had come into his mind, the flowering fruit trees, the green rows well hoed and neat, the pit pony he would rescue from toiling in darkness to carry his produce along the stream side to the coast. It was a vision orderly and beautiful, and it came to him not only here, though here it was stronger, here it seemed almost possible of fulfilment. He might think of it as he was falling asleep, or as he trudged to work in the early morning. Sometimes, at the end of a stint, when his eyes were tired, the shifting glints of the coal seemed like stirring leaves and gleams of light on water.

Occasionally he had spoken to his eldest son, Michael, about this piece of land, not directly as an ambition of ownership but as representing a happy state of existence, a labour that made sense, being on ground that was your own. In fact, the Dene, and all the lands surrounding it as far as the coast, and all the coal that lay beneath, had belonged for several generations to the Spenton family, whose mansion and park and gardens and lake lay on a commanding rise of ground some two miles from where he was standing.

The clouds to the west lifted suddenly and a shaft of sunlight fell across the wooded incline. The voices of the children came to him again. He descended some yards along the narrow path that led through trees down the side of the glen. His sight was confused by the gleam of sunlight on the dark, clustering foliage of the yew trees that grew here on the upper slopes, and the mist of green formed by the first buds of leaf on the beeches. After some moments he came to a point from which he could look down to the valley floor, see again the cold grey of the beck, too far below to be touched by the sunshine, though the change of light had made it possible to see the movement of the current, a whiteness at the edges where the water was whisked in eddies.

Then, quite suddenly, he saw the children; they were at the stream side, five diminutive figures, all boys, crouching by the water. Something about their gestures and voices, the way they crouched so intently, looking down, told him that a competition of some sort was going on. Then he saw a fleeting gleam of white, then another and another: they were racing boats as far as the overhang of rock some dozen yards further down, where the stones in the stream bed rose to the surface and broke the current. He remembered doing the same as a child – just there, just in that same place. You took some loose bark from a silver birch, stripped the pith and set your boat on its bevelled side, well clear of the bank . . . At the same moment that he was recalling this he saw that one of the boys was his youngest son, Percy, who would soon be seven years old.

With some impulse of secrecy, or tact, he turned aside, began to go back the way he had come. As he reached the level of the rough pasture above, the hollow from which he had emerged closed behind him, to be replaced by a new order of familiarity, the slate roofs of the village, the smoke from the coal fires burning in the houses, the fumes of the open salt pans that lay beyond, swathing the houses themselves and all the air above and around them in a mist that was sour and all-pervasive.

Entering the lane that led to the village, he fell in with a miner named Saul Parrish, who lived close by him, he too returning from work and black with the dust of the coal. As they drew nearer to the first houses they heard a sudden outcry, the voices of women raised in shrill protest, the rarer voices of men. A strong smell of excrement was carried to them. Then they saw the coop cart and the black dray horse and the lines of washing running down the alleys below the houses.

'They are aboot the emptyin' of the netties,' Parrish said, in the tone of pleased authority that comes to one who after study has found the answer to a difficult problem.

It was a note of self-satisfaction peculiar to Parrish. And perhaps it was this, the habit of delivering information obvious to all as if it were a special shaft of insight, that caused the beginnings of anger in Bordon, an anger not primarily directed at

Parrish but at the tangle and confusion he knew to be reigning there in the narrow lanes, the washing lines caught up, clothes in danger of soiling, the weaving of the men with the stinking buckets, the confused upbraiding of the women, his wife Nan among them.

'A can see that for mesen,' he said. 'A dinna need nay tellin'.'

The privies were in the yards behind the houses; they were emptied every so often into a cart specially designed for the purpose, high-sided, fitted with a huge tin basin with a sliding cover, to be borne away and tipped into a deep and monstrously reeking cesspool in the moorland some miles away.

'Anyone can see what they are doin',' Bordon said. 'What a want to know is why them fellers always come to us on a washin' day. Tha never knows when they'll come next, but tha knows it will always be on a washin' day, so they can clag everythin' up.'

Parrish's eyes were bloodshot, after the hours of close and dusty work. They gleamed now in the blackened face with the light of superior wisdom. 'Why, man,' he said, 'they have their hours, as we arl do, rain or shine, that's the way of it. 'Tis arl planned out by the manage.'

'The manage?' Bordon felt the rage rising in him, stiffening his jaw. 'Is tha tellin' me that the manage plans it out so them fellers always come to empty the shit in the village of Thorpe on a bleddy washin' day? What is the manage, is it God? There's someone there has a grudge against us.'

He had spoken loudly, and a man who had approached without their noticing, so intent were they on their talk, now spoke from behind him. 'Who is that taking the name of God in vain?'

Turning, Bordon saw the very man least welcome to him at such a moment. It was Samuel Hill, who always had to be interfering and putting his nose in, judging everything and awarding points this way and that. He it was who always tried to set himself up as arbiter in the fist fights that were sometimes chosen, when words failed, as the means of settling an argument. Because of this mania for sitting in judgement he was generally referred to – but never by Bordon – as Arbiter Hill, a title of which he was proud. He had been to a charity school and could read and write after a fashion, an advantage that had got him a place as assistant overman, tallying the loaded corves as they were dragged by the putters from the coalface to the pit bottom.

'Tha takes everythin' personal,' Parrish said. He never liked his words of wisdom to be questioned, and he reacted now with some rage of his own to the rage he had heard in Bordon's voice. 'Tha brings everythin' back to theesen. Does tha think they do it out of spite?'

He turned to Hill. 'He is sayin' there is a grudge against us in the manage because they always comes to empty the privies on a washin' day. Them fellers empty the buckets in pit villages as far as the banks of the Wear, but he thinks Thorpe is the only colliery in the County of Durham that has shithouses in the yards.'

'I think I've understood the issue.' Hill had somehow managed to insert himself between the two disputants. 'Here on my right,' he said, 'in the person of Saul Parrish, we are hearing the opinion that the workings of authority as regards the emptying of the netties in Thorpe do not take account of the likes of you and me, having a wider view of things, ranging farther afield and emptying more netties in the course of a week than what we can imagine. On my left, we have James Bordon, who is stating that there is more to the emptying of the netties than meets the eye, there being some reason lying below why they always come to us on a washing day. There is the further question, not so far touched upon, whether they always *do* come on a washing day or whether it only seems so because of the nuisance. That is the position as it stands at the present time. Now, lads, box on.'

But Bordon's rage had died as he listened, and weariness had returned. The voices of quarrel still came from the village, sounds ugly and discordant, so much at odds with those he had emerged from, which had seemed part of the silence. 'Take it personal?' he said. 'The manage dinna pay them fellers. Him that owns the mine, Lord Spenton, he dinna pay neether. Every man jack of us is docked tuppence a week, as you know well, Saul Parrish. That is personal enough, an't it? Them that pays should have a say in the runnin' of it.'

'It's as well nobody but us is listening,' Hill said. 'Those are words that could be took wrong.'

Bordon shrugged. 'Bad cess to them that would take it so,' he said. He had long suspected Hill for a tale-bearer. Then, realising he had made a sort of joke, though by accident, he smiled a little. 'You two gan on,' he said. 'A'll stay here till they've done.'

He lingered in the lane for some time longer, greeting the men who passed, but remaining alone. Only when the cart was gone did he start to make his way towards the village. He knew now, rage spent, that he had been wrong in what he had said about the nettie-men; he knew they came on various days, he knew there was no plot. He had been angered at the sight and sound of them because washing day was always Saturday and it was the day he looked forward to most in the working week, the clean shirt and trousers, the prospect of rest next day.

There was free coal for all the mining families and fires were kept up all day, in all seasons. Nan was waiting for him with the water already heated for his bath. She was the only woman of the house; their one daughter had died in early childhood. The two older sons worked longer hours than their father, fourteen hours a day, dragging the loaded baskets along the workways from the coalface. It would be after dark when they returned; at this season they only saw full daylight on Sundays.

The hip bath was brought out and set before the fire, the hot water poured out from the big copper pan and mixed with the cold brought in from the well in the alley. His clean clothes were laid over a kitchen chair; there was the pipe to enjoy afterwards. He looked at Nan's face as she ministered to him, and felt a concern for her that came close to sorrow. She had had to endure that chaos and rage together with the other women, after the long day of washing, the poss tub, the mangle, the tall lines to reach up to. There was weariness in her face, but no trace of anger; she was intent, pouring clean water from a tin mug over his shoulders and back.

'A saw our Percy in the Dene,' he said. 'He was racin' with birch boats in the beck. A dinna know if he saw me watchin'.'

'He wouldna have knowed it was you, all black from the pit. Men are different inside of them but tha canna tell much difference on the outside till they wash the coal off.'

Different inside they were indeed, she thought, whether clean washed or not. Bordon was subject to rages and there was violence in him, but it was never directed at her. From the day she had agreed to marry him he had tried to protect her as far as he could, he had wanted her to stop working at the pithead, sorting the shale and slate from the heaped coal, work she had started at the age of nine. It had meant a sacrifice of money, but he had insisted. There were some who made their wives labour at the mine even when they were advanced in pregnancy . . .

His hair had thinned in these last two or three years; she could feel the small ridges of the scars that ran over his scalp. He was taller than average, and the only protection any of them had was the cloth cap; he did not always remember to stoop enough, and so he banged and bloodied his head against the roofs of the galleries as he passed.

'It minded me of doin' the same when a was that age,' he said. He turned his head in an effort to look at her through the blur of the water. Percy's age was frequently on their minds nowadays; this summer would see the end of childhood for him, set him on the long course of becoming a pitman. It was not something to be much talked about, any more than other obvious facts of life. Percy himself was ready to go down, as his brothers had done before him; but he was the last of their children, and both felt a sense of regret they had not felt for the others.

'He should be gettin' back home by now,' Nan said. Then, after a moment, 'He does well to play while he can.'

'Just in that selfsame place,' he said, closing his eyes, seeing the place again. 'The beck runs fast there.'

He was dressed and had finished his tea by the time Michael and David came home. They came back together, as happened now and then, when their hours of work coincided.

There was no hot water for them – that was the privilege of the head of the family. They took buckets to the well that was shared by all the houses in their alley, brought the water back to their own yard and washed down there. Their only light was a candle-lamp, but it was enough for Michael to see that his twelve-year-old brother, with the coal dust washed away, had livid bruises on his arms and legs. 'How did tha get them marks?' he said.

David was reluctant to say. Stoicism came naturally to him; bruises of whatever kind were part of the life of the pit; it did not seem manly to complain, he did not want to look a weakling in his admired elder brother's eyes. But as they fumbled their working clothes back on again in the cold yard, Michael persisted, and finally got the answer that confirmed the suspicions he had held for some time now. David worked as putter's mate with a man named Daniel Walker; together they loaded the coal hacked out by the hewers, together they hauled and pushed the loaded sledges along the gallery ways to the pit bottom, where the quantities were tallied and the corves winched up to the surface. This was piecework; they were paid by the quantity of the coal they shifted. It seemed that Walker, thinking to spur David on to greater efforts, frequently struck him with his fists on the arms and shoulders and kicked him on the legs.

'Is tha doin' the best tha can to share the work?'

'Yes,' David said, with some indignation at this slur on him. 'A canna do more, a canna gan faster.'

'An' yon fool thinks he can make you do more by hittin' you?'

David made no reply to this, standing there with his face averted, as if he had done some wrong. And this unhappy silence, this childish guilt at the fault of another, moved Michael and angered him at the same time. 'Right then,' he said. 'A'll have a word or two with Walker.'

3

It was two days before Erasmus Kemp learned of Sullivan's escape. The news was delivered by the barrister in charge of his case, Thomas Pike, who had himself only heard of it the day before.

'Why was I not told at once?' It was always congenial to Kemp to have someone before him on whom to lay the blame, and Pike had now to withstand the glare of the dark eyes in the level-browed, handsome face. Twenty years Kemp's senior, one of the most eminent advocates in London, he had nevertheless to call on reserves of fortitude to meet this regard without demeaning himself by lowering his eyes. The passionate suddenness of his client's moods still sometimes took him by surprise, combined as it was with a certain rigidness of bearing, slight but noticeable, unusual in so young a man. No doubt due to pride and self-consequence, the lawyer had thought – Kemp was known to be extremely rich; but there was a guardedness in it, as if he were afraid of jarring some old hurt.

'That is a question for the prison authorities, sir, not for me,' he said in a tone he took care to make neutral.

Kemp checked the angry response that rose to his lips at this impertinence – for he took it as such. Calculation was as prompt with him as rage; Pike was a highly successful lawyer, prosperous enough to allow himself the liberty to take offence and abandon the case if he so chose. A mistake to antagonise him . . . His very presence there, in his client's place of business instead of his own, constituted no small concession.

'How did it happen?'

'It seems that one of the debtors was playing host in his

room in the prison, one of the upper rooms of course, those on the fourth floor, well removed from all the misery below. Friends of his and women of the streets, you understand. They ordered up cakes and wine in good quantity.' Pike paused to allow himself a discreet smile. 'They cannot pay their debts, but they can always contract new ones, even in prison. Some musicians were ordered for the dancing. Four, I believe. The fiddler was drunk on arrival, though no one seems to have noticed it. He was handed a bumper and it was one too many for him, he could not keep on his feet. There is no dancing without a fiddle, and this Sullivan, who apparently is noted as a fiddler, was released from his chains and brought up to take the man's place. The jollities went on till well past midnight. In the meantime the jailers were changed and no one thought to pass on the word about Sullivan. So when the musicians finally left, he left with them.'

'Why was he not immediately pursued?'

'This was in the early hours of the morning. By the time it was discovered the man would have been well clear of the prison, and there was no way of knowing which road he had taken. Sir, there are not officers enough in London to conduct a search of that kind.'

A short laugh broke from Kemp, though his face showed no change. 'I cross the Atlantic to bring these men to justice. I spend weeks in Florida, enrolling the force of troops I shall need. I spend further weeks discovering the whereabouts of the miscreants and tracking them down. All this at great expense and to the neglect of my business. And now this wretch strolls out of prison, and no one thinks any more of it till next day, several hours later.'

'That seems to be the case, yes.'

'I shall lodge a complaint. I shall see that those responsible are dismissed. You will understand my displeasure, sir. I have related the circumstances in which my father's ship was lost.'

The lawyer nodded. Even without this relation he would have known a great deal of the case. The impending trial was complicated; in fact, there would be two hearings, one civil, the second criminal. It had aroused considerable interest in legal circles, and the London newspapers had all contained accounts of it, embellished by a good deal of gossip. Kemp's career had become public property in the course of the last two weeks, described in detail, the obscure beginnings in Liverpool, son of a bankrupt cotton merchant, the marrying into money in the person of Sir Hugo Jarrold's daughter, an unhappy match by all accounts. Then the fortune made in sugar, the partnership in his father-in-law's bank – he was head of the bank now, the old man never appeared in public, it was thought that his mind had gone. Kemp had returned from Florida to news of his wife's death . . .

'I swore I would see them all hanged,' Kemp said. 'The loss of ship and cargo ruined my father. And now one of them walks free, as if he had done no more than raid a chicken house.'

'Well, he could be hanged for that, as the times go,' Pike said. He remained silent for some moments, regarding the man opposite him. The bitterness of these last words had brought Kemp forward in his chair. He had raised his hands in speaking, causing pale ripples of reflection on the polished ebony surface of the desk at which he was sitting. He had a habit of occasional rapid gesture unusual among English people, at odds with that slight stiffness of bearing. The darkness of his eyes and hair, and the olive tint of his complexion, these too were unusual. He was dressed with sober elegance in clothes that were fashionable but not ostentatiously so: a solitaire in the cravat, coat of dark blue velvet, cut away at the front to show a white silk waistcoat, unembroidered, buttoned in the new style, all the way down to the hem; he wore no wig and no powder on the hair, which was tied behind with a single ribbon. It was the dress of a man who gave a great deal of thought to the figure he made.

'They will hang, be assured of it,' the lawyer said. 'They killed the captain, but that was in the course of a scuffle, confused in its nature – it might be difficult to establish responsibility. No, it is the sailing off with the cargo of Negroes that will be viewed more seriously, as constituting piracy, an aggravated form of theft, an outrage against property. There is no country in Europe where a man or woman or child, especially of the poorer classes, is more likely to be hanged for offences against property than this great country of ours. According to Blackstone's Commentaries, that are presently being published, there are in this Year of Grace 1767 no fewer than one hundred and sixty capital statutes, an increase of a hundred since the beginning of the century. And they are growing day by day. Murder, rape, maliciously cutting hopbinds, destroying the heads of fish ponds, waging war against the King in his realm, all are equally likely to get you standing room on the cart to Tyburn. In theory, at least – whether juries will convict on a lesser charge is another matter, of course.'

'It is their duty to convict if that is the law,' Kemp said. He was largely in favour of severe punishments, and had not liked the other's lightness of tone. Belonging as Pike did to a trade that could only profit from this proliferation of capital offences, such levity seemed like ingratitude. 'It deters people from committing felonies,' he said. 'It nurtures respect for our institutions, which I believe are the envy of the world.'

Pike had sensed this disapproval, understood it, felt a certain contempt of it. Not much humour there, not much play of mind. He himself had plenty of both – too much, some of his colleagues thought. 'We need to make jokes about the law, sir,' he said. 'It belongs to the profession. Like the doctors, you know. Who better fitted than they to make jokes about sickness?'

He paused on this with a certain sense of constraint, recalling only now that Kemp's cousin, a man named Matthew Paris, had been the doctor on the ship, had taken part in the mutiny, in fact had played a leading role in it, had been wounded when the people of the settlement were captured, and had died of the wound. The embarrassment was needless, however; his remark had been so foreign to Kemp's way of viewing the world that he had failed altogether to understand it, and so made no reply, obliging the lawyer to speak again, before the silence could become oppressive. He could not leave yet, there were things still to be imparted to this difficult client of his. 'Well,' he said, 'it deters those who are hanged, there is no smallest doubt of that. And of course it is an encouraging mark of our national prosperity.'

Kemp stared. 'How do you intend that remark?'

'Sir, this vast increase in the application of the death penalty has coincided with a notable influx of wealth through growth in our manufactures and maritime commerce. To put the matter simply, there is constantly more capital circulating in the country, and therefore constantly more property to protect. Property is the thing, sir, not the life of the subject. Let me give you an example.

Not so long ago, the servant of a gentleman in Taunton, possessed of some grudge, attacked his master with a carving knife, wounding him in a dozen places. He did not die, being blessed with a strong constitution, but he came very close to it. Well, the man was hanged of course, but you will not easily divine why.'

'Why, for attempted murder, I suppose.'

'No, sir. The law we serve with such devotion is not always so simple. They hanged him for attempted burglary. In order to gain access to his master he had to enter by the door that led to his master's chamber. There was no forcing of locks – all he did was lift the latch and go in.'

Kemp regarded the lawyer for some moments without speaking. The instinctive antagonism of his nature, a constitutional unwillingness to react as was expected or desired, unless there was something to be gained, kept his face impassive now. Pike was acting for him, they had agreed on a fee, he saw no cause for seeking to please Pike by raising eyebrows or uttering exclamations of astonishment. 'So long as he was hanged,' he said, 'that answers the matter well enough.'

'Some might take that view, yes. I have been wondering . . . If you wanted the men hanged, the remainder of the crew, I mean, why not see to the business in Florida? It is a British possession by exchange of Havana with the Spanish. The Admiralty has jurisdiction there, no whit less than here in London. And procedures are simpler in the colonies. They could have been hauled off and hanged from one day to the next.'

Kemp hesitated before replying; in fact, at first he was minded not to reply at all. He had never, from earliest youth, liked to avow his motives for anything, feeling it to be somehow undignified, or even demeaning, as if he were submitting himself to judgement. His cousin had been wounded in the capture and had died of the wound before he could be got to the hangman in Florida or anywhere else. Kemp had felt this keenly at the time as a failure on his own part. His view of it had changed since then, the failure was tinged with sorrow now, though he could not bring himself to admit blame or contrition – that would be to betray the mission of justice that had impelled him. He had been guided by principle in bringing the men back to England, and he was a man who set great store by principle.

'That was my first thought,' he said. 'But then it seemed wrong to have them tried and executed in that hasty, scrambling sort of fashion. Twelve years had passed since they took refuge in Florida. I judged it more in keeping that they should stand trial and be hanged here, in full public view, so they should serve as an example of the workings of justice, and make it known on every hand that punishment is certain, whatever the time that has elapsed.'

It was Pike's turn to hesitate now. He was not cynical exactly, but he had seen too many courtrooms to believe altogether in the principle of justice as a determining force in legal process. 'Worthy aims, worthy aims, upon my soul,' he said at last.

'Have there been some further developments? Other than the escape of this scoundrelly fiddler, I mean. Is it not high time that these men came before a jury?'

'We have been successful in our application for the release from prison of the first mate, Barton. As you know, he is turning evidence against the others on the promise of a pardon. His evidence cannot be presented in court while he is in confinement, since it might seem that his words are aimed at securing his own release.' Here the lawyer permitted himself a pause and a smile, though he made no attempt to share the smile with his client. 'That his words will have already served to secure his release is an entirely different matter, of course. He has undertaken to make a written deposition. It seems that he can write.'

'Yes, he told me he could read and write.' With the words there came to Kemp a memory of the mate as he had been aboard ship, when the proposition to betray his shipmates had first been put to him. In the narrow confines of the cabin, Barton, brought down from the open deck, had shivered like a dog and gulped down the rum and talked of his sainted mother, who had taught him to read at her knee. A reek of sweat and fish oil had come from the man's body as he sat across the table. They had used the oil against mosquitoes in that land of swamp and lagoon. Kemp's nostrils contracted involuntarily at the memory. Barton had been naked above the waist except for a scrap of red silk round his neck; and this degraded dandyism had stayed with Kemp as somehow marking the mate's readiness to preserve himself, to serve new masters. How glad he had been to get this evidence against his cousin. Any instrument, however base, however loathsome. Matthew had still been alive then . . .

'That is all satisfactory,' the lawyer said. 'But this case has aroused widespread attention, and I have learned something this morning that might complicate matters and make it more difficult to get a speedy judgement.'

'What is that?'

'Frederick Ashton and some others of similar persuasion have taken the case up.'

The name, coming thus unexpectedly, caught Kemp off guard, and he glanced aside, a thing unusual with him. He had recently met, and exchanged some words with, this man's sister, Miss Jane Ashton, at the house of a business acquaintance, and her face came vividly to his mind now, the eyes particularly, between grey and green in colour and very direct and unfaltering. She had looked at him without coquetry, without any care to challenge or provoke, though some hint of laughter there had been. No other young woman had regarded him so frankly, none that he could remember. He had felt a need to break that scrutiny and he had found a way of doing this by paying her a compliment on her gown. At this she had smiled and glanced slightly away, and this had seemed to him like something won from her. A smile of good augury, as he thought of it now: not five minutes afterwards his host had told him in private talk that a Lord Spenton, a mine owner, desired to obtain a loan from the bank, thus presenting the kind of investment opportunity that he had long hoped for.

The lawyer had noticed his hesitation and misunderstood it. 'You know the man?'

'We have not met, but I know him by repute.'

'So far he has confined his activities to contesting the right of property in slaves brought to these shores from the West Indies, using the argument that England is the home of freedom and that her laws cannot tolerate one man claiming ownership in another.'

'That is all very well,' Kemp said. 'But they don't understand the workings of money, these people. There might be a hundred blacks brought here in the course of a year, all acquired by purchase. Then there are the numbers already here, probably at least a thousand in London alone. It amounts to a very considerable capital sum. Who is going to compensate the owners?'

'That is a question that causes alarm on all sides,' Pike said. 'Of course, if they were declared to be free upon setting foot on English soil their owners would be obliged to desist from bringing them here.'

'But that would be an unwarranted curtailing of our essential liberties as Englishmen.'

The lawyer's own habit of mind caused him to suspect that there might be some intention of irony in these words, but his client's face had remained completely serious. 'Well,' he said, 'it seems that Ashton is now looking further afield; he is intending to use the case for his own purposes. He has already engaged counsel to defend these men, an unusual step in itself, since they are quite penniless. His lawyers have petitioned for a postponement to allow them to seek material for the defence.'

'Defence? What defence can there possibly be? It is perfectly obvious that the men are guilty.'

'A defence of some kind can always be mounted. But certainly it is difficult to see what line Ashton intends to take. They have no independent witness to call into court. All those on board the ship at the time of the mutiny have either died since, or been resold into slavery in Carolina, or are lying in Newgate Prison facing capital charges. With the exception of our friend Barton, that is, and this Irish fiddler. I suspect Ashton will try to make a single action of it and force a decision on the issue of property.'

'But it is one single action, surely.'

'No, sir, you naturally see it in that light because you think of the felonies that were committed, the murder of the captain, the theft of ship and cargo, the clear intention not to return. But there is an action prior to this one. The mutiny can be said to have begun, and so we shall plead, when your cousin raised his hand against the throwing overboard of the sick Negroes, still alive as they were. We shall have Barton's testimony to support us in this. Now there is no question of felony up to this point, none at all. The slaves were cast into the sea in order to claim the insurance on them.'

'Lawful jettison,' Kemp said. 'There was a shortage of water – barely enough for the crew. Barton will testify to that also. I am fully entitled to the insurance money, every penny of it, as owner of the ship through my father.'

'Quite so, sir, we are in complete accord. But the insurers are contesting the claim, as you know; they will say the jettisoning was not lawful, they will say there was water enough. Now it is in our interest to keep these two actions entirely separate, and seek to have the question of insurance settled in the Court of Common Pleas, not at the Old Bailey, where it might become confused with the criminal charges. We cannot know for the time being what line the defence will take, but I am supposing they will seek to have our arguments of lawful jettison absorbed into what they will see as the essential issue, which is that the jettison would have been unlawful, and even criminal, under any circumstances.'

'How can that be? It makes no sense.'

'Well, I think they will maintain that it is a crime under any circumstances to throw living persons over the deck of a ship on the only grounds that they are sick and like to die.'

'It is a contagion of madness,' Kemp said. 'We are talking about the ship's cargo. The Negroes were acquired by lawful purchase on the Windward Coast of Africa. They were to have been sold at Kingston slave market in accordance with established practice. How can they be regarded as other than cargo?'

He had the sensation, frequent with him since his return, of arguing with himself, or with some shadowy person not quite himself, someone whom he urgently needed to convince, but who constantly framed arguments more weighty than his own. For twelve years, in that wilderness, they had lived free, black and white together. Free but not equal: there must have been struggles for power and precedence among them, this was a natural feature of any human society. But the inequalities, whatever they were, would not have depended on colour or race. And the people had lived in understanding of this; they had shared the women, they had shared the parentage of the children . . .

'It is madness,' he said again.

'Entirely so, sir, we see eye to eye on the matter. But the law has to deal with divergent interests.' The lawyer brought his palms together then slowly moved them apart. 'The law has to stretch, sir,' he said. 'They will maintain that it was murder.'

'Killing the ship's captain when he was about the lawful exercise of his duties, that is not murder, I suppose?'

'They might claim, they *will* claim, that it was justified as preventing the numerous murders that might have followed.'

With this Pike rose to his feet. 'I will not occupy your time any further,' he said. 'I judged it needful that you should know of these developments.' He stood for a moment longer, smiling at Kemp, who had also risen. 'Have no fear,' he said. 'We shall prevail. Property is the key to the business. If they fight us on property they are bound to lose. The Lord Commissioners appointed by the Admiralty will have a high regard for property. We must hope for a judge with good understanding, someone with holdings in the West Indies, or at any rate with a stake in the trade.'

When Pike had gone Kemp returned to his desk and remained there for a time that passed blankly, without his noting it. Then he rose and went to his window and looked down for some moments through the thick distorting glass at the blur of the traffic below. When he turned back towards the room it was for a brief while as though everything in it was strange to him. As if seen for the first time, the framed watercolours, the ledgers and the account books on their shelves, the broad table with its silver-mounted inkstand and its japanned tray, where lay his paper-knife with the mother-of-pearl handle, and his seals, and his ivory paperweight in the form of a Moor's head.

He could find no comfort or reassurance in any of these things, even as their familiarity returned. They expressed him, they consorted with his state, that was all. It was the same with his mansion in St James's Square: silk hangings and ormolu clocks and Italian stucco and mahogany panelling – costly furnishings, as befitted his wealth, but no more to him than that.

He found himself thinking now of his parents' house in Liverpool and of his bedroom there, the things in it that had been dear to him, abetting him in his hopes, consoling him in his disappointments: the silver cockspurs and the brace of duelling pistols on the wall, this the gift of his father; the framed embroidery done by his mother, *Blessed are the Meek*, the words picked out in dark blue stitches surrounded by forget-me-nots and white roses. Like many persons of fanatical character, Kemp was deeply superstitious, though he would have been highly indignant to hear the word applied to him. The objects in that room, so clearly remembered, had solemnised his love for Sarah Walpert and his intention to marry her; they had sorrowed with him at her loss; they had witnessed his vows to go into sugar and repay his father's debts.

The rage was spent in him now, to leave a feeling almost of desolation. It had only been the news of Sullivan's escape that had quickened him to fury. Sullivan, who had been so devoted to Matthew, had attended him when he lay dying. The fellow had had the presumption, in chains with the others as he was, to ask for the return of his fiddle on the grounds that it was personal property. Kemp had remembered this insolence and the look of the man as he made the request, the long, dark hair unkempt, tied back with a ragged scrap of cotton, the blue eyes at once vague and quick-glancing, as if he had glimpsed something splendid the moment before and was trying to find it again. There had been tears in those eyes when Matthew was nearing his end, and Kemp had felt it as an insult, this grief for his cousin, who had led the crew in mutiny and murder and piracy, an insult to the high sense of justice that had taken him halfway across the world to bring these men to account for their crimes, his cousin chief among them, and so avenge the father who had hanged himself rather than face the shame of bankruptcy.

His mind flinched away from thoughts of his father fumbling with the noose in the dark. There was no high mission of justice now, it had gone with his cousin's death, gone while he stood on the deck, feeling the immensity of his defeat, clasping the brass button that Matthew had let fall as he spoke his dying words. Something about hope . . . There was no knowing how his cousin came to be clutching the button in these last moments of his life. Kemp remembered that his first impulse, on mounting again to the quarterdeck, had been to throw it overboard, into the sea. Then it had come to him that it was a kind of gift, though accidental, and he had put it away in his pocket. It had stayed in his pocket throughout the voyage home and he had kept it since, without really knowing why. Because of the mystery surrounding it the button had become a sort of talisman. Over the course of time the sense of accident had been replaced in Kemp's mind with an opposite feeling of design, as if he had been meant to have it all along. It lay now in a drawer of his desk; he took it out and looked at it sometimes, and remembered how his cousin had glared across the cabin before he died, and spoken loudly, as if answering some urgent question.

Still he stood there, glancing indifferently at the objects in the room. He had done everything that was practical and needful. He had sold the Negroes in Charles Town and used the money to buy a share in a cotton plantation some miles inland; he had seen his cousin buried in consecrated ground; he had brought the surviving members of the crew back to London to have their crimes and their punishment published widely. He had always been sure of being in the right, always sure that his reasons were impeccable and would stand up to any scrutiny. He was no less convinced of it now, as he stood there. But his conviction of moral rectitude and commercial shrewdness brought no slightest warmth or comfort to him.

He had thought this sense of being trapped in shadows when he should be out in the sun might be due in some measure to his wife's death. She had died while he was in Florida, of a distemper caused by poisoning of the blood, the doctors said. They had not been happy together, and in fact had lived largely separate lives during these last years. He had not loved his wife, though in the days of courtship he had professed love for her. She was Sir Hugo Jarrold's daughter, she had wanted him, and her father was accustomed to giving her what she wanted. He, for his own part, had been driven by the need to repay the debts his own father had left. It had not been long before she discovered the betrayal, and she had gone on to betray him in her turn, many times over. In spite of this, he felt the more alone for her going. His mother too had died while he was away. The knowledge that he had not been there by her side at the moment of her death had clouded his homecoming with a guilt he knew to be unreasonable but was no less real to him for that.

He thought of Jane Ashton again, and with the thought came some lightening of his mood. Not five minutes after the words they had exchanged and her smile when she looked away, his host, Sir Richard Sykes, who sometimes acted as guarantor of the bank's credit abroad, had drawn him aside to tell him that an acquaintance, Lord Spenton, was interested in applying to the bank for a loan.

Sykes had told him something about Spenton's situation, and he had investigated further. There were debts here and there, some of them fairly substantial. He owned large tracts of land in the County of Durham. More importantly, from the bank's point of view, he owned all the coal that lay below these acres. His mines were not so profitable as they should be, considering their advantageous position close to the coast. It had immediately seemed to Kemp an opportunity for investment of a kind long meditated and hoped for. He had told Sykes that the bank would be ready to discuss the loan and he was waiting now for some further word from Spenton, who was taking his time over it. This waiting, the prospect of getting into the coal trade, was at present the only thing that gave any glow of promise to Kemp's feelings about the future.

Not five minutes after that smile of hers, he thought again. It was as if she had blessed the enterprise even before either of them knew of it.

4

Jane regarded her brother with the expression she reserved for his accounts of his doings, solicitous, affectionate, marked by a slight pretence of disbelief. She was the younger by twelve years – they were the only two that had survived childhood – and she admired his earnestness of purpose, though sometimes, when this became relentless, she grew impatient at it and in a way rebellious.

'You look tired,' she said. 'Would you like more tea?' He was not a robust man, and the calls he made on himself taxed him sometimes beyond his strength.

Ashton held out his cup to be replenished. 'I have been rushing to and fro like a madman all day.'

'Did you manage to save the man?'

The question concerned a Negro from the Gold Coast who went by the name of Jeremy Evans. After residing quietly in Chelsea for three years gaining a living as a porter, he had been seen and recognised by his former owner, who had brought him from the sugar fields of Barbados and from whom he had run away once on British soil. On this man's orders Evans had been kidnapped the previous evening, tied and gagged, carried to Gravesend and rowed out to a ship bound for Jamaica, to be sold as a slave on arrival.

'It turned out that the captain was in the plot,' Ashton said. 'I think it probable that he was promised a commission on the sale. As you know, we had obtained from the Rotation Office a warrant for Evans's release, and had it sent to Gravesend, where the ship was lying. But it came to me that with the ship cleared and ready to sail the captain might refuse to obey the summons, or pretend he never received it, which in fact was what he did.'

Ashton paused to sip some of his tea. 'This is doing me a power of good,' he said, smiling at his sister.

Jane kept house for him and made sure the servants performed their duties, just as she tried to make sure she performed her own. She was capable of considerable severity with them, as with herself, at any scanting or neglect. It was a lesson learned from her mother – both parents were dead now. She knew how her brother liked his tea and took care to see it was made as it should be. He was ascetic in his tastes; it was rarely that he touched alcohol in any form.

'I knew that the only thing he would take notice of was a writ of *habeas corpus*,' he said. 'I had to go first to the Lord Mayor and then to Justice Winslow, and spend time waiting, before I could obtain the writ. Then it had to be served on the captain aboard his ship. We were lucky. Two hours more and she would have been setting sail.'

'Mr Evans was the lucky one,' she said. 'He will have cause to remember you.' Others too, she thought. For a good number of years now Fredrick had given all his energy, and spent much of his private fortune, in contesting the right of property in other human beings, particularly when attempts were made to assert this right in England. It had been revulsion at a brutal case of re-enslavement that had brought him to embrace this cause, and so changed his life. Stronger than revulsion had been shame and a sort of remorse that such things could happen on English soil, that they could be condoned, a young Negro brought here, kept imprisoned, beaten and starved, turned out into the street when he was thought to be dying, restored to health free of charge by a doctor who took pity on him, recognised by his former master, seized and shipped to the West Indies to be resold. The charity of the doctor, a Scotsman named Andrews, had been a main element in Ashton's conversion; he had visited the man and the two had become friends, and associates in the cause of abolition.

'So the captain released him without compulsion?' Jane said.

'Yes, he had no choice. He was furious, of course, and violently abusive, but he did not dare to ignore the writ.'

'You are pleased then, with the outcome?'

Ashton paused on this with a certain caution. He was at the opposite pole to the politician, who leaps to claim credit for any success, however slight or incidental. All the passion of his nature was fixed on achieving a success that would not be partial but complete, that would put an end to this iniquitous traffic in human beings. And he feared in his darker moments that his limited means and small political influence made such success unlikely in his lifetime. When he answered now, it was with a sort of reserve habitual to him. 'The officer who served the writ says that he saw the poor fellow chained to the mast in a flood of tears. He was weeping still when they rowed him to the shore, but now it was for joy.'

'So then, we should call that a success, surely?'

Ashton was pleased to hear her including herself in Evans's rescue. He sometimes worried that his sister did not have sufficiently deep convictions. She almost never expressed large or general sentiments of a moral kind, or seemed interested in the broader movements of reform. She was active in charity and good works, especially where the homeless and destitute were concerned; but her zeal was limited, in Frederick's view at least; it lay all in a rage for immediate betterment, for practical measures that might help people to help themselves.

Unlike myself in this, he had often thought, as in other ways. She took little active part in the movement for abolition, though sometimes trying to persuade those among her acquaintance who professed sympathy to contribute to the costs of legal process and of lodging runaway Negroes in safe houses pending the hearings. Mainly the sympathy was more expressed in drawing-room rhetoric than in any alacrity to part with money, as she had remarked to her brother with an assumption of lightness, almost of carelessness, in the irony, frequent with her though in him completely lacking. He did not understand it, this habit of raillery, of assumed indifference, except to think that at twenty-three years of age she had not so far been softened by love. There had been suitors, but none had been acceptable to her. He himself was unmarried and thought it likely he would remain so.

He looked at her now for some moments without speaking. Her temperament was happier than his, he knew. She was very vividly present in this plainly furnished sitting room, in her dress

of blue silk with hooped skirt cut to reveal the frill of petticoats
and the white silk stockings and the pale blue satin slippers. Like
him, she was Methodist in religion from earliest upbringing, and
in her way she was devout; but she was pretty, more than pretty,
and her figure was good, facts of which she was fully conscious;
she was as fond of clothes and as observant of fashion as any
young woman of spirit – and means – might be expected to be.

'Well, as to success,' Ashton said at last, 'that is a very rela-
tive matter, Jane. We have rescued him from being re-enslaved,
so much is true – or at least we have given him a respite. He is
in safe keeping at present. No doubt Bolton will post up a bill
offering a reward to any who find and return him.'

'Bolton?'

'His former owner. Open the *London Gazette* any day of the
week and you will find several notices of the kind. We seek to
uphold the law on behalf of black people held against their will
or made captive when there is no charge against them, because
that is the law of this country and should apply to all, whatever
the colour or the degree. And we can obtain release if there is
clear illegality, and if we act in time.'

'But that says a great deal for the fairness of our laws, does
it not?'

'Oh, a great deal,' he said, and the force of the sarcasm
brought a sudden light into his eyes, always clear in their gaze
and very striking in the narrow, delicately boned face, at present
drawn with lines of weariness and strain. 'And so the injustice
can go on for ever, while we proudly contemplate the perfect
justice of our laws.'

Jane felt the beginnings of a familiar exasperation at her
brother's unyieldingness, his refusal of comfort. 'But you said
yourself that the laws are applied.'

'Most cases do not come to our notice at all. For every one
saved there are a dozen taken by force from these shores to be
sold in the West Indies or our American colonies, and worked
to death there. And those who remain here are caught in the
contradictions of the law. Let us imagine that we are at this
moment attending a hearing on a plaint of unlawful detention
of a black man or woman. The case goes our way, we succeed in
obtaining release. Full of jubilation we leave the courtroom, step

round the corner and find a black child of seven or eight being sold at auction in a coffee house.'

His voice, relating this, had fallen into a rhetorical mode, as if he were addressing more persons than one, the result of a feeling of isolation that descended on him, even with this sister whom he held in deep affection, a sense of the appalling obviousness of what he was saying, this overwhelming truth, which was not, however, by some ugly paradox, immediately plain to others.

'Yes,' he said, 'you can apply to a justice and he will grant you a writ. But no court in this land, in this England of ours, where we are so proud of the pure air of liberty, no court and no judge will take the essential step of denying the right of property in black people brought here from our colonies abroad. We have tried again and again to bring a case that will force the issue, and we have always failed. They do not dare to set a precedent that might bring the right of ownership into question. Liberty is sacred, of course, but only when it favours the slave owner.'

He was silent for a moment or two and then said, with a sort of solemn indignation, 'And now it seems I am to be sued by this Bolton on the grounds that by my intervention I have deprived him of a capital sum, namely the current value of a male slave in good condition at the Kingston slave market, where it was purposed to sell him.' Ashton shook his head. 'It is lunacy,' he said. 'A writ is served on a man for violent and flagrant disregard of the laws relating to the liberty of the subject, release of the abused person is secured, and then you find yourself being sued for his value as a slave.'

Something divided in his expression, some mixture of incredulity and ruefulness, struck her now as comical, and she laughed a little, at which he was visibly surprised for a moment, then smiled himself and nodded, 'Yes,' he said, 'you are right, it is ludicrous.'

'You should laugh more, Frederick,' she said. 'And you should divert yourself more. It does not mean that one cares less. And this is especially so now, with the case of the slave ship that has come before you, that one hears talk of all over town.'

'No wonder there is talk. It is a most unusual case. In fact, I can't remember anything like it. Not only for the circumstances, but for the appalling wickedness of the crime, those unoffending people, our fellow human beings, bound and cast overboard to drown, and all to save a few guineas. However, we may derive benefit from it.'

'Derive benefit?' She had never grown used to her brother's sudden changes from near to far in the way he viewed things. There were times, as now, when she felt a peculiar chill, a sense of dismay, at his ability to pass, in a breath, from compassion genuinely felt to considerations of strategy, to what might be turned to account.

'The case has received widespread attention,' he said. 'It has featured much in the newspapers, people are talking about it, and not only in London. It will give us an opportunity to bring the iniquities of the trade to public notice. There are two actions, entirely separate in law but closely bound together, both brought by the owner of the ship, a man who has made a fortune out of sugar – out of the slave trade, in other words.'

'Yes,' Jane said. 'Erasmus Kemp. We have met.'

'Have you indeed? I did not know that.'

'It was at the house of Sir Richard Sykes, in Lincoln's Inn Fields. It seems that he and Mr Kemp have some banking interest in common. As you know, his daughter Anne is a particular friend of mine.'

'You said nothing of this.'

'There was really nothing to say. Just a few minutes of conversation, quite unmemorable, with several others present.'

Jane had busied herself as she spoke with setting the tea things back on the tray, an operation she would normally have left to the parlourmaid. She was aware of not being entirely frank, but saw no reason why she should be, or why she should be uneasy at not being. Distinctly memorable, in fact, had been Erasmus Kemp's glowering good looks and elegant figure, his lack of smiling, the blaze of his regard, as if he were aiming his eyes at people. She had sensed a sort of unhappiness in him, fiercely contained. His face had lightened a little when he complimented her on her gown, but still he had not smiled . . .

After waiting in vain for something further from her, Ashton said, 'All this happened something like fourteen years ago, and now there is no ship, very few survivors and no reliable witness.'

She was about to ask him more when a footman entered to announce a gentleman visitor, a Mr Van Dillen, who was asking if he might be accorded some minutes of Mr Ashton's time.

'Show him into my study and ask him to take a seat,' Ashton said, getting to his feet. 'Tell him I shall be with him in a minute or two. This is one of the underwriters,' he said to his sister, after glancing at the card the servant had handed him.

Jane too had risen. 'I have some things to see to,' she said. 'I look forward to hearing your account of the visit.'

As they stood together in the light from the wide bow windows, the resemblance between brother and sister was evident. There was the same delicacy of feature and clear gaze, the same fine, dark brown hair, though Jane's had tints of copper that her brother's lacked, the same straight-shouldered, narrow-boned build. The brother's face was grimmer, beyond what could be accounted for by the difference in age, drawn with some expression of endurance or obstinacy, as if the suffering caused him by contemplating the suffering of others had forced him to call on reserves of resistance, taken from him the commoner sort of kindness.

'What will you do?' she asked, as they moved together towards the door. 'About Mr Evans, I mean.'

He held the door open for her, keeping it wide to allow the unhindered passage of the skirts. 'What I shall do,' he said eagerly, 'is bring immediate proceedings for criminal assault on his behalf against Bolton, who ordered it, and the men who seized him and conveyed him to the ship, and the ship's captain who had him chained to the mast.'

She smiled at him as she passed through. 'Dear brother,' she said, 'you will drown in litigation one of these days, if you are not careful.'

He remained in the room for some minutes after she had gone, as if at a loss, momentarily disabled. These moments of arrest came sometimes to him, times at which his purposes seemed suspended, hoisted away from him, and he was recalled to his former life, genteel and pointless, the debating society, the coffee house, the written verses of slight value circulated among friends . . .

He glanced up suddenly, as if to break free. Yes, he would

bring criminal charges against them. He had never before initiated criminal proceedings by a black man against a white. The Grand Jury might throw out the indictment. But it was only by testing the ground that any way forward could be found. Tirelessly, in spite of all disappointment, he persisted in the belief that a judgement would some day be delivered that would open men's eyes, call the entire system into question. If Evans's case went as far as the Court of King's Bench, substantial costs were only to be expected . . .

The maid came in to take away the tea things, and with this Ashton recalled suddenly that he was awaited in his study, and began to make his way there.

The man who rose at his entrance was middle-aged and corpulent, plainly dressed in frock coat and double-breasted waistcoat, and wearing the raised wig with double roll common to men of business. 'Good of you to give me your time, sir,' he said, as they shook hands. 'I am much obliged. Van Dillen at your service.' He spoke with a slight foreign accent.

'Pray be seated. You represent the insurers, I believe.'

'That is so, sir. You have been giving the case some attention, as I understand.'

Ashton's first impulse was to ask the other how he had come by this understanding. But he forbore – it would be common knowledge by this time, at least in the circles frequented by his visitor. 'Naturally, yes,' he said. 'It has some unusual features, would you not agree?'

Van Dillen raised a plump, short-fingered hand and briefly caressed his chin. 'Unusual features, yes, one could say that. You will know that an action has been brought against the underwriters to recover a percentage of the value of sixty-eight male slaves and seventeen females lost in the passage from the Coast of Guinea to the West Indies in the year 1753.'

'I did not know the numbers. What is your warranty for those?'

'The first mate of the ship, James Barton, has made a deposition to that effect and will repeat his testimony in court, if so required. Other members of the crew may be called upon to testify, since it is a question of fact and does not involve them in any criminal charges. Barton has said that they cast the Negroes overboard while the breath of life was still in them. This they did on the orders of the captain, which orders, as he declares, were sufficient authority. He has been freed on the surety of the present owner, son of the former owner, by name Erasmus Kemp. His whereabouts have been kept secret to prevent him from being got at.'

Some snap of resentment in the tone of these last words told Ashton that efforts to get at the mate had already been made, without success. 'Well,' he said, 'if we can bring him before the court, we may get at him there.'

'You say "we", sir. I am delighted to hear you say it. It is in the hope that you will support our case that I have taken the liberty of calling on you at your home. They claim there was a shortage of water aboard the ship. It is our belief, and we will found our case on it, that this is gross falsehood, that these slaves were cast overboard because they were sick and like to die before reaching Jamaica, and that this was done in the full knowledge that death aboard ship, when due to natural causes, is not covered by our policies.'

Ashton passed a hand over his brow. 'Natural causes, is it? Heaven help us. I have not yet understood how I can be of service to you.'

'You can speak for us, you are a man known for your opposition to slavery, known as a generous patron and protector of black people. Who more fitted than you to make an appeal to the court and express on the behalf of the underwriters the sincere indignation and moral outrage we feel at the barbarism of this claim? Thirty guineas a head for the men, twenty-three for the women, that is what the owner is claiming. We will dispute the estimates of value, but if they are taken as correct it will amount to upwards of twenty-five hundred pounds, taking the men and women together.'

'I see, yes,' Ashton said. 'You want me to sound the note of humanity so as to help you avoid meeting the claim.'

'I would not put it like that, sir.'

'No, I dare say not. Well, we shall not quarrel over words. Perhaps we can come to an accord. We for our part will seek to have the cases heard together in the same court. The charges Kemp is bringing against the crew, or what remains of them, are murder and piracy – murder of the captain, not the Negroes. Since the ship was at sea, the case comes under the jurisdiction of the Admiralty, but this will make no difference in practice, as it will be heard at the Old Bailey just the same, with two, or possibly three, Admiralty Commissioners sitting in judgement. If you will raise your voice with ours in a common plea, and argue with us that one set of human beings cannot, in law, have such power over another, that this was mass murder whatever the quantity of water, we may both be victorious. You will avoid payment, and we may obtain a ruling that denies the right of property of one man in another.'

He had leaned forward in the enthusiasm of these words, but Van Dillen remained silent and motionless for several moments, avoiding his eye. 'No, sir,' he said at last. 'No, it will not do. We will press for the hearing to be held at the Guildhall, as is usual in such claims. We cannot confuse the two cases, we cannot hazard the firm's money on an issue of property. It would only lead to muddle, sir. No, we must confine our arguments to the question of jettison, whether these Negroes were cast over the side for some just cause or not.'

'Some just cause?' Ashton rose to his feet, obliging his visitor to do the same. 'I should have known better,' he said. 'I will not take up any more of your time. Be assured that whatever words are uttered on our side in court, they will not be designed to save your guineas.'

5

It was the purse that brought an end to Sullivan's brief period of affluence, while at the same time signalling its peak – the purse, and with it, in disastrous combination, a misplaced sentiment of fellow feeling. In all the years of his life – years of poverty and vagrancy from early adolescence onwards – he had never possessed such a purse; in fact, he had never possessed a purse at all, keeping what coins he had in a cloth bag inside his shirt. And he was, in any case, particularly vulnerable to tricksters during this period of his life, being unused to money and in a way innocent about it after the years in the Florida settlement. They had traded, but there had been no use for coins.

For all it was so fleeting, he was always to remember the sense of wealth and well-being that the beautiful purse and its contents had brought him. They became linked in his mind with his miraculous escape, the supremely fortunate encounter by the wayside, a time when he had been a man at large, a man under a vow, with a destination, in stout boots and a good coat with brass buttons. Though in the end not much was to remain to him but the destination and the vow, he was always to think of these few days as constituting one of the highlights of his life.

The wagon put him down in Bedford on the evening of the following day, when it was already dark. Guided by his new sense of himself as a travelling man with the power of purchase about him, he chose an inn on the high street with a good front, the Golden Cockerel, a name that seemed appropriate to his condition. The landlord, however, was not at first in full accord with Sullivan's vision of himself, perhaps suspicious at the discrepancy between the good clothes and the wild hair and ragged beard. Then there was the Irish accent, the haggard looks, the vagabond's fiddle over the shoulder. He wanted a shilling in advance, he said.

So it was the landlord of the Golden Cockerel who had the first sight of the purse and its contents. Sullivan was later to wonder whether this man, who smiled upon him when he saw the money, was in the plot too. But no shadow of doubt troubled him at the time; he took pleasure in the display, and bore himself in lordly fashion.

He dined well on sheep's liver chopped and grilled, accompanied by roast potatoes, the whole washed down by a quart of ale. It was the best meal he had eaten for months, since the yams and sweet potatoes and marsh birds of the settlement. He slept soundly, breakfasted heartily and paid the balance of his score to the now friendly landlord.

It was a man transformed who walked down Bedford High Street that morning. To make matters even better, the weather had changed; he emerged from the inn to sunshine and a blue sky; it was the last day of March, spring had arrived, he saw a cherry tree with buds of flower in a sheltered courtyard. Always mercurial, Sullivan felt his life to be full of blessings, and he began, as his habit was, to count them over. He was well clear of London, no one could know which way he was headed, there could be no alarm put out for him here. The fetid cell in Newgate Prison, where he had lain in fetters with his shipmates since arriving in England, the fear of the noose that had accompanied his days and nights, all this fell away from him. He was going to do his duty by poor Billy Blair. He was a man who kept his vows. And in the knowledge of this he held up his head and walked with a light step.

He had clear intentions for this morning. He would make the rest of his appearance tally with the coat and boots, the whole to be in perfect keeping with a purse-bearing man. A more prudent person, knowing the long journey that lay ahead, might have kept his money closer about him. But Sullivan was improvident by nature, and he had spent years in the wilderness of south-east Florida, where the future was not much considered except in terms of the weather it might bring.

First he purchased, for sixpence, a canvas bag suitable for a travelling man. Since he had no other possessions at all, it would do well for his fiddle and bow. His next care was to find a barber. The one he found was also a wig-maker and made efforts to sell Sullivan a white silk wig that would have cost him more than half his store. He resisted this, however. He was proud of his hair, which was dark and luxuriant.

'I am not enterin' in the merits of wigs as such,' he said. 'I know well that they are widespread throughout the land. There will be those with a thatch that is wearin' sparse, there will be those that are wishin' to make themselves stand taller. But a man with a head of hair like mine would niver want to hide his light under a bushel, though willin' to admit he is become overgrown, consequent to a neglect that there was no avoidin'.'

After the shave he had his hair trimmed, pomaded and gathered at the nape with a silk ribbon of a dark green colour to go with his coat. The cost of this was tenpence, the greater part of which was due to the ribbon.

From here, the mild sunshine on his face, the effluvium from his scented hair in his nostrils, he proceeded down the street until he found a journeyman tailor sitting stitching behind the window of his shop. From the stock of ready-made clothes inside he chose worsted breeches and a good calico shirt, changing into his new clothes behind a screen in the shop.

'These I leave to your judgement,' he said, dropping his former garments on the counter. 'I have some experience of commerce an' there is no doubt in me mind at all that you will make me an allowance for them.'

But the tailor, after the briefest of examinations, gave it as his emphatic opinion that the garments were of no value whatever. In fact, he barely touched them and seemed displeased to have them on his counter.

'That shirt an' them trousers have been my coverin' in good times an' bad,' Sullivan said. 'How can they have no value to them?'

For only answer the tailor pointed out that the clothes were threadbare, torn in places and stained, and moreover had been of mediocre quality even when new. The price of Sullivan's purchases would remain unchanged at three shillings and ninepence.

'Very well then, I will not bequeath them to you,' Sullivan

said, picking up the garments and stowing them in his bag. 'A man will niver prosper in this world who is lost to all sense of justice an' decorum,' he said over his shoulder as a parting shot. Immediately outside the shop he encountered the gap-toothed smile of a sandy-haired, thin fellow with no great air of prosperity. 'I hear well that you are from Ireland,' this man said.

'I am so,' Sullivan said. 'Though it is long years since I last set eyes on Galway.'

'Galway, is it? Isn't that a happy chance now? 'Tis a Galway man I am meself.'

Often it is some slight cheating of our expectations that inclines us this way or that when dealing with our fellows. Sullivan knew he had a wealthy look about him. He was a purse-bearing man, which the other emphatically was not. In view of this, he had supposed that this fellow countryman of his, who smiled and spoke so friendly-like, would have it in mind to ask him for a small loan. He would have obliged, or so he thought afterwards, highly suited as it would have been to the splendour of the morning and his new sense of himself. He would have given the man a penny or two, together with some good wishes for his subsequent career.

But no such request was made to him. 'This meetin' has done me a power of good,' the man said. 'To see a fellow Irishman risin' in the world, it gives us hope for a future better than what is offered in the present, through no fault of me own. I hope you will be crossin' the water again soon, an' seein' them you hold dear.'

Sullivan, who had been left to his own devices at the age of fourteen and had not set foot in Ireland for more than twenty years, felt some prickle of tears at this reference to home and dear ones. And when the man did not attempt to beg from him, and seemed about to move away, he reached out and took his arm. 'Well,' he said, 'we can take a pot of ale together before we part, for the sake of the dear old days that are no more. You are of these parts, as I suppose, so you will know of a place.'

The man showed every appearance of pleasure at this suggestion. 'Murphy,' he said, holding out his hand. 'Patrick Murphy.'

Sullivan was about to say his name, but then recalled that he was on the run, a fact he had been overlooking all that morning. They might be posting handbills up . . . 'Corrigan,' he said. 'Michael Corrigan.'

If the other noticed this hesitation he did not remark on it. 'I know the very place,' he said. 'You look like a man that might have music in him. There is some come into the town that sings an' plays on the drums an' hautboys. Everywhere they go there is crowds follerin' after. I have heard them meself, an' they are ravishin' on the ears. They are performin' in a tavern nearby this very place where we are standin'. It is the innkeeper pays them, because of the people they bring in.'

'Music, is it? You are lookin' at a man who has lived by his music in days gone by. Me fortunes have changed for the better lately, but it is a power that never quits you.'

He followed his new-found companion through narrow streets until they reached a low-fronted hostelry from which the sounds of singing carried to them as they approached. The taproom was crowded, people were standing close together, there was no room for sitting. They had entered at the close of a song and the applause rang round them. Four men faced the audience on a raised platform. One of them, who had a drum slung across his chest, was black.

Sullivan gave his order to a man in an apron weaving through the crowd with a loaded tray. 'We will do the payin' when you do the deliverin',' he said to the man, and then, to his companion, 'I wasn't born yesterday, there is such a thing as trustin' our fellow man over an' above what is reasonable. He might say he had niver had the money.'

Patrick Murphy's reply to these words of wisdom was not audible, as at this moment there came a rattle from the drum and a sustained note from the oboe, and the group launched into song.

> *No weather can stay us when sailing for home,*
> *No roads too rough for our steps to traverse . . .*

It was in a way unlucky for Sullivan, in these special circumstances, that it should have been a song of exile and homesickness, and that one of the singers should have been a black man. He lost for some moments all sense of his surroundings, swept by a wave of sorrow and longing, remembering the last night of the settlement, when they had gathered to celebrate the birth of Neema and Cavana's baby. He had played like a demon that night, there had been singing and dancing, the widow Koudi had smiled at him and he had felt he would not be unwelcome in her bed. All the while, unknown to them, the redcoats were waiting above them, among the trees, waiting for dawn, for the signal to attack . . .

Coming back to himself, he was aware of tears in his eyes. He turned his head to say something about the beauty of the singing but Patrick Murphy was no longer there. And the sound of the voices was strangely muted as he thrust a hand into his coat pocket and found that the purse was no longer there either.

6

Bordon woke shortly before daybreak, as always; it was a habit that came from the long years of rising for work, an awareness of the changes of light that came to him in sleep and roused him. He was fully awake when the calls came from the alley outside, sad-sounding, more like a lament for the night gone than a welcome to the new day. It was the turn of Hardwick and his sons to shout the hour; they had no clock but they never failed, not like some who had one. Peter Hardwick claimed that he could tell when day was coming by a change in the cries of the owls that haunted the Dene, but this was not believed by everyone.

Nan rose at the call, put on a coat and went to see to the men's bait, tie the lids across the cans to stop the food from spilling while they walked over the fields to the pit. There was a bag for each of the three, with a leather strap to go over the shoulder; they knew which bag was theirs, but what was inside the cans they only knew when they opened them. The contents varied from day to day: bread, pasties, hard-boiled eggs, bacon, cold potatoes – she saw to it herself and used what she had in the house and what she could find amid the sparse stock of the store. With three of them working there was money enough – they were not in debt for groceries, as many were.

Bordon rose and went to the door of the other bedroom, where his sons slept. The cottage was identical to all the others in the village, just as the yards behind were identical: three rooms, not counting the square-built chimney corner, all on one floor. He knocked and shouted, waited for an answering call and retired to the bedside to put on his pit clothes.

Percy woke at the knock, heard David muttering beside him; these two shared a bed, while Michael, as the eldest, had one of his own, a narrow pallet set against the wall. Percy tried to sleep again, turning away from the plaints of his brother, who was always slow to wake. He would stay in bed for another hour at least, not rising till it was full day, a privilege he tried to make the most of, knowing it would not last much longer now. Soon he would be going down with the others, a thing desired and dreaded in equal measure.

This morning sleep did not return to him, something increasingly frequent of late. He was afraid of the mine because he knew it was a testing ground; you had to go down before you could become a man. The sound of clanking and hissing came over the fields to him, as if issuing from some monster under the ground clamouring for victims. The fear was not lessened by the return home each day of his father and brothers because they were bigger and stronger and had stood the test, but perhaps not everybody did. He had a very close friend called Billy Scotland, who was the same age as himself, and he had often wondered if Billy too was troubled by these doubts. But he could not ask because he knew that Billy would deny it, and by asking he would have revealed himself as faint-hearted. Recently it had occurred to him that Billy might be keeping quiet for the same reason.

While he lay there, prey to these thoughts, some seventy men and boys set off in the half-dark, walking in loose groups across the pasture fields that led to the eye of the pit. Michael watched for the light, as he did always; it was the only natural light that he would see that day. The sea still slept in the distance, shrouded in darkness. But there was light enough now for him to make out the tufts of sheep's wool caught in the fences, a soft clogging of the wire, no definite shape to it, only a sort of softness. There were catkins on the hazel trees; he could not distinguish the colour, but he could see how the foliage was thickened by them. Colours came out now, as the light slowly strengthened, tints of dawn that would be lost in the full light of day; he made out the reddish gleam on the trunks of the birch trees higher up, at the edges of the fields, a colour that had seemed menacing to him as a small child, making him always feel relieved when he had got past.

Deeply familiar things, but they had never grown stale for him. From the age of seven he had walked through these fields in all seasons and weathers, walking behind his father, as he did now, as his father had done at that age, and all the fathers before him that Michael could imagine. From open-cut to shaft, they had been hacking out the coal here for a longer time than anyone could reckon. There was nothing but the mining, no other work for the men. The village of Thorpe was there because of the coal, and for no other reason in the world.

He could distinguish his father's back now, among the others, in the forward group of twenty or so. He found himself wondering if his father took notice of these changes in the light, these small signs of the changing season. Such things were too intimate to talk about. He sensed the wound of loss in his father, the rage in him, knew of the long-held desire to possess the plot of land by the stream side in the Dene. This had never been openly confessed, but his father had talked of the acreage, the sheltered position, the ease of irrigation. Practical things – it was the nearest he could come to unburdening himself. It was no more than a dream, in any case. He could never hope to buy the land, he would never have the money, it would never be offered for sale. But a dream nursed so stubbornly, over so long, becomes something more . . .

There was no real hope of saving. There were the three of them, soon to be joined by Percy, who would bring in an extra sixpence a day for the first five years, more after that, maybe double, when he rose to be putter's lad, as David was now. In four or five years David could hope to be promoted to headsman, taking two-thirds of the earnings of the sledge loads. He himself was twenty-one now, he looked forward to becoming a full pitman, a hewer like his father, with fifteen shillings a week. But the family would lose his wages when he married. There was a girl he liked, Elsie Foster, who lived six doors away from them, though he hadn't yet taken the decisive step of asking her to walk out with him. He was hoping to see her now, though it would be only briefly, before he went down; she started work at the same time he did, sorting out the waste from the coal at the head of the shaft.

There was enough money, they could hold their heads up,

they need be beholden to no one. There was even enough for him, with his father's permission, to take three hours a week in addition to Sunday, to practise at handball. He was recognised as having a talent for the game, and would be the Thorpe champion in the annual match with the nearby colliery village of Northfield, due to take place fairly soon now.

One of the men in the group ahead of him was Daniel Walker, who he intended to have a word with as soon as he saw a chance of getting him alone. He thought again of his brother's hangdog look the previous evening when his bruises were revealed. He had been ashamed . . . David was walking beside him now, silent, still not fully awake. He might have hastened his steps so as to come up with Walker, and perhaps find an occasion as they walked side by side. But he did not want to be among the first to go down; in the few minutes of waiting for the rope he could look at Elsie; he looked for her every morning and she looked for him.

He could hear the sounds of the workings as they drew near the pithead, the grinding of the cogs on the drum, the jingling of the horses' harness as they plodded round, the creaking of the stern-pole fixed to the axle of the drum. The first men were going down already. There was a fire burning in the iron basket suspended over the shaft, and by its light he saw Elsie with the other women, crouching over the heaped coal. As he waited, with seven or eight others, for his turn to be lowered down the shaft, she looked up and saw him watching and smiled. The banksman shouted up from below that the shaft was clear, and the men prepared to descend.

There was no platform, only the winding rope that dangled before them. They bound themselves into the rope, each man making a loop and thrusting one leg into it, each using one hand to grip the rope above him, each keeping the other free to guard himself against being dashed against the sides of the shaft in the descent – collisions which had sometimes maimed men in the past. The younger boys sat astride the knees of the men, the older ones clung with their hands to the rope and twined their legs about it. Clustered thus, colliers and boys riding down on a single rope, it was as if they had been spliced together and hung on a string by some giant hand.

The fire bucket was kept burning above them, suspended over the mouth of the shaft, placed there to move currents of air through the mine workings and disperse accumulations of marsh gas. By its light, as they descended, they could see for a while the vitreous glints in the walls of the shaft. These were lost as they went deeper, and for a while they were in a darkness almost total, with only the candlelight far below them on the shaft floor and no sound but that of the rope uncoiling on the drum.

Michael found the occasion he was looking for soon after touching down at the shaft bottom. David had stopped at the entrance to the main gallery, to load empty corves on to a sledge. At a point where the gallery divided into two narrower ways towards the coalface, he came up with Walker and spoke a greeting to him. Walker turned quickly, as if startled. The light of the candle he was holding lit up the lower part of his face, glinted on the fair stubble around the heavy jaw. 'What does tha want?' he said.

Neither of them could stand upright here, the ceiling was too low. Crouching forward, with heads lowered, they faced each other. There had never been much love lost between the two families; small disagreement had been magnified over time, as happens in close-knit communities.

'Tha's been bearin' too heavy on our David,' Michael said. 'Tha's been too free with yor fists.' He saw Walker's mouth loosen with a sneer. 'A'm tellin' you to lay off it,' he said. 'The lad's only twelve.'

'He's been blabbin' then, blabbin' to big brother,' Walker said. 'Blabbin and blubberin'.'

Michael had resolved at the outset to keep calm, but the unfairness of this brought the beginning of anger to him. 'He dinna blab,' he said.

'He's nay bleddy use,' Walker said. 'He dinna put his back into it. He's losin' me a shillin' a day.'

'He does his best,' Michael said. 'A know him better than tha does.'

'Is tha callin' me a liar?'

'Keep yor hands off him,' Michael said. The anger rose in him, impeding his breathing in that constricted space. 'Tha thinks tha owns him. He's smaller than you, he pushes the baskets at

7

'I had hoped the business might be settled privately between us,' Van Dillen said. 'The outcome must be doubtful in law and if we go to the extent of a hearing there are costs to be thought of. Why should we fatten the lawyers, Mr Kemp?'

He was not finding the interview easy. He was physically uncomfortable, for one thing; the seat of his chair was too small for a man of his bulk, and the weather was unseasonably hot. The room had only one window, and the morning sun, strong despite the clogging air of London, slanted through it and lay directly on him. He felt overheated in his bob-wig and broadcloth suit.

He was at the further disadvantage of being a petitioner, of having solicited this meeting. Some men are dressed in authority wherever they go, but the broker was not of these; he was accustomed to wielding what he had of it in the domestic surroundings of his home in Richmond, his modest premises off the Strand, or free and unbuttoned in his booth at Lloyds Coffee House, where most of his day-to-day business was done. This present ground belonged to a man not only younger but very much richer. A wealth not much expressed in display, however, he had noted: plain oak panelling, shelves for ledgers and almanacs, ladder-backed chairs.

'We are in high summer before we have had spring,' he said, in the face of the other's continuing silence. He felt an itch at the side of his neck, some insect crawling there. Conditions however uncomfortable will generally be favourable to life of some sort and the windless days and early heat had produced a plague of small black beetles that flew about blindly, getting tangled in wigs and snared in the corners of eyes, copulating and dying, leaving a scurf of corpses.

The broker took out a handkerchief and dabbed at his neck, turning his head in a way too affectedly elegant, or so Kemp thought, for an honest man. Too many Dutchmen in shipping and insurance these days, too many brokers altogether. He had never had the smallest fellow feeling for opponents; the knowledge of conflicting interests fed an appetite for enmity always keen. 'To my mind,' he said, 'there is no doubt of the outcome in law, none at all.'

'How? After close on fourteen years and most of the actors in it dead?' Van Dillen looked with affected surprise and genuine curiosity at the man before him. It was not so much the certainty of tone; the broker had much experience of disputed claims, and litigants always professed – at least publicly – un unshakeable faith in the justice of their cause. But this man had an air of conviction that came close to ferocity, his eyes blazed with it. A vivid face, not very English, some suggestion of the south in it. From Liverpool, the family, a melting pot of peoples and races . . .

There was again a silence between them that lasted for some moments. In one corner of the window a fly tumbled and buzzed, caught in some hopeless mania of escape. The din of metal wheels on the cobbles of Cheapside came to them here, but distantly; Kemp's place of business looked out over the quiet courts south of St Paul's. There was the occasional scrape of a stool from the adjacent room, where three clerks worked side by side at a long counter. 'What are fourteen years, or forty, if it comes to that?' Kemp said. 'What point are you seeking to make? Time can make no smallest difference to the justice of my claims, mine or any other man's.'

'That is all very fine, sir,' the broker said. 'Impeccable sentiments, egad, they do you credit. If you but had the trying of the case yourself, there could be very little doubt of the verdict. But it is far from certain whether the judge will take the same view.'

He had spoken tartly, provoked at last by the arrogant certainty of the other's tone. Now he saw Kemp relax a little from the braced position he had assumed in the high-backed chair, and he wondered for a moment if the way to get the fellow on terms less stiff was to quarrel with him. The broker was an observant man, and shrewd in his way. There was some absence in the other's face, a kind of blankness, in spite of the fierce regard. This was a man who believed so strongly in his own purposes as to appear stricken by them, afflicted – and he answered this affliction with rage. 'In a case of this kind,' the broker said, 'at such an interval of time and with such flawed and partial testimony, no one can predict the outcome.'

He saw the other pick up a ruler and strike down at the desk with it. 'Filthy little creatures,' Kemp said. 'How do they get in? The window can't be opened.'

'What can be predicted are the legal costs,' Van Dillen said.

'My good sir, the facts are not in dispute, at least as regards the central fact of the Negroes being cast overboard and the necessity thereof.'

'It is precisely the necessity of it that the insurers will dispute if it comes before a court.'

'There was a shortage of water. Lawful jettison is one of the hazards covered by the underwriters. You guaranteed the policy with my father in 1752, through his agent in Liverpool, where the ship was built and fitted out.'

'Not I,' Van Dillen said. 'I inherited the policy on the death of my uncle, when I became one of the partners. I would never have signed an agreement on a per capita basis at a fixed rate. No firm that I know of would insure against loss of cargo at more than twenty per cent of the current market value.'

'Well, sir, like it or not, the insurers accepted the risk at that time to the extent of thirty guineas per head for the men and twenty-three for the women. Come, it is not so unreasonable. In the summer of 1753, when these Negroes were cast overboard with just cause, a male slave would have fetched forty-five guineas in Jamaica, whither the ship was bound, and a female thirty-three or -four. The numbers are not in dispute. There were eyewitnesses, some of them still alive.'

'They will be the surviving members of the crew, no doubt, presently lying in Newgate Prison, men who will be facing charges of murder and piracy once this insurance claim has been settled. Fine witnesses, sir.'

'There is also the chief officer, Barton. He will testify to the numbers and to the shortage of water.'

'The mate on a slave ship, we know what that is. And freed on your surety. Neither judge nor jury will take him to their bosoms. And then, memory plays us false, all men of ordinary judgement recognise that. It was a desperate action, ship and crew were in a grievous state at the time. It is no use whatever to talk about the value of the cargo, as we both know full well. A Corymantee black, for instance, will fetch more than an Ibo, as being more robust and less likely to cut his throat or decline into melancholy and so die.'

Van Dillen smiled and nodded and sat back as far as he was able, smoothing down the white cotton waistcoat over his ample paunch. 'Sir, latitude of thought, the ability to make distinctions, is a main mark of civilised man. I know the Guinea trade, sir, we do a great deal of business in that line.'

'I do not doubt it.' These last remarks had confirmed Kemp in his dislike of the broker, whose quality of civilisation had an odour he recognised. That he was obliged to recognise it, that it was an odour Van Dillen obviously took for granted they had in common – something Kemp could not deny, even if he had so far demeaned himself as to attempt it, since denial would have been tantamount to admission – his visitor could hardly have given him offence more mortal. 'I have business to attend to,' he said. 'What is the nature of this proposal of yours?'

'Well, that is soon said. The underwriters, who have authorised me to speak for them, are willing to make a private settlement. This is not because we feel our case to be weak, far from it, but to save the trouble and costs of an action. We will not dispute the number cast overboard. In view of the time gone by and the difficulty of establishing anything after such an interval, we think it reasonable to set a value of ten guineas a head on the blacks, whether male or female, it makes no difference. At the number we have been given, that would amount to eight hundred and fifty guineas. I am authorised to offer that sum in complete settlement. It is a generous offer, under all the circumstances, and I trust that you will find it satisfactory.'

'No, I do not find it satisfactory,' Kemp said, with a perceptible increase in volume and eagerness of tone. 'Generous offer? Do you take me for a supplicant? Be damned to your generosity, sir.' He paused a moment, then continued more quietly, with a rigid set of the jaws. 'I will have my father's rights in full. I will have a proper settlement by process of law. That ship was my father's. He had her built and fitted out. The blacks were purchased with trade goods he had provided at his own expense. His last days were shadowed by that loss. I will have satisfaction for his name.'

Satisfaction for his investment, the broker was inclined to think, thereby doing Kemp less than justice and demonstrating the limits of his own understanding. His eye had been on the younger man's right fist, which had clenched during this speech and whitened to a bloodless line along the knuckles. Van Dillen was a sedentary man, thick-necked and sometimes troubled these days by shortness of breath. This passion of retribution was disquieting to him. Kemp would seek to use the surviving seamen as witnesses in support of his claim on the insurers, and afterwards do his best to see them hanged . . .

'Well,' he said, 'I see you are set on the courts.'

'It is you who talk of the courts,' Kemp said, slowly opening the fingers of his hand. 'I am set on obtaining my rights.'

The broker nodded. Rights were measured with money, in his view of things. The terms were more or less interchangeable. Kemp had money in plenty, but those with money always wanted more. It was a fact of life, he had never encountered a single exception to it. All the same, he was obliged to recognise now that there was more to this than money. He knew a good deal about the man sitting opposite to him; he had made it his business to know. A career meteoric, even in these days of quick fortunes. Seventy thousand pounds, Jarrold's daughter was said to brought him, along with a share in the bank. The old man had lost his wits, as it was said, and was kept in confinement. The bank he had founded was in Kemp's hands now. No, there was no shortage of money in that quarter. Of course, such a man would want to win all battles. How he had discovered their whereabouts, these remnants of slaves and crew, how he had been able to track them down in the wilds of southern Florida where they had taken refuge, these were matters not yet definitely known – there were conflicting accounts. No doubt much would be made clear in the course of the capital charges at the Old Bailey . . .

Van Dillen's pale, heavy face registered nothing of these thoughts as he got to his feet. 'I will take my leave, sir,' he said. 'I have made the offer that was agreed among us. I am sorry you do not see fit –' He faltered a moment, meeting Kemp's gaze, then said more firmly, 'I think you are making a mistake, but the arbitration of law will settle the business one way or the other.'

Kemp assented to this indifferently and accompanied his visitor to the head of the stairs that led down to the street. Returning to his office, he walked to and fro for a while, possessed by a spirit of discontent. Glancing through the thick and rippled glass of his window, he had a distorted view of rooftops and chimneys. He saw pigeons rise, their wingbeats like a stirring in some opaque and viscous fluid. The window was fixed to the wall and could not be opened. The bank's premises were old, they had been old in his father-in-law's time. Jarrold had always been parsimonious; he had limited the windows in this room to one only, and had it fixed in place, in order to avoid the window taxes of the 1720s.

Kemp had not found it necessary to make any changes. London's skies were fogged by smoke from a thousand chimneys. Lamps would have been needed to work by, in any case, for most of the year. He did not mind spending money where he saw it as necessary, but this was a place of business, he could see no point in trying to make it look like something else. He knew people who were spending considerable sums to make their offices resemble drawing rooms, with sash windows and chintz upholstery and cabinets of porcelain. Such extravagance was enough to ruin a man's reputation for sober and reliable dealing.

Now, however, he would have liked to have a window he could throw open, to admit more air into the closeness of his office, expel the lingering traces of Van Dillen's scent and sweat. As he paused in his pacing and stood still in the middle of the room, it seemed to him that this was also the smell of the world outside, that it came seeping through, thickened by stagnant sewage and faecal dust. He was a fastidious man, clean and scrupulous in his person and clothing, an outward mark of his need to be beyond reproach in motive and behaviour. He had never faltered in the attention he paid to his person, but in the pursuit of money to pay his father's debts he had sometimes come short on the moral plane, had been obliged to breathe a tainted air. He had suffered from this at the time, and continued to do so at the memory.

It was a similar sense of taint, a feeling of being contaminated, that troubled him now. He had been too eager with his explanations to this Dutch interloper, he had lowered himself. As if it mattered a straw whether the fellow appreciated his motives or not . . .

We generally like to regard ourselves in a good light, but the extent to which this matters varies from person to person. For Erasmus Kemp it mattered very much, and for this reason he had never been much given to any closeness of self-questioning. The answers to such questions will be ambiguous at best, motives will usually reveal themselves to be impure. Kemp had generally found it sufficient to assure himself of needing no one's endorsement, whether friend or foe, not merely on particular occasions, but generally. It was a question of dignity. And now here he was, disgusted with himself at the recollection of his vehemence before that foreigner, whom he had not liked, whose interests were opposed to his own.

A betrayal of himself, no less – and not the first since his return. Lately he had been increasingly subject to impulses to explain himself, justify himself, even with people he did not know well, a thing quite foreign to his usual self-containment, and to what he thought of as his true character. It was as though he were striving to shore up certainties previously held that seemed now in danger of slipping away. In an obscure fashion he was beginning to sense why this might be so. The principle of justice, always strong in him, had been violated by his own failure, since returning home, to find any feeling of happiness or cause for celebration at the success of his expedition to Florida. For great success it had been, there could be no doubt of that. He had hunted down the fugitives, white and black. He had used troops from the garrison at St Augustine to flush them out. The remnants of the crew lay in prison now, awaiting trial.

A triumph, no other word for it. Why then this haunting sense of loss and waste? But it was not new, it had always been there, a companion continually neglected and forgotten, continually demanding to be recognised anew. All the successes of his life were consumed to ash in the fire of achieving, in the realisation of his will and intention. Only the energy of planning, the envisaging of success gave him pleasure, only purposes had meaning for him. He had always lived by plans, by vows, by promises made to himself.

He brought to memory now, as if to make his success more real to him, the last hours of that colony of renegades, the approach through darkness, his tension of excitement kept under stern check, the stationing of the troops, the waiting for dawn. From the compound below there had come the sound of drum and fiddle and some kind of whistle or flute, a discordant music, sometimes passing into wild harmony. From the swamps all around the whine of mosquitoes and the strange sharp clicking of young alligators as they snapped at frogs and turtles in the creeks. Those sounds, that night, the anticipation of capturing Paris and his motley associates and bringing them to justice, that had been happiness.

And now this sordid aftermath, this haggler of a broker coming with his 'generous offer'. Kemp was shrewd in matters concerning money, with a shrewdness derived from years of business dealings. He knew he could have increased Van Dillen's offer if he had been prepared to bargain. They would not want to risk an adverse judgement; none of the brotherhood at Lloyds would want a precedent established; increased indemnities on hazards to cargo could too easily be turned to the shipowners' advantage. But this was a problem that did not concern him.

The triumph of the capture had not survived his hated cousin's death. Nor had the hatred survived. This cousin who had mortally offended him in childhood, who had been cast into Norfolk Gaol as a common prisoner and set in the pillory for printing seditious matter and denying Holy Writ, bringing disgrace on the whole family, who had led the crew of the *Liverpool Merchant* in mutiny and murder and made off with ship and cargo. A burden of accumulated bitterness lifted from his spirit by this death, but bringing neither freedom nor relief, only a sort of vacancy.

He had known it as he stood on the quarterdeck of the ship that was to bring them home, below that vast, all-encompassing sky, looking down at the men and women of the settlement and the children of their union. He had felt repugnance at the thought of white and black breeding together. Still in his hand the button Matthew had let fall as he died, a gift to the cousin who had hated him, who had brought the soldiers and ordered the shooting, a gift to the author of his death . . .

A thought of an unaccustomed kind came to him as he moved to reseat himself at his desk and resume the work that awaited him there. He had argued once, while still in Liverpool, with the girl he had wanted to marry, about a painting in her parents' house, whether it was a painting of people in Paradise or just in a beautiful garden. Sarah and he had almost quarrelled over it.

The people in the painting were happy and smiling and elegantly dressed, at ease in their surroundings. Somewhere there might be a place like this, a place where dwelt those who were caught and held in the anticipation of triumph, dwelling for ever in some night of excited vigil, with the wild music sounding in their ears. Or even one for those who had realised their aims and were happy still. Somewhere there might be a piece of ground, a territory, where the following steps are also happy, the steps you take after the victory, after justice has been done and profits made, when you begin to walk away, when you return home . . .

Perhaps the coalfields of Durham might be such a place for him. The papers on the desk before him were mainly concerned with the mining industry. Since learning of Spenton's desire for a loan he had spent a good deal of time studying production figures and methods of extraction in the eastern part of the county, towards the sea. He had talked to shipping agents, studied contracts made by the mine owners or their lessees with the lightermen that loaded the coal at the wharves of Hartlepool and carried it to the collier ships that would bring it down to the Pool of London. He had learned to his great satisfaction that the lease on Spenton's mines was due to expire in a matter of weeks. He had worked out the terms of an offer that might be attractive to Spenton, linking the loan with revised conditions for the lease.

Spenton had not made any move to visit the bank, and Kemp, wanting to avoid all appearance of eagerness or haste, had waited for an invitation to the nobleman's London house. Instead of this, Spenton had sent him a note by a servant, inviting him to be a guest at a party for dinner that he was giving at the Spring

Gardens in Vauxhall in some days' time. Kemp had learned later that Sykes too had been invited. It wasn't exactly what he had wanted; there would be too many people. But he would be able to broach the matter, at least.

Jane Ashton's face came to his mind again. It had all begun there, this prospect for the future, this renewal of purpose and hope, it had all begun with her smile and her glance. Since that moment all had gone well, all was set fair. She had brought him luck. The present lease expired at just the right time for him, and there were no special bidding rights involved in its renewal.

She must have already known about the court cases that were pending. She must have understood that her brother's interests were directly opposed to his, that the man she was looking at stood for everything her brother – and she too, no doubt – considered detestable. Yet there had been no hint of enmity in her regard, and he had been aware of none on his own part as he looked at her. And this was something so far outside his usual habit of mind as to seem almost miraculous.

8

'It is a most amazing piece of good fortune,' Ashton said. 'No, that is not the way to describe it, it is the work of Divine Providence.'

Horace Stanton, who was a friend and fellow abolitionist of long standing, and would be a leading member of the defence when the charges of murder and piracy came before a jury, nodded at these words, but without much appearance of fervour. He was, like Ashton, a devout Methodist, but the name of God did not come often to his lips. Cautious by nature, he was sparing in expressions of faith, not wishing to squander resources. Only in the courtroom, making his final plea to the jury, was this habitual caution relaxed.

'Certainly, it will help our case very considerably,' he said. 'It is likely to help the underwriters too, if they make the right use of it. It is not yet known who will be representing them when the case comes up.'

The two men were sitting over coffee in the morning room of Ashton's house. It was still early; Stanton had come with the news as soon as possible, knowing how much it would gladden his friend.

'I cannot ascribe such a thing to the working of chance alone,' Ashton said. 'There is a blessing in it.'

Jane Ashton entered the room as he was speaking, and bade the two good morning. 'What blessing is that?' she said.

'We have a new witness,' Ashton said.

Stanton's manner had brightened perceptibly at the sight of Jane in her cream-coloured day gown that followed the lines of her figure very much more closely than the hooped skirts fashionably worn for going out. He was unmarried and well settled; he had known Jane Ashton since she was sixteen and had always thought her highly attractive, and not only because of her looks: something careless-seeming in her, irreverent almost, made a challenge to his prudent and sober nature. She was too head-strong, of course, too forward with her opinions – the result of growing up without parental control. But marriage would cure her of these faults . . .

'He is one who was there at the time the Negroes were thrown overboard,' he said. 'One who was neither slave nor crew member.'

'That sounds very mysterious.' Jane smiled at the lawyer, aware of his interest and pleased by it, though privately thinking him somewhat too dry and tending too much to the pompous.

'The interpreter on the ship,' Ashton said and paused, smiling. His face had lost its lines of strain; he looked years younger. 'What they call the linguister, whose work it is to make clear to his fellow Africans the wishes and commands of officers and crew. You understand, there were different languages spoken among them, depending on the region where they were captured.'

'He saw the jettisoning,' Stanton said. 'He saw the crew rise against the captain. He saw everything that took place.'

'He is an African then? I thought they were all sold back into slavery in Carolina.'

'That might have been his fate, certainly,' Ashton said. 'He was not a slave, he was on the ship of his own free will. He was intending to come to England to better his fortunes. None of this mattered to Kemp, of course. The man was offered for sale at Charles Town along with the others. By his own and our good fortune, an army officer just retired and waiting for a ship home, a Colonel Trembath, liked the look of him, discovered he could speak passable English, purchased him and brought him back to England as his personal servant. When he heard the man's story he gave him his freedom and kept him in his service at a wage.'

Ashton paused a moment, and there was a note of wonder when he spoke again. 'He brought him here, to London. He has been here ever since, as a servant in Trembath's house, under the name of James Porter. The interest the case has roused, the frequent mentions of it in the press, brought it to his employer's notice. He has notified us that Porter is ready to testify to the effect that there was no shortage of water at the time, that in fact there had been recent rain when these people were cast overboard. He declares that the decks were not yet dry from it on the morning when the deed was done.'

'Of course, he speaks from memory,' Stanton said. 'But it will carry weight. What makes it particularly fortunate is that there is no charge against him, he has nothing to gain or lose, unlike the people of the crew, and unlike the first mate, who has turned evidence against them. Generally speaking, in my experience, such a witness is likely to be believed.'

Jane regarded her brother's face. It wore an exalted expression, almost fierce in its intensity, as if he were ready to take a sword and strike out. 'I am so glad,' she said, and Ashton, while knowing that her gladness was for his sake rather than the larger issue, was touched by the affection for him in her words and glance. 'It could make all the difference,' he said. 'If we can succeed in having the cases heard together at the Court of King's Bench, and if it can be shown that there was no shortage of water and even that poor pretext was a lie, the hideousness of this crime against our common humanity will be evident to all but the most callous and wicked.'

Stanton, who felt that Ashton was a great deal luckier in his sister than in the reappearance of the linguister, said, 'Well, I must take leave of you. I shall have to examine the wording of this new charge that has been brought against us.' He shook Ashton's hand, lowered his head over Jane's. 'We will talk again later today,' he said, 'or perhaps tomorrow morning. In any case, as soon as I have all the facts.'

'What charge is it that they have brought against you?' Jane asked when he had gone.

'It regards the man Evans. You will remember my telling you that I intended to bring charges for assault and abduction against his former owner, Charles Bolton, in response to his charge against me of theft.'

'Yes, I remember.'

'Well, it has emerged that Bolton had already sold Evans to another man, a sugar planter named Lyons. Imagine it, he had sold him already, even before the abduction attempt, while he was still living peacefully in Chelsea, not suspecting anything. Now both of these men are bringing charges of damages and theft against me. Yes, it is scarce credible, I know, but such are the facts. And with the worship of property that is growing among us, their arguments may prevail. Much will depend on the judge.'

'Let us hope he will be reasonable.'

Ashton smiled. 'Well, not too much so,' he said. 'An entirely reasonable man is likely to conform too closely to prevailing notions of what is reasonable, and put property before all else. No, let us hope rather that he will have a heart open to compassion.'

'You are going out?' She had only noticed now that her brother was wearing shoes instead of slippers and that his hat lay on the table, where he must have placed it.

'Yes, I was about to leave when Stanton came. I am going to the prison. I intend to speak to these men and question them.'

'To the prison? What, into the cell where they are being held?'

'No, I hope to be allowed to see them in one of the yards behind the keeper's lodge.'

'But you will catch your death. Everyone knows it is a hatching place of diseases. No one goes there that does not have to.'

'Nevertheless, I am going.'

'At least let me have some vinegar packs made up to hang inside your coat.'

Ashton was impatient at the delay, but he saw the concern on his sister's face, and he was accustomed to bow to her wishes in matters of this kind, where safety and care of the person were involved.

When, some time later, provided with the vinegar-soaked bobbins, he sallied forth in search of a sedan that would carry him to Newgate Street, Jane remained where she was for a time, without moving. The thought of being anywhere in the vicinity of Newgate Gaol, let alone entering it, was appalling to her. Once, coming down from Bridewell Walk to Clerkenwell, after a visit of charity to the workhouse, she had passed by the prison, and the deathly stink of the place had assailed her, even closed as she was in her carriage, and the voices of the women screaming through the bars at people going by along the foot passage.

She had never forgotten that reek of misery and violence; always now, on her visits to the workhouse, she told the coachman to turn directly into Corporation Lane and so return home by the longer route. She had felt no pity at the time and none since, only a violent disgust, and a sort of rage that people, however low their estate and however ill their deeds, could be treated thus, manacled and pent up in that festering place. Frederick had said that compassion counted for more in a judge than a too-reasonable habit of mind. But it seemed to her that anger was much to be preferred to either, a rage for improvement, for changes in the way things were done – changes that should be effected now, immediately, since the need was so obvious, so pressing. She felt this rage for betterment within her, despite the lightness of manner, the slight air of carelessness she generally assumed in the society of others.

She had acquaintances among her own sex who were zealous in works of charity, but there were none she could think of who felt this passionate need to change the state of things. No man of her acquaintance – and in this she included her brother – would think it becoming in her to give eager expression to such opinions in company; some she could think of, if they were alone with her and felt safe from the judgement of their fellows, might try to please her by pretending to take her words seriously . . .

These thoughts made her feel rebellious and disconsolate at the same time, a mixture of feelings familiar to her. She found herself thinking about Erasmus Kemp and wondering how he would take it if she spoke seriously to him about things that mattered to her. She could not imagine it, she did not know him. But he was different from the other men she had met. His looks and manner came vividly back to her. He had seemed to gather all the energy of everyone else there, gather it to himself and contain it and bring it to her as an offering.

She would not go on with her embroidery, she decided; she would return to her own apartment and have her coffee there, and continue reading the latest issue of *The Ladies' Diary*. Much of this was written by gentlemen in tones considered suitable for ladies. But it contained, amid news of the latest fashions and

9

Ashton alighted from his chair on the eastern side of Bridewell and approached the prison by the covered passageway that led towards the entrance gates to the keeper's lodge. After some twenty yards he emerged into the open at a point immediately below the outer wall of the prison, whose five storeys rose sheer above him. From one of these floors, as he passed, a chamberpot was discharged, and he narrowly escaped being fouled by its contents. Sounds of pain and riot rose to him from the gratings of the cellars where the condemned were held.

He stated his business to the turnkey at the gate, a man of unsavoury appearance and unsteady with drink. Stating his business, however, was not enough to gain him entry. The turnkey asked for a shilling, which he declared to be the usual tariff, but was then visibly content to get the threepence that Ashton handed him through the bars.

Oppressed by the stench and grimness of the place, Ashton took refuge in levity. 'Well, my friend,' he said, 'if it will keep you drunk the longer, I suppose it has to be seen as a good cause. It is not surprising that a gatekeeper to the infernal regions should ask for a sweetener, there is good precedent for it.'

No reply to this was forthcoming. He was led across the short yard to the lodge, where he found two assistant keepers making up a tray of wheat bread and sliced pork.

'You the visitin' gen'leman what ordered up the vittles for the press yard?' one of them said at sight of Ashton. 'Sixpence ha'penny, yer pays beforehand an' takes the tray yerself. If yer wants it taken up, that will be eightpence.'

'I can eat better than that round the corner at half the cost,' Ashton said.

'Ah, yes, sir, but yer not suffrin' from the 'andicap of bein' in confinement, are yer now? Prices is subjec' to circumstance, every mother's son knows that.'

'I see you are a philosopher,' Ashton said. 'I am not he who ordered the food, I have nothing to do with the press yard. I want to speak to the keeper. I want to ask him for an hour or so with the seamen who are awaiting trial on the piracy charge.'

'Them as threw the blacks over the side an' rose agin the captain an' made off with the ship?'

'Those are the men, yes,' Ashton said, impressed again by the way in which these separate events were taken as belonging all together in the popular mind.

The man looked Ashton over for a moment, taking in the cut and material of his clothes, the silk cravat, the ebony cane. His nostrils twitched at the smell of the vinegar. 'The keeper ain't 'ere today, sir,' he said. 'He is rangin' abroad on matters of public concern.' The other man sniggered at this but said nothing.

'To whom can I apply then?'

'There is several of 'em, as I recall. An' yer wants to see 'em all at the same time. That means two armed men to keep a watch out an' prevent 'em doin' you a mischief.'

'That is not likely. I am here to help them.' He had time privately to acknowledge that this was not strictly true, before the man said, 'Goin' by time an' ooman resources that comes to one shillin' an' sixpence, sir. Cash down.'

'Don't you get wages?'

At this both men smiled broadly, the first smile he had seen on either of their faces. 'Wages, ho yes,' the younger one said. 'What is them?'

On handing over the money, he was led to a narrow, evil-smelling courtyard immediately behind the lodge. The gate to this was unlocked to him; he was joined shortly by two taciturn men with pistols at their belts and staves in their hands, and the three of them waited in silence between the high walls of dark brick that enclosed the yard.

Ashton stared at the wall before him, trying to rehearse in his mind the best way to conduct the impending interview. It was of first importance to gain the men's confidence, try to break down the distrust they would feel towards any that came with seeming authority from the world outside. Only thus could he lead them the way he wanted them to go.

Lost in these thoughts, he was startled, almost, to hear the rattle of the gate and see the men being led in. Among the variety of experiences that the case of the *Liverpool Merchant* had in store for him, this first sight of the remnants of the crew was to remain one of the strongest and most lasting. He had thought much of these men, but always as a group, undistinguished one from the other, a single body with a single mind, under the captain's orders at first, then joined in rebellion. It was with a distinct sensation of surprise that he noticed now the differences in feature and stature among them as they came through the gate, and saw the glances, bemused and uncertain, of those who have been thrust out of dimness into light. All were bearded and unkempt, but he noted that one was squat in build and strongly made and vacant in looks, a second ill-conditioned in expression, with jaundiced eyes, another hulking of form with a shambling walk and only one eye that was of use to him – the white blob of the dead one had a steadiness both sinister and droll, strangely at odds, in its fixity, with the blinking of the other.

'I had believed there were eight,' he said to one of the guards.

'One got clear away,' the man said. 'The luck of the Devil, he got hisself mistook for someone else. The fiddler, that was.'

Once through the gate and into the yard, the men wavered forlornly together for some moments. Then, as if by a common instinct, they moved to the near wall and took up positions there, with their backs to it.

'Will you go outside the gate?' Ashton said to the guard who had spoken. They would be out of earshot there, the men would be more at ease. 'You can keep us under observation just as well from there, and intervene quickly enough if there is any sign of trouble.'

'Our orders was to keep close,' the man said. 'Anythin' untoward, an' it is on our heads.'

'There is such a thing as dooty, sir,' the other guard said. 'Me an' Jemmy is very partic'lar in doin' our dooty.'

'I don't doubt it,' Ashton said. 'There is sixpence for each of you if you will do as I ask.'

The hesitation was of the briefest; it seemed to Ashton that he had barely finished speaking before the men's hands were reaching out to him. Only when they were outside the gate did he turn to the men against the wall. 'I have come here to help you,' he said, and the partial lie steadied him, gave force to the words that came next. 'I do not represent the prosecution. I will not take advantage of anything you say to me, unless I can do you good by it. I want you to trust me.'

He saw one of the men, grey-bearded and seeming somewhat older than the rest, glance up, saw a twist come to his face that might have been a smile. 'Trust don't come into it,' this man said. 'Yer might as well talk of trust to a rat in a hole. We are lost men.'

'Your cause is not lost,' Ashton said. He had noticed the total lack of deference in addressing him. 'You are?'

'Hughes, my name.'

'We calls him the Climber.'

This had come from one of the men against the wall, Ashton was not sure which. 'Why do you call him that?'

'He was allus climbin' to get away on his own, up on the top trestles,' the one-eyed man said. 'He don't like anyone close.'

'I see.' A sense came to him of the torment such a man must have suffered, chained and penned up with the others. Even in prison the quality of suffering would vary. Had it come home to Hughes that he had helped to inflict suffering even worse on the slaves below decks? Probably not . . . 'Is there one who will speak for all?' he said.

There were some moments of hesitation, then one of the men raised his head to look squarely at Ashton. 'I can speak for the others, sir,' he said, 'seein' as I was the carpenter, an' therefore rankin' above, as is so considered aboard ship.'

'What is your name?'

'My name is Barber, sir, William Barber.'

'Can you tell me how it came about that the Negroes were thrown over the side?'

'It was the capt'n's orders,' the one-eyed man said before the carpenter could speak. 'We was only obeyin' orders. We was all in it together. On a ship you does what you're told to do by them that is set above you.'

'That is true, I suppose,' Ashton said. 'But surely there is still a choice to be made? After all, there is a higher law than that of a ship's captain. No man can be obliged to act against his conscience.'

Hardly had he uttered the words before he knew them for untimely and out of keeping. But it was his habit to utter general statements of a moral kind and though these were felt sincerely he did not always pause to consider whether it was the right moment for them.

'Them that has not been at the orders of a slavin' skipper can have no opinion. Show me a conscience that will stand up to the cat-o'-nine-tails, I would like to see one.'

This had come from Hughes, and Ashton was wondering whether he should attempt a reply to the effect that the threat of flogging would have been of no avail if the crew had been united in opposition, when another voice was raised. 'Beggin' your pardon, sir, I was in the galley, I did not come out on deck till hearin' Mr Paris call out an' then the pistol shot that came after.'

'That is Morgan, sir, the ship's cook,' Barber said. 'It is true that he was in the galley at the time, we can all swear to that.'

'Will you go on with your account?'

'The slaves was dyin' in numbers, sir, both the men and the women. There was the bloody flux among them, an' it was gainin' ground day by –'

'What is that?'

'It is when they passes blood, beggin' your pardon. What they eat is turned to blood inside of them, they passes it with their excrements an' they gets weaker an' dies from one day to the next. The ship run into squally weather, we had to fasten down the hatches on them, they had no air, sir. On that mornin' we are talkin' of, when we opened the hatches we found twelve dead, countin' men, women and boys. I remember well the figure because it was what Thurso began by tellin' us. He called us to a meetin', you see, sir, the ship's officers that was left.'

Hughes let the words wash over him, without paying much heed to the meaning. It was an old story, too much had happened since. He looked up to the strip of sky above him. It was blue, hazed with the smoke of the city. With what seemed something more than an accident of timing pigeons flew across that narrow space as he looked up, glinting in the sun, birds of silver. Even amid the stench of his person and that of his shipmates, even in the misery and filth of this place, he seemed to sense the burgeoning of spring. He scanned the wall across from where he was standing. Sixteen, eighteen feet. There were cracks in the brickwork and small hollows where the mortar had crumbled from the joints. Given time, given a bit of luck . . . He did not really believe it; he was old now, nearly fifty, his muscles had stiffened in prison; a bad fall, and he could cripple himself. On crutches to the hangman . . .

He had always been a climber, always first in the tops. In the dark misanthropy of his nature he had found joy in sleeping away from the others, slung high aloft, swaying in his sleep with the sway of the ship. In the years of the settlement too he had kept apart, always happiest at a distance from his fellows, making platforms up in the trees where he could hide away. Suddenly now, in the midst of the voices, a memory came to him. He had been high up in a jungle cluster, overlooking a freshwater pool. The white-tailed deer came to drink there; bow and arrows on the platform beside him, he had been waiting to see them come stepping through the trees. If you chose the right moment, when the deer lowered its head to drink, you could break its neck with a single bolt. Waiting there in solitude – it was one of his last memories of happiness. And it had been then, in those moments, that he had looked seaward and seen the schooner, wondered why it dallied there at anchor, not knowing that aboard her was a man named Erasmus Kemp, who had come to destroy them.

This was the man who had taken him and set him here in this hateful, choking closeness to others, a closeness there was no escaping, that had brought out a spirit of murder in him, not against his mates, who were caged and helpless as he was, but against those outside, those who had done this to him, who still lived in freedom.

'He put it to us fair and square,' Barber said. 'There was the bosun an' the first mate an' the cooper, Davies, an' me. We was all the officers what was left, d'ye see, sir?'

'Not the doctor?'

'No, sir, Mr Paris was laid up with a fever. Well, he was comin' out of it, but he was keepin' to his quarters below. I think we all knowed that was why Thurso called the meeting when he did.'

'What do you mean?'

'Them two never got on. Thurso didn't want no argument, he never liked anyone goin' agin him.'

'I see, yes. So he put the matter to you . . .'

'The slaves was dyin', we had been blown off course, we was still a good many days from Jamaica. Them as died aboard was of no value, but if they was jettisoned with lawful cause the ship's owner could claim insurance. Thurso said he would make sure every man jack of us got a piece of that money.'

'It is easy to promise money that is not your own,' Ashton said. 'Would you be ready to swear in court that the captain offered you a bribe to do as he wished?'

It was a false move, too precipitate, he saw it immediately in the faces that were turned to him, the stillness that seemed to descend on the forms of the men as they stood there against the wall. No answer was made to his question. After some moments the carpenter said, 'Then there was the shortage of water, sir, that was what made it legal like.'

'Are you sure water was short? Had you been placed on rations?'

'That I don't remember,' Barber said. 'Any of you lads remember if we was rationed for water?'

No reply came to this, and there was no movement among the men.

'There had been copious rain during the night, or so I am given to understand,' Ashton said.

'Water was short,' Hughes said. 'We was aboard the ship an' you wasn't.'

In spite of himself and the resolution of forbearance he had made, Ashton stiffened at the insolence of this, and raised his head to meet the man's gaze directly. He saw dark eyes that made no move to evade his own; there was a fire of violence in them such as he had rarely seen. For the first time he felt glad of the presence of the armed guards just beyond the gate. He needed only to raise his hand to summon them.

'Please listen to me,' he said. 'I understand why you should want to maintain the legality of drowning your fellow human beings – for that is what they were, made in God's image, just as you and I are, and completely unoffending. But there is no protection for you in this, even if it could be proved. It is no defence, with the capital charges of murder and piracy you will be facing, to plead that the jettison was lawful, that you were labouring under necessity. That is the line the ship's owner will take, Mr Erasmus Kemp. He will be supported in it by the testimony of the first mate, Barton. By asserting that there was a shortage of water, you will only succeed in helping Kemp to obtain the insurance money he is claiming on the deaths of these poor people. Surely you can see that? Kemp is the man who brought you to this ruin.'

No answer came to this, and he saw no change in the attitude of the men. He had been too optimistic. How could they regard him as a friend, as someone who desired to help them? He came from the world outside the prison, the world that asks questions, calls people to account. He needed their trust, he was exerting himself on their behalf, but it was not to save them from the gallows – this he admitted freely to himself; their ultimate fate did not really matter to him, he did not feel concerned in it. Through them, through the public notice they might draw to this atrocious crime, thousands of lives might be changed, might be saved.

He still had his appeal to make. He had been wrong to hint at blame. It was essential now to get them back to the narrative, bring them together again in the effort of recollection. 'So all the crew were involved in it?' he said. 'In the casting them over, I mean.'

'Yes, all of us,' Barber said. 'That is, all of us 'cept for Morgan and Hughes. Morgan was in the galley an' Hughes was up aloft, keepin' an eye out for the weather.'

Once more Ashton encountered that fearsome regard. Unlike Morgan, Hughes had not tried to exculpate himself, he had not deigned to.

'We had to make a ring round them in case they tried to run,' Barber said.

'I was one of them that done the handlin',' the one-eyed

man said. 'Me and Haines an' Wilson was the ones that hoisted them over.' It was clear that he had misunderstood the whole tone of the conversation, the defensiveness of his shipmates. He had spoken in an ingratiating manner, addressing himself directly to Ashton, as if it were a mark of his virtuous character that such a trust should have been placed on him. 'Us bein' the strongest,' he said. 'Me and Haines was close, both bein' London men.'

'Haines was the bosun, dead now,' Barber said. 'He was killed by Indians in Florida when we was first tryin' to settle there.'

'Haines got what he deserved. He was a bastard of a flogger an' you was his lickspittle, Libby.'

This came from Hughes, who had briefly transferred the anguish of his rage to the hulking man beside him. That Libby made no direct reply to this was a sign, as it seemed to Ashton, both of the truth of the assertion and the menace that emanated from the speaker.

'Haines was set over us,' Libby said, for all answer, adding after a moment, 'I am a man what respects them that is set over us.'

His single eye was flickering, as if the light in the yard was too strong. It came to Ashton that he might be on the way to blindness. He was clearly a man by nature subservient, eager for the protection of authority, a tendency likely to grow stronger if sight were failing him. He might be useful. If handled in the right way he might be persuaded to go counter to the version of events the others had collectively agreed on. Worth remembering in any case . . .

'And so this business was halted by the appearance on deck of Matthew Paris, the ship's surgeon?'

'That is correct, sir, he came up from his sickbed on to the quarterdeck an' he held up his hand an' cried out agin it.'

'I see, yes.' A sudden vision of that distant intervention came to Ashton: the rain-washed deck, the cry, the raised hand, the violent aftermath. 'That is what gave you pause,' he said.

A thin, fair-haired man standing beside Libby now spoke for the first time. 'We was busy keepin' the ring, keepin' a watch for any that tried to run, we didn' know at first where the shout come from, it was like it come from the sky, an' he was pointin' up to the sky when he come forward.'

'That is Lees, sir,' Barber said, performing once again the

duty of introduction he had assumed. 'He is in the right of it, I think we all felt somethin' sim'lar. There was two that didn' wait for us,' he added after a moment. 'A man an' a woman. They run an' jumped over the side together before anyone could lay a finger on them. They might of been related, I dunno. Mebbe like man an' wife or brother an' sister. We took them aboard an' stowed them below, men on one side, women on the other, without thinkin' much if they might be related. It was a thought that only came to me later. To tell you the truth, sir, it is not easy to recall these things an' not easy to talk about them, for most of us at least.'

He had glanced round at Libby as he uttered these last words. It was clear that this self-proclaimed friend of the dead bosun was not very popular among them. Also worth remembering . . .

'Why is that?'

'We lived together, we got to know one another, good and bad. Twelve years, sir, you gets a diff'rent view. There was fewer women than men, the women had to be shared by agreement, so as to avoid fightin' over it. The women had to agree too, as it was decided – there was to be no forcin' of the women. When you are all sharin' together, who is black an' who is white don't weigh much on the scale. As a way of judgin' folk, I mean.'

The legal case that could be made out of the murder of the slaves and the mutiny that followed had mainly occupied Ashton's thoughts up to now; he had not speculated much about how the survivors had lived afterwards in their settlement, and it had not occurred to him that there would have been this sharing among them. He felt immediately repelled, and faintly sickened at the thought of it, black and white fornicating together by turns, a thing displeasing to God and man alike, producing a mixed race. It was not to further promiscuity of this sort that he was fighting to free the enslaved. Once free, they would be happy to return to Africa, to find dignity and prosperity among their own people. On the other hand, the deeper understanding that had come about through this experience of life together in community, if it could be voiced in court, might have an effect on the jury, as showing the absurdity of asserting a right of property in one's fellows on the grounds of race or colour . . .

He took care to let nothing of these thoughts show in his

face or manner. It was time now to make his promise to them – first the promise, then the appeal. 'You are kept in chains, I believe,' he said. 'Everything has a price here, so it seems, and I will make sure that you are not fettered again, at least until they bring you for the hearing. And I will contrive matters so that you will get regular and wholesome meals.'

He saw Barber glance sharply round at the others. Libby smiled in ugly fashion, and a look of wondering delight appeared on the half-witted man's face.

'We are beholden to you,' Barber said, and there were nods among the men, and one or two exclamations of agreement. There was no softening in Hughes's regard, however.

'I want to make an appeal to your reason and your self-interest,' Ashton said. 'There is only one way for you to escape hanging. If you will plead that you mutinied on grounds of conscience, that you rose against the captain because you realised that you were engaged in murdering innocent men and women, then you will have a chance of life. There would be no real falsehood in such a statement, only a shifting of the time. After all, you came to this realisation later, during your years in the settlement. It will be argued against you that this change of heart was belated, too much so to carry conviction, as it did not occur until many had already been cast overboard to drown. But you can make reply that you were under the orders of the captain, whom you were accustomed to obey. When Divine Mercy intervened, in the person of the ship's doctor, you saw the hideous error of what you were about, and immediately ceased from it. If we can succeed in swaying the jury to that effect, it is more than likely that they will dismiss the capital charges on the grounds that there was no intention of harm, and you will go down in history as heroes of the anti-slavery movement.'

And if we fail, he thought, and you end on the gallows, there is a chance that you will be seen as martyrs, and that is almost as good . . . But no, they were not the stuff of martyrs, or heroes either; they had no voice, no attitude, they represented nothing. If by some miracle of advocacy true justice could be done and these men declared guilty of murdering the slaves and hanged for it in full view, that would be the best solution of all. Beyond hoping for – Stanton would not risk such a plea. But what a wonderful thing it would be, what a triumph! A clarion call through all the years to come, sounding the note of justice and humanity to future generations . . .

With this thought, his sense of differences among the men, a perception that had earlier taken him by surprise, altogether disappeared. They became once again in his eyes the featureless, amorphous body they had been before, a body that circumstance had deprived of all rights, made entirely subject to considerations of utility, of the higher and nobler purposes they could be made to serve.

'If you do not make this plea,' he said, 'you will have no defence against the charges of murdering the captain and making off with ship and cargo, since the slaves will be regarded in that light. You will be condemned and you will end on the cart to Execution Dock.'

No reply of any kind came from the men assembled there. Ashton regarded them in silence for some moments, then he said, 'I leave the matter to your consideration. I will pray to Almighty God that you be guided to the right decision.'

On this, he raised an arm and signalled to the guards waiting outside the gate.

10

'I should have suspected somethin' there and then, when he said that about seein' the power of music in me. How can anyone see the power of music in a man only by exchangin' a few words? He must have been followin' me, he must have seen me fiddle. But the notion did not enter me mind at the time, I was puffed up with pride an' vainglory, I am not the man to deny that.'

Several people were listening to this, or appearing to, all in a medium state of drunkenness, as was Sullivan himself. They were sitting around a fire of scraps and rags on a piece of waste ground in the town of Peterborough. 'They is terrible cunnin', some of these beastly fellers,' somebody said.

'Lookin' at it another way, I had spent a good part of the money, so the loss was not so grievous. Then there was this shillin' that was left to me. Small things can lead to great, as various sages has observed at different times. A shillin' is not a large sum, but when I discovered that shillin' in me pocket I knew the Blessed Virgin was still keepin' me in the lamp of her eyes. It was at the first partin' of the ways, one road was leadin' to Watford, the other to St Albans. I took a shillin' out of me purse an' tossed it an' it come down for St Albans.'

'Aye, St Albans, is it?' another man said. 'I bin there.'

'What it was, you see, I was only lately a purse-bearin' man, an' I was not intoirely in tune with the condition of it, so I did not think to put the shillin' back in me purse, I stowed it in me pocket. Then it come back to me, a picture of meself, standin' at the crossroads, spinnin' up the coin.'

He had seen the group round the fire, seen the Hollands

passing among them and brought a pint from the nearby taphouse, so as to be friendly. 'Then there was the pleasure of it,' he said, 'feelin' the edges of the shillin' in me pocket. Pass the jar down, will you, it is stayin' too long at that end.'

Not much was left of his shilling now. Sixpence had gone in the course of the four days it had taken him to get here from Bedford, and twopence had gone on the gin. He felt entitled to a fair share of this, as also, it seemed, did the man sitting next to him, who had contributed nothing but readily seconded his request for the jar to be passed along. This was a lank, lantern-jawed unshaven person, from the folds of whose being there emanated an odour of neglect strong enough to prevail against the fumes from the burning rags.

'My friend, I understand you, I understand you well,' this man said. 'It was the force of habit that saved you.' The gin was beginning to slur his speech slightly, but he had the accent of an educated man. 'One of the strongest forces known to human-kind,' he said. 'I would put it on a level with instinct, in the sense that it is antecedent to reflection. If you had paused for thought, you would have replaced the shilling in the purse and so lost it along with the rest. You may find it hard to believe, but I have known force of habit to be urged in a court of law as a defence against the charge of murder.'

'You know somethin' of the courts then?'

This had come from the man on the other side of Sullivan; there was a woman sitting close by him – it seemed that these two were together.

'Know something of the courts?' The man paused to take a drink from the jar. 'I should think I do.'

'Steady with the fluid,' Sullivan said, reaching out for it. He had to keep his hand extended for a considerable time before the jar was yielded up to him. Half of the gin was gone already. 'My name is Michael,' he said. 'Names are in order, seein' as we are takin' swallers from the same font.'

'Know something of the courts?' the man said again. 'Simon Reedy is the name, a name that should have been known throughout the land, but for adverse circumstances, and conspira-cies against me. I was intended for the law, sir, I might say I was born for it. I practised at the Bar and was widely recognised as an up-and-coming man, a man marked out for greatness. Lord Chief Justice Reedy was the title prophesied by many, until through the plots of envious colleagues I was wrongly accused of falsifying documents and other malpractices of a similar kind, and struck off the list. As a consequence, I was forced to descend to the lower level of lawyer's clerk in the London firm of Bidewell & Biggs.'

'What was the case you was speakin' of, where force of habit played such a part?'

The question came from a ragged man sitting across from Reedy, on the other side of the fire.

'The defendant had struck his wife a blow that knocked her off her feet. In falling she struck her head on a kerbstone, fractured her skull and died on the spot. It emerged that it was this man's common practice to strike his wife in moments of irritation. He had been doing so for many years. His counsel mounted an extremely effective defence on the grounds that the blow had been occasioned by pure force of habit, and that the defendant could not therefore be said to have intended harm, in the sense that the law understands intention, as there had been no interval of time for intention to be formed. I will not disguise from you that I was the barrister who mounted that brilliant defence.'

'What happened to him then?'

'He was sentenced to five years' penal servitude.'

'The son of a whore, he got off light, they should of stretched his neck,' the woman said, speaking for the first time and with unexpected violence. 'I would give 'im force of habit, I would put a bellyache in his broth every night till he croaked.'

'No, no,' the lawyer's clerk said. 'The fact that you administered poison to him on a number of successive nights could not be said to constitute habit. On the contrary, it would argue premeditation, it would be viewed as *malum in se*. Capital punishment should be inflicted in such a case, by the command of God to all mankind. You will remember His words to Noah, our common ancestor. "*Whosoever sheddeth man's blood, by man shall his blood be shed.*"'

'You could train it up to be force of habit,' the woman's companion said. 'If you kept at it night after night with very small doses, just a grain or two, in the end you would do it without thinkin' twice.'

'You misapprehend,' Reedy said. 'This is the law of the land we are talking of. There is need to make distinctions. The ability to make distinctions is the mark of a civilised society. It is necessary for the welfare of the people, *salus populi suprema lex est.* Pass the jar this way, will you?' His speech had thickened now and his mouth had developed an occasional tendency to slip sideways a little, but there was no faltering in the flow of his words. 'You see, it is very different from the theft of your purse,' he said to Sullivan. 'In that case there was clear intention of harm.'

'Well, it was meditated on beforehand, so much is true. But I contributed to me own downfall. The thought that he might be given to thievin' niver strayed into me mind. He was a Galway man, like meself.' Sullivan paused for a moment, then added, 'Leastways, that was what he gave himself out to be. I have thought since that it might not have been the truth. Losin' the purse was a blow to me, I am not the man to deny that, even though the gravity of it was reduced by the spendin' that had gone before.' He remembered as he spoke the brightness of the weather, the world full of promise as he stepped out into Bedford High Street, well fed and well rested, spring in the air. 'There was a blessin' on me,' he said. 'An it is on me still.'

'You have no cause to reproach yourself,' Reedy said. 'It may have been unwise to trust a man on such short acquaintance, but it was neither rash nor heedless as the law understands these terms.'

In his seagoing days Sullivan had seen much strong drink consumed, and it impressed him now that the lawyer's clerk was able to maintain such command over his speech while slowly losing it over his features and the bearing of his head. It argued a great deal of practice. 'I am not sure in me mind how them words differ,' he said. He had always liked to pick up new words and use them in conversation; it added tone to a man. A great deal of his vocabulary had come from songs he knew by heart and sometimes sang to the accompaniment of his fiddle.

'They differ profoundly,' Reedy said. 'Rashness consists in failure to perceive, or give full consideration to, an error in the surrounding circumstances, when an action is being contemplated or is about to be taken. Heedlessness is a wrongful failure to advert to and give due weight to, the surrounding circumstances, when an action is being contemplated or is about to be taken.'

Finding no immediate response to this, Sullivan contented himself with nodding sagely. Reedy's head was declining on to his breast. His words came more slowly now and were more difficult to follow. 'Both in their different ways are forms of failure to take care, and both are deserving of punishment if harm or wrong should ensue. I lost my place as a clerk in the firm of Bidewell & Biggs because of the gross heedlessness of Bidewell, who frequently left money in a drawer in the anteroom of his office without ensuring that the drawer was kept locked, thus bringing about the ensuing harm of my dismissal. This criminal heedlessness of my employer was compounded by . . .'

The voice died away. Something between a sigh and a snore came from Reedy and then no further sound.

'Force of habit,' the woman's companion said. 'He knows somethin' about that, I dare say. He already had a skinful before you brought the extra. He is here without shelter an' night comin' on because he has found his true level, never mind all that talkin'. It is different with us, we got nothin' to blame ourselves for. Till three months ago me an' Betty here an' our three children were livin' as we had allus lived, as my father lived before me. We had some strips of land in the open fields on the edge of the village of Thetford, not very far from here. We kept fowls, we had a cow, we got our firewood from the common land. Then the new law come in. They enclosed the village an' shut us out. Most of the common land was taken by the squire, an' so we lost our livin'. We couldn't pay the rent, they didn't want us on the parish poor rates, so they put us out of our cottage, bag and baggage. We found people in the village, freeholders, who were willin' to take the children for the sake of the work that could be got out of them. We been on the move ever since, livin' as we can. There is a new factory opened in the town, an' they wants people for frame-knittin'. We are goin' to try our luck there tomorrow.'

'We stay together,' the woman said, and Sullivan saw her smile at the man beside her. 'Sharin' makes it easier,' she said. 'We been unlucky in some ways, but we still together.'

Sullivan considered for a few moments. The jar was finished, the fire was dead; most of those who had been sitting around it had melted away without his noticing. He had enough money left for two pallets on the floor of a lodging house, but not more. The lawyer's clerk had no coat to his back, only shirt and waistcoat. Just as I was meself, he thought, when I walked through the prison gates an' set off for the County of Durham, holdin' me vow inside me . . .

He shook Reedy by the shoulder to rouse him. 'You an' me will find lodgin' for the night, so we can be in better case to welcome the mornin'.'

Roused from his stupor, Reedy affirmed that he knew of a place not far away where a bite to eat and a space on the floor could be secured for twopence a head. 'This is a true act of friendship,' he said. 'Simon Reedy will be eternally grateful.'

With Sullivan supporting his uncertain and wavering steps, he led the way through a maze of streets until they came to a house that had no inn sign or mark of any kind, only a brass candle-lamp set over the door. They were received by an elderly woman of unsmiling looks and short words, to whom Sullivan handed over his last pennies.

The sleeping spaces were straw with strips of hessian laid over them; there was a row of chamberpots along the wall at the far end. There were a dozen people already there, three of them women. Sullivan soon disposed of the slice of bread and the bowl of thin gruel, but Reedy could not stomach more than two spoonfuls of this, so Sullivan obliged by having the rest. 'I have always been a foe to waste,' he said.

The two found space to lie side by side, and the candles were doused and borne away, all save one. Reedy reaffirmed his eternal gratitude, relieved himself in one of the chamberpots and was soon snoring. Sullivan looped the straps of the cloth bag containing his few possessions over his arm in such a way that no one could detach it or fumble inside it without disturbing him. He did the same with his boots, tying them together and looping them into the handle of the bag. His head was heavy with the gin and sleep came soon to him.

When he awoke, the pale light of morning was coming through the solitary window. The groans and sighs of reluctant awakening came from various parts of the room. His bag and boots were with him still, but when he sat up he discovered that the brass buttons no longer adorned his coat – they had been neatly snipped off. Where the lawyer's clerk had been there was only an empty space.

11

As Michael Bordon, walking close behind his father, drew nearer to the eye of the pit, he saw, in this first light of day, what looked like stones falling through the sky, and knew this for the plunging flight of peewits, the first of the year, the courtship flight. Because of the mist that lay over the fields he could not watch the recovery from these downward plunges, but he had seen it often enough before, the way they flirted with catastrophe, saving themselves at what seemed the last possible moment, rising again on strong wingbeats.

The sight of the birds did something to uplift his mood, which was sombre this morning. It was Saturday; next day he was due to meet Walker in the corner of the big field. He was not afraid of hurt, but he was afraid of losing. He felt now that he had been unwise to force the issue in this way; he had allowed his temper to get the better of him. It might have been possible to ask the overman if his brother could be shifted to another putter. Too late for that now; he could not withdraw from the fight at this late stage, on any pretext at all. If he lost, David would be worse off than ever. He had some advantages: he was very quick in the reflexes of his body; he had good balance and he saw well on both sides. But he was not a natural brawler, and his adversary was two years older and a good deal thicker in the shoulders.

Walker was among the men waiting at the head of the shaft to be winched down, but the two did not look at each other. They had to wait there some minutes for the banksman's call of all clear. Michael saw the women and girls arrive, a little later than usual. Elsie was among them and he could see her face and form clearly because of the lamps around the mouth of a new shaft that was being sunk to serve for ventilation – the sinkers were only three feet down, they needed a good light at the surface. The smile she gave him was different from one you might get when passing in the street or talking together among other people. It stayed with him as the banksman's call came up, as side by side with his father he clutched at the rope and made a loop in which to bind his right thigh, as he secured his grip and took David astraddle over his knees, as they were winched down and the light from the fire bucket overhead slowly faded, leaving them to descend in a darkness relieved only by the flickering light of the candles far below.

Elsie's face and the movements of her body as she worked came to him intermittently as he toiled through the day. The routine of his labour varied little. He had a youth to help him, a little older than his brother. Together they loaded the corves with the coal hacked out by the hewers; together they loaded these on to the wooden sledges, though the heavier part of this fell to the elder – the boy was not yet strong enough to take his full half of the weight. Michael wore thick strips of leather attached to the back of his belt and known to all as bum-flaps; with the aid of these he would crouch to get his backside against the loaded corf and heave against it, while the boy hauled on it from the other side, until together they got it shifted into position on the sledge. Then, with one pushing from behind and one dragging from the front, they moved the loaded sledge to the pit bottom, where the corves were tallied, hung on the rope by the onsetters and drawn up.

This series of actions they continued for the fourteen hours of the shift, with two breaks to eat and drink – brief, because their wages depended on the amount of coal they moved. In the final two hours neither man nor boy had any thought at all. There was only the ache of the muscles, the patient endeavour to keep on till the time was up, the wish to be out of the dust and the shifting light, to get to the rope and wrap themselves in it and be drawn up into the open, into the friendly dark.

It was not until evening, when he was washing down, that Michael thought of Walker again, and then only because David was with him, and it was there that he had first noticed the boy's bruises. David had said he wanted to be there, to see the fight, and Michael had found no reason against it, though knowing that if he were beaten David would suffer a double blow, forced to witness his own defeat and the loss of his champion.

From the beginning he had sworn his brother to secrecy. He had said nothing about the matter to anyone else in the family, hoping particularly to keep it from his father, who was violent in his rages and quite capable of challenging Walker's father to a bout – or any other member of the family – if he saw things going against his son. Michael was glad, that Sunday morning, as he walked the half-mile or so to the big field – so called because it was a hundred acres in area – that he had made no mention of it. It was a personal quarrel; he had no desire at all for any public triumph. The only thing that mattered was that Walker should stop taking things out on his brother.

He had chosen for his seconds, first making them promise to say nothing to anyone, two men of his own age whom he had known for as long as he could remember – they had all three started down the mine at the same time. One of them was a cousin of Elsie Foster. There was no source of water anywhere near the field; it had to be carried, and the two took turns with the bucket and sponge, as they walked beside him. It would have made more sense to choose a place nearer the Dene, where water could have been fetched from the beck, but the corner of the big field was the time-honoured place for such encounters, and it would never have occurred to anyone to suggest anywhere else.

At the far end of the field the ground sloped down, then levelled out near the corner, so there was a clear space bounded on both sides by fences and giving a certain sense of enclosure. Michael and his small party were first to arrive, and while they waited he stood a little apart from the others, tense now with knowledge of the test he knew to be coming. In spite of this tension he was curiously detached, taking note of his surroundings as though he would be required afterwards to give an account of them. It was a misty morning, with a pale radiance of sunshine. In the copse at the top of the field there was a colony of rooks, and he could hear the bleating of lambs somewhere beyond that. The cries of the rooks had the same wild, plaintive note as those of the lambs; they echoed back and forth until it became difficult to distinguish one from the other. Through this confusion of sound there came the song of a lark overhead, steady and unfaltering, as he felt his own purpose to be now. He thought again of his brother's face, wide-eyed with the guilt of the bruises.

Across the fields, in the direction of the village, he saw a group of five or six men approaching, dressed in Sunday best, dark suits, caps, white mufflers. As they drew nearer he made them out: Walker was in the centre, flanked by his father, two of his uncles and his two older brothers, one of whom was carrying the bucket.

'He's browt the family with 'im,' Elsie's cousin said.

Michael's heart contracted with contempt for Walker, who had blabbed to his people. 'Numbers are needed if tha's in the army, an' facin' the same way as arl the others,' he said. The scorn was unreasonable, even childish; in some part of his mind he knew it. But it came by necessity; it gave strength to his purpose; for the first time he felt that he had a fair chance of beating Walker.

Greetings were of the briefest. The respective seconds took up position with their buckets roughly ten yards apart. Michael took off his jacket and Walker did the same. The two men advanced towards each other, and they came in a fighting crouch, fists raised – there were no preliminary words, no handshake.

Because the other had adopted a boxing stance, Michael was braced for an exchange of blows, but at the last moment, when they were scarcely a yard apart, Walker dropped his hands, lowered his head and put all his weight into a shoulder charge. There was no time to step aside or give ground, no time to draw back an arm and deliver a punch. Michael took some of the impact on his forearms, which were still extended before him, but the main force of Walker's head and right shoulder took him in the chest, in the region of the heart, winding him so that he fell on one knee, fighting for breath.

It was fortunate for him that he did not try to remain standing, or the fight would have ended there. His seconds came forward to bring him to his corner – this was technically a fall, and he had a right to two minutes of breathing space. But he waved them away and struggled to his feet again. Walker came forward in a rush, as if to repeat the manoeuvre, but in the midst of the pain that breathing still caused him, some instinctive cunning told Michael that this was a feint, designed to make him lower his guard, that the other would stop short and strike at his face, reversing the trick that had served so well at the beginning. In a pretence of being deceived, he took two steps back and lowered his fists as if bracing himself for another charge, at the same time drawing back his right shoulder and keeping his right arm low. As Walker stopped short and swung with his right hand, Michael raised his left arm to block the blow, stepped in close and put all his strength into a hooking punch to the upper part of his opponent's midriff. He saw Walker's face twist with pain, saw the droop of the body as the breath left him. He struck again, first with the left, then more heavily with the right. Despite his hurt, Walker had tucked in his jaw and lowered his head, so these blows were too high to clinch the fight, but the second, landing on the left cheekbone, was enough to send him staggering sideways. Underestimating his opponent's toughness and power of recovery, Michael made the mistake now of advancing too eagerly, and received a blow that split his lip and sent him back on his heels. Again he was lucky. Walker, in haste to make the most of his advantage, slipped on the grass as he advanced. He did not fall, but he lost some moments, and Michael was able to slow him down further with a desperate blow, somewhere between a swing and a lunge, landing on the left temple.

It was a wild blow, but it turned out to be the one that decided the issue. Walker had made no move to block it, though it had been clumsy enough and clearly signalled. It came to Michael now, as he tasted the blood running into his mouth, that his opponent had not seen it coming, that perhaps he did not see well on that side.

The impetus of the fighting – always fiercest in the opening minutes – had lessened now. The two men circled each other for some moments, then Michael repeated the blow, this time giving a wider angle to the swing. Again the blow landed on the temple, but now more heavily. Walker shook his head slightly as if dazed. Michael jabbed at the other's left eye in an effort to close off his vision on that side altogether. He received a flailing blow across the bridge of the nose. Through the tears that this occasioned he saw that Walker's head was hanging low. He swung against the left temple again, putting all the weight of his body into the punch, and Walker went down.

He was supported to his corner and the wet sponge pressed to his forehead to revive him, but the two minutes passed and he did not rise to come forward. Looking across at him Michael saw that he was conscious. The left eye was obscured by blood, despite the bathing, but the other was open and regarding him sullenly. Walker was beaten and he knew it – he had no heart for more.

Michael knew better than to utter any words. The men with Walker had faces of rage. He stood waiting a half-minute longer, then turned away. As he did so he experienced some moments of giddiness and a certain doubt as to whether the ground was firm enough under his feet. He backed against the wires of the fence for support. The corner of his right eye gave him pain, his ribs on the left side ached from Walker's charge and the blood from his upper lip was still flowing, staining his shirt. He closed his eyes, and in a darkness shot through with fire he heard a girl's voice: 'A canna reach up so far, sit thesen down against the fence.' He opened his eyes to see Elsie Foster's face before him, very serious and intent. She was holding the bucket and sponge. 'Tha's too tall for me to reach up,' she said, almost as if it were a failing on his part.

He sank into a sitting position against the fence. A moment later he felt the wondrous cool of the water on his brows and on his mouth. 'Tha's in a right mess,' Elsie said.

'She must have got wind of it somehow,' the cousin said. 'Mebbe she heard some talkin'. She must have follered behind us. She took the bucket, it was nay use arguing, she's a terror when she's set on summat.'

Through the blessed touch of the sponge, he saw her face, full of care. 'Can a call round nex' Sunday?' he said, in something of a mumble because of the split lip.

Now at last he saw her smile. 'A thowt tha'd never ask me,' she said.

12

Wednesday afternoon was the time in the week which Erasmus Kemp had chosen for his visits to his father-in-law, Sir Hugo, in the attic apartment of the house in St James's Square, where the old man was kept confined. The day and the time never varied, and it did not on this occasion, though later Kemp was dining at the Spring Gardens as a guest of Lord Spenton, to whom he was intending to make an important proposal – one that he hoped would be seen as mutually beneficial.

At the last moment, before leaving his office, he thought of the brass button lying in the drawer of his desk and remembered again how his cousin had struggled to say something, to answer some question, as he was dying. Something about hope. How had Matthew come by it? How had he come to be clasping such a thing in these last moments of his life? The mystery surrounding the button had endowed it with a sort of power in his eyes, something you might touch to save you from danger or bring you luck. It came to him now that this encounter with Spenton, if it went well, might transform his life, and that he needed all the help he could get. He went to the drawer, took out the button and tucked it into his waistcoat pocket.

On this day he always quitted the bank premises a little earlier than usual, leaving Williams, his chief clerk, in charge. Williams had grown old in the service of the bank and knew more about its affairs than anyone. He had virtually run the bank during Kemp's absence in Florida. Now, with this new interest in the coal industry promising to bring about further absences, perhaps prolonged, Kemp was contemplating the offer of a limited partnership in the firm, though he had said nothing of this yet to Williams.

The two chatted for some minutes while Kemp waited for his horse to be brought from the stables. As usual on this day of the week, the clerk – who knew very well the significance of Wednesdays – made polite enquiries about Sir Hugo's state of health, speaking in tones deferentially lowered, as if his former employer's insanity were cause for enhanced respect. And Kemp answered as he always did, briefly and rather nonchalantly, as if they were discussing the weather.

He took his accustomed route, passing south of St Paul's in the direction of the river. The usual array of traitors' heads adorned the spikes above Temple Bar, and the usual enterprising characters were offering spyglasses for rent to any passers-by who might be taken with a fancy for a closer look at the features of the decapitated felons. In Benton Street he passed a water cart, pulled by two hollow-ribbed horses. A ragged fellow was sprinkling water outside the shopfronts to lay the dust – the shopkeepers would generally give a halfpenny for the sweetening of their premises.

The smell of the wet dust came to him as he rode by. The water brought out a sort of impure sweetness, a compound of dust and warm cobbles and sewage, recalling to him scenes of childhood, his parents' house in Liverpool, in Red Cross Street. On summer mornings the servants would bring out buckets from the houses to lay the dust, and it was as though the water released odours of lime flowers from the trees lining the little square, and pastry smells from the houses and the muddy smell of the Mersey, not far away.

Thoughts of the Mersey brought memories of the docks to his mind. He had sometimes gone with his father to see the unloading of the raw cotton. Smells of tar and molasses, and the smell of the slave ships waiting to be loaded with trade goods, a smell unlike any other, a dark odour of blood and excrement; the timbers were impregnated with it, no amount of scrubbing or sluicing had been able to take that smell away . . . It had not even been necessary to visit the dock for it, he suddenly remembered; at times it had lain over the whole town. On certain days in summer, with the breezes coming from the west, it had invaded the houses, dark, indefinite, all-pervasive, entering parlours through open windows, contending with the scents of flowers in the gardens.

It had been the reek of all captivity to him as he grew up. Neither he nor his father had ever had doubts about the legitimacy and commercial desirability of buying and selling Africans. The trade had brought an influx of capital to Liverpool and to the country as a whole, capital which had helped to fund the nation's progress in industry and manufacturing. Nevertheless, in his present darkened and disillusioned mood, the oppression he felt at the imprisoning circumstances of his life, the sickness of heart that had accompanied his return to England, it seemed to him that this remembered odour enveloped the whole of London too.

He thought of turning down Sutcliffe Street and following the Embankment for a while. But there was too great a press of people in the vicinity of Charing Cross – more so than usual, as it seemed to him – so he took the more direct route towards the Haymarket. As he neared home, his spirits lifted. In a matter of a few hours now he would be joining Lord Spenton and his party at Vauxhall. He would have an opportunity to take a look at the man and sound him out on the possibility of an agreement between them regarding the leasing of the mines on his land. He would be going unaccompanied, which suited well with his purpose of talking privately to Spenton. But Margaret would not have gone with him even had she been alive; they had followed different courses and kept different company; for a good deal of the time neither, if asked, would have known the whereabouts of the other.

Nevertheless, as he entered the house and felt the accustomed silence of the hall settle around him, he experienced a sort of half-resentful nostalgia. It was at this hour that he had sometimes ascended to her apartments on the first floor and taken tea with her. She had never made any special preparation for these visits of his – her preparation was all for the evening's entertainments, in which he had no part. He would find her with her hair set in curling pins and drawn back over a little cushion on top of her head, and her face, more often than not, masked with white paste. Fritz, her poodle, and Marie, her French maid, united in hostility towards him. He had felt uncomfortable in the overheated room with its silk drapes and Italian stucco moulding. Half an hour was the time allotted for these visits, and he had always been glad to leave, and always aware that she was glad to see him go. Now it was as if she had chosen to die while he was away in order to spare herself the tedium of further visits from him on his return. An illness mysterious in its causes and symptoms: increasing languidness, ravagement of the features, a drawn-out distemper or disorder of the blood. Ladies of fashion were more subject than others to this ailment, the doctors had told him. It was suspected that an excessive use of cosmetics played some part in it.

He thought of Jane Ashton's face as she had looked on the occasion of their meeting – the only occasion so far. She had a radiance that needed no help from art. Perhaps there had been a little rouge on her cheeks. Her face had not really left him since that evening. Eyes that had not fled from his – it had been something like flight on his part that had brought him to compliment her on the gown she was wearing. The gown too had stayed in his memory, the bodice close-fitting, with a trimming of lace ruffles on the sleeves, and a lace fichu, transparent as the fashion was, allowing the beginning of the division between the breasts to be glimpsed. White silk, the petticoat . . . No detail could be left out, all had equal importance, all were somehow associated with his new enterprise. He had memorised them as he might have memorised a poem, a verse of magic power. Candid, that was the word for her looks. He felt a rush of need or desire, he could not tell which, somehow made keener by the impending visit to his father-in-law, a duty always disagreeable to him. He must find a way of seeing her again, in spite of the hostile brother; he would tell her of his plans, gain her approval . . .

These thoughts had unsettled him. He washed his face and hands in cold water, and had tea brought to him by his manservant, Hudson. Then, wearing a plain calico dressing gown over his shirt and breeches, he made his way to the top floor of the house, where Sir Hugo had his quarters. He spoke first to Sadler, the keeper, who was quiet-voiced and stout of build, qualities he needed in equal measure, as there was occasion sometimes to soothe, sometimes to restrain his charge.

'Well,' Kemp said, 'how is he today?'

'Much as usual, sir. We had a bit of trouble with our soup. We have written a letter to the Lord Chancellor and another to a wig-maker in Leadenhall Street, and there is a note for Lord North, to be delivered by hand.'

Kemp looked at the sheets of paper covered in his father-in-law's spidery handwriting. The letter to the wig-maker was an order for a silvered-silk toupee with bucklers, a pigtail queue and three rolled curls, the rolls to be hollowed.

'He has a great grasp of detail, sir.' Sadler was always deeply confidential when speaking of the deranged banker. 'He leaves nothing to chance.'

The note to Lord North was in the form of a petition, urging him, as a friend of the King and close in counsel to His Majesty, to do all in his power to resist the movement for abolition of the Atlantic slave trade. Kemp picked out a paragraph at random:

If abolition of the slave trade were to be carried out without reserve or condition, emancipation of the Negroes would soon follow, and with this the interest of England in the West India islands would inevitably decline and die, the capital and property invested therein would at once begin to lose value and would before long entirely disappear, a sum of seventy million pounds by conservative estimate sunk without trace, causing a loss to the revenue of three millions. Sugar, now generally regarded as a necessity of life, will be quadrupled in price, to the discontent and dissatisfaction of the people, with the consequence that our Empire will be rent with dissension and ultimately dismembered . . .

The note would never be delivered. Sir Hugo would forget he had written it or forget when he had written it or believe it was something he still intended to write. So it was with the letter to the Lord Chancellor and that to the wig-maker. The old man spent most of the day at his writing desk and lived in the midst of a plethora of papers, which Sadler gathered from time to time and bore away.

Keeping Sadler still in attendance, Kemp went in now to see

his father-in-law. 'Well, sir,' he said, 'and how are things with you today?'

'Ah, Erasmus, I am glad to see you.' The old man's voice had lost nothing in clarity, nor in decisiveness and authority of tone. He never failed to recognise his son-in-law. Indeed, he recognised everybody. But his memories had lost all order and sequence, and he was often confused as to the time that things had happened – the distant past was the same to him as yesterday.

'There is something I particularly want you to do,' he said now.

'What is that, sir?'

The old man gave him a glance at once fiery and fearful under grey, dishevelled eyebrows. His shirt was open at the neck to show the stringy tendons of his throat, and his scant hair stood in wisps of disarray around his head.

'We were all dressed and ready a half-hour ago, sir,' Sadler said. 'But we have started a new game now, hiding things in odd corners. Orders for wigs are issued frequent like, but we will not on any account keep one settled on our head for more than a few minutes. As soon as your back is turned, the wig is off and stowed away somewhere.'

The old man plucked at Kemp's sleeve, drawing him forward. 'A word in private,' he said, directing a look of sharp suspicion at Sadler.

Kemp allowed himself to be led into the inner room, where Sir Hugo had his writing implements and his desk, with drawers that could be locked. It was in this sanctum that the old man spent his days, entangled in financial dealings that went back half a century.

'I am no longer sure that I can trust Sadler,' he said now. 'More than once lately I have felt inclined to dismiss him.'

He went to one of the drawers in the bureau, unlocked it with a key that he took from his pocket, and took out two folded sheets. 'I want you to see that these are properly delivered,' he said.

Kemp opened them and read them, one after the other. The first was a bill drawn on the Bank of England to be discounted by a Manchester firm for the export of woollen goods to Lisbon in exchange for an equivalent value in gold bullion. Sir Hugo had founded the bank's fortunes on Portuguese bullion obtained from the country's mines in Brazil and he had lately returned to the obstinate belief that this was still a hugely profitable trade, despite the fact that the supply of gold had dried up thirty years ago. The other paper was a promissory note addressed to the bank's agent in Jamaica for a sum of two thousand pounds. This was one of a regular series; the old man was still purchasing Negroes, or so at least he believed.

Kemp had tried and failed on various occasions to reason with his father-in-law, but he could never resist the temptation to try again. It was this obsessive buying of slaves that had led Sir Hugo into madness, and if he could be argued out of it he might be restored to sanity – or so, at least, his son-in-law believed. Kemp had little patience with mental disorder, regarding it in the main as an acute form of error, something that could be mended if sufficient evidence to the contrary were advanced. The old man clung to the belief that abolition of the trade was imminent, a matter of days or weeks; he was constantly issuing instructions for the purchase of Negroes, whatever their age or condition of health, convinced that when abolition passed into law he would be compensated on a per capita basis at the market price, regardless of value.

'Sir, there is no reason whatever to think that abolition will come soon, there is no sign of it, the movement has almost no following in the country. Let us consider the figures a little.' He had himself, as deriving large profits from the West India sugar trade, given considerable attention to the figures over a good many years. 'The nation needs sugar, as you rightly asserted in your recent note to Lord North.'

'I wrote to His Lordship, did I? I know 'twas my intention.'

'Yes, sir, you did. You do well to keep the matter present to His Lordship's mind. The consumption of sugar is deeply entrenched among the people. There would be great unrest in the land if the supply were to decline, let alone fail altogether. It is purchased in British colonies, it is brought here in British ships. So long as this holds good, there can be no falling-off or slackening, we will continue to sell Negroes and buy sugar. In fact, the movement is rather the other way. Last year eighty-two slave ships sailed out of Liverpool. When I went into sugar in 1755, only twelve years ago, there were fewer than forty. In the last half-century there has been a tenfold increase in the tonnage engaged in the trade. In the last decade alone the amount returned on some thirty thousand Negroes was well over a million pounds, and not much less than a million remained when the gross value of the trade goods was deducted. The average maintenance cost of the cargo during the Middle Passage amounts to only ten shillings a head, and this leaves a balance of gain on the whole equal to –'

But he saw now that the old man had grown agitated and distressed at this parade of figures, attacking as they did his cherished plan of buying sick Negroes cheaply and striving to keep them alive for the short period before abolition came. He had began plucking nervously at his clothes and hair, and after some moments he said, 'I was not a member of the committee at the time, I issued no instructions to buy those pieces.'

'Which pieces are those, sir?'

'It was all a plot against me. The cloth was bought through Goddard & Fisher, they had their placemen on the purchasing committee.'

Kemp remained silent for a short while. His father-in-law was back in 1754, when some bales of cloth, of a quality inferior to the sample sent but still marked up on the price, had been sold through a company in which he had a share. 'The court exonerated you, sir, as you will remember,' he said at last.

He met again the old man's eyes, at once enraged and fearful under their disordered brows. Once more he was pierced by the irony of his present relations with this wreck of a man before him. He had never wanted to go into sugar; it had been the quickest route to wealth at a time when he was beleaguered by debts. He had wanted to take active part in a future he saw coming, build the roads and cut the canals that would transport the products of the factories and mines to where they were most needed. And now here he was, extolling the sugar trade as an antidote to madness. In his father-in-law's plight he felt a quality, not of justice exactly, but of appropriateness. After Sir Hugo's long and successful career of chicanery and aggrandisement, his avenging angel had arrived in the form of this demented gamble, this delusion of a race against time. The bank's estates in Jamaica were no longer very extensive; most of the plantations had been sold, the land and the Negroes on it. Little more than a sideline now, but magnified in the old man's mind to enormous proportions, a terror of impending ruin that only desperate remedies could prevent.

Such perceptions of incongruity came frequently to him now; they were unwelcome, they undermined and subverted what he thought of as the proper order of things, like the forcible intrusions of a stranger, and he entertained them only half willingly, as if they involved some betrayal of principle. Sir Hugo's confusion was past mending, it would only get worse – he was obliged to recognise this at last. But he was aware as he quitted the room that his own motions of mind were very far from possessing the order and clarity that he would have desired and thought proper.

13

Some hours later, dressed with extreme care in a suit of dark green velvet, close-fitting at the waist as fashion dictated, but severe of cut otherwise, Erasmus Kemp issued from his house and engaged a sedan to take him to Westminster Bridge, where he found boats plying for hire all along the Embankment. The light was fading when he arrived at the river, but a deep stain of sunset still lingered in the sky. The hot, dry weather had continued, the air was grained with dust, giving a spreading splendour to the sunsets during these days.

The crowd by the water was jostling and noisy, with people thronging for boats and waiting in lines on the quays. Today had been a hanging day at Tyburn, one of the eight in the year – he had not known this, but Hudson had made mention of it while helping him to dress, and he had immediately wondered whether Spenton had chosen the day with this in mind.

Hanging days were occasions for public holiday, and there was a festive, jubilant air in the crowd. Street musicians and beggars and performers of all kinds were taking advantage of this concourse of people. There was a man juggling with pointed spikes, a troupe of dwarf acrobats, a legless ex-soldier, still in tattered uniform, on a little wheeled cart. Pies and sausages were being offered for sale, and a bareheaded gypsy woman was holding out to passers-by a single white rose that she claimed had come from the buttonhole of one of the men executed that day.

Kemp was put out by the proximity of so much humanity, most of it unwashed and vociferous. His clothes were not ostentatious, but they were clearly expensive, and he was aware that he would be an object of interest to pickpockets in such a press of people. He should have brought Hudson with him to guard his back . . . He was annoyed at his failure to do this, and annoyed at having to wait. Anything that came to delay or impede his purposes irked him as if it were part of a deliberate design. He thought of attempting to hire one of the boats for his use alone, but this would have aroused the hostility of those waiting and exposed him to risk of violence.

He hesitated for a short while, then began to walk away in the direction of Lambeth, keeping close to the Embankment. After ten minutes or so he found a small barge with a single oarsman, who agreed to take him to Vauxhall Stairs for two shillings. It was twilight as they set off, and the passenger boats out on the river were lit up with small lanterns set along the rails. As the air darkened, the shapes of the boats were defined by these lamps; beyond them, moored out in midstream and flooded with light, were the bigger boats, Bishop's restaurant and the floating brothel known as the Folly prominent among them. Voices of revelry and the sound of orchestra music carried clearly over the water.

Reaching the Stairs, Kemp paid the boatman and made his way to the Corinthian columns and triumphal arch of the portico that gave admittance to the Gardens. An old man with a powdered wig, dressed in the red and silver livery of those employed in the Gardens, was taking the money at the turnstile; two younger men, wearing the same livery and armed with batons, stood at the sides of the counter to make sure no one tried to enter without paying.

He had arranged to join Spenton's party at their supper box in the front arcade of the pavilion, and he made his way there now, passing up the river stairs and thence along the central avenue, crowded with strollers, its trees ablaze with lamps, to the main garden and the supper rooms. He had not met Spenton, and had no idea what he looked like, but there were only three boxes in the gallery at the front of the arcade and the whole area was brilliantly lit, so he was not troubled by fears of failing to find him. And in fact, while still at some distance, he recognised his banking associate, Sir Richard Sykes, who was standing at the balcony of the box on the right. Sykes saw him at the same time, and waved.

As he drew nearer to the pavilion he was approached by a liveried footman, to whom he gave his name and who led him, not to the box containing Sykes but to the middle one of the three. This directly overlooked a raised platform that had been set up amid the shrubbery; he noticed that four men with musical instruments were seated there. There were several people in the third box too, and someone he did not see called out a greeting to him. So Spenton had hired all three of the supper boxes, the best ones, allowing a view over the avenue and the passing crowds . . .

It was Spenton who stood up now, as he entered the box, to shake him by the hand and perform the introductions. Kemp heard the names and uttered the prescribed phrases of acknow-ledgement without paying a great deal of attention to the faces: the Honourable James Conway, Viscount and Viscountess Mowbray, Sir Joseph Golding, Miss Sheridan, Major and Mrs John Winslow. His main interest was reserved for his host, who gripped him lightly by the arm and said, 'Come and sit here, by me, my dear sir.'

As he sat down Kemp noticed that Spenton had Miss Sheridan on the other side of him, and that she was young and full-breasted and good-looking, with dark hair dressed up on her head and large eyes whose colour he could not determine. Sykes had said that there was a Lady Spenton but that she did not care for London life and spent most of her time on the family estates in the north of England.

'I am glad to make your acquaintance, sir,' Kemp said.

'And I yours. I believe we have matters to discuss. But we will save that for a stroll together after supper. So we can aid digestion at the same time, eh?' He turned in his chair to smile full upon Kemp. 'If you are agreeable, that is.'

'Yours to command.' A man of affable touch and conde-scending gesture – so much might have been expected. There was a good deal of charm in the manner, but the face that was turned to him was strangely at odds with itself; the high, clear forehead and the delicate moulding of bone at temple and cheek were at war with the narrow-lidded, rather protuberant brown eyes and the heavy jaw with its strongly marked cleft, like a dimple that continued too far. He was resplendently dressed in a dark crimson suit with a high collar and buttoned sleeves, and a lace-edged cravat tied in a bow under his chin and secured at the throat with a diamond stock pin. 'Yes, yes,' he said, 'all in good time, we will kill two birds with one stone.'

He looked away as he spoke, and Kemp allowed his face to relax from the smiling expression it had assumed. Smiles never came easily to him. His gaze fell on Miss Sheridan, and she raised her head slightly and widened her eyes at him in a way that seemed provocative. It came to him that this was a lady who had seen some mixed company in her time, for all she was so young. He was wondering what more he might say to Spenton, when he found himself being addressed by the Viscount, who was sitting at his left.

'We are to hear some singing, sir. This gifted young lady is shortly to oblige us. Did you ever hear La Petunia sing "Lasciami piangere"? Egad, sir, she could melt a heart of stone. I once wrote a sonnet to her nipples. Do you enjoy the opera? The English are generally too coarse for it.'

'The ballad is a form more congenial,' Kemp said coldly. He did not like to hear his fellow countrymen criticised and thought the reference to this foreign woman's nipples in very questionable taste, with the Viscountess at the table and within earshot, arguing as it did an acquaintance that went rather further than merely listening to her sing. However, glancing at the lady, he could detect no sign of displeasure. 'We do not like all this Italian posturing and gesturing and pretended passion,' he said.

'We are patriotic, I see,' the Viscount said. 'Very commendable.' He gestured towards the rococo decorations in the columns of the arcade. 'It was those same posturing fellows that designed all this,' he said.

Kemp checked the sharp reply that rose to his lips. He had not come here to quarrel, and it had occurred to him that the other might be slightly drunk. The whole back of the box was occupied by an enormous painting of Britannia Victorious, receiving the victor's wreath from Mars. He turned his head pointedly away from Mowbray, and fell to studying that.

Perhaps feeling some strain in the silence that ensued, the Major's lady, Mrs Winslow, said, 'They have very good concerts at Ranelagh Gardens nowadays too. Did any of you go to hear

Mozart perform there on the harpsichord? His own composition, you know. Only eight years old, quite amazing.'

Conway, a thin, languid man with eyeglasses, now spoke for the first time: 'He will not last, he will burn out. Charles Blenkinsop, the organist at St Paul's, now there is a man.'

'Now would be the time for your performance, my dear,' Spenton said to Miss Sheridan. 'I will escort you.'

Leaning forward and resting his arms on the outer rail of the box, Kemp saw the couple emerge from the arcade and walk arm in arm through the crowd, which was growing denser as the evening advanced. He saw them reach the stage, watched Spenton hand his companion up then mount the steps himself and exchange some words with the musicians waiting there. It was all for her benefit then. Spenton had hired three supper boxes in the front arcade, the most expensive part of the pavilion; he had filled them with his acquaintance, a good many of whom, judging from those in his own box, had an interest in such concerts and probably some influence in the world of opera; he had engaged musicians to accompany her; he must also have hired the space for the stage and paid for its construction; no doubt he had also ordered supper for everybody, to be served when the performance was over. Miss Sheridan had her charms, there was no doubt of that. But for a man in need of a loan it seemed a lot to spend.

At the suggestion of Mrs Winslow, the two ladies of the company took the occasion to go down and join Spenton, who had descended from the stage but remained close by: the three would constitute the beginning of an audience; others would join them, as is the way of passers-by, and Miss Sheridan would get off to a good start.

Something, perhaps the departure of the ladies, or delayed excitement at the thought of La Petunia's beauties, seemed now to rouse the elderly Sir Joseph from a state of apparent torpor. He leaned forward confidentially and said, 'The loveliest of all was Miss Lily Somers, she was a most exquisite performer, a voice that was as clear as it was sweet, there were nightingales within her.'

'One can well imagine where they would make their nest,' the Viscount said, as if to himself.

'I heard her sing Cleopatra at the King's Theatre in the

Haymarket. "Da tempeste il legno infranto". Forty years ago now. I had roses sent to her dressing room. She gave me the two ribbons she had used to tie up her hair, red ribbons.' His voice had risen in the excitement of these reminiscences. For some reason he had fixed his eyes on Kemp. 'Sir, I tied them together and knotted them round my testicles. For years I put them on with my clothes. I wore them till they rotted away.'

'Egad, sir, rotted away, did they?' The Major cast a droll look round the table. 'Nothing lasts for ever,' he said.

Before any more could be said on this subject of mortality, the musicians struck up, and Miss Sheridan's voice rose to them from below. She had chosen her opening song very well, the patriotic ending to 'The Kept Mistress', well known to everyone after the success of the play.

> *This island, this rocky ribbed coast,*
> *This jewel strong set in the sea,*
> *Nor gold mines, nor vineyards can boast,*
> *But boasts she has sons dare be free . . .*

She followed this up with 'Art thou troubled? from *Rodelinda* and, in artful contrast with the stateliness of this, several spirited airs from works by Vivaldi. She had a soprano voice, strong and warmly modulated, and it carried far over the Gardens. Mrs Winslow had been right: a considerable audience had gathered to listen, and there was a good deal of applause at the end of each piece.

Kemp was content to watch the crowd and listen to the singing and wait for the private talk that Spenton had promised him. From here he could see a good way across the Gardens. The columns of the pavilion were lit with glass lamps, and these cast a brilliant light over the singer and the orchestra and the crowd round the stage. There was no breath of wind and the day had been sultry, but there was a freshness in the air, which he thought must be due to their nearness to the river. Perhaps it was full tide – he fancied that there was a faint tang of salt. Light rained down from the lamps in the trees along the avenue, falling on to the standing or moving figures in a way that was curiously capricious in spite of its fullness, making bright, metallic shoots of emerald among the foliage, casting a deep glow on the dyed feathers in the ladies' hats, glittering briefly on powdered wigs.

Miss Sheridan quitted the stage to renewed applause, and Spenton conducted her back to the box. In spite of his nonchalant manner, he had planned the evening with considerable care, or so it seemed to Kemp. The timing was impeccable. As soon as everyone was again seated, while Miss Sheridan was still smiling at the compliments being showered on her, two attendants, they too in the livery of the Gardens, began to mount with supper trays. There was fricassee of quail, the slices stewed in wine and butter, and a good quantity of the legendary Spring Gardens ham, the slices so thin that it was said you could read a newspaper through one, though no one at the table claimed to have tried this. Champagne and claret accompanied the meats, and there were custards, tarts and cheesecakes to follow.

Kemp could not forbear making further calculations while he ate. There must be at least twenty-five guests, he thought, taking all three boxes together. The price normally charged here for a bottle of French claret was five shillings, already far from cheap; ordered up thus for the occasion, it would cost considerably more. Then there was the champagne, then there was the food, then there were the musicians to pay, and the waiters. This was a man in straitened circumstances! The thought came charged with feelings of resentment; Spenton was heedless of expense because he had been born to money, whereas he himself had had to fight and scrape and resort to questionable methods in his pursuit of it.

After supper Spenton suggested a stroll, and this was generally agreed upon. Emerging from the arcade, Kemp saw that there were men engaged in dismantling the orchestra platform, confirming his suspicion that it had been erected there solely for Miss Sheridan's benefit. Spenton took his arm, and together they turned into the first of the gravelled walks that led off from the central avenue. This extended some hundreds of yards and ended in a series of triumphal arches. Beyond there was a further vista, what appeared to be a ruined Roman temple with Corinthian columns, a recent addition to the Gardens that Kemp had heard spoken of but was seeing now for the first time, not a building at all, but a triumph of illusion – a *trompe l'oeil* painting on a huge scale. The walk turned off from this at right angles, leading past a small Chinese pavilion and a statue of Handel playing a lyre in the character of Orpheus. At this point they heard the ringing of a bell not very far away.

'That is the bell for the water show,' Spenton said. 'I always make a point of seeing it when I am in the Gardens. I am having some hydraulic features installed in the grounds of Wingfield, my house in Durham, and so it is of particular interest. Would you care to give it a glance?'

Kemp assented, though somewhat taken by surprise; he had been expecting his companion to broach the subject of the loan, not this one of waterworks. Spenton was obviously a man who dallied and delayed – or perhaps merely affected to. But he was in need of a loan, they would come to it, otherwise they would not be walking here together.

There was a gated turnstile at the entrance to the show, and another liveried attendant there to take the money. It was considerably more expensive than the general charge for entry to the Gardens, half a guinea a head. Spenton insisted on paying for them both. 'Come this way,' he said. 'The figure with which they begin is particularly impressive.'

They were in time to see the figure of Death, a skeleton with an hourglass, slowly rising from the surface of an oval pool, and pointing with his dart at a pillar on which the hours were marked. He had a lamp inside him, lighting up his skull, and his progress upwards was menacing and slow.

'He is standing on a board with a hole in it,' Spenton said. 'The dropping of the water out of the cock and through the hole in the board makes him rise up little by little. Ingenious, ain't it? When he is clear of the water he will strike with his dart at the pillar, and it is this that releases the clockwork and starts up the show. I am presently constructing something similar in the grounds of my house.'

There was no sound of a blow, but the movement of the dart was swift when it came, and the effect was immediate. The pillar was only one of several; all were brilliantly lit up now, and the water came out in a sheer flow, breaking into forms of dragons and swans and fish. At the top of the structure there was Neptune riding a whale, out of whose nostrils the water glittered and jetted through small openings.

'Ingenious, ain't it?' Spenton said again. 'You see the figures but not the devices that set the whole thing going. There are cisterns behind the pillars, a three-level frame, pumps, jacks, weights, springs, piping, a whole mechanical world. You don't see them, they are concealed by the brightness of the light.'

He had spoken with a liveliness of interest quite at odds with his usual nonchalance of manner. Turning towards him, Kemp saw his face full in the light, and was again aware of that strange mixture of delicacy and brutality in it. At this moment Spenton, still gazing raptly at the endless forming and dissolving of the images, said, 'I believe your bank is prepared to advance me a loan.'

It was not in such garish light, nor with before him an image of Hercules drawing a bow at a hissing, water-jetting dragon, that Kemp had envisaged conducting the discussion now finally arrived at, but he took the opportunity that was presented and set out as clearly as he could what the bank was prepared to offer. Spenton's request would be granted – he was asking for a loan of five thousand pounds; he would be given five years to repay the money, and no interest would be charged. These terms were conditional upon the bank being granted a twenty-year lease on Spenton's mine at a cost to the lessee of a thousand pounds a year, payable annually in advance. The bank would be responsible for the running of the mine, and the profits on the coal would go to the bank.

'Yes, yes, I see,' Spenton said. 'We should return now, I think. The best of the show is over.'

Hercules had now been replaced by a fiery bird revolving on an axle. They turned away from the light and began to go back the way they had come. For some minutes they walked side by side without speaking. Kemp was beginning to think that the offer had not pleased Spenton. More favourable terms than this the bank could not offer . . .

They turned on to the avenue known as the Grove, where the lights were sparser and the shadows longer, designed for the use of those who might wish for a more solitary and meditative promenading. Quite suddenly Spenton said, 'Well, I find it a generous offer on the bank's part and I am quite ready to accept it. If you would be kind enough to give me some of your time and visit me the day after tomorrow, in the morning, we will have the agreement drawn up in the presence of my attorney. Then I hope you will come up to Durham as my guest, and have a look round. I am intending to go up there next week. I have to talk to my tenants, and there is the annual handball match with the neighbouring colliery village – I never miss that. We have a particularly promising champion this year, I am told.'

The casualness of this acceptance, coming after the silence and mixed as it was with talk of tenants and handball, struck Kemp as extraordinary, so different was it from his own style when anything concerning money was being talked about. Unexpected too the wave of relief and jubilation he experienced at hearing the words – he had not altogether realised how much his heart had been set on obtaining the lease.

He was looking towards the river as they walked. From the darkness that lay over the water a fiery bolt of light rose into the sky and burst there, descending in a golden shower. Where have I read or been told about a shower of gold falling on a girl? he wondered. A naked girl . . . The rocket was followed by another, then another. The bright shower of their descent filled the sky. Of course, it was a hanging day, there were always fireworks on hanging days in the spring and summer months.

At some prompting that he was afterwards to think of as not due to chance alone, he turned to look towards the line of trees bordering the avenue. The glow of gold lay on the foliage of those more distant. He saw a group of people pass through this zone of radiance. One of them was a young woman, who raised her face to the sky just as a rocket burst and a shower of gold began to descend. In these few moments, as the red turned to gold, her face was lit up, and it was the face of Jane Ashton.

14

The day had begun badly for Ashton, and things did not improve in the course of it. Stanton came to see him in the morning with the news that Evans, the Negro they had rescued at Gravesend hours before he was due to be forcibly transported to the West Indies, had disappeared from the house where they had been keeping him out of harm's way until his case could be heard.

'He is gone without trace,' Stanton said. 'He must have been inveigled out somehow, perhaps on some false summons from us, then seized and carried off. He was aware of the danger to him, he knew by experience what these men are capable of for the sake of the fifty guineas they claim he is worth. It is a tidy sum, after all. No, it is unlikely that he left the house of his own free will. And if he did, why has he not returned?'

'But how could they have known where he was?'

'It is possible that the man who had Evans in his care, whom we have been paying to keep him safe, saw a chance of some more immediate profit. No doubt they would be ready to offer a reward, perhaps two guineas or so.'

'Townsend? No, I am unwilling to believe that. He has been providing this service for years, there have been others before Evans. Why should he betray us now?'

Stanton smiled at these words and shook his head. 'You are always ready to take things on trust, Frederick, and it does you credit. But it is not a habit of mind we can afford to cultivate when we have to question witnesses in a court of law. Under certain circumstances loyalty can wear thin. Townsend may have had losses we know nothing of, he may have had expenses we know nothing of.'

'I cannot believe it. I think it more likely that Evans was followed to the house. Those two, the slave-takers, as they call themselves – and why not, since it is their trade? – the two that seized Evans and bound him and carried him to the ship, whom I was intending to sue for assault and abduction along with the ship's captain, they have not been found, they have not been named. They were nowhere to be seen when the writ was presented to the captain. I think they may have waited, unobserved, and followed us when we accompanied Evans to Townsend's house.'

'It is possible, yes,' Stanton said. 'Then they would offer the information, at a price, to those two gentlemen who are claiming damages from us, who would allow some time for things to settle down and vigilance to be relaxed, meanwhile spying on the house, waiting for a moment when there was no one else about.'

Ashton nodded. 'However it happened, we have lost him,' he said. It was bad news indeed. Evans would be held in captivity somewhere. London contained numerous prisons of one sort or another, many of them disguised as private houses; people could be kept in confinement indefinitely at small cost. 'There is nothing we can do for the moment,' he said. 'Merely his disappearance gives us no grounds for action. Without a definite knowledge of his whereabouts we cannot lodge a complaint on his behalf. It would be answered that he might have simply run away. I am sorry for the poor fellow, he has done no wrong and he is being made to suffer.'

'We must hope for the best,' Stanton said, and on this he took his leave, somewhat disappointed to have had no sight of Jane Ashton – she was out on a visit of charity, Frederick had said.

Ashton remained in his study, sunk in gloomy thoughts. This new violence done to Evans had brought about one of the lapses into depression to which he was prone. There had been so many disappointments, so many setbacks. The odds were too great, the forces of avarice and cruelty would carry the day, as they had done for all the centuries of man's habitation on earth.

His mood was not lightened when in the early afternoon he

received a note from the judge appointed to hear the insurance claim on the jettisoned slaves. After due consideration Mr Justice Blundell had found it more in keeping with the dictates of due process to have this civil case heard separately at the Guildhall at a date yet to be determined; the criminal charges would more appropriately be heard later, before the King's Bench. He had therefore decided not to refer the matter to the Lord Chief Justice, a decision which lay within his powers . . .

Nowhere contained in this carefully worded document was there any hint of Blundell's private awareness that to trouble the Lord Chief Justice with such a request could seriously impede his own further career, and might well put an end to his hopes of a title. In fact, it had not taken him long to make up his mind; the delay in communicating his decision had been merely to lend an impression of weight and deliberation. He knew the public interest this case had aroused and he knew Ashton by repute, knew him for a troublesome fellow who was set on disturbing the social order. But he had not had any direct dealings with him before, and the petition he had been sent, eloquently urging that the two cases should be tried together, had given him a glimpse of nightmare, a vision of the bottomless pit – this also, of course, not hinted at in his reply. In particular, the improper use of Holy Writ had troubled him. The words taken by Ashton from the Book of Job had gone on echoing in his mind. *What then shall I do when God riseth up? And when He visiteth what shall I answer Him? Did not He that made me in the womb make him?*

His appetite had been affected for two days running. Instead of presiding over a case of insurance liability he was being asked to request the senior judge of the land to transform this simple matter into a formal and explicit deliberation as to whether the Negroes thrown overboard were to be regarded as something more than goods, an issue to be left to the judgement of a dunderheaded jury, unpredictable and given to crude sentiment. Who could tell what the outcome might be?

He had refreshed his memory by referring to the definition of piracy delivered in the case of *Rex* v. *Dawson* of 1696: *Piracy is only the sea term for robbery within the jurisdiction of the Admiralty . . . If the mariner of any ship shall violently dispossess the master and afterwards carry away the ship itself or any of the goods with a felonious intention in any place where the Lord Admiral hath jurisdiction, this is robbery and piracy . . .*

This was all very well, as far as it went. But the felonious intention, in this present case, was not altogether evident. He could not recall any case of piracy in which no attempt had been made to profit from the stolen goods. Why had these men run off to Florida without attempting to sell the slaves or the ship? There were cases on record of persons taken prisoner by pirates, but these were persons of rank, for whom a ransom might be asked. What ransom could be asked for a parcel of blacks, and who could conceivably ask it? It was this appalling tangle, and the thought of discharging it on to the Lord Chief Justice, on whom his advancement largely depended, that had so much affected his appetite. And he had felt released from an incubus after dispatching the note announcing his decision.

In spite of the blow to his hopes, and his continuing depression at Evans's disappearance, Ashton did what he could in the course of the next few hours to institute a search for the Negro's whereabouts. He sent for two men who had helped him on occasion in similar searches, and gave them Evans's name and description. If they found him and brought word of where he was, they would have a guinea each. He did not tell them the address at which Evans had been staying, though one of them asked for this. They could not be trusted with such information. No reliance could be placed on the men themselves, only on their hope of a reward. Slave-takers and slave-finders belonged all within a single confraternity; had the paymaster been other, these two would have sought out any fugitive Negro in London and returned him by force to those who claimed to be his owners. They knew the communities among which the fugitives took refuge, as they knew many of the houses where those recaptured were kept confined until a ship for the plantations was fitted out and made ready to sail.

Ashton had no clear idea of how many black people there were in the city; the numbers were nowhere recorded. Some had been manumitted and lived as free men and women; others fled and lived as they could, as labourers, market porters, street musicians, beggars; yet others remained in the service of those who had brought them here, slaves still, liable to be sold to another master or carried back to the West Indies. This growing population had created a new trade: the man-hunters, who combed the streets for runaways and lived on the rewards.

It was late in the afternoon when Jane returned. She had spent most of the day, in company with two ladies of her acquaintance, in the Pass Room at Bridewell, where the female vagrants and prostitutes and unmarried mothers were kept confined for short periods, before being moved on. She was engaged, together with the others, in trying to teach the women useful skills, such as weaving, frame-knitting and basketwork. She often encountered resistance, but today there had been progress, or so she felt, and she was happy at this – so much so that she launched into speech immediately at sight of her brother, giving him no opportunity for the time being to relate the doleful news he had received that day.

'They have been harshly used since earliest childhood, most of them,' she said. 'No one has ever thought of them or taken any care for them in all their lives. They have been whipped out of one parish after another. Why should we be so shocked that they have bastard children or take to thieving and whoring? Is it any wonder?'

'No, certainly not.' Ashton had never grown altogether used to his sister's impetuous habit of speech when she was excited in her feelings, nor to her forthright use of terms not usually regarded as polite in young unmarried ladies.

'They feel of no use to themselves or anybody, that's what it is. Today we had two silk weavers with us, we paid them for the day's work, they set up their looms and the women took turns to try their hand, they saw things made and finished, small things, handkerchiefs, braid, ribbons.'

Jane's face was alight, her eyes were shining. 'They took part in it themselves, you see, Frederick, that is the great thing about it, they could see what they had produced. Only give these women power over themselves and they will be saved from so much misery. A few shillings a week, I know it is not much, but it would give them some self-respect, some control over their own lives.'

All the force of her conviction vibrated in the words. People must be given means to act, to change things. It was no use wringing one's hands and doing nothing. Pitying people was only useful as a spur to action, it had no value as a state of mind. Sometimes Jane wondered if she were really such a good Christian after all. Compassion made her feel uncomfortable and impatient, and it could turn quickly to anger unless there was some immediate scope for rendering it superfluous. She could not feel that it was good for the soul to contemplate the sufferings of others – or one's own, for that matter.

'Houses of Correction, they call them,' she said. 'That is correction, is it, covering women with shame?'

Only now did she notice that her brother's face was not showing the degree of gladness at her success that she might have expected. 'How has your day been?' she asked.

Prompted thus he related the double blow he had received, told her how he had set the men on to discover Evans's whereabouts. 'Without some luck they have small chance of finding him in time,' he said. 'Evans's new owner, as he considers himself, this sugar planter, Lyons, may be the one behind it, or perhaps he is in league with the previous owner, Bolton. Both were intending to bring an action against me for trespass and theft in the sum of two hundred guineas.'

'Yes, I remember you speaking of this.'

'Well, they keep finding reasons for postponing the action, and this is because they cannot be sure of winning. Two witnesses to the first assault, when they carried him out to the ship, have now come forward. I believe that is why they have anticipated the judgement by securing Evans's person. Better to have fifty guineas in hand than wait for a doubtful ruling.'

'They have gone to a great deal of trouble for the sake of their fifty guineas.'

'That is true. There is more than money in this, much more. Their sense of property has been outraged. Both are convinced they have an absolute right of ownership in him, and will wave a bill of sale to prove it.'

Ashton was silent for some moments, then said, more quietly, 'This business is taking on the look of a feud, an issue of principle on both sides. If we can only rescue the man and get him safe to court, preferably with the bruises of his ill-treatment still upon him . . . If we can get a favourable ruling we might, with God's help, add some real momentum to the movement for ending this foul trade. It is strange, perhaps it is regrettable, the heart can take no account of numbers.'

'How do you mean?'

'Evans's life and circumstances are no less in importance, in their value to us, than the lives of all the Negroes that were thrown from the deck of the *Liverpool Merchant*. Both have to be measured against the many thousands of lives we hope to redeem.'

'But Evans is only one and his life is not at immediate risk, only his liberty. You cannot really mean what you are saying, Frederick.'

But she knew, with sinking heart, and without needing to look at his face, that he had meant every word of it.

It was at this moment, when this stricken silence had fallen between them, that the housemaid tapped on the door, bearing a note that had just been delivered. It was an invitation, addressed to both brother and sister, to an evening reception to be held the following week at the house of Mr Jonathan Bateson.

'I don't think I know him,' Ashton said. 'Perhaps you have some closer acquaintance with the family?'

'No, I have never been to the house and have no acquaintance in the family at all.'

'Strange.' Ashton was silent for some moments, then said, 'Bateson, Bateson, yes, now I think of it, I recall the name. He sits in the House of Commons. He represents the West India interest. The sugar trade, in other words.' He looked at his sister more closely. 'Perhaps he is an associate of Mr Erasmus Kemp,' he said.

Jane turned away, as if there were something that needed her attention. But he was in time to see that she had changed colour. 'The man will be waiting for an answer,' he said. 'I think we should accept, don't you?'

15

'Snippin' off me buttons without wakin' me would have needed a light touch,' Sullivan said. 'He cannot have been so drunk as he made himself out to be. It is troublin' to the spirit to think that he must have had a knife about him.'

Just beyond Chesterfield, heading north on foot, he had fallen in with another wayfarer, a thickset, shaven-headed man, and had confided to him the story of the stolen buttons.

'Lookin' at it another way,' he said, 'the weather is improvin' day by day, an' where is the need for a coat like that?'

'That's right, that's what I allus say, look on the bright side,' his new companion said. 'You can't win every bout, you will get beat sometimes an' lose the purse money, but you ain't lost it cos you didn't have it without you won the match.'

'My feelin's exactly,' Sullivan said. 'Then there is the further argument that a coat like that, whether equipped with buttons or not, will tend to cramp the style of a fiddlin' man, an' reduce the power of his music.'

He had pawned the coat in Peterborough before leaving, together with the bag in which he had been carrying his fiddle and bow; these were slung over his shoulder now, as they had been when he walked out of Newgate Prison. His old shirt and trousers had also been in this bag but the pawnbroker had not been interested in these.

'He tried to make out that a coat that has lost its buttons has thereby undergone a grievous loss in its value. I wasn't born yesterday, I said to him, I am a travelled man, I said, I know somethin' of commerce, an' it is obvious to me that you are exaggeratin' the importance of them buttons for your own purposes. Buttons is a variable thing, I said, buttons can be gold, they can be silk, they can be cloth, but a good stout coat is not subject to changes of quality.'

In the end he had obtained five shillings on coat and bag together, more money than he had possessed since the day of his escape from prison. Some of it had gone in the course of the days it had taken him to get this far. But he still felt affluent, and was planning to treat himself to pork pies and ale when he got to a likely-looking tavern. He said nothing of his resources to the man beside him, having suffered twice already through being too forthcoming. And the man asked him no questions of that sort, asserting merely that pawnbrokers were an unholy tribe.

'You goin' far?' Sullivan asked.

'There is a fair at Redfield, startin' tomorrow, if I can get there.'

'You are a wrestlin' man, as I understand it?'

'That is so. William Armstrong, at your service. Strong by name an' strong by natur'. What I does is challenge any man in the crowd to come up an' try his luck. Who gets the best of three falls takes the purse. All comers, any style, Irish, collar-an'-elbow, free-for-all. Strong young fellows, they are lookin' for some easy money an' the chance to show off for the girls.' He shook his head and smiled a little. 'Not many gets to try a third fall,' he said.

'Where does the pledge come from?'

'I allus keeps a shillin' or two about me to begin with.'

'Well, I wish you luck tomorrow.' It had occurred to Sullivan, while listening to the wrestler, that he could make for the fair too and maybe increase his stock by providing a bit of music. 'Redfield is north from here, isn't it?' he said.

'That's right, it's on the Doncaster road. About twenty miles from here.'

'Well, this is turnin' out providential,' Sullivan said, gladdened by this prospect of adding to his capital. He had no slightest idea of geography, or distances, but thought he must be past the halfway mark by now. 'All the same,' he said, 'it is strange how things will get repeated as the years pass. I had a coat with brass buttons once before, years ago now, an' the buttons was cut off an' stole from me.'

He paused with momentary caution; but he was elated, speech came readily to him, as always, and the further he got from London the less likely he felt it that anyone should discover that he was a man on the run, or care who he was and where he was making for. So long as he remembered to leave out the name of the ship and all reference to Florida and the settlement . . . 'Yes,' he said, 'I was pressed aboard a slave ship bound for the Guinea Coast, an' a man named Blair was pressed along of me – neither of us had any choice in it. We knew each other before, havin' sailed together, but that time it wasn't on a slaver – we would niver have signed on for a slaver. I was wearin' a coat with brass buttons when we went aboard, an' it was took off me back on the grounds it was verminous, which was an outright falsehood. I niver saw that coat again, but I know the buttons was cut off it, I know that for a fact, an' I know who done it – it was the bosun. Haines was a bad man an' he come to a bad end, an' I thought me buttons was gone for good, but twelve years later I tripped over me own feet an' fell down in a ditch, an' there was one of the buttons just under me nose, not by chance but by a blessin' that was intended. It was the very place where Haines met his end at the hands of the Indians, it must have fallen from him then. I was guided to it with the purpose of restorin' me faith in justice. That button was a mark of grace an' I gave it to a dyin' man who had been the doctor on the ship, intendin' it as somethin' for him to hold, somethin' to see him through, if you take me meanin' . What became of it after that I niver knew. Billy Blair was dead by then. It is because of Billy I am on the road now. I made a vow to meself that I would find his folks an' tell them what end he had made. They are minin' people in the County of Durham, an' that is where I am headin'.'

It was a story he had told at various times to various people in the course of his journey, amplified and embellished as he drew further from London and felt safer. Getting to Durham had by now assumed the character of a divinely guided mission. His solemn vow, the grace of his escape from prison, that marvellous encounter by the wayside, the scrapes and vicissitudes of his journey so far – small misfortunes designed to teach him, by the mercy of his recovering from them, that he was watched over

– all this combined to give the destination of Billy's birthplace a significance that no other destination had ever had for him. His life on land had been spent in dockside Liverpool, where the boat from Ireland had set him down, and then as a fugitive in the wilderness of southern Florida. He had never before been north of the Humber, and had not the remotest idea of what life in a pit village might be like.

'Durham, is it?' the wrestler said. 'Well, you have a good way to go yet. It is not often that I meet a man who is travellin' under a vow. I think I see a means to help you on your way.'

'What would that be now?'

'I have three shillin' in my pocket at this present time. I am keepin' them safe. Two shillin' of that will be my stake when I gets to the fair. Anyone who comes forward will have to match that stake, winner take all. So with every bout I win I double my money, do you see? Now I don't put it all back in the pledge, I keep a shillin' out every time, so if I lose – an' there is no man that can win every bout – I still have my stake money, I can try again somewhere else. If I start with two shillin' an' there are three challengers an' I win all three of the bouts, I will end up with twenty-three shillin' in my pocket, includin' the money I have put by. You are a man that knows something of commerce, an' I think you will agree that it is a handsome profit. Now here is my idea. Let's say you trust me with sixpence. Keepin' the same course of three bouts, instead of sixpence you would have three shillin' at the end of it.'

'Well, it is a temptin' offer, I am not the man to deny that,' Sullivan said. 'In the language of commerce we would call it a good reward on the investin's. But there is a snag in it of very considerable proportions.'

'What might that be?'

'You might lose the first bout an' then me sixpence goes up in smoke.'

'It is not often that William Armstrong loses a bout, particularly the first one, when he is still fresh. But you haven't understood the finances of it. I will do the same with your money as I do with my own, keepin' a bit back every time. So you will still have your sixpence whatever happens. You can make it a shillin' if you like. I'll tell you what, you can mull the matter over while we are steppin' out together. No hard feelin's either way. William Armstrong bears no grudges.'

There was no further discussion between them concerning this proposition, and in fact Sullivan had scarcely gone another mile before he decided against it. A man could be robbed twice and it could be set down to his trusting nature. But a man who allowed himself to be robbed three times in a row was a fool and deserved no better. Besides, he was hungry and felt the need to rest his feet for a while. The thought of pork pies and ale – though why this particular combination he could not have said – had been steadily gaining in radiance, and he did not welcome the idea of postponement.

He therefore, when they came up to a roadside inn of promising appearance, announced his intention of going inside for a bite to eat and an hour or two of rest. His companion was eager to press on, wanting to cover as much of the distance as he could so as to get some hours of sleep in the early morning and be freshened up and restored to full strength for the wrestling. So the two parted here, with mutual assurances that they would seek each other out at the fair.

It was approaching midday on the following morning when Sullivan arrived at the small town of Redfield-on-Trent, and made his way to the fairground, which was on a field by the river. He passed stalls selling gingerbread, paused to watch a ladies' smock race and the pursuit of a greased pig – there was a guinea for the man who succeeded in catching the beast and keeping hold of it. He was looking for the bit of ground that would be quiet enough for his fiddling and singing to be heard, and open enough for a crowd to gather. This was not easy to find; the field was thronged and the general jollity was increased as people had recourse to the beer stall. Not far from this there was a cockfight in progress with a great shouting of bets and cries of encouragement to the bloodstained adversaries. He saw at a distance the wrestler with a crowd before him, but he kept away.

Finally he found a quieter area, where a game of skittles was going on, and near this a raised platform, on which a very fat and smiling man in a wide-brimmed black hat sat at a table before a row of bottles containing a reddish liquid. Below the platform, at the foot of the three steps up to it, a youngish man in the kind of white cotton apron worn by apothecaries was shouting in a high-pitched, slightly cracked voice. The words came from him with the unfaltering flow of long habit, and Sullivan paused to listen.

'Come forward, ladies and gentlemen, do not hold back, we shall be moving on within the hour and your last chance of obtaining a cure for all human disorders will be gone for ever. Our much-famed Hypodrops, if taken for three days in succession, will infallibly cure hypochondriac melancholy in men and vapours in women, so as never to return again, and that by striking at the very root or true cause as well as remedying the effects of these perplexing maladies and all their variety of symptoms, all the diseases we poor mortals are afflicted with, vicious ferments in the stomach, flatulent or windy disorders, gout, giddiness, impediments in locomotion, dimness of sight, swollen veins, kidney stones, choked lungs. Only two shillings and sixpence the bottle, chemically prepared from the most valuable specifics in the mineral, vegetable and animal kingdoms . . . The man you see behind me is the world-famed Dr Ebeneezer Muir, his Hypodrops are in demand by the crowned heads of Europe, to you for this occasion he is offering this universal cure for only two-and-six a bottle . . .'

People came forward, among them a number who were visibly ailing, hobbling on crutches or half blind. The shouter mounted the steps for the bottles and took the money. The smiling, immobile man at the table kept a very sharp eye on the coins that were changing hands. All the takings found their way into a black leather bag that lay on the table before him.

Sullivan moved some distance away and took up a position with his back to the table and the inventor of the Hypodrops and the one employed to do the shouting. He took off his waistcoat, spread it on the ground before him and dropped coins to the value of one-and-six or so – half his remaining stock – into the middle of it, as an indication of where people should lay the hoped-for offerings. He took up his fiddle and played a reel, with all the verve he could summon. There was nothing like a reel for attracting attention. Before long there was a small knot of people gathered before him. When he judged the number sufficient, he embarked on 'Tarry Trousers', playing first the air and taking some short dance steps as he played. It was a song he knew well, belonging to the dockside taverns of his other life, before the slave ship, before the days in Florida. After some minutes he lowered his fiddle and sang the first verse:

> *Yonder stands a pretty maiden.*
> *Who she is I do not know.*
> *I will court her for her beauty.*
> *She can answer yes or no.*

His voice was pleasing, a slightly husky tenor, not very strong but sweet in tone. From childhood on he had been a singer, and had often enough kept body and soul together through the gift; many of the words he used in talking came from his memory of songs.

A countrywoman in a bonnet came forward and dropped a coin to join the others on the outspread waistcoat, and Sullivan smiled and ducked his head in thanks – there was always a first one needed to set the others on to it. The song he had chosen to start with had the rhythm of a jig, and this was not by chance: if he could get people dancing he stood to finish off with a pocketful of pennies . . .

> *My love wears the tarry trousers,*
> *My love wears the jacket blue,*
> *My love ploughs the deep blue ocean . . .*

He broke off to play the tune again. The crowd was getting bigger, one or two more coins landed on the waistcoat. He was raising the bow when the man in the white apron who had been shouting the virtues of the Hypodrops approached from behind and tapped him on the shoulder.

'Dr Muir requests you to go further off,' he said. 'Your music is drowning out my pitch, the people cannot hear me.'

He looked younger, now that he was close, and he had a general air of unhappiness.

'A singin' man has as much right here as a shoutin' man,' Sullivan said. 'More, as the sound is more agreeable. The doctor has not purchased the intoire field, I suppose.'

'No, but we were here first. Those who come late must find their own places.'

Sullivan considered for a moment. He could not emerge with any advantage from this disagreement. The other would stay there and argue the matter, and in the meantime the people who had gathered would drift away – one or two had already done so, the others would follow. 'I'll go then,' he said. 'We are losin' custom while we stand here.' As he was about to take up his waistcoat and the coins lying on it, he asked the question that had been vaguely in his mind since arriving. 'Why does the doctor not do his own shoutin'?'

The young man hesitated and seemed at first not disposed to reply. Then he said, 'Well, I'll tell you, I don't care who knows, I am fair sick of it, he pays me next to nothing and keeps all for himself. The reason he don't do the shouting is that he has no breath, his lungs are gone – as soon as he makes any effort he starts gasping and wheezing. If they knew that the inventor of Hypodrops, the wonder-working universal panacea for which he is charging two shillings and sixpence a bottle, cannot raise his voice above a whisper and cannot get to his feet without breathing heavy, they would add to his ills by breaking his bones. Mine too – the one shouting is just as much in danger. It is only watered-down beetroot juice and minced-up sloe berries and a bit of sugar. There, I have told you, and I am glad of it. I will leave him, he can stew in his Hypodrops. He has started making me wear this apothecary's apron, so as to look more worthy of trust. I have told him it is dangerous, but –'

Suddenly he broke off and his eyes widened as he looked over Sullivan's shoulder. 'I knew it,' he said, and he turned and began to run.

Sullivan had no time to gather up his belongings. Three men armed with staves jostled him violently aside, trampling on his waistcoat and the coins lying there. Dr Muir was slow in movement even when highly alarmed, and he had only just succeeded in getting to his feet when they were upon him. Sullivan saw him go down, saw the heavy sticks rising and falling, heard the smash of breaking glass. The constables would be on the scene before long, he might be taken and questioned. He grabbed the waistcoat, took up what coins he could see – they were few – and fled in the same direction the doctor's assistant had taken.

He lost no time in getting clear of the fair and setting off on the road that led towards Doncaster. He was hardly out of the town, however, when he was hailed from the yard of an inn and recognised William Armstrong sitting there with a pot of ale before him. The wrestler beckoned and shouted an invitation to join him in a drink.

'I had best be pressin' forward,' Sullivan said.

Armstrong heard the reluctance in this and repeated the offer, and Sullivan had not the fortitude to say no a second time, feeling the need for a good draught after the fright he had had. When he was seated with a tankard before him, he told the wrestler about the fracas he had run from.

'I will niver forget that man,' he said. 'One minute sittin' there smilin', watchin' the money come in, next minute gettin' his bones broke. He will stay in me mind as an example of shiftin' fortunes just round the corner.'

'That's right,' the wrestler said. 'You can never tell what kind of a hold to take, you have to live day by day.'

'An' there is somethin' else in it. It is a difficult matter to get across, but when I saw him go under with them fellers rainin' blows on him, what struck me as the most calamitous was that he could not make a sound above a whisper, he was beaten out of his senses with no voice to him. That man will niver get his bones together again after the beatin' they gave him.'

'I have known it before,' Armstrong said. 'It is the apothecaries of the town that sets them on, because they lose their trade. So you didn't do well with the fiddlin'?'

'I started off well enough, but it all came to nothin'. It was me own money that I put down, so I am worse off than I was before.'

'Well, I had a good day myself. I was thrown once but I still won best of three. Four bouts an' I won them all. I have money enough to stay in this inn tonight. Tomorrow I'll be makin' towards Chester. That is westward, a different road from what you are takin'. I am glad we have met again because there was somethin' I had in mind to say to you. I been travellin' these roads now for close on twenty years. I meet people by the way, an' sometimes we go along together for a while, an' we talk, as people will. There is various reasons for bein' on the road. There is those lookin' for somethin', mebbe some work or somethin' that will change their luck. There is those that are runnin' away from someone or somethin'. There is those that can never stay long in any place an' have always to be movin' on. But in all these years I never met anyone who is not on the road for his own sake but because of a vow of friendship that he has made. It struck me, I don't mind tellin' you. I would like to help you on your way. I have had luck today, an' mebbe it was brought by you. I want to give you the two shillin' that was my stake when I started off this mornin'.'

The wrestler dug in his pocket, took out a handful of coins, and pushed some of them across the table to Sullivan. 'This will help you get to Durham an' keep your promise,' he said.

Sullivan looked at the money before him, and he felt tears gathering in his eyes. 'You have restored me faith in human nature,' he said. 'I was robbed twice before, but if one man in three has a generous heart it will mount up to something in the years to come.'

'I am forty-three years old, near as I can work it out,' the wrestler said. 'The lads I am wrestlin' with are half my age mostly. I won today but the time is comin' when I won't. You are goin' on a mission of friendship, what happens to you afterwards don't matter so much, once you have carried it out. I am not goin' anywhere except to a bad fall and the workhouse.'

Looking through the mist of his tears, it seemed to Sullivan that he was seeing the wrestler's face for the first time. One cheek was bruised from the fall he had taken. The eyes were short-lashed and blue and as guileless as a child's.

'I thought you were plannin' to rob me of sixpence,' Sullivan said, 'an' you are givin' me four times as much.' He reached out to take the other's hand. 'I will remember this kindness till the end of me days,' he said.

16

The inflammable gas known to the miners as firedamp was colourless and odourless and it could gather anywhere below the ground, in newly opened workings or in old hollows where work had been abandoned. As the shafts got deeper and the leakage of water more controlled, the currents of air that the water had caused were much reduced, and the gas at the deeper levels became more frequent. It could lurk undetected for long periods and could be exploded without warning by the flame of a candle, carrying death and destruction throughout the mine.

Four hours into his work at the coalface, his stint of coal only half hewed out, James Bordon saw a pale, bluish cap appear at the tip of his candle, a kind of ghost flame that he knew, that he had seen before. By accustomed practice this had to be reported immediately to someone in authority. Shielding the flame with his hand he made his way back along the gallery, found the assistant overman tallying the corves at the pit bottom and told him he suspected that firedamp had gathered in the area where he was working. The men would not be cleared from the workings until the presence of gas was definitely established. Bordon offered to do the testing himself, and this was agreed. He asked for a knife to trim the wick of his candle, and one was found for him. He scraped off the layers of semi-liquid sheep fat from the top of the candle, snuffed the wick short and carefully cleaned away the fiery particles that had collected on it. When he was satisfied that the flame was as pure as possible, he returned to the section of the face where he had been working, accompanied by the overman, whose duty this was, having once been informed of the danger.

Holding the candle between the fingers and thumb of his right hand, Bordon made a screen with the palm of his left, so that nothing but the spire of the flame could be seen. The gas was known to be lighter than air, and he began close to the floor, raising the flame, and his screening hand, very slowly. At a height of five feet or so the flame took on a slight tinge of bluish-grey, shooting up from the peak of the spire and ending in a fine point of deeper blue that was neither flame nor air. This, as the candle was raised slightly higher, increased in size and deepened in colour. It was an infallible sign: they were no more than two feet from the firing point, and both men knew it. They retreated to the pit bottom and the overman rang the bell that was kept there as an emergency signal for the men to return to the surface. There were a dozen men and boys working in this section of the mine; they were checked by name as they came out from the workings, and were winched up to the surface.

So it was that these men returned to the village before midday, an event of rare occurrence. Percy Bordon had no notion of it and did not see them come, engrossed as he was in a game of marbles with his best friend, Billy Scotland. These two had known each other since the toddling stage and were bound by their shared knowledge that they were only weeks away from the first step towards manhood and the dignity of wage-earners.

In spite of this friendship, there was very keen competition between them when it came to marbles. This was so even when the winner stood to gain only the small and common marbles called pot alleys, made of baked clay and stained in dull colours. But today it was keener than ever, because in a spirit of mutual challenge and bravado they had agreed to stake a glass alley, larger, much more beautiful, with a blaze of colour at the heart of it, red or blue or yellow. Whoever won would dispossess the other, a sore loss as they were rare and greatly prized.

'*Cow-cow-diddio, there's rings round it,*' Percy chanted as his friend took aim. It was a magic formula designed to put Billy off his stroke and make him miss. Whoever got his alley into the small and shallow scrape of ground known as the mott had the right to shoot it between forefinger and thumb and strike, if his aim was good, that of his adversary. This mott-and-strike, if repeated three times, decided the winner. Billy was ahead by two to one, and Percy was seriously worried.

The game was played on the waste ground adjoining the back lanes of the village, and for this reason neither of the boys was aware of the men's return until they heard the voices from the front of the houses. Billy had so far failed to make the winning stroke and Percy had caught up, so they were two games each. However, now that the issue was so much on a knife edge and could go either way, both of them were regretting the reckless challenge of earlier. It seemed much preferable not to risk their glass alleys after all. And the voices of the returning miners came at just the right moment, providing grounds for curiosity and an honourable reason for abandoning the game.

The two made their way to the lane that ran past the front of the cottages. There they found the older miners sitting together in the yard of the alehouse – it had been agreed that this break from custom warranted a jar or two. It made no difference whether or not they had the money to pay; many of the men were in permanent debt to the landlord and had their wages docked every week, on pain of being barred from the tavern if they defaulted. The yard was bordered by a low wall, and the two boys sat with their backs against this, invisible from the yard but still within earshot.

'They will have to get the firemen in,' the overman, whose name was Campbell, said. 'I cannot say I envy the lads that job.'

There were six firemen employed in the colliery, all of them below the age of thirty. The one on duty in the section of the mine where firedamp was found would soak his clothes in water and crawl along the workway with a lighted candle attached to a long pole held out before him until he arrived at the concentration of gas. When the explosion came he would fling himself face down against the ground. Fortune assisting, he would escape the rush of flame which shot along the roof over his head. For this he received a daily wage of five shillings, which put him among the highest paid workers, not only in the colliery, but in the country as a whole.

'Aye,' said another man, 'the money is good, but naybody would do it with a family to think of. The wife would never know if tha'd come back with a whole skin.'

'It is all a question of weighing things up.' Arbiter Hill was one of those who had come out of the pit, and he was at his usual game of clarifying the issues and trying to control everybody. 'On the one hand we have a desire for betterment of the finances, on the other hand we have the risk of serious hurt by fire, a risk accepted freely by agreement with the manage. That is the issue lying before us. Now, lads, box on.'

Bordon, always irritated by Hill's habit of laying the law down and telling other people the way they should think about things, said, 'We can all see why they do it, there is nay mystery in that. Does tha think them fellers sit around and balance it all out? So long as we have nay light to work by but a bare flame, lads will gan on gettin' the skin burned off their backs.'

'It is a matter of luck,' Campbell said. 'Do you mind when them six men went down to repair a wall that was fallen in? About eight years now, one of them shafts with a long workway, longer than is usual nowadays.'

'Aye, sinkin' a new shaft is cheaper than roofin' a long gallery, so they say in the manage,' another man said.

'Well, this one ran underground for a good three hundred yards, mebbe more, an' they had built the wall to go from the shaft bottom nearly as far as the end, right down the middle, to shift the air down one side and back down the other. No one had been working the coal there for six months or so, an' the firedamp had gathered, unbeknown to anyone. They sent these six fellers down to put the wall right, and they hadn't been at it long before the candle flames exploded the gas an' there was a great flow of fire from where they were working, back down the tunnel towards the shaft bottom. They started crawling back on hands and knees, hoping the fire would pass over them, but they never got back, they were frazzled one after the other as the fire caught up with them, burned to a cinder in no time, all except one, name of Harry Matthews. They had to fetch him up, he had lost his senses an' that was the saving of him, he fell flat on the ground and the greater part of the fire went over him. He was badly scorched but they got him out alive. That's what I mean, see, it is a matter of luck.'

'What became of Matthews?'

'He never went back down. He was scarred by the fire but

that wasn't the reason. He never got over the fear of it, an' the thought of what had happened to his mates. The family moved away to Castle Eden. I've heard since that Harry is fit for nothing.'

'Well,' Bordon said, 'he was luckier than the other lads, but that's about all tha can say.'

'Putting the matter in a nutshell,' Arbiter Hill said, 'and weighing up the pros and cons of it, on the one hand you have the state of being overtook by fire, on the other hand you have the state of being a human wreck.'

'Water can be a worse enemy than fire sometimes.'

This had come from an elderly man known to all as Bushy, who had worked underground for almost fifty years and whose face was darkly veined with coal dust.

'A first went down the mine when a was six years old,' he said. 'Before any of you lads was born. A Tyneside colliery it was, near Jesmond. There was an old pit nearby that was fallen out of use, but there was coal left standin' in the pillars holdin' up the roof. They went down to get this an' they were workin' in a dyke between two galleries when the water burst through from the old workin's, an' they were cut off, seventy-seven men an' boys. It was deep down, they didna have pumps that could deal with that much water, an' they still don't. It took eight months to dry out the pit. When they got down to them they found them all starved to death. They had eaten the pit ponies, they had eaten their candles, they had eaten the bark of the roof props. They had lingered an' died in the dark. The lads that found them said that some had died only recent.'

In the silence that followed upon this grisly story, Percy and Billy, still behind the wall, looked at each other with wide eyes. Now, more strongly than ever before, Percy was tempted to ask his friend if he too felt fear at going down the pit – fear and pride mixed, he would make a point of saying. The imagined hiss and burst of flame, the crawling, doomed men, the terrible washing and slapping of the water – like laughing – while the men and boys, some not much older than themselves, were slowly dying in the dark, all this seemed to Percy the doing of the great beast that lived in the pit, whose breathings and thrashings carried across the fields and accompanied his days. Did Billy feel the same? It would have been a comfort to him to know that he was not alone in these feelings, that his best friend shared them. But, as always, another kind of fear kept him silent. Supposing Billy professed not to know what he was talking about, supposing Billy declared himself to be counting the days to starting down the mine? Even if it were not true, he, Percy, would have shown himself up as cowardly, and that would be worse – much worse – than losing his glass alley . . .

17

The insurance claim on eighty-five African slaves, cast overboard while still alive from the deck of the *Liverpool Merchant* on grounds of lawful jettison, was heard at the Guildhall, Justice Blundell presiding. In contrast to the long course of postponements and delays that had preceded it, the hearing itself was brief, occupying no more than three hours of the court's time.

The insurers were represented by an elderly lawyer named Price, who had a large experience of such cases. Kemp's lawyer, Pike, had wished to hold his fire for the criminal trial at the Old Bailey, which was due to be held at a date not yet specified; he had recommended a young barrister named Waters to represent the ship's owner.

The claimant, who gave his name as Erasmus Kemp, made a short statement to the effect that he was applying for compensation in the name of his father, now deceased, whose property had passed to him. Price declined to put any questions to him, and declared that the underwriters did not dispute his claim to be the present owner of the vessel.

It was only when stepping down that Kemp saw Jane Ashton sitting at the back of the court with a man who he thought must be her brother. She was looking straight at him, and for some moments, as he descended the steps, their eyes met. His own place was in the forward part of the court, in the same row as the insurance broker, Van Dillen, and the two associates that had accompanied him. When he was again seated Kemp became intensely aware of her presence there, not far away, and of the fact that he would be seeing her the following evening at Bateson's house. Press of business had prevented him from enquiring whether the Ashtons had accepted the invitation, but even had he been less occupied he would hardly have thought it necessary to ask; he knew beyond question that they – she – would be there. Their destinies were linked; he had seen her face, lit up by the shower of gold, smiling upon his enterprise, just minutes after Spenton had replied so favourably to his proposal for the lease. A blessing, no less. So strong was this feeling, as it returned to him now, that for some minutes he ceased to follow the proceedings of the court, and so missed Barton's opening words, which of course did not much matter, as they had agreed together on the ship returning to England as to what the mate's evidence should be.

Barton had dressed for the occasion with all the elegance he could summon on straitened means, in a fustian coat with broad lapels, a short wig and a high stock that kept his head upright and restricted his usual loose-necked, peering way of looking about him. He took the oath with aplomb, but then made the mistake – the kind of mistake he would always be prone to – of leaning forward and resting his elbows on the rail, in an effort, as it seemed, to convey a sense of ease and a confidence in his own veracity, only to be told by the clerk of the court, in no uncertain terms, to stand upright and bear himself properly, instructions he obeyed with comical alacrity.

'The capt'n put it to us,' he said. 'Capt'n Thurso that was. We was hassembled below in the capt'n's cabin an' he put it to us fair an' square, hunnerd per cent.'

'Will you tell us who was present at that meeting, in addition to Captain Thurso?' Waters asked.

'There was myself, the bosun, the carpenter . . .'

'The ship's officers, in other words.'

'That is right, sir, yes.'

'The men who represented responsibility and authority on board the ship. And you decided, taking counsel together, that the cargo would have to be jettisoned. Is that so?'

'Hunnerd per cent, sir.'

'Fellow, what is this way of answering?' Justice Blundell said, red-faced and irritable in his heavy wig. 'You must answer yes or no.'

'Yes, sir, beggin' yer pardon.'

'A collective decision taken by the responsible members of the crew,' Waters said, addressing himself to the jury. 'And on what grounds was this decision taken? It was taken on grounds of dire necessity. The witness will relate the circumstances.'

'We was short of water, sir. There had been stormy weather an' one of the casks was holed, unbeknown to us, an' the water had leaked away.'

'So there was insufficient water to go round among the crew and the slaves?'

'Hunnerd per – yes, sir, right in hevery detail. We 'ad no choice, sir, we was still ten days off Jamaica, we 'ad to throw 'em over so as to be sure there was water enough for the crew.'

'No choice, Your Worship, those are the key words. It was a question of life or death for the crew. And if the crew perished, who was to manage the ship? That constitutes lawful jettison and that is the contention of the ship's owner, Mr Erasmus Kemp, whom I have the honour of representing in this court today.'

Barber, the ship's carpenter, was brought, still in chains, from the yard outside. His evidence substantiated that of Barton, though with one significant difference. Ashton's words had had an effect, but not the one he had wished for. Conferring together after his visit, the men had decided that the best course was to deny having made any judgement whatever as to the amount of water on the ship.

'We was informed by Capt'n Thurso that there was not water enough,' he said. 'We took it on trust. On a ship you takes the word of the capt'n.'

'Are you seriously asking us to believe,' said Price, with significant glances at the jury, 'that there was a lack of water urgent enough to justify the throwing overboard of those men and women while the breath of life was still in them, and that you weren't aware of this urgency until the captain told you of it? Are you seriously asking us to believe that a damaged water cask would not be noticed by any single member of the crew until the water had all leaked away?'

'We was rushed off our feet, we was undermanned, there was no time to look at the casks.'

He was led away, and Price turned to the jury. 'There was no time to look at the casks,' he said. 'Of course there wasn't. They were afraid the slaves might die below decks before they could be thrown over the side to drown. The reason for that hasty dispatch had nothing to do with damaged casks or a shortage of water. There was no shortage of water. Were the crew placed on rations? No. Did the ship put in anywhere for fresh supplies? Again no. They were in haste to jettison the sickly because they knew that those dying aboard ship were not covered by the insurance.'

'But what had the captain to gain by this, or the crew either?' Justice Blundell leaned forward to put this question to the impassioned Price. 'I cannot see that they would take such action only for the sake of the owners.'

'Your Worship, we cannot know the captain's motives. Some promised reward, some prospect of commission, perhaps mere habitual fidelity towards the owners. We cannot examine far into the state of mind of a man long since dead.'

Some commotion was now caused in the court by the calling of James Porter, who was seen to be a Negro. Before he could be questioned by Price for the insurers, Kemp's lawyer intervened.

'May I enquire into the quality of this witness? What is his state?'

'He has been manumitted by his former owner, who brought him back from the West Indies, and in whose service he has since remained as a free man. We have a deposition to that effect by his employer, a Colonel Trembath, a retired officer who has served his country well and whose word cannot be impeached.'

'That is all very well,' Waters said. 'It is not his present condition that concerns the court, but his condition as it was on the deck of the *Liverpool Merchant* at the time these events took place. At that time he was a slave, and therefore his evidence is tainted and inadmissible.'

Price said nothing to this, but he allowed himself a broad smile of superior understanding, and he was still, for the benefit of the jury, keeping this smile in place when Porter surprised the court and brought a frown to Justice Blundell's face, though no reprimand from him, by addressing the hostile counsel directly. 'No, sir, you are quite wrong,' he said, in excellent English. 'I was not enslaved, I was on the ship of my own free will. I was employed as an interpreter.'

Waters would have done better to yield the point, but he still hoped to discredit the witness and arouse some prejudice against him on the grounds of colour. 'How can we believe that?' he said. 'What need for this great title of interpreter aboard a slave ship? It is all an invention of your own.'

'Sir, you reveal considerable ignorance,' Porter said. 'The Africans we took had never heard English spoken before. Do you suppose they became gifted with knowledge of it the moment they stepped on board the ship?'

'My man, you are here to answer questions, not to ask them,' Blundell said.

'I beg your pardon, sir, but he was calling me a liar.'

The rebuke had been a mild one, and Price took heart from this mildness. He could sense a general sympathy in the court for Porter, who was bearing himself with dignity under these heavy-handed attacks. 'If it pleases the court,' he said, 'Barber can be recalled to testify in support of the witness's claim.'

But Blundell was beginning to feel oppressed by the tedium of these proceedings; and he was aware that his dinner hour was not far away. 'No, let us go on,' he said.

With a series of questions Price elicited from the witness that he had been present at the jettisoning but had taken no part in it, that there had been no shortage of water whatsoever, that in fact there had been recent rain, that the casks were regularly inspected and there had been no report of damage.

It was when Porter stepped down that Waters made his great mistake. He was ambitious and was at an early stage in his career. He had been gratified by Pike's recommendation and had greatly wished to justify the trust that had been placed in him. There was also the fact that Kemp was a powerful man and might have been a source of favours. Now he sensed that things were going against him, and that the victory he had hoped for was slipping away. The discomfiture enraged him, brought out a strain of fierce antipathy never far below the surface. He had seen Ashton in the courtroom and now, instead of making a reasoned address to the jury and giving what emphasis he could to the case for the owners, he embarked on a personal attack.

'There is a person in court at this present moment,' he said, at the same time turning and looking directly at Ashton, 'who I am told on good authority intends to bring on a criminal prosecution against the persons who took part in this lawful and eminently reasonable jettison, those of them that have survived. That is dangerous folly – more than folly, it amounts to madness. I am sure that I express the sentiments of the members of this court, and every good citizen throughout the land, when I say that the blacks thrown overboard were property and nothing else, they were cargo, as bales of cotton might have been. No charge of murder can be brought against the crew, no charge even of cruelty in any degree whatever, their actions were not in any degree improper –'

He was halted at this point by Justice Blundell, whose scowl, in the passion of this address to the court at large, he had quite failed to see, and who now spoke to him loudly and irascibly. 'How can you permit yourself such animadversions in my court, sir?'

The judge had felt his heart begin to beat in his ears, a sure sign of rising blood pressure. This, instead of warning him to remain calm, increased his rage. This presumptuous young fool was reviving the nightmare of Ashton's petition, raising questions of property and humanity, which had nothing at all to do with the issue before the court. 'We are not assembled here to discuss the beliefs or the intentions of any person whatever, whether present at these proceedings or not,' he said. 'I am surprised at you, sir. Do you think you are on the hustings, soliciting votes?'

Waters knew better than to attempt an answer, and in fact the pleas of counsel ended here, Price being more than content to wait for a verdict. In somewhat calmer tones Blundell directed the jury's attention to the fact that they were there to decide whether the throwing overboard of the Negroes was a genuinely necessitous act of jettison, in which case the insurers would be liable, or whether it was a fraud on the policy, in which case they could not be required to make any payment. Was there a shortage of water or was there not? How was it that the first mate on the ship, the man Barton, knew with such certainty what no one else knew until the captain informed them? Was not this strange and contradictory? Counsel for the owner had produced no evidence that the ship was foul or leaky. Barton was freed from imprisonment on the surety of the claimant. Did not this taint his evidence and incline greater belief in the declaration of James Porter, the interpreter on the ship, who had nothing to gain by lying, that in point of fact there was no shortage of water at all?

The jury, thus guided, came in a matter of minutes to the conclusion that the claim of lawful jettison had no substance, and therefore the insurers were released from all obligation of payment.

18

The following evening, while he was waiting below for his sister to complete her toilet and make herself ready, Ashton had a glass of claret, an unusual thing for him. He had felt a spirit of celebration since the insurance verdict, while knowing that the victory was partial, in some ways hardly a victory at all, since no issue of principle had emerged from it, only a ruling as to insurance liability. With a man like Blundell on the bench, this was hardly surprising; he had reacted with fury to the ill-judged attempt of Kemp's lawyer to discuss the nature of the cargo. Ashton had hoped for something more but without any great belief. Once the decision to hold separate hearings had been made, he had known that any attempt to enter a plea of murder against the remnants of the crew was unlikely to succeed, though he was no less set on it.

They were unworthy of saving; they had proved it in court with Barber again as their spokesman. They had not given heed to his advice, they had pleaded ignorance and blind obedience. Nevertheless, the judgement in favour of the underwriters had done some service to the cause. It was true that it had not been stated, or even implied, that the Africans were to be regarded as other than merchandise. But there had been journalists in the court; he had seen a correspondent of the *Morning Chronicle*, a man he knew fairly well, who had a certain discreet sympathy for the abolitionist cause. He could not express this directly without incurring the risk of dismissal, but he could be trusted to stress the fact that casting the Africans overboard had been unlawful and fraudulent, that it had been a deed entirely gratuitous, without ground or reason other than the desire to claim on the value. A monstrous crime, it had to be so regarded, in any court, in any system of law . . .

Once again the appalling obviousness of it came to Ashton, accompanied as always by the bafflement he felt at the failure of so many to see it. How could such an offence against God and man be adjusted, compensated for, shuffled away out of sight by a judgement that related only to the regulations governing insurance claims? He was intending to write to the Lord Commissioners of the Admiralty to petition that the surviving crew members should be prosecuted for mass homicide. He rehearsed some phrases in his mind as he waited. *I believe it my duty to lay before Your Lordships the circumstances of multiple and felonious murders carried out by captain and crew of the* Liverpool Merchant *in 1753 . . . I have done my utmost to discover and publish the full facts in regard to this most inhuman crime, so that justice may be done, and the blood of the murdered may not rest on us all . . .*

No, it was clear that the crew had forfeited their rights. They would not now be able to escape from the contradiction of having risen up and killed that very embodiment of authority to whom they claimed to have owed absolute obedience. Unlikely that they would change the nature of their evidence now, advance at this late hour the only defence that might have saved them, a crisis of conscience, the sudden realisation that what they were doing was hideously wicked.

There was no way out for them now. They were bound for the gallows, either as mutineers and pirates, which he was compelled to admit was the more likely outcome, or, Divine Providence assisting, as the murderers of eighty-five innocent men and women made in God's image like themselves. Again he reflected on what a wonderful stroke of fortune it would be if the judgement went that way, how it would resound in the annals of humane endeavour. Finally, a key ruling . . .

He sipped his claret, and the warmth of it on his tongue and in his throat was also the warmth of this imagined success. With one of the upsurges of spirit characteristic of him he felt that everything was possible, a new age of freedom was about to be ushered in.

From this he fell to considering another matter, also

promising in its way. It presented itself as a series of images or memories. Jane had kept very quiet about having met Kemp before. She had said nothing about it for a week or more. She was not usually so reticent, and there were particular reasons why she should have spoken of this meeting. Kemp's return from Florida with the surviving members of the crew was being spoken of on every hand; she had known that he, her brother, was involved in the case; she had known that Kemp was an adversary, and this should have argued a readiness to say what she knew of him in the hope that it might be useful. But she had done the exact opposite. And when she had finally spoken of the meeting it had been with what seemed to him now in retrospect a sort of studied casualness. She had turned away and busied herself with the tea things, though there had been no immediate need for this, they were scarce finished drinking their tea . . .

These were things not much remarked at the time, given significance now by certain impressions of later. When they had received the invitation, when he had recalled – and mentioned – that Bateson was a Member of Parliament representing the West India interest, she had known, she had guessed who was behind it; she had flushed, even before he uttered Kemp's name. Her nature was honest, any slightest subterfuge brought unease to her, brought colour to her face. She had been eager to attend the hearing with him yesterday, but not too much could be made out of that – she knew his interest in the case, knew how much weight he attached to it. Of course, she would have supposed that Kemp too would be at the hearing . . .

He was still occupied with these thoughts when Jane entered the small room adjoining the hall where he had been waiting for her. 'Well, you are a vision and no mistake,' he said as he got to his feet. And indeed it was clear to him that his sister had taken great care with her appearance for this occasion. She had recently rebelled against the hooped skirt, one of the first he knew of to do so, as being awkward to manage and too restrictive. She was wearing now a gown of silver muslin with a close-fitting bodice and a skirt cut at the front to show a white embroidered petticoat, simple in style, without flounces. Her hair was combed smoothly back from the forehead and temples, and drawn up behind with some pearls interwoven. But to the affectionate gaze of her brother it was the radiant pallor of her face and the spirited brightness of her eyes that gave her beauty.

Ashton's valet, the only manservant in the house, was sent to whistle up a cab for them. Bateson's house was in Grosvenor Square, and they descended amid a number of persons, also alighting from coaches, who thronged at the steps up to the house, were met by liveried footmen in the large entrance hall and guided to the foot of the broad, curving staircase that led up to the ballroom on the first floor. As Frederick, with Jane by his side, reached the top of the stairs he gave their names to the steward waiting there, who shouted them in stentorian tones. A further few steps brought them to the welcoming smiles of their host and hostess.

From his chosen point of vantage, Erasmus Kemp had seen the couple reach the head of the stairs and heard the names called out. Her appearance, her shouted name, her entrance into the ballroom, were the culmination of a design he had been maturing ever since learning of his colleague's intention to hold the reception, which was mainly for the benefit of various business and political acquaintances and prominent members of the West India Association. He had lost no time in asking Bateson if the Ashtons might be added to the list of guests.

He had been painstaking and methodical, as always, arriving early, planting himself where he had a clear view across the room. But – and it was one of the several contradictions of his nature – this care and preparation, designed to give him a feeling of calm control, was far from having this wished-for effect; he was not made calmer by it, rather the contrary, as when in listening to music we are not calmed by the gathering notes, however quietly they gather, because we know they are a prelude to some tumultuous crescendo.

It was with the sense of some imminent clash of cymbals that he waited some moments longer and then began to walk towards them through the crowd. He was walking in step to this music of the mind when by a coincidence he felt to be strange, and in some way significant, the orchestra in the gallery overlooking the room struck up with some martial music, which seemed familiar without his being able to recollect where and when he might have heard it.

'Music from the heavenly spheres,' Ashton said, glancing up towards the gallery. He had not known the musicians were stationed there.

Jane was never to remember how she replied to this, or whether she replied at all. As her brother was speaking she had observed Erasmus Kemp making his way towards them, and she needed to collect herself for what she feared might be an awkward moment. He had lost his case yesterday, and her brother, though without being one of the parties to the dispute, had in a certain sense been victorious. It had been a prelude, in a way, to the Admiralty case that was to come, when they would be direct and self-declared opponents . . .

'Miss Ashton, a great pleasure to see you again.' Kemp lowered his head over her hand.

Not entirely unexpected, however, Ashton had time to think, as he smiled a little and waited for introductions. These came, and the two men inclined their heads.

The meeting, the sight of each other at such close quarters, was for both of them something in the nature of a shock, both having formed judgements of the other that now turned out to need revising. Kemp had set Ashton down as a sentimental sort of fellow, probably given to preaching and hand-wringing, not on close terms with the realities of life. He found himself looking at a face that was ascetic but far from meek, at eyes that were closely observant and penetrating. Ashton, in his turn, instead of the coarse-grained trader he had been expecting to find, saw a face that was acquainted with pain and bewilderment, whatever the striving for an arrogance that would conceal this.

Ashton could find no immediate words, and Jane too was silent, both feeling that some reference to the previous day's judgement should be made, both fearing to sound a note of triumph. There were the strains of the orchestra falling from above, there was a hubbub of voices and a bustle of movement about them, but Jane felt caught in a web of silence and unease. She sought for something to say. The music, perhaps; it was a piece by Haydn they were playing now . . .

It was Kemp, however, who broke the silence and in a way that was totally unexpected.

'I would not wish you to think,' he said, looking squarely at

Ashton, 'that the lawyer representing me yesterday was acting on my instructions when he singled you out and made personal remarks about your plans to prosecute the case further.'

'I am very glad to hear you say so,' Ashton said. 'Since he was representing your interests directly and no one was representing mine – in fact, I had no direct interest in the case – it was natural to suppose that his outburst was part of some tactic previously agreed upon.'

'No, nothing of the sort.' Kemp raised his head and spoke with more emphasis now, as if he had been contradicted. 'I would not descend to that,' he said. 'If I cannot win by fair means, I would not wish to win at all.'

Ashton nodded, not really believing this, not really believing it was true of himself. Fairness was not a fixed value, it depended on the nature of the end to be served. 'Well, it does you credit,' he said.

'The fellow went far beyond his instructions,' Kemp said. 'I believe he lost his temper, as a matter of fact. I shall on no account employ him again. I hold him partly responsible for the unfavourable judgement we received.'

Ashton made no immediate reply to this. It was clear to him that despite the assurances of probity and fair dealing Kemp still believed he was in the right, would always believe so; he had been angry to see his lawyer obscure this fact by antagonising the judge. Something of this anger had come into his eyes as he spoke, eyes that were long and narrow, very dark, with a singular intensity of regard. He had worn the same look when the jury returned their verdict. Ashton had noted it, as he had noted the triumphant smiles of Van Dillen and his associates seated not far away. He had thought it due to the sting of defeat, but it seemed now that Kemp believed he had been dealt with unjustly . . .

After the initial greeting he had not looked at Jane again, as if the necessity of making things clear, removing any suspicion of underhand dealing, were of paramount importance to him. In fact, it was suspicion on Jane's part, not Ashton's, that he wished to remove. Ashton was an opponent, and he had never had much care for the feelings and opinions of opponents. But that Jane Ashton should think ill of him, should think him capable of such contriving, that was a very different matter.

And Jane, with the pleasurably heightened perceptions that come from a growing interest in the mind and person of another, knew that he was speaking to her, knew with the kind of certainty that needs little in the way of evidence, that the reason he did not look at her was that he wanted to do so very much, that he had dwelt long upon her and had arranged this meeting – she wondered with a kind of indulgent irony whether such an arrangement came under the heading of fair means.

Ashton glanced around him. The moment was propitious. 'If you will excuse me for a short while,' he said, 'there is someone over there I would like to exchange some words with. An old friend,' he added, smiling at Jane, who had turned in some surprise to look at him.

This left the two of them standing alone together. And alone for the moment they felt themselves to be, in the midst of all the people there. Not far away were long tables loaded with things to eat and drink; there was wine and champagne, pastries and sweetmeats of every sort, pies, tarts, moulds, charlottes and betties, trifles and fools, syllabubs and tansies. But thoughts of eating and drinking came to the minds of neither. Kemp's plans for the evening had not ended here; he knew the house, had visited Bateson on several occasions before, usually to discuss the business of the West India Association or the state of the sugar trade.

'Let us go this way,' he said. Passing below the gallery where the orchestra was playing, one came to a French window that opened on to a covered portico. Here they stood, leaning against the balustrade, looking out over the garden below. The evening air was cool, and Jane was glad of the quilted linen shawl over her shoulders. Somewhere among the trees, undeterred by the voices, the music, the clatter of plates and glasses, a bird she thought might be a nightingale was singing.

It was now that Kemp – not by calculation, but by sheer force of feeling and need for her understanding – hit upon the way most likely to secure Jane's sympathy and approval. Instead of the compliments and close regards that she had been half expecting – standard behaviour among the men of her acquaintance, and generally tedious to her – he began to talk about the Durham coalfields, and the colliery village of Thorpe, and his plans to go there soon and look at the mine, on which he had taken a lease. Within a few days, he told her. He spoke of his ambitions, his wish to build, create, improve the way things were done. He had studied, he had read a great deal about the mining and transport of coal, he already, even before going there, had ideas about how things could be done better.

He kept his eyes on her face as he spoke, and he saw that he had captured her attention, and something more; her expression showed the warmth of interest he had hoped for but not altogether believed he could arouse. He grew in eloquence, carried away by the feeling that she was entering into his designs, sharing them. There was so much that was antiquated and inefficient in the methods of extraction and marketing, so much scope for improvement . . .

'I think it is a splendid thing for a man to want to do,' she said. With her enthusiasm for action and reform, her hatred of resignation, Kemp's words had struck a deep chord in her. He could not have paid her a greater compliment than this, to tell her of these plans, take her into his confidence. He was inviting her approval, her judgement, seemed even to have need of it, not only regarding his intentions in Durham, but for himself personally. And he was vividly present to her, with his darkness of colouring, the intensity of his gaze, his habit of occasional sudden gesture. He had lost the slight stiffness of bearing; he leaned towards her as he talked, as if in eagerness to convince her.

'There are so many things closed to women,' she said. 'If I were a man, I would like to do something like that, something useful and positive, something to improve the lot of those people who spend their lives toiling in the darkness of the mine.' Her eyes were shining. 'It is a noble aim,' she said.

These words brought something of a check to Kemp, who had not much considered this aspect of things. Of course, it was becoming in a woman to harbour such sentiments . . . 'Well, you know,' he said, 'increased efficiency is bound to bring benefits to the working people.'

He paused on this, looking at her face, and at this moment she turned a little towards him and the light from the room behind them fell on her more directly. The brows and eyes, the slightly smiling mouth – it was the same face, the face he had seen at Vauxhall, momentarily lit up by that shower of gold, celebrating his success. He was persuaded of it, but he could not risk asking her, not now, not this evening. If she should say, no, I was not there, it was not I, the face was not mine, the blessing would be dimmed, they would both come closer to the light of common day.

They were interrupted at this point. Others had found the door and entered now, several people talking loudly together. Kemp had time to say in low tones, 'When I return from Durham, may I call on you?' and she to answer, with the one word only.

This word once obtained, and now that they could no longer be alone together, Kemp saw no need to stay. They rejoined Ashton, who was in the midst of a group, involved in an animated discussion as to the prospects of the government remaining in power now that the Earl of Chatham had retreated into madness and was spending his days in a darkened room in Hampstead with Lady Chatham as his only link with the outside world.

Kemp did not join in this, and after restoring Jane to the company of her brother, he took his leave. It seemed to Jane that the light was dimmer for his going, and she felt a little empty, as if the best of the evening were over. This feeling she translated into a need for comfort, and she had a glass of burgundy and ate a chicken leg, followed by a tansy pudding.

19

In the course of the following days, helped along by the wrestler's two shillings and by farthings and halfpennies from his fiddling and singing, Sullivan got across the Humber at Hartgate, bypassed York and was approaching Bridlington when he found a fair in progress at a seaside village called Rushburn. It was late afternoon, he was tired and footsore, and it came to him that this would be a pleasant and healthful place to stay the night. He had sixteen pence; half of that would get him a plate of bread and cheese and onion, and a bed. If he could add to his stock by playing and singing for an hour or two, he would be off to a good start next morning on what he felt would be the last leg of his journey to the birthplace of Billy Blair. In pursuance of this aim, he found a corner, spread his waistcoat and began, as usual, with a lively air to draw the people in. This time it was a tune he had first heard as a child in Ireland, 'The Galway Piper'. To add to the performance he shuffled his feet and nodded his head and turned his body this way and that in time with the tune. When a knot of people had gathered, he lowered his fiddle and broke into song. He knew a great many songs and did not think much beforehand of which to choose. Now, stirred to a sort of nostalgia by what he had just been playing, he sang some of the words to it:

> Loudly he can play or low,
> He can move you fast or slow,
> Touch your hearts or stir your toe,
> Piping Tim of Galway.

The crowd grew a little. He heard a coin strike against those of his own he had previously laid there to serve as good example. He repeated the air on his fiddle, then chose another song, a melody slower and more lingering, requiring a raised head and a look of yearning:

> *When like the dawning day*
> *Eileen Aroon*
> *Love sends his early ray*
> *Eileen Aroon*
> *What makes his dawning glow*
> *Changeless through joy and woe*
> *Only the constant know*
> *Eileen Aroon*

He continued until nightfall. When he counted the takings he found they came to fivepence halfpenny in coins of small denomination, a reward he considered reasonable. As he was leaving he noticed a beer tent crowded with people, open at the sides and roofed over with canvas, brightly lit now that darkness had come. He felt dry after his singing; the thought of an energising draught was suddenly tempting and after some moments more became irresistibly so.

He entered, fiddle and bow slung over his shoulder, made his way to the long counter where several people were serving from the barrels, and asked for a pint of ale, which cost one penny. He was tired, he did not feel sociable, he would have preferred to drink outside in the open, away from the crowd. But he could not leave the tent without returning his mug: there would be men posted to watch out for any move of that kind, the mug being worth more than the ale contained in it. So he made his way to a far corner of the tent, where the lamps did not reach with full strength and there was a twilight zone.

However, he was no more than halfway through his drink when a woman came up close to him, bade him good evening and – finding he did not draw away – rubbed the front of her thigh against him. 'You could give us a swaller o' that, you could, mister fiddler,' she said.

This rubbing, and the thinness of the material of the woman's skirt, worked an immediate effect on Sullivan. He had not been with a woman for a long time now, not since the days of the Florida settlement. There had been the long return to England, during which he had been kept in irons; there had been the weeks he had spent, still fettered, in prison; there had been the miracle of his escape, the sacredness of his vow, the urgent need to get away from London and escape pursuit . . .

'Here,' he said, handing her the mug. 'I am not the man to deny a sup of ale to a lady.'

He watched her drink, saw the movement of her throat.

'I knowed you was a gen'leman soon as I set eyes on you,' she said, and paused, and drank again.

'I will go and get you a pint for yourself,' Sullivan said, but she laid a hand on his arm. 'No,' she said, 'don't go away, you might forget me.'

She was not very pretty and not very young, but she had bold eyes and a painted mouth, and when her hand slipped from his arm and came gently to rest on his abdomen, he felt very constricted in his trousers, and began to lose all thought of consequences.

'S'ppose you an' me was to go for a stroll outside,' she said. 'It's a nice night, ain't it?' She handed him back the mug. 'You better finish this.'

A final, feeble impulse of caution came to Sullivan. 'How much?' he said.

'I asks two shillin' in the usual way of things.'

'I have not got two shillin'.'

'How much have you got?'

'One shillin' an' eightpence halfpenny.'

'Well, I have took a fancy to you, that was a lovely song you sang, that one about Eileen. I will take a bit less this time.'

Sullivan, too much in haste to return the mug to the counter, let it fall, empty now, into the dark grass at his feet. The sense that he was getting a special price destroyed the last of his reserve, and they stepped out of the tent together.

They walked away from the lights, went through a gate into the next field, found a place near the hedge. 'First we pays, then we has our fun,' the woman said, and Sullivan handed over the money. 'I would spread me coat for you, if I had one,' he said. 'I had a fine coat once.' The echo of an old obsession came to him, even in this moment of high excitement: 'I had a fine coat once but it was took off me back, twice I have had me buttons stole . . .'

'Well, I ain't goin' to steal 'em now,' she said. 'You better unbutton them what you have got left.'

No time was wasted on further speech. The woman went down on her back, lifted up her skirt and spread her legs. There was no impediment of undergarments. Sullivan found his way and was very soon in the throes of delight. But these had barely subsided when his peace was disturbed by a light on his face, and he saw two men standing above him, both armed with heavy sticks.

'Aye aye,' one of the men said. 'What 'ave we got 'ere? A pair o' nightbirds, ain't we?'

Sullivan scrambled to his feet and with a gallantry he felt to be commendable at such a time held out his hand to help the woman up. 'Who might you be?' he said.

'It is the constables,' the woman said.

'That is right, my pretty. You've 'ad to do with us before, ain't you?'

'Don't know you from Adam, I don't.'

'She don't look at the faces,' the other man said.

'I have seen somethin' of the world an' you do not have the look of constables to me,' Sullivan said. 'You must have watched us and follered after.'

'No need for talkin'. All you needs to do is show us you have got money enough about you for a night's lodgin', an' we will let you alone.'

Sullivan said nothing to this for some moments, hoping that the woman would come to his aid and say they were together and had money in common. But she remained silent.

'I have no money,' he said at last. 'Owin' to a combination of circumstances which I have not the leisure to go into at the present moment.'

'Sleepin' in the open, no abode an' no money. You are a vagrant, an' you will 'ave to come along with us to the parish workhouse.'

'Show me your badge of office,' Sullivan said, and received a violent push in the chest that sent him back several steps.

'Any more o' that an' you will get a batterin'. An' don't try makin' a run for it, you will not get far.' He turned to the woman, shining the lamp in her face. ''Ow about you?' he said. 'Betsy, ain't it? 'Ow much did he give you?'

'He give me a shillin'.'

'Ho, yes. Very likely. Well, you gives us the shillin' an' you keeps the rest, an' everythin' is fair an' above board.'

With the sad, belated wisdom that follows upon passion spent Sullivan saw his bread and cheese and his bed for the night transferred to the pocket of one of the men. Betsy left the scene at a good speed and without a backward glance, and he was taken by the arms and led away.

20

As the time approached for the handball match with the neighbouring colliery village of Northfield, Michael Bordon spent his Sunday mornings and evenings practising, alone or with anyone who cared to play, at the handball court, which lay alongside the alehouse. He was now, by the consent of a large majority, Thorpe's appointed champion, and he took the responsibility very seriously. Sunday afternoons he spent walking out with Elsie Foster. They had now reached the stage of walking hand in hand.

His mother had been the first to notice the change in him. He would previously, after the practice session, put on his pit clothes and go to play chuck farthing or sit in talk with the other men. Now he would spend a long time over combing his hair, and ask her more often to trim it for him. He would get out his best suit, the breeches with embroidered knee-bands, the coat close-fitting, cut in at the waist.

Nan was carried back to the days of her courtship. She had been lucky in Bordon, she knew that; he was sometimes violent with others, but never other than gentle with her. There was something unfulfilled in him, something rebellious and unresigned, that made him often sombre, and this was more evident now that he grew older. He knew that Michael was walking out with Elsie Foster and that the family would lose income when the boy married; this would not be yet, but probably as soon as Michael went from putter to hewer – Bordon had married then himself.

Both of them approved of the girl and the family. Elsie

worked on the tips, just as Nan had done. Bordon had taken her from that work, as it was likely Michael would do with Elsie.

Her husband's best clothes were still there, in the trunk, though it was seldom that he wore them now. She went and got out the cravat, remembering how smart he had looked when he first came calling, so tall and straight, turning his cap in his hands. Her brother Billy had run off to sea before that . . .

She decided to give the cravat to Michael as a special thing to wear for this first walking-out. It was very fine, muslin edged with lace. He was dismayed by it. Fancy cravats of this kind were no longer worn by anyone he knew. But he said nothing. He looked at his mother's face, which was lit up, the lines of work and weariness all smoothed away by the memories this totally unwearable cravat had brought her. He put on the cravat, tied it properly in a bow and set forth. When he was out of the sight of the house he took it off and put it in his pocket.

Elsie too wore her best clothes for these outings; they were always much the same, but he was always smitten anew by the look of her, the white hose and short dimity petticoats, the printed cotton gown, the stomacher with its bunches of variously coloured ribbons, the straw hat tied under the chin – it was what the other girls wore for Sunday best, but on her it seemed uniquely fetching.

They took the path that led across the big field, where Michael had fought with Walker. It was a fine afternoon, others were walking there, they exchanged greetings as they passed. Ahead of them, to the north, the sky was divided by a broad, straight-edged band of cloud that seemed precisely ruled across from verge to verge. Above this band there was still the blue of day, deep and luminous; below it the delicate and reticent shades of evening were gathering, bronze, silver, slate grey, palest apricot.

Michael slowed his step. 'Shall we gan through the Dene?' he said.

There was a pause before the reply came, but it was of the briefest. 'If tha likes.'

She would have thought it improper in Michael to suggest this at any earlier stage. Like holding hands, it was a necessary and time-honoured step in the progress of courtship, the first experience of enclosure, of being screened off and out of view.

Generations of couples had traversed these paths above the beck, many were the children that had been conceived here.

Talk was more personal and intimate with them now, and as they crossed the pasture fields and began to descend towards the deep cut which marked the beginning of the Dene, Michael told her of the attempts he had made to get the overman to shift David from being Walker's marrow to being his. 'Walker an' me are both puttin' the coal, just the same,' he said. 'Why not keep it in the family? Walker can find someone else – he can have the lad that works with me, if he wants.'

'Well, but,' she said, 'tha wouldna be doin' him nay favour. Walker would just start knockin' him about. What a mean, he'll keep his hands off yor David, now that tha's had it out with him.'

'Well, that's one way of lookin' at it,' Michael said. It was an aspect that had not occurred to him, or to his father either.

Elsie turned to smile at him as they walked. ''Tis sometimes better to let things be,' she said. Michael was like the men of her own family, set on having his own way and keeping close to his own idea of things. But he would listen to her, and she liked him for this – it was one of the things she liked most about him. 'My uncle would be alive to this day if they had only let things be,' she said. She had been fond of this uncle, her mother's brother, who had died in an accident at the pit some two years before, killed by a haphazard fall of stone from the mouth of the shaft. 'They changed the work hours,' she said. 'The men went off without puttin' the timbers across where the stone was loose, an' the basketman had just come on an' he didn't know it. Usual game, tryin' to get more work out of the men for the same money.'

Anger had come with the words into her voice and into her face. Michael made no answer, allowing silence to mark his agreement and sympathy. He knew the circumstances of Thomas Fenby's death; pit deaths and injuries formed part of the collective knowledge of the colliery. But Elsie's quickness of feeling was still strange to him. She had gone from a smile to a flare of anger in two shakes of a duck's tail. 'Look,' he said, with a certain relief at finding a change of subject. He pointed down at the path as it began to descend through the wooded slopes of the Dene. There were the trot marks of a fox in the dried clay.

There had been high winds in the previous days, and they

could see a tangle of damage higher up on the slope, where the trees were more exposed. Branches had been torn from some of the elms there; they lay in a jagged debris of timber, the pale yellow of the breaks deepening to reddish in the core of the wood. In places the bark had been stripped off in the fall, leaving raw-looking, ochreous patches. Chaffinches fluttered among the tangle of boughs, repeating a single sharp note.

They fell silent as they went further in. Both were aware of the momentousness of the occasion. Elsie was nearly eighteen. She had come here often as a child, with other children, played hide-and-seek, gathered primroses, splashed in the stream. But this had ended for her at the age of ten, when she had started working on the tips. Since then she had come only rarely. Girls did not go alone into the Dene, and it was not customary for women of any age to go on excursions of this sort together. Now it seemed to her altogether a different place, hushed and strange.

For Michael too these slopes felt unfamiliar and new. For the first time he felt truly alone with Elsie, in spite of the presence – felt by both – of others here, occasional muted voices and rustlings of movement among the trees.

They took the path that led downward, towards the beck. From somewhere on the other side of the narrow valley they heard the voices of children. Elsie was having some difficulty in walking now, on this steepest part of the slope. She had hesitated over the choice of shoes and finally, not thinking they would be going into the Dene, chosen the only pair she possessed with raised heels – Italian heels they were called, she had no idea why. She was walking in front of Michael – the path was too narrow for them to walk side by side – and she feared she might seem ungainly to him. But he – able now for the first time to look as much as he liked at her – was too much taken with the carriage of her shoulders and the sway of her hips to pay much attention to the way she set her feet. This too she sensed might be the case, but the thought did not make her less eager to reach easier footing.

As they drew near the beck the ground levelled out. There was a gleam of sunshine on the wet stones, and they saw a green leaf, fallen before its time, go drifting by, edged with bright specks of foam. They followed the stream as it curved sharply and ran through a broad sweep of fern and tall grasses with plumy, bluish heads. There was a blaze of yellow from the kingcups that grew along the wet border, following the line of the curve.

'My father has always wanted to own this piece of land,' Michael said. He had never shared this knowledge of his father's wish with anyone before – it was like admitting Elsie into the family. 'For a market garden, tha knows, to grow vegetables and fruit. About two acres, it is, two an' a bit, all on this side of the beck.'

Elsie looked about her. 'It feels different,' she said. It was completely still here, out of the breeze that had been in their faces as they walked. 'It feels warmer,' she said. 'A never marked it in arl the times a used to come here.' She paused, seeking for words. 'Mebbe a did mark it. When tha's little tha sees things, then they gan out of yor mind, but tha dinna truly forget them.'

'Just an idea of his,' Michael said. 'A mean, he never had a chance of gettin' it.' He pointed up the slope. 'Nay shortage of water, the beck never dries.'

She looked up to where he was pointing and saw the glint of water as it came down to feed the stream. There was a drift of bluebells alongside the spring and a rowan tree in flower.

'Everythin' here comes out early,' he said. 'Tha sees butterflies here before tha sees them anywhere else. He said so once. An' dragonflies, he said. He comes down here on his own, tha knows, just to stand an' look.'

They looked at each other in silence for some moments. Then he said, 'Would tha like to sit down for a bit?'

'Yes,' she said, and her eyes rested steadily on him. 'If tha wants.'

'A wanted to bring you to this bit of ground,' he said. 'A wanted to tell you . . . there is nowt I canna tell you. A long time a was watchin' out for you, every mornin' a was waitin' to see you. Seein' you in the mornin' was like a light a took down with me, down the pit.'

'A was hopin' tha'd speak,' she said. 'But tha needed a good batterin' first. Walker done us a good turn. Without him we might still be just lookin' at each other an' lettin' the days gan by.'

They went some way up from the stream to where the ferns grew thickly. Elsie sat very straight for a while. Then she untied the strings of her hat, which were knotted in a bow under her chin, and took it off and laid it beside her. Below the hat was a mob cap drawn tight across her head, and when she loosened this and took it off, her fair hair, which had been contained in it, fell round her shoulders.

'That's better,' she said, smiling. 'My head was feelin' hot.'

'All of me is feelin' hot,' he said.

Whether her balance was precarious and easily upset by his hands on her shoulders, or whether he pushed her gently down, was not something that occupied the minds of either. Hidden among the thickly growing ferns on this so much desired piece of ground, they lay embraced together.

21

On a rainy morning, not long after the insurance ruling, Ashton's manservant knocked at the study door to tell him that a man had come to the house declaring himself to be the bearer of a message for Mr Frederick Ashton. He had been asked to wait outside, and the door had been closed on him, he being of a ragged and unkempt appearance and also very wet.

Ashton went down into the front hall and opened the door to the man, who was waiting in the rain, at the foot of the steps. 'What it is you want of me?' he said.

'Beggin' yer pardon, sir, am I lookin' at Mr Frederick Ashton?'

'You are.'

'I been entrusted with a message, personal for Mr Ashton, from a Negro man, name of Jeremy Evans.'

Ashton was long to remember the man's starved looks and the rank odour of his wet clothes and the sudden leap of hope that came with his words. 'Come up the steps,' he said. 'Here, under the lintel, out of the rain. Where is he, where is Evans?'

'He is in the Poultry Compter, sir.'

'What, in prison? Is there some charge against him?'

The man smiled a little at this. Water from his drenched hair ran down into his eyes, but he made no move to clear them. 'There is many ends there with no charge agin 'em. There was no charge brought agin me, properly speakin'. Suspicion, they calls it. I was passin' by, I had nothin' to do with any fightin' or woundin', but they took me in along with the others, they kept me locked up till someone spoke to say who it was that done it.

They let me out early this mornin'. Evans managed to get some words to me in passin'. It had to be Mr Frederick Ashton, but he didn't know where you was. He told me the house he was taken from. I went there first. I been goin' round in the rain all mornin'. Evans told me you was a gen'rous gentleman.'

'I am very grateful to you for this information.' Ashton took out his purse and counted five shillings into the man's palm. 'I hope you will find the means to get close to a fire and dry yourself before you catch a chill.'

'Thank you, sir. Evans spoke true of you. I will eat before I dry – they doesn't give you much in the way of vittles.'

Ashton did not wait to watch him through the gate, but went immediately for hat and cape and boots. Within ten minutes he had found a hackney coach and was on the way. The prison was in Marylebone Road close to the junction with Chapel Street. Progress was slow – the rain had brought out more vehicles than usual.

On arrival he was led by a jailer to a kind of office, dank and malodorous, adjacent to the cells. After he had waited for several minutes with mounting impatience an assistant keeper arrived, and Ashton at once demanded to see Jeremy Evans.

'There is no one of that name committed here,' the man said, with a slow shake of the head.

The denial steadied Ashton and brought a more deliberate process of calculation to him. It meant of course that this man, and almost certainly the head keeper too, had been bribed to conceal Evans's presence there. They would know there were no grounds for his detention, and so the safest course was to deny knowledge of him.

'Fellow, you are lying,' he said. 'You have been paid to lie, is it not so? I have it on good authority that Mr Evans is here. You will fetch your superior to me, or I will see that you have cause to regret your part in this.'

He spoke with the voice of his class, in the tone and with the assurance of one used to being listened to. His cape was open to show the manner of his dress beneath. He saw on the keeper's face the usual unhappy doubt of the corrupted under-ling confronted by an authority which, though indeterminate, was inimical to him and threatening and far larger in scope than that which he was accustomed to wield over the wretches in his charge.

'Go and fetch him now at once.'

The man hesitated a moment longer then turned and went without further words. This time the wait was longer, but Ashton was no longer prey to impatience. His purpose was clear to him and he was intent on it.

The head keeper was an older man, bulky, bald-headed and wigless, with a look of ill temper. It seemed to Ashton that he had been aroused from sleep, or some state of torpor.

'What is it, what is it?' he said. 'I am much occupied, sir, I have little time for visitors.'

'You have time enough for brandy, one could get drunk from the breath of it on you.' Ashton could not keep the contempt out of his voice. 'I will tell you what it is soon enough,' he said. 'You are keeping here, in unlawful custody, a man named Jeremy Evans. I know you have been paid to do so and I know by whom. This is not a private prison, you are answerable to the public authority for the way it is conducted. I intend to see this man and talk to him, here and now. If you deny this to me I will bring an action against you and against those who brought him here and laid false charges and against whoever it was that signed the order for custody, if ever such an order was made. I will see you hounded out of office, sir.'

'You cannot obtain an order for his release without you bring a writ, you nor any man else.'

The words were sullen, but it was no more than a token defiance that they expressed; even as he spoke he nodded to his assistant, who at once left the room.

'Have no fear, I shall apply for the writ without delay,' Ashton said. 'And if you deliver him now to any who come without a writ signed by a magistrate in proper form, you will live to regret the day, I promise you.'

When, some time later, he saw a black man enter, accompanied by the assistant keeper, it came to him with a strange effect of shock and temporary bewilderment that he would not have known that this was Evans, knew it only now that he saw him led here under guard. The night of his rescue from the ship it had been dark, the violent altercation with the captain had taken up his attention; others had released Evans from his bonds and brought him back to shore. Not once had he looked the man in the face. Now, as their eyes met for the first time, he was perplexed to think of all the concern he had felt, the importance of this man to him, the sense of failure and defeat at his disappearance, the hope this day had brought – all for a man whom he could not have picked out among a crowd of others . . .

'I am Frederick Ashton,' he said. 'I shall get you out of here, you may rely on it.'

Evans's eyes were deep-set and luminous in the strongly marked face. There was the bruise of a heavy blow, still unhealed, on his forehead and right temple. He made a movement towards Ashton as if to take his hand, but this was roughly checked by the keeper.

'Take your hand from him,' Ashton said sharply. 'You have no rights in him.' He went some steps towards Evans and held out his hand, which the other took in both of his.

'Have you committed any offence, that you should be brought here?' Ashton asked.

'No, sir, none. Three men come to the house at a time when the house is empty, not those same who take me the first time. Only one comes to the door, says he has a message from you, sir. Then the others come at me from the sides, take a hold of me at the door. I fight with them.'

Evans raised his head and straightened his shoulders. 'I don' go easy,' he said. 'I fight with them. But it is too many for me. I try to shout but one of them hits me about the head with a stick. I lose my senses, don' know where I am.'

'What, they dragged you like that through the streets, half conscious as you were, and nobody intervened or even enquired into the matter?'

'Nobody, sir, no. People think black man slave run away.'

'What a famous example of humanity,' Ashton said. 'And these fine fellows here locked you up without question – except regarding the price. Before I can obtain your release I shall need an order for it, signed by a magistrate. It will be an order for your immediate appearance in court to answer as to whether you have done any wrong that would justify your being kept imprisoned. Once we have established that you have no charge to answer, you will leave the court a free man. Do you understand?'

'Yes, sir, and Heaven bless you. I ask it in my prayers.'

'You are a Christian then?'

'Yes, I been baptised.'

'That very probably will help us,' Ashton said. 'The courts are more favourably disposed to those who are not heathens. I am sorry you will have to stay longer in this foul place, but it should not be more than a few days.'

'I will not mind it. I know you do not forget me.'

Ashton saw that tears had come to Evans's eyes. 'I am your friend,' he said. 'Keep it in mind that I am working for your release. On no account must you leave this prison unless you are accompanied by me.' He turned to the head keeper. 'When I come for him,' he said, 'I will enquire of him, not of you, how he has been treated in the meanwhile. I advise you to bear this in mind.'

On this, Evans was led back to his cell, and Ashton took his leave, not ill-satisfied with the result of his visit. He went immediately to the Lord Mayor's chambers to lay the information that a Jeremy Evans was confined at the Poultry Compter without any warrant.

He did not have long to wait. The writ was issued the following day. Charles Bolton and Andrew Lyons were commanded to produce before the Lord Mayor at his chambers the body of Jeremy Evans, and to show cause for the taking and detaining of him. The action was heard at Mansion House in the presence of the Lord Mayor himself. The cause of detention of Evans was stated to be that he was the slave and property of Lyons, by purchase from Bolton, who had held him in Jamaica as a slave; that when brought to London he ran away from the service of his master, but was recovered and detained until a ship was ready to return him to the West Indies.

The Lord Mayor, having listened to Ashton's claim of imprisonment without warrant, as voiced by his lawyer, Horace Stanton, took very little time to ponder the matter. No evidence had been produced that Evans was guilty of any offence, and therefore his detention was unlawful. He was discharged and declared free to leave the court.

He had scarcely finished pronouncing this judgement and Evans, with Ashton at his side, had just come to his feet, preparatory to leaving the courtroom, when a man strode forward and seized Evans by the arm, announcing his identity as Captain William Newton of the *Arabella*, the slave ship designated to transport Evans to Jamaica. In his other hand he waved the bill of sale certifying to the purchase of Evans by Andrew Lyons.

'I secure his person as the property of Mr Lyons,' he said in loud tones.

Ashton saw two rough-looking men pressing behind, obviously hired for the occasion. Evans struggled to free his arm, but the captain held on to it. Newton's face was red and congested-looking, and veins stood out at his temples. A sort of reciprocal rage of violence was aroused in Ashton, and he felt a sharp impulse to strike at the arm that was still holding Evans. Fortunately for him – he would have stood small chance in a physical conflict with the captain – he heard Stanton's voice immediately behind him: 'Threaten to charge him with assault if he does not immediately release the man's arm.'

'This man has been discharged by the court,' Ashton said. 'There is no charge against him, he is free to leave. That document you are brandishing has no validity here. The issue of property must be decided in another court. Remove your hand from his arm at once, or I will issue an immediate summons of assault against you. There is no shortage of witnesses.'

He saw the fury in the captain's eyes, saw the convulsive clenching of his jaw. 'Remove your hand from his person at once,' he said.

Newton struggled with his rage some moments longer, then released Evans's arm. 'God damn your liver and your eyes,' he said. He turned away and his hirelings turned away with him, leaving Ashton swept by an exhilaration he had scarcely known himself capable of.

It was this release of triumphant joy that he began with when later that day he was telling Jane what had happened in the courtroom. 'He had brute written all over him,' he said. 'A brute of a slaving skipper. God help those unlucky enough to be subject to him when he is master of that small world of a ship – not so very small either, when we think of the hundreds of poor souls shackled below decks. I must confess that I felt a great surge of triumph when he was forced to let go of Evans. I felt that I was acting as God's minister to see justice done, justice and mercy.'

'They are not often combined,' Jane said. She smiled at her brother with full affection. He had told her of his visit to the prison the day before, and now his account of events in the court-room, and the part he had played, had aroused an ardent admiration in her, so completely were they in accord with her idea of how a man should bear himself in such circumstances, or a woman, for that matter – she liked to think that she too would have acted and spoken in the same way. 'I am proud of you, Frederick,' she said, 'and I am proud to be your sister.'

'Oh well, it was only for a few minutes, you know.' His tone was deprecating but he was deeply pleased by her words and by the look on her face as she said them. 'Just for those few minutes, I felt I was carrying out God's wishes and His purposes. All the same, it is a most amazing thing that in this England of ours, nowadays so abounding in refined legal argument, with a new generation of penal theorists who claim to rest their policies on humanity and common sense, that a man can be hauled off to prison, committed on a false order of custody and kept under lock and key for an indefinite period without any charge being made against him.'

He paused and shook his head, with the rueful smile common to him. There were degrees of corruption, as there were of all moral states. The venality of the keepers at the Poultry Compter, who would sell a man into captivity, seemed deeply criminal to him as compared to that of the starveling turnkeys he had encountered on his visit to Newgate Prison when he had gone there to speak to the surviving crew of the *Liverpool Merchant*.

'It is there we should begin,' Jane said. 'It is there we should try to mend things. Not with theories and philosophies and adding wise books to the stacks of them already written, but seeing the wrongs and abuses where they are, and striving together to mend them.'

'Yes,' Ashton said, though with some hesitation. It was a favourite theme of his sister's – her face had lit up with enthu-siasm as she spoke. But he had never been altogether in sympathy with it. Like trying to stop a flood with your hands, he thought.

You needed a law that would block the source. In the meantime, of course, people got drowned . . .

'But even more amazing,' he said, 'and almost defying belief, is that there and then, in the presence of the Chief Magistrate of the City of London, in his residence, in his court, after he had just declared a man free to go, this same brute of a ship's captain, with two hired ruffians at his shoulders, should dare such a thing, should dare such open defiance. You will not believe it, but we had to ask the Mayor to provide us with an escort for Evans so we could get him away from the premises of the court without his being waylaid and carried off by those waiting outside.'

It had shocked him, yet again, this blindly tenacious sense of property in another human being on no more grounds than that the skin was of a different colour. It went far deeper than any question of value, the price Evans would fetch if brought to the slave market. Bolton and Lyons between them had already spent a good part of this on bribes and rewards. It was the presumption of absolute right, the sense of outrage when this – to them – natural order of things was disputed.

Jane had been out somewhere; it was only now that he noticed this by her dress – he had been too occupied with his account to notice it before. At once, by some obscure association of ideas, he thought of Erasmus Kemp. The two would not have met since the evening of the reception at Bateson's house; Jane was not one to make assignations, and Kemp would know that visiting her at home was the only way of being granted a private conversation. She had not referred to Kemp since that evening, but Ashton remembered how they had disappeared together, how they had shut themselves away. The very absence of comment, in one so open and frank as Jane, was significant – or so he reasoned.

'I am glad that I was able to become acquainted with Mr Kemp,' he said. 'It is good to have a face and form for one's adversaries.'

'Yes, I suppose he must be regarded as an adversary.' The word had no weight in her mind; there was only his face, the blaze of the dark eyes fixed on her own. As if he could only explain, only express himself, as if his purposes only seemed real to him while his gaze was locked on hers. As if only she could meet his need. He was everything her brother detested, everything she too should detest. A man who had founded his fortune on the sugar plantations, on slave labour. But he wanted to change, he wanted to build, to create, to improve the lot of common people . . .

'A lot of force in him,' Ashton said. 'I am not sure what kind of force it is. I would hesitate to call it moral. He seems equally intense in the pursuit of his financial interests as in the sphere of personal feeling. Not a man to sacrifice his time except on issues important to him, perhaps I can say dear to him. He was set on conversing privately with you, so much was clear to see.'

'It is true that he paid me particular attention.'

'Indeed, yes. That is to put it mildly.'

'He asked me if he might call when he returns from Durham.'

'And how did you answer him?'

'I consented to it.'

'I have been thinking . . . you know he is a very important figure in the Admiralty case that is pending – it is to be heard very shortly now. In fact, it is he who has instituted the charges of mutiny and piracy. If it could be put to him that it is close to your heart . . . that you would be happy for a judgement favourable to our cause . . . If he could be persuaded to declare some change of mind, some new order of feeling – he has had time to consider and so on, he sees now that a charge of piracy cannot be sustained, as the Negroes were not property, and those surviving much outnumbered the crew. He might even be brought to state the belief that the killing of the captain was justified, and even lawful, as it put a stop to a process of murder. In short, if he knew it was your wish, he might be prevailed upon to withdraw the suit and make a public statement of his reasons for so doing. Think what attention such a statement would receive, what a great triumph it would be for us, for the cause of abolition. Of course there is the evidence of eyewitnesses, but in the absence of a plaintiff, in the absence of anyone calling for a judgement, the case might founder, yes, it might founder . . .'

He had been walking back and forth, possessed by the splendour of this vision. Now he stopped and looked at her, perhaps becoming aware of her silence, the absence of approbation. He saw a look on her face he could not recall ever having seen there before, a look in which there was no slightest indulgence for him. His sister was regarding him coldly, as one might look at a stranger, someone for whom there was no kindness.

'Do you really think that I would ask such a favour, such a large favour, on the strength of the acquaintance I have with Mr Kemp, an hour of conversation, less than an hour? Do you not see that to ask such a thing of such a man as he is, as I sense him to be, or indeed of any man . . .'

The ugliness and unseemliness of her brother's suggestion, coming so soon after her admiration for him, threatened her composure now, and her voice trembled as she continued. 'Do you not see that it would mean, seem to mean, offering something . . . promising something in exchange? You are asking me to serve your turn, and without even any surety of the result you desire, to claim a right of property in him and thereby to put myself in his hands. How can you be so careless of your sister's dignity? How can you be so coarse and selfish?'

'Selfish?' he began. 'Selfish when I have at heart the liberation from bondage of many thousands, whose faces I do not even –'

But she swept out of the room without waiting for him to finish.

22

Jane was to see Erasmus Kemp again sooner than she had expected, before his departure for Durham, in fact, as the case against the surviving members of the crew of the *Liverpool Merchant* was heard at the Old Bailey only three days after the quarrel between brother and sister.

Despite the constraint that still existed between them, she accompanied him to the courthouse, though with divided motives, as she fully admitted to herself. There was the long habit of support for her brother, her sympathy for the cause so dear to him; and there was the wish, felt no less strongly, to see Erasmus again – for it was certain that he would be there.

It was not the first time that Ashton had attended a hearing at the Court of King's Bench, but he had never lost his sense of the strange isolation, in the midst of the bustle of the city, that the Old Bailey conveyed as one drew near to it. Having turned off the busy thoroughfare connecting Newgate Street and Ludgate Street, the only approach to the courtyards and outbuildings, and to the Sessions House itself, was by means of a single narrow alleyway, and as one proceeded along this the rattle of wheels and the cries of the street vendors fell away behind one.

They emerged on to the Sessions Yard, where a considerable number of people had already gathered, most of them there to watch the proceedings and hear what they could, but there was a scattering of turnkeys and court attendants and some witnesses waiting to be called – Ashton saw Barton and James Porter, the ship's interpreter, among them.

They passed through the gate into the bail dock, where what

was left of the crew of the *Liverpool Merchant* were chained and under guard. Hughes was the only one of them to meet Ashton's eye as he passed, and it was the same look of ferocious hostility that he remembered from the time when he had questioned the men in the prison yard. They crossed the dock and were admitted through one of the gates flanking the portico and led by an attendant to the places reserved for them in the gallery overlooking the court.

Erasmus Kemp was there already, in the balcony on the other side of the courtroom, almost exactly opposite them. He and Ashton inclined their heads in the barest of greetings. Jane made no motion of greeting but when she raised her eyes to look at him she found his gaze fixed on her, the space between them was cancelled, and it was as though they were continuing some conversation, close together in a pause between words. Just so he had looked at her on the terrace of Bateson's house, excluding all the other people there, all the rest of the world. She was stirred by the memory and by something close to pity for him in his tenacity, so strong as to make him seem helpless, though still she was flattered by it. Thereafter she did not meet his eyes again.

The judges now entered from the upper floor, where they had been assisted in donning their scarlet robes and full-bottomed wigs. All those present in the courtroom rose to their feet as the Lord High Admiral, with the Lord Commissioners on either side of him and the Chief Justice of Common Pleas following behind, mounted the steps to the judges' bench and took their places. When they were seated the High Marshal of the Admiralty advanced, bearing the emblem of authority, the replica of a silver oar, which he laid on the table before the judges. The jurors, having been assembled in the Yard, now entered and took their places in the enclosures on either side. The crier called for silence and Kemp's lawyer, Pike, rose to open the case for the prosecution.

The first witness to be called was one Captain Philips, a stout, bluff-featured man recently retired from the sea and resident in London. He related to the court that in the year 1765, while passing through the Florida Straits bound for Norfolk, Virginia, he had anchored at a latitude of some 27 degrees, south of a point on the coast known as the Boca Nueva. He had sent a party ashore to take water from the fresh springs he knew to be there, and gather firewood and shoot any game they came across. These men had returned to tell him of finding the remains of a ship named the *Liverpool Merchant*, and he, aware of the general belief that the ship had been lost at sea with all aboard her, had gone ashore himself and found the story to be true. He had felt it his duty, on returning to London, to inform the ship's owner, Mr Erasmus Kemp, of the discovery.

Horace Stanton, for the defence, endeavoured to show that the mere discovery of a wrecked ship did not prove any intention on the part of the crew to remain in Florida and evade justice. 'Shipwrecks occur, do they not?' he said to the captain. 'Is it not true that those waters are treacherous to ships that come too close in?'

'Yes, sir, so much is true.'

'So there is no reason to suppose that it was other than accident, that the ship was wrecked in some storm, making it impossible for these people to return home?'

At this point Pike intervened. 'Please tell the court the circumstances in which the ship was discovered.'

'Strange circumstances, sir.' On the captain's face there had come a look almost of incredulity, as if even now he could not fully reconcile himself to the improbability of his account. 'I will never forget it,' he said. 'Out of sight of the shore she was, tilted over in the bed of a dry creek, in the midst of swamps and lagoons, where no man would ever expect to see a ship. Her name was still there, on the scroll.'

'How did the vessel get there, do you suppose?'

On Stanton's objecting to the introduction of supposition into the evidence, Pike rephrased the question: 'How, in your professional opinion, could the ship have been in that place?'

'There can only be one explanation,' Philips said. 'She must have been hauled up the channel by men pulling from the banks on either side.'

'But you have testified that the bed of the creek was dry when you came upon the ship,' Stanton said. He turned and addressed the judges on the bench. 'My Lords, this witness's evidence is contradictory and cannot be believed.'

Philips's face had reddened. 'Take care who you call liar, sir,' he said. 'That coast is full of creeks and inlets, large and small. I know it better than most. The courses of the water are constantly changing. The creek was broad enough, it could have held deep water at one time.'

'Only one way the ship could have got there,' Pike said, with expressive looks at the jury. 'And only one reason for taking it there, so far out of sight of the shore. It is obvious that the aim was to conceal all traces of the vessel. Were these the actions of men who intended to return and yield up the cargo they had stolen?'

In the course of further questioning of the witness, Stanton elicited the fact that the crew alone would not have been able to tow the ship so far. All the men available – and the women too – would have been needed for such heavy and prolonged labour.

'So,' he said, 'whether hale or sick, whether black or white, all took equal part in this hauling of the ship. Whatever the purpose – and this we can only speculate about – it is very clear that this cargo, these stolen goods that my learned friend speaks of with such nonchalance, were in fact the people of the ship. They heaved on the ropes along with the others. They outnumbered the crew – they could have taken flight but they did not. Without their cooperation the enterprise would have been impossible. A strange notion of cargo, My Lords, a strange notion of theft.'

Philips stepped down and Kemp was called. He descended from his place in the gallery and went to stand at the bar and take the oath. He related how Captain Philips, conceiving it to be his duty, had come to his London house and told him of the finding of the vessel in the wilderness of southern Florida, and of the strangeness of the ship's position, so far from the sea and hidden from sight. The news had come as a shock to him. For twelve years he had thought the ship lost at sea with all aboard her. The loss of the ship had brought ruin to his father, who was hoping to recoup his fortunes by selling the slaves in Jamaica and returning with a cargo of sugar to sell on the Liverpool Exchange. His father's death had followed soon after the loss of the ship. On the strength of the news brought by Philips, he had thought it probable – indeed almost certain – that men who had taken such care to cover their tracks must have intended to take refuge in that waste and remain there. And since they could not have gone far on foot in such country, he had felt sure that the survivors would not be very distant from the place where the wreck had been found. He had decided to mount an expedition, track the miscreants down, bring them to justice.

He was aware of only one person in the courtroom as he spoke, and that was Jane Ashton, who was sitting above in the gallery, looking down at him and listening to his words. No one else there mattered much to him. He believed it was just that these remnants of the crew should be hanged for their crimes, and he hoped for a verdict to that effect. But this hope, though held with deepest sincerity, took second place. The important thing was that Jane should understand his motives, appreciate the stern and heroic part he had played.

It was inevitable that this bid for her blessing should bring about certain omissions and distortions in his account of things. He stressed the high and lonely mission of justice that had taken him so far and cost him so much. He made no mention of the hatred of his cousin Matthew that had so impelled him, nor of the urge for action he had felt, the need to escape from the general unhappiness of his life at that time, of which the hatred had been merely a symptom, as he judged it now. Naturally he did not try to relate, then or in his later accounts to Jane, that he had been responsible for his cousin's death, that he was still trying to fend off remorse for this, a remorse which he felt should be resisted, as it threatened to nullify the justice of his cause. Nor did he make any reference to the fact that his father had made unwise investments and would still have been bankrupt even if the ship had come safely home. But he was aware of no falsehood as he spoke. It was the truth of himself, purified of obscuring dross, that he was offering up to her.

And she, listening to the conviction that rang in his voice in that hushed courtroom, thought him entirely truthful, also very distinguished in his bearing and altogether splendid in his dark blue velvet suit. Until that moment the proceedings of the court had seemed largely theatrical to her, the judges in their bulky crimson robes and heavy wigs sitting on their high platform, several feet above the common mortality of the court, the opposing counsel with their gestures and glances, as if they were reciting parts. But when Erasmus Kemp started to give his evidence these actors looked dusty and shoddy beside him. So strong was this impression that she did not pause to ask herself, though she was to do so very soon afterwards – with the appearance of the next witness in fact – quite how the accused men had merited such a relentless pursuit, why they should be required now, after all this time, to render up their lives, and in what way they could be thought to have benefited from their misdeeds. They had spent the years as fugitives in that desolate place . . .

No doubt was cast on Kemp's account; the facts were clear and they were not in dispute. He was followed by Barber, the ship's carpenter, who was brought into court still shackled. And it was the wasted frame of this man and his shuffling gait and the clanking of his fetters, so much in contrast to the fine figure that Erasmus had made, that raised questions in Jane's mind that should perhaps have come earlier.

Under Stanton's questioning, Barber confirmed that all the people of the ship who could keep to their feet had taken part freely in towing the vessel to its last resting place. Some of the blacks had collapsed and died as they toiled, he said, and their bodies had been left there on the banks of the creek or in the water.

'There was no time to bury them, we could not help it,' he said.

'What, you would have buried them?'

'Yes, sir, so we would.'

'But this was cargo, as the court has been told.'

'No, sir, things was different by then; we had sailed with them, sir, we needed the help of them that was able-bodied to bring the ship inshore.'

'Can you describe the relations that existed at this time between the crew and these former slaves?'

Pike interposed here to object to the word 'former'. The Africans were still slaves, he said, they had been made property by the fact of purchase. The crew had no right – and no power – to revoke their status.

Stanton did not pursue this argument; he allowed a brief pause, then repeated the question in more simple terms: 'What was the feeling between the members of the crew and the Negroes at this time?'

'We felt we was companions in misfortune, sir.'

'Companions in misfortune,' Stanton repeated with lingering emphasis. He looked to right and left at the jury on their different sides of the courtroom, allowing his face to show no hint of his pleasure at this fortunate reply – the judges never took to a smiling advocate. 'Companions in misfortune,' he said again. 'I beg that you will bear that phrase in mind, gentlemen.'

He had decided, after long consultation with a reluctant Ashton, not to press a charge of murder against the crew for the throwing overboard of the sick Negroes, as being too unlikely to succeed. Instead, he would seek to rebut the charge of piracy on the grounds that there had been no robbery, and seek an acquittal, which would be almost as great a stroke, if they could bring it off, as it would establish that the Africans had not, at any time, been merchandise, had never been other than human creatures.

'Pray where was the robbery?' he asked now, addressing the judges. 'Can any man say at what point in this series of events, and by what miraculous intervention, these black men and women ceased to be goods and reverted to humanity? Can we say that they were goods while lying chained below decks, goods while being cast overboard still alive, yet not goods shortly afterwards when their chains were struck off and their help was asked for? Where is the evidence that these men presently on trial for their lives had intended to realise value on the black people or on the ship? If they did so intend they took a very strange way of going about it. The fact is that the Africans were never, at any time, mere cargo, mere property. Their humanity was not stripped from them by the fact of purchase, as the prosecution would have us to believe. The people of the crew, though not realising this at first, came to understand it later through the experience of shared hardship. They know better now. May we not all know better now? Are we to be lesser in humanity than these very men who are being called pirates, *hostes humani generis*, enemies of the human race?'

Pike came forward to claim the right of reply, and this was accorded to him. The court was not on trial, he said, in spite of the endeavours of counsel for the defence to make it seem so. The learned and illustrious judges had not convened this court in order to have the nature of their humanity made subject to question. No hindsight, no shared experience, no subsequent change of heart, could be offered as matters affecting the issue. They must restrict themselves to the actions of the time. A particular morning on the deck of a particular ship. On that morning the master of the ship and all the members of the crew regarded the Negroes as cargo, as it might be timber, or sacks of grain. He took leave to remind the jury that piracy was only a term for sea-robbery, meaning robbery within the jurisdiction of the Admiralty. To bring home the charge of piracy it was not necessary to show what use it was intended to make of the stolen goods or to calculate the profit arising from the crime. Piracy *jure gentium* consisted in destroying, attacking or taking a ship, or taking any part of its tackle or cargo from the owners on the high seas, by acts of violence on the part of a body of men acting without the authorisation of any state. If the crew of a vessel revolted and sought by armed force to convert the ship or cargo to their own use, this also was piracy.

Stanton expressed his thanks, with some degree of sarcasm, for this clarification, and followed this with the declaration that in point of fact there had been no revolt on the part of the crew at all.

'What?' Pike addressed himself to the jury with real or pretended astonishment. 'These men rose against the master of the ship, who was set in lawful authority over them, and they murdered him and they took control of the ship and they sailed away. And yet it is asserted that there was no revolt.' He paused here, glancing round with a pantomime of bewilderment, at one with the jury and everyone in court, good people all and well intentioned, struggling to understand this perversion of reason. 'This is the logic of bedlam,' he said. 'This is to turn the world on its head indeed.'

'Your Lordships,' Stanton said, 'if we can but set aside the connotations of the word "murder", we will be enabled to see that this was no more than a scuffle, unplanned, unexpected, occurring on the spur of the moment, without thought of conse-quences. There can have been no intention to kill the captain.'

One of the the Admiralty Commissioners now spoke for the first time. 'Not much comfort for the captain in that.'

Pike nodded with an air of admiration for the shrewdness and penetration of this remark. 'Indeed not, My Lord.'

Stanton now begged the court's patience and asked for the first mate of the ship, James Barton, to be called to the dock in order to elucidate the circumstances in which the killing of the captain took place.

Barton was waiting in the Sessions Yard for such a call. Accompanied by the court attendant who had been sent to fetch him, he passed through the gate into the bail dock, where his former shipmates waited in their fetters for the verdict. This brought him, for the few moments of his passage, close before the men he had betrayed. And Hughes, standing with the others under close guard, the stench of his captivity in his nostrils, saw Barton pass, saw the peering glances, hatefully familiar, as if the mate had caught a whiff of something promising in the air, saw that he was dressed for the hearing in a good coat and a wig of pristine whiteness – no doubt purchased with his reward money – and made in that single moment of the mate's passing, a vow to his dark gods: if it was granted to him to escape death, he would find Barton, wherever he was, and would deliver that death to him, a death by strangulation . . .

Even had he known of this, Barton would not have been greatly troubled by it, feeling fairly sure that all the men would hang. Standing at the dock, he answered Stanton's questions with notable assurance – he was becoming, he felt, a highly accomplished witness.

Yes, the intervention of the ship's doctor, Mr Matthew Paris, had sparked off the mutiny. Mr Paris had raised his hand and shouted against it, against the jettisoning of the slaves. Upon this, Captain Thurso had drawn his pistol.

As always, in the desire to be on good terms with authority, and to establish confidence in his own veracity, Barton went too far. 'It is my belief he was hintending to shoot the doctor,' he said.

'We are not interested in your beliefs,' the Lord High Admiral said, with a bad-tempered snap of the jaw. Time was passing and he had already decided on how he would direct the jury. 'Tell the court what happened next.'

'Yes, sir, beggin' yer pardon. Before he had time to fire Cavana threw an iron spike and it struck him in the right eye and sent him staggerin' back. Then he fired, but he was off balance, he aimed into the midst of the men. The shot hit Tapley in the leg an' he fell to the deck.'

'Cavana, Tapley, these men are dead now?' Stanton asked.

'Yes, sir. Tapley died aboard ship when his wound got hinfectious, an' Cavana died later, in Florida.'

'What happened after Tapley fell?'

'The cap'n couldn't hardly see, sir. There was blood streamin' down his face. He was fumblin' with the pistol, tryin' to reload. I dunno if he reloaded, but he never fired. Rimmer stepped forward and stabbed him to the heart.'

'Rimmer is among the accused,' Stanton said. 'You see how it was, gentlemen. A ship blown off course, disease below decks, desperate and driven men, a fortuitous intervention on the doctor's part – he was not seeking to overthrow the captain's authority, only to protest at the barbarous crime, yes, I persist in calling it so, that was taking place before his eyes. In the bloody scramble that followed, there was no concerted action on the part of the crew. One of them had been brought to the ground, there was fear among them of the captain's pistol. They were left in command of the ship, so much is true, but that was never their design.'

Pike had only two questions to put to Barton.

'The captain went armed, then?'

'Yes, sir.'

'Is that usual on a merchant vessel?'

'No, sir, it is not, but there was feelin' agin Cap'n Thurso. He felt hisself to be threatened. I was with the cap'n, sir, hunnerd per cent. Barton is always faithful to them that is set above us.'

'Well, it does you credit. Thank you, that will be all.'

When Barton had stepped down, Stanton called his final witness, the ship's interpreter, James Porter. He had wanted this man's testimony to follow close upon that of Barton, who had – as anticipated – striven to make the captain appear the victim of premeditated violence.

Having established Porter's condition as a free man, his situation aboard the ship as belonging neither to the slaves nor the crew and the fact that he had been present on deck throughout the events of that distant morning and had witnessed the intervention of the surgeon and the violence that followed upon this, Stanton asked him if his memory of these matters was clear and obtained the assurance that it was.

'And will you tell the court the precise moment at which the captain drew his pistol?'

'It was immediately upon the doctor calling out, sir.'

'And he had raised the pistol and pointed it, he was intending to fire?'

'Yes, sir, it was clear he was intending to fire.'

'Was any move to harm the captain made before he raised the pistol?'

'No, sir, none.'

Stanton asked no further questions, allowing this emphatic negative to resound, as he hoped, in the minds of both judges and jury.

When the witness had stepped down, Pike embarked on the case for the prosecution. The facts were not in dispute. And it was facts they had to deal with, not sentiments, not pious wishes for a better world. There was no doubt whatever that at the time these events took place both the captain and the crew regarded the Negroes as property, as goods, with a precise and ascertainable value, a value determined by the most reliable indicator known to us, what people were willing to pay for them, the price per head they could command at Kingston market. It made no difference whether they were well or sick; while there was the breath of life in them they retained their value. At the moment that these men rose against their captain and took unlawful possession of the cargo, thereby depriving the owners, represented here today by Mr Erasmus Kemp, whose moving testimony they had heard, at that same moment they became guilty of an act of piracy. In any other light than this it could not be regarded. And the penalty for piracy, when accompanied by violence, was death.

Pike paused on this, looking from side to side at the jury in their narrow enclosures. The decisive moment had arrived. 'Honourable members of the jury,' he said, 'the defending counsel has sought to portray the murder of the captain as something not intended, as being in the nature of an accident. But it was no accident, gentlemen. You heard the testimony of the first mate, James Barton. *There was a feeling against him.* Those were the words used. He went armed, against all custom and usage. Why did he do so? Because he knew that these men were waiting for an opportunity to rebel against him and do him harm. Let me remind you – and it is not disputed by the defence – that the first wounding, the first act of aggression, was not committed by the captain but by one of the seamen, the man named Cavana, who threw the spike that destroyed the captain's right eye. Where was the need for the man named Rimmer, at present awaiting sentence, to deliver a death blow with his knife? The captain could have been overpowered and made captive. These were not men urged on by legitimate grievance. This was a mob, gentlemen, driven by hatred of authority, by envy of those fortunate enough to be possessed of property. If you find in favour of the defendants, you will be laying down a precedent of utmost danger, you will be delivering the rule of law into the hands of the mob.'

He ended there and withdrew to his place in the court. Stanton, making the final address for the defence, summarised the arguments of earlier, reverting to the scrambling and haphazard nature of the business, denying that there had been an act of robbery in any sense in which the term could be understood. He made an impassionate plea to the jury, appealing to common humanity, dwelling on the phrase that Barber had used, 'companions in misfortune'. He asked them to imagine the state of mind of the crew on that morning, half starved, exhausted after managing the ship through days of bad weather, engaged in a task they knew in their hearts to be hideously wrong, under the orders of a brutal and despotic captain who would visit savage punishment on them at the smallest sign of dissent. Then the surgeon's appearance, the cry, the hand raised to Heaven. It must have seemed, to these driven men, like a divine intervention.

Stanton paused now to gather himself for the peroration. He could see nothing on the faces of judges or jury that might indicate the nature of their feelings or thoughts, but this, in his experience, was almost invariably the case.

'And then, what did they do then?' he demanded. 'Did they attack the captain? No, they did not. All they did was to desist, to pause in their task, no more than that. It is not true that the first act of aggression came from the crew. You have heard the testimony of the ship's interpreter, James Porter. The first act of aggression was that of the captain, in drawing his pistol. Before this, no harm came to anyone. It is clear that there was no initial intention of harm on the part of the crew. Where is the conspiracy in this, where the concerted uprising? Their only crime was to listen to the dictates of a higher law. I beseech the court to grant true justice to these men, the justice all of us here present would hope for in this world and the next, that which is tempered with mercy.'

On this he fell silent and returned to his place in the court. The Lord High Admiral conferred briefly with his colleagues on the bench, all of whom nodded their heads in agreement. Then he addressed himself to the jury. He pointed out that, while it was true that in England the offence of piracy had not been defined in any statute, a great deal of legislation had been enacted dealing with the punishment of robbers at sea. He referred them to the two most recent Piracy Acts, those of 1699 and 1721, which had further defined and amplified the nature of this felony. He would take leave to deliver the essence of the matter shorn of needless complications. If, in any place where the Lords of the Admiralty had jurisdiction, the mariner of any ship should violently dispossess the master and afterwards carry away the ship itself or any of the goods aboard her, that was robbery and piracy and carried with it, if proved, a sentence of death. They did not need to concern themselves with the nature of the cargo, or whether there was intention to return, or with any subsequent relations between the crew members and the Negroes. The law was very clear. Was there a mutiny? Was there violent dispossession of the master? Was the vessel carried off? They should decide on their verdict in the light of these questions.

Almost as soon as the presiding judge began his direction of the jury, Ashton knew with intense disappointment that the case was lost. It came as no surprise, though with an increase of bitterness, when the jury, after conferring briefly among themselves, standing together in the body of the court, brought in a verdict of guilty, without reference to mitigating circumstances and with no recommendation to mercy.

The crew members were led in from the bail dock to take their places before the bench. They stood facing the robed figures raised above them, whose faces and great wigs only were visible to them above the nosegays that had been placed on the table to sweeten the air and protect the judges from the stench and foul breath.

The courtroom was silenced by the crier with the time-honoured words: 'My Lords, the King's Justices, strictly charge and command all manner of persons to keep silence while sentence of death is passing on the prisoners at the bar.'

However, there was still a surprise to come, and it was contained in the manner of the sentencing. The Lord High Admiral did not rise immediately but remained seated and spoke to the court as a whole. 'We, through the powers vested in us by the grace of His Royal Highness, King George the Third, do represent the power of the law but do also represent the mercy of the law, and in this blend lies the majesty of the law and also its mystery, as not lying within the common prediction. We hereby acquit and pardon the men Morgan and Hughes, who were for different reasons not present on deck at the time of the mutiny, and therefore took no direct part in it. These men may walk free from the court.'

The two were immediately led away to have their fetters struck off by the turnkeys in the Yard. The justice waited for some moments until quiet was restored, then got to his feet. He laid the black cloth over the crown of his wig and observed an impressive pause before speaking directly to the men standing below him, who waited dumbly for the words they knew would signal their death. In this shared knowledge they stood side by side, enfeebled by the weeks in prison, exhausted by the weight of their shackles, convicted of a crime too distant for them to recognise. Only Rimmer and Barber made the effort to raise their eyes to the figure standing above them; the others kept their heads bowed. And in the contrast made by this wretchedness with the solemn ritual of the court, the august judges in their scarlet apparel, the rhetoric of the advocates, the silver mace, emblem of authority, lying among the nosegays on the table, the Lord

High Admiral's remarks about the majesty and mystery of the law
were given abundant illustration.

*The Law is that ye shall return from hence to the place whence ye
came, and from thence to the place of execution, where ye shall hang by
the neck till the body be dead, dead, dead. And the Lord have mercy on
your souls.*

23

Bitterly disappointed as he was, and enraged by the verdict, Ashton lost no time in quitting the courtroom, and Jane was obliged to hasten away with him. He was not sufficiently in possession of himself to stay for any words with Stanton, a discourtesy he afterwards regretted; his friend had made a good case, the blame was not his but that of the world at large, as represented by the judges and the jury. This hasty retreat of brother and sister left Kemp feeling obscurely cheated, though of what he could not easily have said; there could have been no exchange of words with Jane, not at such a time, not when her brother had suffered such a defeat, and he himself was dressed in victory.

The judges had left the bench and mounted to the upper floor to be disrobed, but Pike was still in the courtroom, and Kemp made his way towards the lawyer with the intention of expressing his pleasure at the verdict and his congratulations on the way the case had been conducted. He had never taken much to Pike, while admitting his quality as an advocate. But now, as he approached, it came to him that the suitable thing was to suggest sharing a bottle together and drinking to their success.

Pike showed every sign of pleasure at the suggestion. 'There is the George, just round the corner, in Ludgate Street,' he said. 'It is a tolerable place, I have used it before.'

It was only when the two of them were seated together over a bottle of Madeira that Kemp began to express his thanks and congratulations. 'I must say, you chose your words extremely well,' he said. 'And not only the words but the right time to utter them.'

'Long practice, sir.' Pike smiled, clearly pleased at the compliment.

'I was sorry, though, to see Hughes and Morgan get off scot-free. It is the merest quibble to suggest that they were not part of the mutiny.'

'We may owe that to Mr Stanton's final plea, though not in the way he intended it.'

An expression had appeared on the lawyer's face as he spoke that Kemp had seen there not infrequently before and did not much care for, a look that went with the tone of his voice, amused, sardonic, in a way regretful.

'How do you mean?' he asked, with a certain coldness.

'Well, you will remember that he urged the court to show mercy as they themselves would wish for mercy? Perhaps you did not glance at the Lord High Admiral's face as these words were uttered?'

'No, as a matter of fact I did not.'

'He was not pleased, sir, he was not pleased at all. He did not care to be included in that way, lumped together with common mortals. He sits in judgement, you see, he delivers the sentence. While he is up there on the bench in his robes of office he is not in need of mercy. It is those below him that are in need of that – in sore need often enough. No, I think Stanton made a mistake there. It is one often made by zealous reformers – they are too set on benefiting the human race, they forget to make allowance for divergent views of what is beneficial.'

'Well, but the two men were pardoned, after all.'

'Having first been found guilty. That was not Stanton's aim, nor was it Ashton's. They wanted them all acquitted. The Lord Admiral, on the other hand, wanted to show that he it is who doles out justice and mercy. In the right measure and proportion, of course.' Pike smiled and raised his glass. 'He and no one else,' he said. 'Here is to the law, sir. If the judge had not wished to assert his prerogatives, those two would probably have been condemned to death along with the rest.'

Kemp nodded. 'I see, yes.' But even as they drank together, even though grateful to Pike for his efforts, he found his old disapproval returning, and for the same reason. Pike made light of the institution that gave him his reputation and his living – a

good living too. It was ungrateful, it was even duplicitous . . .
And Pike grew aware of it now, as before, this disapproval, and
as before felt a kind of contempt for it, the lack of humour, the
rigidity of mind, impelling him – and this too not for the first
time – to do further outrage to his client's sense of propriety.
Propriety and property, the fellow's guiding lights . . .

'I am not altogether sure that it was wise to appeal to the
jury's sense of common humanity either,' he said. 'Or to urge them
to imagine the state of mind of the crew on that distant morning.'

'I don't see much wrong in that.'

'The jury is open to pity, both singly and by a sort of contagion, as are we all. But the ability to imagine the thoughts and
feelings of others is a great deal rarer than might be thought,
and people will quickly grow hostile if urged to exercise a faculty
they do not possess. Nor will they always wish to share their
humanity with the accused persons in the dock, especially when
these persons are common seamen, and ragged and penniless
into the bargain. They would rather recognise common humanity
in persons more closely resembling themselves or, better still,
persons higher up in the scale of things. The jurors are men of
property, sir, they are landowners. Small landowners, to be sure,
but landowners nevertheless. There is a property qualification at
present set at fifteen pounds a year.'

'That is very little.'

'Indeed it is, sir, indeed it is. But it must be remembered
that probably close on three-quarters of the inhabitants of this
great city will be too poor even to pay taxes, much less be in
possession of freehold or copyhold to any extent of value at all.
This huge mass of humanity lies just below the noses of the jurors.
They can smell it, sir. Their greatest fear is to slide back down
into it.'

He paused for some moments, raising his glass to drink.
With the case ended and his connection with his client about to
be dissolved he felt a lightening of the oppression he had always
felt in Kemp's company. 'No,' he said, 'they want to share their
common humanity with the creditor, the landlord, the masters
of ships, the employers of labour. And these last want to share
their common humanity with those of wider acres and larger
possessions.'

'Well,' Kemp said, 'it is natural for men to want to better themselves.'

'So it is. And the trick of it, in the courts, is to play on this natural wish as much as possible. That is why I spoke as I did of the mob. The fear of the mob is stronger among those who have small possessions, because they are closer in dealings and in neighbourhood to people of violent and disorderly life. And the fear has grown stronger than ever in these last years with the fluctuations in the price of bread and the rioting that has resulted. It is not a month since the militia had to be called out again. The protesters were more than a thousand strong and they would not disperse until a dozen of them had been shot.'

Kemp drank some more of his wine without making any immediate reply. He felt that justice had been done that day, in the main at least – two had escaped, but five would hang. There was Sullivan too, still at large. His long journey, the time he had lost, the money he had spent, the rightness of his cause, all had been justified by the verdict and the sentence. But this quick-tongued fellow made no mention of that, dwelling instead on tricks and ploys. 'We were in the right and that was recognised by the court,' he said at last, resolving to take his leave before very much longer. The other's way of looking at the world was distasteful to him; Pike took everything together, as if the distinction between right and wrong were shadowy and obscure, when every man of good character knew that it was abundantly clear. And yet there was no indulgence, no complacency of acceptance in the lawyer's tone; his voice had an edge to it, in spite of the smiles, something of bitterness even, as if he would change things if he could . . .

'The thing most to be hoped for,' the lawyer said now, 'is that the common run of people, that great riotous mass within the range of the nostrils of those with fifteen pounds a year, people who have never owned anything, who could hardly be said to own themselves, might somehow be persuaded to share their common humanity with the property-owning classes and help to keep them in their places, in the hope that by so doing they will be more likely to become property owners themselves.'

Pike did not exactly smile as he said these words, but he stretched his mouth and shook his head slowly, in a way that seemed theatrical to Kemp, making him suspect that the lawyer was not entirely serious in what he said, whereas he himself found the words eminently reasonable and felt they represented a hope for a better and safer society. 'Not many would realise such an ambition,' he said. 'One in a hundred perhaps. But it would be of great benefit to public order and the security of the realm. Fewer windows would be broken, fewer people would be shot.'

'Indeed, sir,' Pike said, though still with an expression that seemed to Kemp less than properly earnest. 'Above all, it would give the people hope. Hope deferred, sir, hope of betterment endlessly deferred, that is what binds people together.'

'I suspect that your adversary of today would see the matter differently,' Kemp said, as he rose to his feet.

'Stanton? I have known Horace Stanton for a good many years now. We have met both in the courtroom and out of it. An excellent advocate, with great resources of feeling – and that makes for effective argument, you know, juries can be swayed by feeling when they are not closed off from it by fear. All the same, Stanton has one great fault.'

'What is that?'

Pike smiled slightly and looked directly into Kemp's eyes as the two men shook hands. 'He needs always to believe he is entirely in the right, which no one can ever be, you know.'

Kemp was more than halfway home, quite close to Aldwych, before it came to him that Pike's final words had been aimed at him as much as at Stanton, that the lawyer had wanted to give him something in the nature of a parting shot. Following immediately on this realisation, there came a strange, extremely unwelcome feeling of envy for Pike. Pike didn't need to feel justified, he didn't need to feel in full possession of the truth, he could go this way or that, he could stand back and take a look and choose, he needed no blessing, no angelic guidance. Pike was a free man . . .

So perverse and appalling to him was this feeling that he spent the rest of the way home rebutting it, repairing the breach, restoring his previous disapproval of the lawyer. What was such freedom worth? Pike had no goals, no overriding purposes. He shifted with circumstance, he could recite any part. How could such a life be tolerable? He himself was soon to depart for

Durham, and his goals were clear to him: he would survey the mine, he would determine what was needed, he would improve working methods, achieve higher production and increased profits. These were things that a man could aim at, could believe in. He it was who had a firm grip on reality, not Pike. On his return home he would call on Jane Ashton, he would have her face before him, he would tell her of the plans he had made during the time of their separation. One day, but not just yet, he would ask her if she had been at the Spring Gardens that night, the night of the fireworks . . .

24

'Lookin' at it another way,' Sullivan said to the man working beside him, 'I had the woman before they took me off, so me money was not lost an' obliterated intoirely, I had some value from it, I am not the man to deny that, though the pleasure was fleetin'.'

'No regrets, that's my motto,' the man said. 'I never 'ave no regrets. There is bad things that happen, but we still got our arms and legs, ain't we?'

'I was expectin' her to tell them misbegotten creatures that the money belonged to the both of us, that it was joint stock, to use the language of commerce. But she kept mum, she had no scrap of a notion of sharin'. If she had spoke up, I would niver have found meself here in this workhouse.'

'Well, whores is various, one from another. They have all got the same thing between their legs, but their character is widely different. No regrets – next time you might come across a good 'un.'

Side by side at their task of plaiting strands of hemp fibre into rope, they spoke in low tones so as not to attract the attention of the overseer.

'This work is takin' the skin off me fingers,' Sullivan said. 'It will reduce the power of me music. I will have the law of them for robbin' me of me livelihood. I am not the man to deny that there is always the prospect of a rainbow just round the corner, but what I am sayin' is that them watchmen would niver have fetched me here if that woman had shown a drop or two of the milk of human kindness.'

His companion was a thinly clad, emaciated man with a light of fever in his eyes. 'Them was not reg'lar watchmen,' he said now. 'Far from it. You won't find reg'lar watchmen goin' round at night lookin' for vagrants, you will find them at home by the fire.'

'I thought as much. I knew there was somethin' about them fellers that didn't tally. I suspected somethin' from the start. I wasn't born yesterday, I told them, show me your badge of office, I said, but of course there was no answer forthcomin'.'

'What it is, you see, they farms it out. The watchman what is appointed by the parish has the task of bringin' in vagrants wherever he can find them. He gets fourpence a head. So he hires two men to do the rounds in his place, an' for every one they brings in he gives them a penny each. He halves his fee, but he stays at home out of trouble. An' he gets his wages in any case, a shillin' a day.'

He paused here for a series of racking coughs, and the man on the other side of Sullivan, who had drawn near enough to hear these last words, now broke in. He was a stocky man with reddish hair and a rhetorical style of speech. 'What are we doin' here?' he said. 'We are wearin' our fingers to the bone, makin' rope. Do we get paid for our labour? No we don't. What do we get to eat? Stale bread an' thin gruel. Who makes the profit? Them that sells the rope an' them that runs the workhouse.'

'He is right,' the other said, having recovered from his fit of coughing. 'I been in bridewells before, more than once. I get brought in for diff'rent reasons – this time it was for beggin'. No regrets. But it is always the same story once you get here. They will set you to work. I been set on to makin' candlewick for the chandlers, pickin' feathers for the mattress-makers, beatin' old bricks to dust for the brick-makers. I can't do heavy work no more, because of my chest – it was the brick dust done that. An' never a penny for any of it.'

'No choice an' no pay an' benefitin' only the manufacturers,' Sullivan said. 'That is forced labour an' I will denounce it to the proper authorities once I get free from here.'

'Don't do that,' the red-haired man said. 'Why not? Because you will end up in prison. On what charge? Bein' a public nuisance. Punishment? A good whippin' an' a term of hard labour.'

'One hand washes the other,' the other man said. 'Mootual

benefit they calls it. The manufacturers give somethin' out of their profits to them that run the workhouse.'

'I see well they have worked out a good system. I know somethin' of the law, bein' a travelled man, an' I know that you cannot keep a man confined without lawful cause. How can empty pockets be a lawful cause? There is a paper you can get, with writin' that says you have got the body in captivity, show reason or deliver it up. But how can you get hold of a paper like that when you are the body that has to be delivered up?'

'What is a vagrant?' the red-haired man demanded. 'He is someone down on his luck. Who has the right to call his fellow man a vagrant? No one. Why do they do it? They do it so they can own that man an' sell his labour.'

'It is the same when they cart you off from here,' the other said. 'You are a charge on this parish where you are now. When you have done your time here it is for them to remove you to your own parish an' pay the cost. But a lot of us ain't got no parish, or none that will own to us. No regrets. An' nobody wants to spend money on us in any case. So they gives you a pass that takes you to the next parish an' they carries you there on a cart. The constable that gets paid for the cartin' farms it out to others what will do it for less. If he gets twopence a head for the people in the cart, the one that does the cartin' might get a ha'penny or three farthings. An' all you gets is a ride to the next parish, where they will be waitin' to put you in the workhouse again. Everyone is makin' money on you. Vagrants is very good for business.'

'When they asks you where is your place of settlement,' the man on the other side of Sullivan said, 'what do you tell them? You tells them you want to return to Ireland an' start your life anew. Why do you tell them that? Because you know that they will never send you back there, not in a hundred years. Why not? Because it costs too much. So what do they do? They takes you to the nearest county border an' dumps you there.'

'The nearest county border is the border of Durham County, if I am not mistaken,' Sullivan said. 'Holy Mother, you don't mean to say that they will take me on a cart to Durham free of charge?'

25

It was a mark of Ashton's resilience that not many hours after his fury of disappointment at the piracy verdict, and still suffering from it, he set himself to considering the next battle to fight. The cause of abolition, which had rescued him from a prevailing sense of futility and made him profoundly grateful to Divine Providence for such redemption, had at the same time brought him to a fuller knowledge of himself, his capacity for devotion, his readiness to spend everything he had, all his resources, health and strength included, in the fight against a traffic in human souls offensive to God and man alike.

The summons for theft and damages in the case of Jeremy Evans, which Bolton and Lyons had threatened to bring against him, had not so far been pursued. The two had repeatedly postponed the application for a hearing on the grounds that they were still preparing their case. It came to Ashton now that this delay could mean only one thing: they were afraid to proceed because they could not be certain of winning. He had announced counter charges of aggravated assault against all concerned in Evans's commitment to the Poultry Compter, those who had ordered it, those who had carried it out, the notary who had signed the order for custody, if there was one, the keeper of the prison, who had incarcerated the man unlawfully.

This it was that had frightened them, he now began to feel sure of it. Their position, their claim to right of ownership in Evans, had been seriously weakened by the Lord Mayor's ruling that Evans could go free, that he could not be detained in prison without just cause. The claim of right by purchase, the production of the bill of sale, had not been accounted just cause . . .

On his knees, in the loneliness of his bedchamber, he prayed for guidance. And in the spaces between the words and the silence that came after them God spoke to him and gave him counsel: he was to take the initiative; he was not to wait on the flickering intentions of Messrs Bolton and Lyons; he was to become the plaintiff and press the charge of abduction, not in regard to the taking of the man by force and holding him in prison, but in regard to the earlier attempt to deny his right of residence in England and transport him to the West Indies. Abduction, not criminal assault, as he had originally intended.

Next morning, in the full flush of resolution, he went to see Stanton at his chambers in Chancery Lane. He announced his new intention and asked for the services of his friend in the conducting of the case.

'We will drop all charges against the agents of the business, slave-takers, corrupt prison officers, whoever they may be,' he said. 'We will charge only the instigators, the two men who lay claim to ownership of Evans by purchase and contend that they have the right, by the fact of purchase, to remove him by force from England and return him to the West Indies. We will charge them with kidnap.'

However, he saw no answering enthusiasm on the other's face but instead an expression of increased gravity. 'Frederick, I think it unlikely in the extreme that we could win such a case, in view of the prejudice that exists. Mounting a defence against the claim of damages they were to bring against us, that is a different matter, it raises no fundamental issues.'

'But that is precisely why I want to bring the case, because it *does* raise fundamental issues. If it went in our favour we might, at long last, get a ruling that brings into serious question the status of former slaves now domiciled in England.'

'The Lord Chief Justice would almost certainly refer the case to the Court of King's Bench. He would preside over it himself. He has always avoided making any pronouncement from the bench that would go counter to the West India interest. He has demonstrated this again and again. It would be the same again now. And if we fail, think what harm there would be to the cause of abolition. It would entrench the right of continuous ownership, perpetual ownership from the point of purchase, irrespective of national boundaries.'

Ashton looked at his friend in silence for some moments. The same prudence he had always valued, the same weighing of words. Yet now it was almost as if he were looking at a stranger. 'So then,' he said, 'we rescue the man from the ship that was returning him to plantation slavery, we secure his release from the prison where he was unlawfully held, we find a house where he can be safe while the action for damages is pending. And having done all this, we draw back from questioning the fundamental issue of his right to residence on English soil. Horace, we must take risks, we cannot wait till we are certain of the outcome or we will never achieve anything. We did not get the verdict we hoped for in this piracy trial, but all was not lost, your eloquence was not wasted. The case attracted great public interest and there will now be many, as a result of it, who re-examine their consciences on the issue of slavery.'

'It was a specific issue,' Stanton said. 'It is true that we brought the nature of property in Africans into question by disputing the notion of robbery under such circumstances, but the circumstances themselves were very particular. We had a prospect of success on grounds of mitigating circumstance, but our main chance lay in the fact that no one's pocket was threatened. It is far otherwise with the case you want to bring now. Think of the capital value of the Africans who have been brought here as slaves with the intention of returning them sooner or later to the plantations. You will be familiar with the words of Yorke and Talbot in 1729 when a deputation appealed to them for a clarification of the status of African slaves in England. The two highest law officers of the realm, Attorney General and Solicitor General. They gave it as their considered opinion that a slave by coming from the West Indies to England does not thereby become free, and that his master may legally compel him to return to the plantations.'

'Yes, I know what they said. It has been a slave-hunters' charter ever since. It was never more than an opinion, probably delivered after a good dinner, but it has been elevated to a judgement of high authority, and no one dares to question it.' As you do not dare, he thought, with a sense of desolation.

'Something more than an opinion,' Stanton said. 'It was reaffirmed by Yorke, as Lord Chancellor Hardwicke, in 1749, from the judicial bench in the case of *Pearne* versus *Lisle*. That is not so long ago, Frederick.'

'So you are unwilling to take the case?'

'I am afraid so, yes. For both our sakes.'

'No, Horace, it is not for my sake you are refusing.'

He stopped here, but the implication was obvious and both men felt it as a rent that would take long to mend in the fabric of close cooperation and trust that had stood the wear of so many years.

'You are determined to go on with the case, then?' Stanton said.

'Certainly.'

'I know of a young barrister in these chambers, a very promising man, who sees eye to eye with us on matters of principle. His name is Harvey. I will speak to him if you like.'

It was now that Stanton, indirectly, confirmed the judgement of his motives that Ashton had formed. 'He has his way to make,' he said. 'Appearing in court, making a stir, is more important than winning cases at that stage of a man's career. He will fight hard, even in a losing cause.'

Ashton accepted the offer, and the two parted, without great warmth. Once more at home, Ashton lunched with his sister and lost no time in telling her of Stanton's refusal.

'Well, I am not so very surprised to hear it,' she said. 'He always struck me as being more cautious than was good for him, or good for anyone.'

Brother and sister had returned to more cordial terms now. Jane had sympathised with her brother in his distress at the piracy verdict, and had come again to understand – it formed part of a regular cycle in their relations – the spirit of dedication that made him what he was, and the sharply declining order of importance he gave to the sensibilities of others, and even their welfare, when they were not instrumental to his cause.

'He tried to make amends by offering to find a barrister to take the case,' Ashton said. 'He thought it was unwise to bring the action in any case, as being virtually certain to fail. I think he was mainly guided by a reluctance to challenge the Yorke and

Talbot opinion that slaves remain slaves on English soil. And he was afraid that the Lord Chief Justice would be too much in sympathy with the West India faction. But I think that his chief fear was of attacking vested interests and thus doing damage to his own career.'

Jane felt some sympathy for this, though she did not give expression to it. After all, Horace Stanton's income came entirely from his fees – he had no independent means, unlike her brother in this. But it was not an aspect of the matter that Frederick would think of the least importance, even if it had occurred to him, which she thought doubtful.

'I told him that without challenging these beliefs we would never find out how rooted they really are,' he said.

'Indeed not.' Like testing the water, she thought. You can't tell just by looking at it. Horace Stanton would always hesitate too long before even putting one of his toes in. Not like Erasmus. She thought of him as he had been in the court, that epic tale of pursuit and capture, the spirit of justice and the desire for revenge confused together. Mixed motives, even if this was not fully confessed. But Erasmus was a man of action – he would never hesitate, never hold back. Suddenly, and with a vividness that caught at her breathing, she pictured him standing at the brink, braced for the plunge.

26

In contrast to the custom at Tyburn, there were no fixed hanging days at Execution Dock, where those found guilty of crimes at sea under the jurisdiction of the Admiralty were taken to pay their last dues. Within a week of the death sentence being delivered, Barber and Calley and Libby and Rimmer and Lees were led out from Newgate Prison and found the cart waiting for them in the yard outside, together with a great crowd of people who had come to follow the procession and see the hangings. The men would have been brought out earlier even than this, but the hangings by tradition took place in the mornings, on the foreshore of the river, and they had to wait four days for a low tide at the right time of the morning so as to remain on ground that lay within Admiralty jurisdiction.

Calley, who was the strongest of them in body, but childlike in mind, began to weep when he saw the cart, and Barber, who had sometimes protected him from ill usage by Libby and one or two others aboard the slave ship, though hindered now by his bonds, contrived to put a hand on Calley's shoulder as they walked to the cart and climbed up on to the platform that had been raised there, several feet high, so as to give the spectators a clear view of the condemned men. Here they took their places, sitting together side by side on the narrow bench. On a bench behind them, already waiting, were the executioner and his two assistants.

Erasmus Kemp was not among those who saw them emerge, nor was he stationed anywhere along the route or waiting at the place of execution. He had no smallest desire to witness the sufferings of the condemned men, even avoiding – as far as he could – any picturing of the hangings. The sentence was fitting, it had met the needs of justice and retribution, it had recognised his rights and those of his dead father. But all this was an abstraction to him, like drawing a line in some cosmic ledger. It was necessary too that there should be a measure of pain in the punishment, but he could take no pleasure in the thought of this. The sort of cruelty or vindictiveness that might have given gratification to another in the witnessing of such pain, or even in the knowledge of it, formed no part of his nature.

The cart moved off from the prison, turning into Newgate Street, passing St Paul's and proceeding down Cheapside towards Cornhill. Ahead of it, riding at a slow pace, were the Marshal of the Admiralty and the Deputy Marshal, who bore the silver mace – the same that had lain on the table before the judges – over his shoulder. They were followed by two city marshals and a number of sheriff's officers. The whole cavalcade was conducted with great solemnity and with no sound but the horses' hooves on the cobbles.

This stateliness was in marked contrast to the hubbub of the crowd thronging around the cart. The case had aroused a great deal of public interest. Hangings at Execution Dock were relatively rare; there had only been one so far that year, for a murder committed at sea. Commercial Road was lined with people and resounded with shouts of greeting, jovial witticisms as to the condemned men's impending fate and the shrill sound of tin whistles that were being sold to children along the way. Rimmer, he who had dealt Captain Thurso his death blow, was the only one to show defiance, shouting insults at the people as the cart passed.

Hughes had positioned himself among the crowd in the yard of the Turk's Head in Wapping. From here there was a public right of way that led down to the river and came out near Wapping Old Stairs, where the gallows were erected. The cart would stop at the inn, by long-established tradition, for the condemned men to be served with a quart of ale. He wanted this last look at his shipmates before they were struggling on the rope, but he did not want to be seen by them, for obscure reasons that were to do with the severance of spirit, the detachment from his fellows that he always felt and that reached a kind of paroxysm at such times of crisis as this, with the need to make a solemn farewell, unknown to them – the stronger to him for that – to men he had sailed with and suffered with and joined in half-willing community with in the twelve years of their time in Florida.

He saw the cart come into the yard, saw the aproned landlord come out to hand up the tankards, saw the men raise their pinioned hands to drink. They were white-faced, but Calley, tears still on his cheeks, was half smiling now, as if being the centre of such public attention had overlaid his fears. The landlord was smiling too, as he handed up the ale and saw the men drink. Unlike Calley, he had good cause for smiling, Hughes thought: he would be selling a good many quarts that day.

He followed the cart when it resumed its way along Wapping High Street. The prisoners were helped down the stairs to the foreshore, where the posts and cross-beam had been erected at the low watermark, with five separate stakes embedded deep in the river mud, just beyond. There was a priest on the platform of the gallows and he spoke to the men in tones that were perhaps audible to them but certainly to no one else.

Boats crowded with spectators were moored along the riverside, and barges, also thronged with people, lay further out in the water. There was a ship anchored out in the Pool, and Hughes thought briefly of trying to get out to her, getting up into the topside and seeing his shipmates breathe their last from high above, just as he had watched from high above, and heard the cries of pain, when the first slaves were brought aboard and branded, just as he had watched when the sick were cast overboard and seen the doctor come forward and the confused struggle that had led to Thurso's death and all that had followed upon that. The thought gave him a fierce sense of symmetry, but he knew he could never get there in time, the nooses were already being settled around the men's necks as they stood in line below the beam.

By orders of the Admiralty those convicted of piracy were hanged with a shortened rope, so that the drop would not be long enough to break the men's necks. Calley was whimpering as they adjusted the noose and might have fallen to his knees if one of the assistants had not held him up. Rimmer spoke to the executioner and it seemed that he joked, for both men smiled. At the last moment Barber raised his head and called out in a loud voice: 'God have mercy on us!'

Then the drop was released and there were no more words and only the movements that men make when they are fighting for breath. Hughes watched this terrible slow strangling of men he deemed guiltless, waited through the frenzied jerking of their limbs, the Marshal's Dance, as it was called, because of the raising of the knees and the shivering of the body below the waist.

He stood still there while the struggle lasted, waited while the bodies were taken down and chained to the stakes, which were already being lapped by the incoming tide. He remained in his place as the water rose and slowly submerged the bodies, rising over their chests and finally covering their bowed heads. He knew the procedure, as did all those who had followed the sea. They would remain chained there for the space of time it would take for three full tides to rise over their heads. Then their bodies would be smeared with pitch, taken to the Isle of Dogs, hung on gibbets and left there to rot.

When he finally moved away it was with the sense of solemn farewell renewed in his mind. He knew more clearly now why he had not wanted the leave-taking to be cheapened by words of recognition and farewell. The silence was pure; it gave sanctity, and an endorsement from beyond the grave, to his vow that he would visit the same fate on Barton.

This vow he nursed in the days that followed, allowing no doubt to enter, no lessening of resolve. He felt that he owed his life to the promise he had made in that moment when the mate was passing before him, and this gave him a feeling of dedication he had never known before.

He spent his days at the Gravesend docks, doing what work came his way, sleeping rough. It was here, where the river began to widen, that the slave ships were fitted out. Barton would sign on for a slaver when his Judas money ran out. It was work he knew, the wages were slightly better, he might think to be taken on again as mate.

After twelve days his patience was rewarded. There was a ship fitting out, the *Indian Prince*, that carried the stench of the trade and had the build – high in the stern so that the swivel guns could more easily be brought to bear on the deck in case of slave revolt, thickened at the rails to make death leaps more difficult. One evening he saw Barton coming down the gangplank, following a man in a long coat and cocked hat, who looked like the skipper. He guessed they were bound on a mission to make up the number of the crew, enlist the men they needed, either by force or persuasion. If this was so, the ship must be ready to cast off her moorings and move out into the Pool.

He waited through that night, saw two men dragged aboard by those that had been hired to do it, saw the return of Barton. At dawn the wind shifted and the tide began to ebb. The ship was roped to her tugboats, her moorings were loosed and she was towed out to the deeper water of the estuary. While she lay there, in the last hour before her sailing, Hughes paid what money remained to him to be rowed out to the ship. He climbed aboard her, gave his name to the bosun and signed on with his mark. It was only now, when the anchor was weighed and it was too late to quit the ship, that Barton came up from below and saw him. Hughes was smiling, a rare thing indeed.

27

Sullivan, once more in possession of his fiddle and bow, shared the cart with three fellow vagrants, who like himself were being passed on to the nearest county border. They were set down just north of the Tees, a day's walk from Darlington, and from here they went their separate ways.

On the outskirts of Darlington Sullivan came upon a cattle market and a few stalls offering eggs and cheeses for sale. There were a good number of people about and he decided to give them a song or two. He took up a position at a good distance from the compound where the beasts were herded and the auctioneer was shouting, and began with 'Ned of the Hill', a lyric he had always been partial to.

> Oh dark is the evening and silent the hour.
> Oh who is that minstrel by yon shady tower
> Whose harp is so tenderly touching with skill
> Oh who could it be but young Ned of the Hill?
> And he sings 'Lady love, will you come with me now,
> Come and live merrily under the bough?'

Lingering tunes and words of love stopped people in their tracks sometimes, as he had learned early; they could work just as well as a more lilting start. And he liked this song because he could feel at one with the sentiment as he sang; he was the outlaw minstrel, the words of invitation were his and he put a lot of feeling into them.

As the time passed, there was a scattering of farthings on

his spread waistcoat and he kept a close eye on them; it was not
unknown for a fiddling man to have his earnings scooped up
and fled away with if he got too lost in his music. There had been
many mishaps along the way, but he was so near his goal now,
he was resolved to be careful, make no mistakes, keep a guard
on his money. He was not quite sure what he would do when his
vow was fulfilled and his compact with the Holy Mother carried
faithfully through. He would then be like the wrestler he had
met on the road, of whom he sometimes thought, wandering
from place to place, getting older. He might lay his fiddle aside
and seek work on a coaster, carrying freight down south or across
the sea to Holland. But the *Liverpool Merchant* had given him
enough of the sea to last a lifetime. He was well past his first
youth and did not really care for the idea of hauling on the ropes
again and risking a rupture.

It took him four days to reach the village of Thorpe, place
of his pilgrimage, and he was never to forget his first sight of it.
He had approached through high moorland country, and a turn
in the road brought him in late afternoon to a sudden view of
the village lying below him. This then was where Billy Blair had
come from, this was what he had run away from. Four streets,
seventy or eighty low-built, crouching houses with grey slate roofs.
The sulphurous smoke from coal fires lay like a mist over the
whole village, hanging motionless under an overcast sky. He saw
what looked like a store at the crossing of the streets, and close
to this a stone-built tavern. Beyond the shrouded houses he saw
the vaporous gleam of salt pans, and the sour smell of heated
brine carried to him. Seen thus from above, it seemed like a
vision of the inferno to Sullivan, with in the far distance the dark
silver, luminous strip of the sea, like a land of the blessed, a
promise lost for ever to these souls succumbing amid the smoke.
It was as if this dark cluster of houses had been set down within
the fields to live in eternal malodour, and for no other reason.

The sight of the sea brought him a sort of reversed memory:
standing off the coast of Africa, looking from sea to land, the
smoke rising from the shore fires, first sign of life, announcing
that there were slaves for sale. Then the fumes of smoke from
the deck, like an answer, rising from the braziers where they were
bringing the branding irons to red heat . . .

As he descended the long slope and drew nearer to the village, he heard the hiss and clank that came from the shafts of the mine, and saw here and there, approaching the village from the fields beyond, figures walking slowly, as if summoned by these noises. He saw with something of a shock that their faces were black. He was an impressionable man and he had never seen a mining village before. He was so taken with the sooty, infernal looks of the returning miners that it did not occur to him to ask himself what these people would make of a wild-haired, staring, shambling man with a fiddle over his shoulder. He had cause to do this, however, not much later. As he came to the foot of the slope, where the ground levelled out and the moor gave way to rough pastureland, he saw the figures of children running this way and that in the field next to the one he was crossing. Five or six small figures he made out. He could see no pattern in their movements at first, they seemed aimless; then he saw the dip and rise of some fluttering creature struggling to be free, flying trammelled in a way no bird could have flown, and he realised, as he drew nearer, that the boys were flying a kite, diamond-shaped, with long, trailing streamers.

Intent on watching the erratic plunges and soarings of the kite, the children did not see him until he was through the gate in the hedge and halfway across the field where they were. 'Hey, lads!' he shouted, raising his right arm in greeting. For some moments they stared at him across the decreasing distance. Then, without the slightest pause or consultation among themselves, three of them took to flight in the direction of the first houses of the village.

The boy managing the kite was Percy Bordon, and he could not run without letting go of the bobbin that held the string and so consigning the kite to the final freedom of the skies. For a moment or two, as alarmed as his mates by this apparition with a mane of hair and a stump growing out of his shoulder, he thought of doing this. But the kite was precious to him, and he was heartened by the fact that Billy had stayed by him and not run off with the others, though nothing had impeded him from doing so.

Then, as the stranger drew nearer, both boys saw that he was not deformed with an extra limb but was merely carrying something slung over one shoulder. And Sullivan, for his part, having understood that he was a fearsome figure, stopped at a distance of some yards and did not come any closer.

'I had no wish to startle you,' he said. 'That is a fine kite.'

'My da made it,' Percy said. 'He made it an' he give it me.'

'Did he so? I see well that you are a lucky boy. What might your name be?'

'Percy Bordon.'

'An' your friend here that stayed beside you when the others ran away?'

'He is Billy Scotland.' Emboldened by the gentleness of the stranger's voice, he added, 'He is my best friend, we are the same age, him an' me are gannin' doon the pit together this year.'

'It is a great blessin' to have a faithful friend,' Sullivan said.

Billy now spoke for the first time. 'A was waitin' my turn for the kite,' he said. 'Tha talks funny.'

'Well, so do you for that matter. Do you know if there is someone by the name of Blair livin' here in the village?'

The answer to this was delayed, because the kite, which Percy had taken his eyes off during this conversation, now encountered some mischievous downward current and after struggling some moments took a sharp tilt and came to rest on the ground, where it lay dishevelled, its streamers still fluttering slightly, like an expiring bird, while Billy ran to retrieve it.

'Kites will not hurt themselves when they fall,' Sullivan said, and a vague memory came to him of his boyhood in Galway, helping to fly a kite that never belonged to him, always to someone else. 'Me father made me a kite once,' he lied.

'My uncle John has Blair for his name,' Percy said. 'That is my mother's brother an' he lives in our street.'

Sullivan looked at the boy with a sudden closer scrutiny. The cropped hair and snub nose, the blue eyes and fair lashes, something pugnacious in the small face – he could see, or persuaded himself that he could see, a resemblance. This was Billy's nephew then. Billy would have been proud of the lad . . .

'Well now, Percy,' he said, 'I see you are a good boy as well as a lucky one. I am not the man to go intrudin' into people's homes, causin' disconcertment an' disarray. When you go home now, will you tell your mother that there is a travellin' man with news of her long-lost brother, name of Billy Blair, who run away to sea? Perhaps she would ask her man to come over an' have a word with me. I will be waitin' in the alehouse. There is an alehouse, as I believe? It is a poor place indeed that has niver an alehouse.'

'Yes,' Percy said. 'They call it the "Miners' Home".'

'Well, it will be home to a fiddlin' man for the time bein'. Will you do that for me now? Will you promise to tell me words to your good mother?'

'Yes, a'll tell her soon as a get home.' Percy said. 'What is that hangin' on yor shoulder?'

Sullivan did his best to explain what a fiddle was, but did not meet with much success, so he took up the instrument and played the tune of 'I'll Away No More'. This had a strong effect on both boys, and in fact it was what Percy began with when he got back home and spoke to his mother. The music and the way the man moved his elbow, now quick, now slow, and the strange look of him and his strange way of talking. Only after this did he remember to pass on Sullivan's message, and when he did so he saw his mother's face change. She reached and took a grip on his shoulder. 'He said he had news of our Billy?'

'He said so.' His uncle Billy was something more than a name to him, but not much; a figure in a distant story, a lad who had run away from the coal. He was taken aback by this serious-ness of his mother's, and could think of nothing more to say than what he had said already. 'He had long hair an' he seemed to be lookin' at sommat else all the time an' he talked funny an' he said that it was us who talked funny but it was him that did, an' then he played sommat on this fiddle he was carryin', there is strings stretched over an' tha scrapes across with a stick.'

'An' he said he would be waitin' at the alehouse?'

'Aye.'

'Well,' Nan said, 'he can bide where he is for a bit. A'll have to wait for Bordon. A canna gan there on my own an' he canna come here till Bordon is back from work an' washed an' ready.'

And so it came about that Sullivan waited longer at a quiet time of day and drank rather more ale than he had foreseen, which was fortunate in various ways. It led to a franker conversa-tion with the keeper of the alehouse than might otherwise have been the case, and it led to his getting a good look at a widow woman named Sally Cartwright, who served there.

The keeper had nothing to do with the mining of the coal; he was a tenant of the company, to which he paid a fixed monthly sum, all the proceeds over that going into his own pocket. When he learned that Sullivan's total resources, once he had paid for the beer he had drunk, would amount to only fourpence, and that he had no further travels presently in mind, he served up a pint free of charge and asked for a tune.

Sullivan obliged with a lively rendering of the 'Galway Piper' and followed this with the first lines of the song;

> *Every person in the Nation*
> *Or of great or humble station*
> *Holds in highest estimation*
> *Piping Tim of Galway.*

The keeper rubbed his nose reflectively for a moment or two, then said, 'Do you know any of the songs from round here, the miners' songs?'

'No, niver a one. I know some of the Irish songs an' some of the seagoing songs an' bits of songs that I picked up in Liverpool but that is the sum of it. I was niver in these parts before.'

'Well, but you could learn some. There is Sally, who does some serving round the tables. She is a local woman, she knows some songs, she sings to herself as she goes about.'

He went across the taproom as if to call down to the kitchen, three steps below. But before he could do so a woman came in, drying her hands on her apron. 'That was a nice bit o' singin',' she said. 'It was you, was it?' She smiled at Sullivan.

'This is Sally Cartwright,' the keeper said. 'She could teach you some songs if she chose.'

She was brown-haired and brown-eyed and buxom. She said nothing more but she gave Sullivan a smile he found distinctly beguiling. 'I dare say she could,' he said.

'An Irish fiddler,' the keeper said. 'Playing and singing. That would be something different. There is not another tavern between here and Hartlepool that would have the match of it. It would bring the lads in, and maybe the lasses too. Listen now,

I'll tell you what. You get board and a bed in the outhouse and a shilling a week and a quart of ale a day, and you entertain the company in the mornings after eleven and in the afternoons starting at around four and going on while there are people to listen. What do you say?'

Sullivan was never afterwards sure whether it was Sally's smile and the promise of such a teacher or the prospect of bed and board and a regular shilling that swayed him, but it did not take him long to make up his mind. 'I'm your man,' he said. And I would not mind being yours, he thought, glancing again at Sally. Subject to there being no one else in the offing . . . 'Shillin' in advance?' he said.

'No, I cannot go so far as that. With a travelling man trust has to be built up gradual like.'

So all was settled, and Sullivan's prospects had undergone a radical change by the time the company arrived. This was more numerous than he had envisaged. There was Nan and Bordon and their three sons; there was Nan's brother, John Blair, and his wife and their two daughters and two sons. And there were several hangers-on who had got wind of the business, among them, much to Bordon's irritation, Arbiter Hill.

Sullivan had requested the loan of a comb and had done something to restore order to the wildness of his hair. He had washed the dust of the road from his face and laid aside fiddle and bow. So it was a modified version of the apparition that Percy Bordon saw now. He was reassured, however, to find that the sounds that came from the man's mouth were as strange as ever.

Women did not come very often to the tavern and the landlord had nothing that might meet the needs of more delicate palates except for gin, so this was mixed with water and, after some expressions of reluctance, proved acceptable. The men had ale in pint pots, and Sullivan allowed his pot to be refilled. When all were seated in the taproom – Sally among them, he was glad to see – and when the lamps had been lit and hung on the walls, he began his tale.

So grateful had he been to the Virgin for securing his release from prison, so set had he been on carrying out his vow, unfaltering through all the trials and tribulations that had beset him during the weeks of his journey, that he had not paused to give much thought to the mode of his narrative, the way it should be presented. He began confidently enough with the relation of how he and Billy had seen and recognised each other in a dockside tavern in Liverpool.

'We had sailed together,' he said. 'A ship called the *Sarah*. Long years before, but when you have been shipmates together, haulin' on the ropes together for the best part of a year, you niver forget a man's face, for good or bad. I was playin' me fiddle for the dancin' when Billy came in. He was off a ship, purse full of money.' Skin full of rum, he remembered, but he said nothing of this to the assembled company.

Darkness had fallen outside and the faces of the listeners were ruddy in the lamplight, their bodies motionless. No sound came from them.

'Billy was tricked out of his money. They threatened him with prison for debt unless he agreed to sign on for this ship that was gettin' ready to sail – she was due to cast off with the tide next mornin'. He could not pay his score, d'you see, his purse was robbed out of his pocket. They were all in it together. Billy put up a fight an' I got in the middle of it an' got knocked on the head. The long an' short of it all was that we both ended up aboard the ship, an' she was a slaver, she was bound for the Guinea Coast.'

It was as he pronounced these last words and looked at the unchanging faces that the first shadow of doubt came into his mind. What could the Guinea Coast mean to them, what kind of picture could it conjure up? They could have no more an idea of it than the inhabitants of that coast could have of a Durham pit village. He saw suddenly, and with a sinking heart, that his story, which he had looked forward to telling in fulfilment of his vow, was dressed in the wrong colours. 'That was the Windward Coast of Africa,' he said. 'We traded for slaves there an' when we had number enough to cram the space below decks we set off for the island of Jamaica, where it was purposed to sell them an' buy sugar with the money.'

He paused now as if he had come to a wall with no gate in it. Silence descended on the room, broken after some moments by John Blair, Billy's brother, though not much resembling him to Sullivan's eye, being taller and longer-faced and having eyes closer set.

'Billy was workin' in Sunderland before he run off to sea, a know that for a fact. He was workin' in the shipyard.'

'No,' another man said, 'it was South Shields where he went. He was loadin' coal on the freighters – a was told that by a lad that worked there alongside him.'

Arbiter Hill now intervened, seizing, as was his wont, on the difference of opinion. 'There is some as says Sunderland, there is some as says South Shields, depending on witnesses and memory. There might be others as would say something different again, Hartlepool for example. With the time that has passed we will not obtain the final answer, we will have to box on without it.'

'What the hell does it matter?' Bordon said with sudden violence, and Sullivan saw the woman beside him lay a hand on his arm. He spoke again, but more quietly now. 'Yor listenin' to the story of what befell my wife's brother, yor hearin' talk of Africa an' Jamaica, an' you gan on with tittle-tattle about Hartlepool an' Sunderland.'

This was the husband, Percy's father, he who had made the kite. Sullivan found himself being regarded with eyes of a singular intensity, even shadowed as they were by the brim of the cap, which he wore well pulled forward. Here was one at least under the spell of the story, and Sullivan's spirits lifted with the perception of this. He had wanted his words to grip and enthral, to crown his long journey, even though Billy's death was contained in them. He was taking a risk and he knew it. It was not very likely that news of the part played by the crew of the *Liverpool Merchant* would have reached such a remote place – these men and women did not have the look of newspaper readers. But that it was possible he had known from the beginning. His vow had always involved this risk, and the miracle of his escape had made it worth taking. The interest written on Bordon's face confirmed him in this feeling and gave him heart to go on.

'We niver got there,' he said. 'We niver got to Jamaica at all. We were blown off course. The skipper was dead by this time. We were beached up on the coast of Florida.'

'Florida,' Bordon repeated, and his voice lingered on the name.

Sullivan did not try to describe the efforts they had made to haul the ship up the creek and so conceal all traces of it. 'We had no choice but to stay there,' he said. 'The ship was wrecked. We lived there twelve years, Billy an' me an' the others, white an' black together, them that were left. We made a life for ourselves.'

Out of duty to Billy's memory, so they would understand the way he had lived, as well as the way he had died, he tried to describe the life they had had, the ocean never far away, the lagoons and jungle hummocks and mangrove swamps, the alligators and snakes and deer, the great flocks of white herons that rose all together with a great beating of wings, flying up suddenly for no reason anyone could know or determine, settling again as if it were snow or big white petals.

'Twelve years,' he said again. 'Billy came to his end there.'

'What end was that?' Nan said. 'What happened to our Billy?'

'Unbeknown to us, the sojers were comin'. The man that owned the ship took some redcoats to get us. He said we had stole the ship an' the slaves aboard her – in his way of thinkin' they were still slaves, even after the years we had all lived together. The sojers were closin' round us, but we niver knew it till they started shoutin' for us to come out an' give ourselves up. Billy wasn't in the compound, he was outside, mebbe a mile away, he was fishin' in the creeks with his mate, whose name was Inchebe, a man from the Niger. It was just gettin' light and these two were on the way back with the catch . . .'

He paused here, aware of having arrived at a difficulty but impelled still by the sense of duty, the need to do justice to Billy's life in the settlement, all their lives. 'These two were close,' he said, 'because they were sharin' the same woman. You see, there were more men than women, more than twice as many, so the women could have two if they were inclined that way an' mostly they were.'

'What, our Billy an' another man sharin' the same woman?' John Blair said. 'A never heered of such a thing, it's nay decent.'

'Tha'd rather have it t'other way round, woudn't tha?' his wife said. 'It would be decent enough then, a'll be bound.' There had been a note of bitterness in this, as it seemed – some strain between them had been brought out by this revelation.

'Our Billy only done what the others was doin'.' Nan said. 'A wouldna want two men mesen, one is enough for me.'

'More than enough sometimes,' Bordon said and he smiled

at her, the lines of tension on his face softening into tenderness.

'He shared a woman with a black man?' Michael Bordon said, but there was more curiosity than disapproval in his tone. He was wondering, though he did not say so, whether they ever came to blows over whose turn it was. How he would hate to share Elsie with anyone. Even another hand, touching her lightly . . .

'Yes, he did so, we all did. The woman was black too, all the women were black, d'you see, they were brought aboard as slaves.' This diversion about the sharing had distracted the people from his narrative, even as he was nearing the moment of Billy's death. 'We were there,' he said. 'There were no churches an' no priests. We niver chose to go there, we had to live as best we could.'

Bordon helped him forward again now. 'What were they gannin' to do, kill one another, fightin' over it?' he said to Michael. 'You an' me is black a lot of the time, for the matter of that. So Billy was comin' back with the catch then?' he said to Sullivan.

'As they drew near, they came upon some of the redcoats, hidin' there among the trees. Billy was in front an' so he saw them first an' he shouted to warn Inchebe an' one of the sojers lost his head an' he fired an' the ball took Billy in the back as he was tryin' to get away. Inchebe was caught with the rest of us, an' he told us what befell, he told us on board the ship that was bringin' us away. He said Billy took some steps before he fell, but he was a dead man before he come to the ground.'

He sought for some fitting way to close. The final words were the only ones that he had rehearsed in his mind while on the road, feeling that he owed it to Billy to give the death full detail and sum up the life at the same time. 'It was a misty mornin',' he said. 'There was always strange sounds in among the trees at that time of the day – strange till you got used to them, I mean. The feller that shot him was full of fears, I dare say, an' would niver had done it if he had been of sound mind. Billy wasn't took with the rest of us an' brought back in chains, he died there, where he had been happy and free for all them years. It would be misguided to feel sorry for him. We had a good life there till the sojers came. Everyone respected Billy an' listened to what he had to say. He was plannin' to come back here one day, an' see his folks again, but he died before he could do it, so I have come in his stead.'

No one made any answer to this, and after some moments people began to get to their feet preparatory to leaving. Nan took Sullivan by the hand. 'Tha's been a true friend to our Billy,' she said. 'A'll never forget the service tha's done us. It always pained me, not knowing what became of him. A was only twelve when he ran off, an' we never heered more of him from that day on. It comforts me to know that he didna forget us, that he was meanin' to come back.'

John Blair and his wife left without words, though whether it was disapproval that kept them silent or some sort of displeasure with each other, Sullivan could not tell. He was feeling spent – it had been a tiring day and he had eaten little – but he was not dissatisfied with the way he had told Billy's story. He was thinking of trying to get a bite to eat in the kitchen and a word or two with Sally, who was rinsing out the tankards there, both of these things falling, as he felt, within the terms of his new employment, when he saw that Bordon, having accompanied the others out into the yard, had now returned to the taproom.

'There was sommat a meant to ask,' he said. 'What did they live on there, what did the people do to keep alive?'

'There was fish in the creeks,' Sullivan said. 'There was turtles, which can be partly consumed if you know the trick of it. There was game most of the year, quail, wild turkey, pigeons. There was deer you could get a shot at when they came to drink.'

'No, what a mean, did they grow veg'tables an' suchlike, did they work the ground?'

'Not to begin with. We had nothin' in the world to plant. There was sea cabbage an' acorns an' berries an a kind of wild oats you could contrive to make porridge with. Then with time and lucky chance we came to be friendly with the Indians that lived along the coast. We made them gifts from the trade goods that had been left aboard the ship, kettles, beads, scraps of cotton. We never could fathom what use they were, but it was like a treasure to them. They brought us gifts in their turn. There was a root they knew of that you could grind an' make cakes from, an' there was yams an' pumpkin seeds an' tubers of sweet potato.'

Bordon listened intently to this and nodded several times

when Sullivan had finished speaking. 'You lacked for nothin',' he said, 'you had all you needed,' and Sullivan saw on his face the light of a vision and knew in that moment that he and this miner were fellow spirits. 'We did so,' he said.

Bordon remained silent for a space of time, head lowered. He did not look at Sullivan when he spoke again, but kept his eyes on the stone flags at his feet.

'Tha made me a gift, comin' here.'

Only the strangeness of such a visitor with his way of looking and talking, his tale of wanderings in far places, his wildness, could have brought Bordon to words like these, words safe to utter, inviolate, sealed off by the difference between the two of them. 'A rare gift,' he said. 'An' a'm nay talkin' only about Billy Blair.'

And Sullivan, who was quick to sense feelings in others, felt the gratitude and unhappiness in the words and experienced an urge to protect Bordon by shifting the talk before regret could enter into it. 'Speakin' of gifts,' he said, 'that was a fine kite you made for your son.'

'My father made a kite for me when a was gannin' on for seven years old, in the time just before a went down the mine. When a had sons of my own a carried on with it. Now it's Percy's turn, he'll be startin' soon. Once they start down the mine they dinna play no more.'

He was looking squarely at Sullivan now, and something of a smile had come to his face, though there was no gladness in it. 'They come to the end of playin',' he said. 'How did tha come to be a fiddler?'

'Me father was a fiddlin' man an' he passed it on to me. He travelled about, playin' an' singin' at fairs an' weddin's. There were seven of us, brothers and sisters, we went beggin' by the way, but I was the only one of them that had the power of music in me. He taught me how to find the notes. He always meant me to have the fiddle. He gave it to me when he was dyin' – he had not much more than that to leave, an' it will be the same with me, 'cept that I have no sons to leave anythin' to, our children were all sold, along with the mothers.'

'What use did they have for a fiddler on board of a slave ship?'

'Well, I had been to sea before as an ordinary seaman, so I knew the work. But they like to get a fiddler on a slave ship because he can play an' the slaves can dance to the music.'

'Dance to the music?' Bordon's smile had disappeared. 'Tha's makin' game of me,' he said. There was the beginning of anger in his voice and Sullivan sensed in this quickness to take offence a battle more or less permanent against a world that showed him no mercy.

'No,' he said, 'they needed to be danced because they were in chains, d'you see, they spent long hours cramped up below decks with scarce space enough to move a muscle. Without exercise they would get ill an' melancholy an' their value on the market would take a plunge. So they were brought up on deck an' made to dance to the fiddle music.'

'Still in their chains?'

'Yes.'

'What if they didna have nay fancy for dancin'?'

'They would be flogged.'

Bordon was silent for a while, as if in reflection. Then he nodded, and the same smile came back to his face. 'Not much choice,' he said. 'Better to dance than to bleed.'

With this he made for the door, leaving Sullivan feeling that he had made a friend, though one of uncertain temper. Sally was still in the kitchen, and he made his way there now in the expectation of her smile and the hope of something to eat.

Bordon slept badly that night, assailed by dreams of snapping jaws and clanking chains. He saw the white birds rising up and stalked the deer through close-growing trees. Waking from this, lying wide-eyed in the dark with Nan breathing deeply beside him, he thought of the freedom of that life in Florida, taking the hours as they came, living in the open and the light of day, doing things because they needed doing, so that life could go on, not because you were summoned to do them, not because someone you never saw owned the labour of your body. He felt a deep sense of envy for that band of men and women, even for their toil, even for the dangers they must have faced.

Following upon the envy, softening it with a sort of consolation that he knew to have no basis in reason, there came thoughts of the plot of land by the stream side, in the Dene, the sheltered ground, the falling water, the fertile soil, two acres, perhaps a bit more . . . The apple trees, the green rows of vegetables, the laden pony following the path to the coast where he would set up his stall and sell his produce. Somehow, in a manner that defied logic, this wandering Irishman's story had brought the possibility nearer.

28

It took Kemp forty-eight hours to reach the city of Durham, the journey broken by an overnight stay at an inn in Nottingham. Spenton was expecting the visit and would have sent a coach to bring his guest the twelve miles or so from the city, but Kemp had decided well in advance that he would hire a mount from the stables of the inn where his coach set him down. He was not carrying a great deal in the way of luggage; what he had would go into saddlebags. The thing of overriding importance to his mind was having independence of movement during his stay, being able to range freely; he had much to see, and wanted to choose his own time for the seeing. Spenton would have stables, but borrowing a horse would mean making arrangements, stating intentions, and so limiting the freedom he felt to be essential. As always, he was single-minded, formidably so; all of his being was concentrated now on learning what he could, assessing the levels of investment that would be needed, striving to apply what he had learned from his study of the industry to the actual workings of the mine, which would be entirely new to him.

It was mid-afternoon when, after some questioning of people along the way, he reached the gates to the house and grounds, though as yet no house was visible. Stone pillars on either side were surmounted by reclining lions, bemused and emaciated by time and weather. A man emerged from a small lodge and opened the gate to him. The drive, broad enough for two coaches to pass, wound upwards through rolling parkland, with copses of oak and ash cunningly laid out to give a sense of limitless vistas. The land fell away on his right as he neared the house, and he caught a flat gleam of water in the distance from what he supposed was a lake.

The house was of grey stone, broad-fronted and imposing, with wings that looked more recent than the main body of the building. A footman in livery appeared instantly, descended the steps between the parterres and with much deference took charge of Kemp's horse and led it away. As he began to mount the steps, a youngish man, plainly dressed in a dark twill suit, came down to meet him and held out his hand. 'Welcome to Wingfield, sir,' he said. 'My name is Bourne, Roland Bourne. I am a half-cousin of Lord Spenton and I act here as his steward. His Lordship asks me to apologise for his failure to be here in person to greet you on your arrival. There is a meet of the hunt today, and it is expected of him to be present at it.'

'I quite understand,' Kemp said, relieved at having time to gather himself before being required to encounter Spenton again and find the right face to put upon his host's blend – remembered from their meeting at Vauxhall – of studied nonchalance and sudden fits of enthusiasm for what had seemed entirely marginal matters, tricks of water, clockwork toys, this handball match that was soon to take place. 'Great possessions bring duties,' he said, summoning a smile. 'That is a general rule.' This fellow seemed pleasant enough – probably a younger son and more or less penniless, otherwise he would hardly be at Spenton's beck and call . . .

'Indeed it is, sir, indeed it is. Lady Spenton is still enjoying her afternoon repose, and so it falls to me to show you to your apartment. It was thought that you might like to take your ease for a while, after the journey.'

The room was on the first floor, reached from the main hall by a broad flight of steps that ascended directly, with no hint of the curve now thought fashionable, attesting to the age of the house, at least in this main part of it – well over a century, Kemp thought, noting as he mounted the stairs the heavy Jacobean oak rails of the banister. The Spenton family was not newly arrived at wealth and large estates, so much was obvious . . .

It was clear to him, however, that money had been spent on the house, and perhaps fairly recently. His room was more spacious than it would once have been; walls had been demolished to make space for the canopied bed, the broad writing desk, the marble bust of an unknown worthy, the easy chairs, the smooth extent of Turkey carpet.

There was a lingering warmth of sunshine here, and he noted the two large windows that had replaced the narrow casements of a former age. He approached these now and looked out over extensive views of the grounds. The long approach to the house, with the tree-lined drive rising gradually, had brought him to an eminence he had not fully realised until now. He could see the whole shape of the lake from here, a perfect oval, its shores clustered with willows, a small boat with a Chinese-style pagoda moored to the landing stage. Beyond this was what looked like a ruined abbey, with Gothic towers and ivied columns.

By approaching the edge of one window and widening as much as possible his angle of vision, he was able to look eastwards and see, at the furthest limit of sight, a pale suffusion in the sky that he thought must indicate the line of the coast. Before this, rising towards it, there was a thickening of the light, a low mist, pale sulphurous in colour, and he guessed this to mark the distant presence of the mine. He noticed a narrow seam of green, two or three miles in length, running directly towards the sea. Some wooded cleft in the land . . .

He was left to his thoughts and plans for an hour or so and he was beginning to grow sleepy, as he half reclined in the high-backed chair with its deep cushions and footstool, when an elderly retainer came tapping at his door to tell him that Lord and Lady Spenton were below and looking forward to the pleasure of his company for tea in the drawing room.

He was struck by the difference they showed in the style of their greetings. Lady Spenton bade him welcome with none of her husband's languidness of manner. She was a tall woman, angular in figure and brisk of speech. She had made little effort to dress for the occasion; her hair was combed loose to her shoulders, without ornament, and she wore a day gown with a long apron of the sort she would wear when going about her usual duties. Spenton himself had come in straight from the hunt, still in riding habit and top boots.

There had been a fall during the chase. A neighbouring farmer had been thrown and had suffered a twisted wrist and two cracked ribs. 'It is all in the way you take the fence,' Spenton said. 'The horse must be sure of its rider, or it will baulk. Personally, I think the beast was taking revenge. Davis is a heavy-handed fellow, I have seen myself how he wrenches his mount. A horse has a memory, sir, and sooner or later it will square accounts.' He paused here to take some tea, then turned to his wife. 'And how has your day been, my dear?'

This would be the first moment of the day they had set eyes on each other, Kemp thought, as Lady Spenton began speaking of some wrangle with a tenant over delayed rents. And it would probably be more or less the same every day while Spenton was up here, a situation which he suspected might well accord with the wishes of both. She would see to the running of the house, the management of the servants, the day-to-day dealings with the local tenant farmers. Helped in all this, and perhaps in more than this, by the pleasant-mannered steward . . .

Kemp delayed any talk about his own plans until that evening at supper, which he and Spenton took alone, the lady of the house having sent her excuses and retired early. He had no very definite intentions for next day; he wanted to see the way things were run, the way the mine was managed, before starting to make plans for cutting labour costs and increasing production, though sure there would be scope for this. He knew – though he did not speak of it – that the mine was not making profits commensurate with capacity. With 130 men and boys at work in the colliery, and in spite of its favourable position near the sea and its extensive deposits, Spenton's income from the mine was considerably short of two thousand pounds a year. He would make a good deal more from his land rents, so much was certain; but Kemp had studied the figures, and he knew that the balance was shifting from year to year in favour of the wealth that lay below, with the growing importance of coal for the steel industry and the decreasing costs of transport as the roads improved.

He asked one or two questions regarding matters not yet clear to him, depending as they did on local practice: the levels of advance payment at the time of hiring, the extent to which the miners absented themselves from the work when they felt they had money enough to last the week. But for information on these counts he was referred to the steward and the head overman,

Spenton professing himself to be entirely ignorant of them. Only once in the course of the meal did his host show any degree of interest in the conversation, and that was when he spoke of the impending handball match. They had a new champion this year, a young man named Michael Bordon, who worked as a putter in the mine.

'Back-breaking work, you know,' Spenton said. 'He won't go on much longer with the handball, he will be past it before he reaches thirty. But for the present he is very gifted at it, he has the eye and the speed, quite out of the common. I talk to my tenants when I come up here, it is expected of me, I have always done it. But I make a point of coming up at this time of year so as to see the handball match – I never miss that if I can help it. It is an annual event, you know, with the neighbouring colliery of Northfield, which is owned by the Pemberton family. It has been going on for many years now, it was started in my father's time. Pemberton and I have a few guineas on the result. We were defeated last year by their man, who I am told will be their champion again this year, a formidable player, a man named Dickson. You are lucky in the timing of your visit, Kemp, the match is on this coming Sunday.'

Kemp expressed a pleasure at this prospect that he did not feel. He thought it extraordinary that Spenton should be entirely ignorant of hiring levels at the mine and yet fully conversant with the names of the handball players. It was possible of course that the vagueness was mere affectation and that he knew a great deal more about the workings of the mine than he allowed to appear. Acquainted as he was with his host's spending habits, he suspected that the few guineas would in fact be a few hundred. He was not a gambling man himself. His superstition, passionate as it was, lay all in the search for certainty, for assurances and portents, signs that would guarantee a success total and unqualified, impervious to the quirks of accident. That the signs themselves might be no more than accidental was not a suspicion he permitted himself, except in rare moments of discouragement.

That night the moon shone through his window, a summer moon, full and reddish, like a night-time sun. He did not close the shutters against this luminous intrusion, which made the objects in the room – the posts of the bed, the marble bust, the outlines of the chairs – into shapes of enchantment. As he lay awake and watched the slow shifting of the shadows, the strangeness, the unearthly light seemed like a promise to him, a good augury for the change in his life that he was planning.

A lot would depend on the next few days, what he saw, what he was shown. Spenton obviously took little interest in the day-to-day management of the mine; his steward, Roland Bourne, would know more, and there would be deputies responsible for hiring labour, for upkeep, for the rendering of accounts. But Bourne was there because of family connection, not because of any proved capacity. It seemed to Kemp, as he lay there in the moonlight, a distinctly haphazard way of doing things. He would introduce more method, a closer control. There were many abuses in the industry. He had read of the frauds of the coal dealers, the malpractices in the relations between the coal owners and the lightermen who carried the coal from the wharves at the mouth of the Wear out to the collier ships that would bear it south to Hull and London.

Vigilance would be needed, but the times were auspicious. Blast furnaces fed by coke were growing in size and number, an expansion greatly helped by the wars with France, which had increased the demand for all manner of weaponry. They still had to use charcoal for converting the pig iron into bar iron, but it could not be long now before coke alone was used for the whole process, bringing about a huge increase in the demand for coal.

As he lay there in an excited reverie of possibilities and prospects, Jane Ashton's image was never far from his mind. She was a luminous presence there in the room. He thought of how he would explain his plans to her, he saw her face in the moonlight, bright-eyed with interest as she listened to him.

He remembered her face as he had seen it, glimpsed so briefly in the Spring Gardens at Vauxhall just at the moment when he had come to an agreement with Spenton, made radiantly beautiful by the descending shower of gold. One day he would tell her of this quintessential moment, but not yet. He had a sudden strong erotic feeling for her, the white neck with its pearls, the gemstones in her hair, the straight shoulders and slender waist, the close-fitting bodice of her dress. He pictured her undressing in the moonlight of this room while he lay waiting for her. She would feel a maidenly demur at undressing completely, she would retain an undergarment of some diaphanous material, thin enough for her to feel his touch on her body as she lay beside him, touch of a man's hands, never felt before . . . All was propitious for invention and expansion, every factor, every indication. The fall in the rate of interest, coinciding as it did with a growth in the markets at home and abroad, had provided strong incentives. The return of peace in 1763 had eased the pressure on the price of consols and brought with it a rate of public borrowing which was unlikely to exceed three per cent . . . The quickened breath of her excitement as she turned towards him, as he rose above her . . .

Limitless possibilities of pleasure and profit filled his mind as the moon rose across his windows and the light of it ebbed slowly from the room. He did not sleep until long after midnight but the morning found him fresh, and eager to begin his explorations. He would have liked to set forth at once, immediately after his hot chocolate and buttered toast, but Spenton had an hour to spare before meeting some of his tenants and he was eager to show his visitor some of the features of the grounds.

The lake came first. A huge basin had been scooped out and water fed into it by diverting a tributary of the Wear that ran behind the house. Clumps of trees had been artfully disposed to break the view and give an air of naturalness to this blank sheet.

'No vista is complete without water,' Spenton said. 'I have also constructed a grotto with cascades, which I shall show you shortly. It was designed by Repton, you know. I first had the idea while on a visit to Chiswick Park, which was laid out for Lord Burlington in the Romantic style by William Kent. Kent was virtually unknown at that time, but he became famous afterwards, he laid out the grounds for a good many houses, generally contriving a lake and waterfalls and a folly or two, and planting trees to give a natural look. Repton learned much from him. It was Repton who built the medieval ruin for me. I had to extend the park on that side by taking over some of the common ground.'

Guided by his host, Kemp was able to see, across the motionless expanse of water, beyond the boat with the Chinese pagoda, through a fringe of weeping willows, the broken towers and arches that he had glimpsed the afternoon before from the window of his room.

'You will scarce believe it,' Spenton said, 'but in my father's time these grounds were still laid out with formal walks and straight avenues, in the old, outmoded style, you know. I took care to have copses planted out with oak and beech and ash. These are trees with a quality of the picturesque, of course, but that is not the only reason. When the time comes for thinning, they are the most profitable timber to sell.'

Only a politeness deriving from self-interest held Kemp back from some expression of sarcasm at these words. His host had spent enormous sums on these improvements, he had appropriated common ground, perhaps destroying woodland in the process at a loss to the local people. And all this not for any sound commercial reason, but simply to extend the view, make space for a totally unnecessary ruin. And now here he was, congratulating himself on the small profits he would make from the sale of timber!

The grotto had a pool and a waterfall divided into three streams that descended over the face of a shallow cave. The central stream fell on to the boards of a water wheel and kept it turning, and this, by the aid of some instrument that Kemp did not see, caused a water nymph, fashioned in polished tin, with a painted smile and painted nipples, to stand clear of the water for some moments, sink to her midriff, rise again, dripping and smiling.

'My own invention entirely,' Spenton said. 'It was inspired by the water show at the Spring Gardens which you will recall we visited together. I am planning to introduce another wheel, which will revolve in the opposite direction and bring forth a Triton or perhaps a seahorse.'

As they returned, Spenton led Kemp up a short rise, which brought them to the highest point in the grounds. There was a gazebo on the crest, with steps that led up to an open lantern. From here the views were extensive, and Kemp remarked on the yellowish mist of smoke that thickened the air at a distance below them. 'I suppose that marks the colliery,' he said.

'Indeed, sir, yes. It does something to spoil the vista, but up here it does not much trouble us. We may see it, but it does not accede to the nostrils. Bad odours keep close to the ground, they lurk, sir.'

From here there was a clear view across to the sea, more now than a difference in the quality of light, as it had seemed earlier from Kemp's window, but a definite territory of water, slate blue in the morning light. He could see gulls wheeling above, not the forms of the birds but the flashes that came from them as they turned in flight. However, what mainly took his attention was the long seam of green that lay towards the sea, in fact appeared to join it. It was the same wooded cleft that he had seen from his room, but from this point of vantage he had a stronger sense of the strangeness of it, this deep scrape in a landscape of pasture fields and sparse trees. Impossible from here to determine how deep it was, how deeply it had gouged out the land. But the cleft must be narrow and the sides steep, he thought, otherwise the depth of the cut would be easier to judge from a height so far above.

'That valley down there,' he said. 'Strange in such a setting. It looks like a kind of ravine.' In fact, it is like a wound, he thought, a wound stitched by the vegetation that had sprung up, but still not healed.

'A kind of ravine is what it is. The people here call it the Dene. There are a number of such narrow valleys here in east Durham, where rivers have cut trenches in the limestone. Scientific gentlemen from London have sometimes asked permission to visit this one, botanists, naturalists, people of that kind.'

'Why is that?'

'It has its own climate, quite different from the land surrounding it. The sides are very steep and they are thickly wooded, so they can sometimes protect the valley floor from winds, sometimes expose it to the blast by acting like a tunnel. This makes for extremes of light and temperature, or so I am told. There are parts of the Dene that keep warm even in winter. It seems that butterflies extremely rare elsewhere in Britain are commonly seen here. A gentleman from the Royal Society once told me that he had identified more than a hundred different kinds of moss and liverwort bordering the stream that runs through. I allow the mining folk to go there, provided they set no traps or snares. My gamekeeper keeps an eye on things. The people know I would close it off if there was any trouble of that kind. Meanwhile, you know, it is a resource for them. The children play there until the time comes for them to start work in the mine. There are mushrooms and berries to be gathered. Courting couples find refuge there, among the trees.'

He paused, smiling. 'I believe that agreeing to venture in there is an important step on the road to matrimony,' he said.

There was a sort of easy paternalism in this that grated on Kemp, and aroused a degree of hostility in him, not because he felt any great sympathy for the mining folk, but because it brought his own early struggles back to mind. He had had to scrabble for money, fight for his place in the world. Spenton could afford to take this indulgent tone, here in his gazebo, surveying the extent of his dominion – a dominion never challenged or brought into question except by his own extravagance and excess . . .

Naturally, he said nothing of this. 'It runs towards the sea,' he said. 'It goes down deep, I suppose. How far does it extend?'

'It is three miles or so in length.'

As his interest in this valley mounted, Kemp found himself, without being aware of any conscious intention, fingering the brass button nestled in his waistcoat pocket. It had proved its worth, it had served him well on his first meeting with Spenton. He carried it with him always now and was glad to know that it was there, accompanying him as he took these first steps in exploring the mine's potential for development and profit. 'And it reaches the coast?' he said.

'Yes, it opens on the marshland adjoining the sea.'

Kemp had a sense that his host was growing slightly perplexed at the particularity of these questions, so he said nothing further. But when he afterwards thought of the matter it seemed to him that the idea was born here, in this view from the gazebo, this instinct of caution. Spenton's land, his untrammelled property – there could be no question of compensation. Perhaps a mile from the colliery to the beginning of the ravine. Did he own the marshland, the stretch of shore? There must be someone in the district, someone not too far away, who acted for Spenton, dealt with matters of land tenure, boundaries with neighbours, things of that sort.

'There are one or two things I should like to enquire into while I am up here,' he said. 'Mainly concerning the charges fixed by neighbouring landowners for bringing coal from the mine across their property. Is there someone you have appointed to see into these things?'

It seemed that there was, though Spenton, with the usual vagueness – genuine or assumed – seemed to have utmost difficulty in remembering anything of him but the name, a Mr Bathgate, a notary. 'Bourne will know more of him,' he said. 'I believe his place of business is in Hartlepool. Perhaps you would like to have him brought over here?'

'No, no, it is only a few miles, I will ride over. It will give me some exercise.' The last thing he wanted just now was for Spenton or his steward to be present when he questioned the man.

Nothing more was said on the subject as the two retraced their steps to the house. The head overman, who had also, as it turned out, been employed as an agent for the previous lessee, came for him soon afterwards, and they set off on horseback on their tour of the mine.

Kemp, in borrowed leather apron and cap, with a muslin mask over his face to protect his lungs from the dust, had himself lowered down in a wicker basket, with the overman beside him to guard him from collisions with the walls of the shaft. He saw the hewers kneeling or crouching in the candlelight to cut and hack into the coalface; he saw the labour of the putters and noted the length of the galleries and work ways along which they had to drag the loaded corves; he questioned the overman closely on the methods of dealing with marsh gas and chokedamp; he had the problems of flooding explained to him and learned much about the various methods of ventilating the mine both by fire and by the use of trapdoors – these last worked by children during their first three years at the pit.

By the end of the day he had learned a great deal about the working of the colliery and the methods of extraction. He had also learned, from Roland Bourne, the full name, and the address, of the notary in Hartlepool.

But the great moment of his visit came early next morning, when he rode alone to the mouth of the Dene and saw that, though the sides were steep and thickly wooded, the path that led down from the opening of the ravine to the stream below descended by much more gradual degrees, and that the land immediately adjoining the stream continued roughly level on either side, at least for the mile or so that he walked along it.

He arrived in Hartlepool towards midday and had no difficulty in finding Mr Bathgate's place of business. The notary was a tall man, advanced in age, stooped a little at the shoulder, with a solemnity of utterance and manner belied by bright, quick-glancing eyes.

'Pray be seated, sir,' he said. 'How can I be of service to you?'

Kemp had been kept waiting for twenty minutes or so in an outer room while the notary continued to converse with a client already there, who looked like someone in a small way of business, perhaps a shopkeeper – in any case a person who should have been ushered out immediately when he, Kemp, had arrived on the scene. This, coupled with the fact that he felt free for the moment from Spenton's presence and the constraint this entailed of appearing agreeable and obliging, brought out a strain of arrogance in him that was never far away.

'I am a guest of Lord Spenton,' he said, ignoring the offer of a chair. 'I have need of information regarding His Lordship's estates.'

'Have you so?' The notary regarded his visitor for some moments, taking in the expensive and fashionable cut of his riding suit, the stiffness of his bearing, the dark eyes that were turned from him. He had registered the high-handed manner without being set in awe by it – he was not a man easily set in awe. 'You will have a paper of some sort?' he said.

'A paper, what do you mean?'

'Some note from His Lordship authorising you to make these enquiries.'

'No, I have nothing of the sort. I cannot see that it is necessary. I informed Lord Spenton that I was in need of certain information and I obtained your name from him.'

'I see. So I am expected to take it on trust. I am afraid that sets certain limits on the nature of the information I can give you.'

Kemp checked the angry reply that rose to his lips. For the first time he deigned to look directly at the notary and found himself being regarded with a certain curiosity, but without any hint of deference. Belatedly he realised that it had been a mistake to take such a peremptory tone – the fellow was insolent beyond what could have been expected in a provincial lawyer. 'Well, it is nothing of a particularly confidential kind,' he said more mildly. 'The valley known as the Dene, does it give access to a stretch of shore that forms part of Lord Spenton's property?'

The notary maintained a silence for some moments, looking down at his hands, which lay clasped on the desk before him. Then he said, 'The line of the shore is common land, sir, for fifty yards from the tidemark.'

'I understand that Lord Spenton has once already encroached on common land in order to enlarge his park, and this without penalty to him.'

'That is so, yes.'

'It is likely that he would have the same power of expropriation in this case.'

'It would be a reasonable assumption. The Spenton family have had the land in their possession for four generations. Possession confers rights, sir, that is the way of things.'

On this Kemp took his departure. He was reasonably satisfied with the interview, though bearing away an unfavourable opinion of the notary. Even if compensation for the enclosure had to be paid, it could not be so very much for a short stretch of shore. It would be money well spent in any case, it would give unimpeded access to the sea and with that the right to construct wharves and a harbour . . .

Occupied with these thoughts, it did not occur to him that Bathgate might have learned more from the interview than he had himself, but such in fact was the case. As the notary remained at his desk, in the silence following upon Kemp's departure, certain questions exercised his mind. Why would his visitor, not a local man and apparently wealthy, wish to make such an enquiry? Why had he ridden a dozen miles to do so when Spenton, whom he had claimed as his host, could easily have furnished the information? Why just there, just at that point, where the Dene opened out?

They were different sorts of questions but there was an answer that fitted them all.

29

The morning of the handball match was clear and sunny and practically windless, a cause for general rejoicing as it meant that the game could be played in the open, allowing a much greater number of spectators than did the covered court.

It was a day of heavy responsibility for Michael Bordon. The hopes of the village were centred on him; there was a good deal of money – hard-earned money – resting on the result. Lord Spenton himself had shaken him by the hand that morning and wished him success. Two days before, Elsie had told him she had cause to believe herself pregnant, and he had asked her to marry him, and she had said yes.

So as he waited with his opponent in the shed behind the court while the spectators took their places, it was with a sense that much depended on him and a determination to do his best not to disappoint. He was matched with Charlie Dickson, the man who had won the year before, three years older than himself, stocky but very light on his feet – he was a notable dancer in his village. The two spoke little as they waited, cultivating a certain hostility in the silence.

There was seating for twelve persons only in the area immediately facing the wall of the court, and these were reserved for people of rank. Colonel and Mrs Pemberton were among them, and Roland Bourne, but Kemp, seated beside his host, noted that Lady Spenton had not made an appearance. Behind this row of seats the ground opened widely and sloped upwards, so that the ranks of spectators, standing close together, were able to get a clear view of the court.

While these ranks were forming Spenton explained something of the game to his guest. 'This court was constructed in my grandfather's time,' he said. 'It is the Irish game we play here.' His face wore the same expression of lively interest it had worn when he was explaining the mechanism by which the water nymph was hoisted and lowered.

'Why is that?'

'There was an influx of migrant workers from Ireland at the turn of the century. They came to look for work in the mines here. They brought the game with them and it caught on with the Durham men. At first they would play against any wall, on a clay floor. We have tiled the floor and marked out the lines but it is still played by the same rules and with the same type of ball, very hard, a wooden core covered with strips of rubber. They don't wear gloves, you know, they can bandage their hands if they like, but usually they don't choose to. The ball has to be struck, catching and throwing are against the rules, but the feet can be used. The ball must always be struck directly against the wall and taken on the rebound.'

Kemp listened with an interest at first assumed then growing genuine as his host's enthusiasm was communicated to him, and the sounds from the people assembling behind them grew in intensity. Spenton had to raise his voice as he pointed out the zones of play, the serving area, the short line that divided the court in two, the sidelines and the long line at the back. Points gained by the server were added to his score; a fault in serving or a failure to return the ball meant that the service would pass to the other with the score unaltered. There were three strokes only, apart from the kick: the underhand service stroke, the overhand for balls that bounced high and the sidearm. One player could not block another from playing the ball; if he did the ball was judged dead and had to be served again. The first man to reach twenty points won the game. Five games were played, the winner was he who had the best of the five . . .

'But who is it that does the judging?' Kemp asked. 'There must be someone, surely, otherwise the time would be consumed in dispute and quarrels.'

'There is a man chosen to be the arbiter, one who knows the rules and is accepted by both sides. He must not come from either colliery – the man we have today is from a colliery north of the Wear.'

'He is there in the midst of the court then? He will need to be quick on his feet to keep clear of the ball and the players.'

'He keeps to the sidelines,' Spenton said. 'He will come in with the players . . . Here they are now.'

There was a sudden shouting from the packed ranks behind them as the three men appeared and made their way on to the court. The arbiter was dressed in suit and cap, clearly his best; the players were bareheaded, in shirtsleeves, their trousers tied round at the ankles with twine. The shouting was followed by an absorbed silence as the two began some minutes of warming up, taking turns to serve.

'That is our man, Bordon, the slightly taller one,' Spenton said.

Kemp, who had seen the putters at work some days previously, found it hard to imagine how anyone could emerge from such heavy labour, in such cramped conditions, and move with the lightness and speed both men were showing now as they circled round the court. He could see nothing in either that might be taken as a determining advantage. Bordon had an inch or two of height and perhaps a wider reach, but the other was thicker in the shoulder and altogether stronger-looking in build, and he seemed to move no less quickly for this.

The arbiter spoke to the two men and they came together in the centre of the court to toss a coin and determine who should serve first. It came down in Michael's favour. The minutes of practice had warmed him but he was still nervous and tense, as always at the beginning of any contest in which he was involved. He had not found the coolness of mind that might already have given him some clues as to his opponent's style of play. For this first serve he stood well forward in the service area, as close as possible to the short line that marked the division of the court. He dropped the ball, struck it on the first bounce with the palm of his hand. It came high off the wall, and Dickson, who had stayed well back, was able to leap and strike it with great force. The rebound was very fast and very high – too fast and too high for Michael who had stayed too near to the wall to get his hand to it. With this he lost the advantage of the service.

Dickson won the next six points in a row, then lost the service through a fault, setting one foot outside the service line as he dropped the ball. Michael meanwhile had understood that he could not hit the ball with the same force as his opponent and that he would lose the match if he allowed it to become a trial of striking power. He was being obliged to stay at the back of the court, a position which deprived him of initiative. Dickson seemed to be assuming now that the contest would take this form, remaining in mid-court where he could use the sidearm stroke to slam the ball hard against the wall.

Only a short bounce was any defence against this tactic, and Michael served from as far back as possible, almost a lob. It struck the wall rather low, obliging Dickson to move forward very quickly. So near the wall as this, with the ball dropping, there was little he could do but strike underhand at it and so present Michael with a perfect passing shot.

This exchange in the first game set the pattern for the next two. Dickson gained most of his points with a slamming forearm stroke, delivered across court to widen the angle of the bounce; Michael lured his opponent forward and then passed him with shots that were out of his reach.

Three games had been played and Dickson had won two of them before Michael realised another crucial difference in their styles of play. Dickson had so much force in his right arm and was so quick on his feet that he based his whole game on these strengths, counting always on getting across the court fast enough to deliver the sidearm blow. Michael knew that he lacked the other man's power in driving the ball, but he was a two-handed player, and his returns on the left were hardly weaker than those on the right. In the fourth game he adopted the strategy – which involved high risks, especially as he was a game behind, and behind on points in this one – of striking the ball straight forward instead of aiming at angled shots, using his left hand whenever possible, hitting the ball as low and as hard as he could. By these means he was able to achieve a number of what were known as kill-shots – shots that came off the wall so low as to be virtually impossible to return – and he won the game by a margin of two points.

Dickson's play in the fifth and final game was as aggressive as ever, but Michael sensed a certain wildness in it and thought he knew why: his opponent had made the mistake of counting victory as assured, as a foregone conclusion; he had been winning by two games to one and well in the lead in the fourth game – a win here would have given him the match; now, by a change in the other's tactics that he had not been flexible enough to respond to, he had seen this lead melt away and the two of them return to an equal footing.

The decisive point in the fifth game came when the score stood at fifteen to twelve in Michael's favour. Dickson served strongly across the court, bringing the ball rebounding at a sharp angle and very low, no more than a foot from the ground on Michael's left side. There was only one stroke possible if the ball was to be kept in play. He struck upwards with clenched fist in a kind of blow that was half-hook, half-uppercut, felt a sharp pain in his knuckles, saw the ball come off the wall, saw it spin and bounce short, saw Dickson lunge at it and miss, deceived by the bounce.

With this it was all over. The serve passed to Michael and he closed the game with a series of five wins over a now demoralised opponent.

A great storm of shouted applause came from the ranks of the Thorpe men. The two opponents shook hands with an appearance of good grace. Spenton, beaming with delight, got up from his seat and advanced into the court to shake Michael's hand; Colonel Pemberton followed suit, having first, however, congratulated his own champion on a hard-fought match.

Michael was making to leave the court, but he had not gone far when an exuberant group of his fellow miners surrounded him, hoisted him to their shoulders and bore him up the slope of the yard and along in the direction of the alehouse, followed by a good number behind, all singing his praises. He had upheld the honour of the colliery, and there were those who had won some shillings that day.

Kemp had risen with those beside him at the culminating moment of victory, as the arbiter held up Michael's hand. He had seen the winner hoisted up and borne away, but it was only after this that he looked behind him, and then only to follow the course of the victorious cavalcade as it mounted the slope of the yard. He, like the others who had been seated there, was obliged to wait until the mass of spectators had departed before making his way out. But as he glanced up to follow the hero's progress, he saw a face he thought he knew, one different from the others, not only because of this half-recognition, but from its ruddier colouring, as if the man had been more in the sun. The hair, which was long and very dark, was tied behind with a ribbon, not the common way among the miners, who wore their hair close-cropped because of the dust that got into it from the coal and slate. The face passed in profile across his line of vision and in a second or two was gone, lost in the crowd that was following behind the champion.

He stood still for some moments as the voices retreated, struggling with a wild sense of improbability. It was as if the sounds of jubilation had not faded through distance but were somehow muted out of deference to this struggle of his, as he was carried back in mind to the quarterdeck of the ship that had borne them away from Florida, the people of the settlement, black and white, there in chains below him, the pain from the brass button, which he had been gripping so tightly that it had scored marks in his hand. Before this, the vague and beautiful eyes of the fiddler, his tears, his insolence . . .

He could not believe it still. But as the crowd thinned away, as some moments later he followed Spenton to the carriage that waited to take them back to Wingfield, he thought he heard sounds of fiddle music carried to him on the air.

'Is that the sound of a fiddle?' he said to the coachman, who was hovering nearby, ready to assist him in climbing up.

'Yes, sir,' the man said, 'there is a fiddler come to Thorpe, the first that was ever here, he plays for them at the tavern.'

He sat up late with Spenton, who was in festive mood. Between them they disposed of three bottles of champagne, and though Spenton drank much the most of this, Kemp, abstemious by nature and wary of indiscretion in his dealings with business associates – for this was all that Spenton was to him – felt his head clouded and confused as he made his way to bed, the ghost of the Irish fiddler still with him.

The phantasmic impression of resemblance came back to him in the moments before the fog of sleep descended, stronger, more distinct than before, bearing with it a conviction that owed its power to the superstition of his nature, grown more definite since his meeting with Jane Ashton, a sense of forces and currents that guided human destiny, controls that were arbitrary, accountable to nothing and no one . . . But if it had really been Sullivan, would he not have fled at once? Faced with the renewed threat of the hangman, would he have gone blithely on to the tavern to celebrate the occasion with his music? In the last moments of wakefulness the explanation came to him: the man could not have seen him, he had stood up only at the last moment; Sullivan, if it were he, had already gone past by then; before that, with the people standing packed together and the yard sloping only just enough to allow a view over the court, the people sitting below would probably not have been visible at all to any but those in the front rank.

The question was in his mind, throbbing at his temples along with the effects of the wine, when he rose next morning. It demanded an answer. Spenton, who seemed none the worse for wear, was intending to spend most of the morning closeted with his steward. This left Kemp free for some hours. He was planning to return to the mine to inspect the pumping equipment for use in the event of flooding, and after this – more important now to his mind – to ride over the fields that ran alongside the Dene and examine the lie of the land at the far end, where it opened out towards the sea.

But before he did anything else he was resolved to pay a visit to the alehouse and have a look at this newly arrived fiddler.

30

'He was the only one of them that had the power of sharin',' Sullivan said. 'The sister was grateful an' the others took an interest, but he was the only one that could touch it in his mind. He shared Billy's end, he shared the life we had in the wilderness, the kind of crops we had, the creatures that lived there with us.'

He was standing in the taproom close to Sally – as close as he could get without impeding her – while she restored the tankards, rinsed and dried, to their shelves. 'An' the reason for that,' he said, 'the reason for that sharin', lies in the power of imaginin' a thing that you have niver lived through. It is the power of imaginin' that makes a man stand out, an' it is rarer than you might think, it is similar to the power of music.'

His back was to the yard door, which was open, and it was only when he heard steps that he turned.

'I see you know me,' Kemp said. 'You are Sullivan, the fiddler, are you not?'

It was at this point that the interview, or confrontation rather, rapidly rehearsed by Kemp on his way here, began to deviate from what had been envisaged. Instead of cringing like a guilty man for whom the gallows were waiting, this vagabond raised his head and looked him in the eye, and he was suddenly reminded of the man's habit of seeming to gaze after some lost splendour, glimpsed a moment before, gone before it could be seized. He himself was not that longed-for sight, so much was certain. But whatever the gaze he got, there was no fear in it.

'I am so,' Sullivan said. It seemed to him now that he had always known that his freedom had a term to it, that the Holy

Mother's protection would run out once he had fulfilled his vow, and that this was only reasonable and to be expected. 'You are the one that set the sojers on to us,' he said. 'I niver thought to see you here. Have you come all this weary way just to find me?'

'I did not come to find you, I did not know you were here.' He saw that the woman, who was brown-haired and fresh-faced and ample of form, had drawn closer to Sullivan, and stood beside him now, her shoulder against his. Again he had the sense that this encounter was in some way going awry. He was surprised to feel none of the righteous anger he had expected to feel at having run to earth this fugitive from justice, who should have been hanged and tarred and hung in chains like the others. But of course he had not run the fellow to earth at all; there had been no pursuit, no high quest, it had all been accidental. How could justice triumph by accident, at random? 'What are you doing here?' he said.

'I came to tell Billy Blair's folks what became of the lad. I made a vow to do it if iver I got free, an' the prison gates were opened to me.' There was no thought of flight in his mind – he had nowhere to run to. This man had the power that came from money, he would send people to seize him, as he had done once before. Sally was close beside him, listening to his words, noting his bearing. He would make a good figure in her eyes, even if they were never to rest on him again.

'I made a vow to bring you all to justice and see you hanged,' Kemp said. 'I crossed the Atlantic to do it.' He felt an immediate sharp regret at having said these words. It was as if he had lost all guard on his tongue. To compare his own high purposes with the petty vows of an Irish vagrant! He felt weakened by the admission as though he was seeking to share – a notion abhorrent to him. 'Who is Billy Blair?' he said, not really caring to know.

'He was my shipmate. He was killed by the redcoats you set on to us. He was shot in the back.'

It had the ring of an accusation. Kemp looked at the couple before him for some moments without speaking. She still stood there beside the man, keeping close to him. Sullivan had found the support of a woman, just as he had himself . . . Forgiveness was weakness, it was lack of energy, a dereliction of duty. He remembered again how Sullivan had wept as Matthew lay dying.

An insult at the time, it had seemed to him, grief for the cousin who had done him such wrong. Now a grief he could feel too. Again this sense of sharing, strangely less repugnant now. This was the man who had attended Matthew on his deathbed, almost to the moment of death, the last to show love to him. The button Matthew had held so tightly, had only let fall as he breathed his last . . .

'It was you, wasn't it?' he said. 'It was you who gave my cousin that button?'

'I am not the man to deny that,' Sullivan said. 'It was all I had to give him. It was the last of me buttons that was left.' In the stress of the moment the old grievance came back to him. 'The others were robbed off me aboard the *Liverpool Merchant*. Fourteen years ago now. When I come aboard I was stripped of a good coat on the grounds that it was crawlin' with fleas, which was an outright falsehood. The bosun it was that stole me buttons, though they brought him no luck.'

'This one has brought luck to me,' Kemp said, and only the sense of shared ground, accepted now, could have brought him to make such a confidence. As he uttered the words the truth of them came home to him in a luminously glinting flood. The great possibilities of the mine returned to his mind, the improvements he would make, the rewards of expanding trade and increased profits. It was a worthy enterprise, a noble enterprise, one that a man could give his life to. Spenton would feel the pinch of debt again, he might be persuaded to sell the colliery outright. He would ask Jane to marry him, he would have a fine house built. Together, here in Durham, they would make a new life. There was the Dene, the wonderful discovery of the Dene, a direct route to the sea, only three miles, a loaded wagon on a good road would take less than an hour. He would have wharves constructed, he would have his own barges to take the coal out to the collier ships. No middlemen, no dues, no rights of way to argue about, no problems with labour . . .

He looked again at the man and woman standing there together. In the few minutes since he had entered they had stripped his purpose from him. It had ceased to make any difference to him now what happened to Sullivan, where he went, what became of him. The high mission lay all in the past. It was Sullivan who had made the gift of the button. He had always thought of it as a gift from his cousin, though accidental, but Matthew had merely passed it on. Nothing was accidental, he ought to have known that. The true giver had been the man before him. He dug finger and thumb into his waistcoat pocket, took out the button, held it out on the palm of his hand. 'This is the button, is it not?'

Sullivan took a step forward and lowered his head in scrutiny. 'It is so,' he said. 'It is the selfsame button.' When he looked up it was as if he had glimpsed more closely the glory his eyes always seemed to be seeking. 'How did you come by it?' he asked.

Kemp made no answer to this. He replaced the button and paused a moment, then he said, 'You need have no fear of being apprehended. I shall not report you. I shall say nothing of your presence here. It has been a lucky button for you too, my friend.'

On this, without glancing again at the man on whom he was thus conferring life and liberty, he turned away and walked out of the room.

He took leave of Lord and Lady Spenton, and uttered his thanks, that same evening. Next day, at first light, with no thought in his mind but that he would soon be seeing Jane Ashton, he had his mount made ready and set off for the city of Durham in time to take the morning stage.

31

At about the same time that Erasmus Kemp was making his way to the alehouse for a word or two with the fiddler, a servant of Spenton's was knocking on the door of the Bordon cottage with the message that his master would greatly like to have a word or two with Michael Bordon.

Michael at this time was well into his fourteen-hour shift. The labour was the same as always: with the help of the boy, a thirteen-year-old named Jack, he gathered the coal cut from the face by the hewer, loaded it into the corves, dragged and pushed the sledge with the full corves on it to the foot of the shaft, where they were tallied and hoisted to the surface by the banksmen. But the ceiling was low in the gallery where they were working this morning; he had to keep his head well down and move in a sort of a half-crouch, and he was beginning to feel this in the tendons of his neck and the muscles of his shoulders. It was only when he reached the foot of the shaft that he could stand upright, and it was here that the deputy overman found him and relayed the message.

He had to walk back home, wash in the yard, get into his best suit. He was driven to the house in a two-wheeled carriage. The manservant, who had come from London with Lord Spenton, was supercilious and spoke little to Michael in the course of the journey, though he strove to give the impression that he was fully conversant with his master's wishes and knew the reason for the summons.

Michael had never been to this house before, and a certain awe descended on him as the trap proceeded smartly up the broad driveway and came to a stop before the great stone facade. He was handed over to another servant, conducted to a sitting room and told to wait. He spent a quarter of an hour in company with furniture of a grandness never before seen. There was an imposing table surmounted by a mirror with lamps on either side fixed on a brass rail and drawers below with lions' heads carved on them, each lion with a brass ring through its jaws, by means of which, as he supposed, the drawers could be pulled open. There was a smaller table, for which he could see no need, two easy chairs set facing each other with a stool between them so one could either sit or lie, a settee of a type he could scarcely have imagined, specially designed to fit into a corner of a room. The armchair he sat in was deep, the back and sides were thickly padded, the wings cut off his vision, making him feel strangely enclosed and imprisoned. On the walls were pictures of hills and lakes. The abundance and elaboration and uselessness of the objects in this room made a deep and abiding impression on him.

The servant who had led him here came now to inform him that Lord Spenton was ready to see him. He followed this man down a carpeted corridor, through a small anteroom and then into what he thought must be His Lordship's study, as the walls were lined with books. Spenton was at his desk and without rising waved him to a seat opposite. 'Well, young man,' he said, 'perhaps you would care for a glass of wine?' Without waiting for an answer he spoke to the servant, who had remained at the door, and asked him to bring a bottle of the white and two glasses.

While they waited for this Spenton contemplated his guest in silence for some moments, noting the stiffness of his posture as he sat bolt upright in his chair, turning his cap in his hands. 'I asked you to come here so I could thank you,' he said. 'You played a splendid game yesterday, all who saw you thought so. I was delighted with our win over Pemberton – over Northfield colliery, I mean to say – and I am resolved you shall be our champion again next year.'

Michael uttered thanks for this praise, but the stiffness of his bearing was not relaxed, and Spenton, in an effort to set him more at his ease, began to question him about his family. The intention of kindness was obvious, and Michael was emboldened

by it. He spoke about his parents and his brothers, especially
Percy, the youngest, who was soon to be going down the mine.
'We dinna know how old the lad is, not to the day,' he said. 'The
births are not written nor the deaths neither. So my father says
come mid-August he shall gan doon.'

Spenton nodded. 'Are you walking out with someone?' he
said.

'Yes, sir, Elsie Foster, we are plannin' to wed.'

'You will be getting a barrowman's pay?'

'Two shillin' for shiftin' the stint, sir. It is nay so much to
start a family on, but a'm gannin on for twenty-two, a can hope
to be cuttin' the coal soon, an' then a'll be on six shillin'.'

'You will make your way, I have no doubt of that. But I would
like to help you on a little. I have felt that it would be a fitting
way to mark the occasion of our win yesterday.'

At this point the wine was brought in. The servant waited
for some moments but Spenton dismissed him, rose to pour the
wine himself and brought Michael's glass to him, setting it down
on the small table beside his guest's chair. 'Here's to our victory!'
he said, raising his glass.

Michael drank and found the taste distinctly agreeable – he
had never drunk wine before. He was puzzled by this repetition
of 'our', not really seeing how it could be thought of as Lord
Spenton's victory, though of course His Lordship had always
shown great interest in the handball matches, and seen that the
court was kept up and the lines freshly marked out. He must
mean the colliery too; it was a victory for Thorpe, certainly. Then
a further reason came to him like a shaft of light: everyone he
knew with any pennies to spare had bet on the result; his own
father had put a shilling on him, he knew that for certain; Lord
Spenton and the Colonel would have done the same.

He drank some more wine, settled back in his chair. A bit
more than a shilling, he thought, a canny bit more. The idea,
once lodged, took on the immediate force of conviction. This
was the explanation for all the condescension and affability, there
could be no other. The belief that there had been material gain
on Lord Spenton's part did more to give him self-assurance than
all the words that had gone before.

There was a short silence between them, then Spenton said,

'I would like to show my appreciation of your performance by making you a small gift, no more than a token really, in recognition of the skill and spirit you showed yesterday. I thought that fifty guineas might meet the case.'

It took Michael some moments to follow this ornate phrasing and arrive at the meaning. Fifty guineas! He could barely imagine what so much money would look like if it was all put together – he had never seen coins in a quantity great enough to do more than cover the palm of one hand. Had it not been for the warmth of the wine and the reassuring thought – so reassuring that it had to be true – that Lord Spenton, so powerful and grand, had cause to be grateful, had made money out of him, Michael Bordon, a common pitman, he would never have found the courage even to think what he thought now, let alone say the words that came to him to say to this man at the desk, whose face had lost all expression at his hesitation.

'It is generous in you, sir, more than a could ever have thowt, only for winnin' at the handball. A dinna know if it would be enough . . . Would it be enough to buy the bit of land doon by the beck?'

Taken completely by surprise at this, Spenton raised his head to look more closely at the young man. 'I don't quite follow you, I am afraid,' he said.

On this, clutching his cap, eyes lowered, Michael began to speak about the piece of land down in the Dene that his father had always wanted, always dreamed of having. 'Ever since a was a bairn,' he said, 'before ever a started doon the pit, he would make mention of that bit of land. He never took to the work underground, you see, sir, he never could see nay sense in it.'

How could he explain to this man, who nodded as he listened, who owned thousands of acres, who might for all he knew have as many rooms in his house as there were cottages in Thorpe colliery, how could he explain his father's rages, the mask of sufferance that the years had brought to his face?

'His strength is not what it was,' he said. 'He has been workin' doon the mine, man and boy, for forty year or more. There is nowt else for a man to do in Thorpe.' He raised his eyes to look squarely at his benefactor. 'So much money a would never have thowt to get, never in the world. A dinna know if it would be enough. It is about two acres, measurin' to the bord of the beck, so my father says.'

Land well watered and sheltered from the worst of the weather. His father's idea was to grow vegetables and fruit and take his produce by packhorse to the seaside and sell to folks that were passing. 'A dinna know if it would be enough,' he said again, and fell silent.

Spenton said nothing for some time. He was well disposed towards the young man before him, though this had little to do with the fact that he had won five hundred guineas on the result of the match – it was the winning that mattered to him not the sum. He had noted the bearing of the Thorpe champion, the natural dignity; he admired the athleticism and the fighting spirit he had shown in yesterday's game. But it was something deeper than this that weighed with him now. In every syllable Bordon had uttered there had been love for the father, strong and unashamed, a love that might never have been directly expressed – Spenton knew the taciturn habit of the mining people. He himself had two sons. For the younger he had bought a commission in the Dragoon Guards; the elder, who would one day inherit the estate, had no profession other than that of man-about-town. Sometimes he had paid the tradesmen's bills and on occasion the gambling debts. They were civil to him, but neither of them had ever given him cause to think he was held in any particular affection. Neither of them, really, had ever had to fight for anything, any more than he had himself. He met with money problems from time to time, but these could always be solved in one way or another, they had never obliged him to change his style of life, or even to think of doing so. He rarely went anywhere near the mine, had never been down it. He had his rents, the leaseholders saw to the running. For the first time, listening to Bordon talk of his father, it had occurred to him to wonder what it might be like to toil and hate the toil and never have any freedom from it that was not consumed in weariness.

'It would be enough and to spare if you take the value by acre,' he said. 'Young man, the Dene and all the land surrounding it as far as the coast have been in the possession of my family for a very long time.'

He saw his visitor relax the posture of his shoulders in a

movement that was not a slump exactly, but a kind of drooping. 'No,' he said quickly, 'I am not refusing to sell you the land, but there must be a reversion of ownership after a fixed term, I must retain the right of repossession. Wingfield and all that belongs to it must pass to my son when I am gone, and so it must to his son, in due course. We shall insert a clause defining the term of the leasehold. Shall we say forty years? That should be long enough for your father, eh? At the expiry of that time, the land, the acreage, whatever is done with it or built on it, will be returned to the estate. Would such an arrangement be satisfactory to you?'

Hardly believing the words, after the anticipated refusal, Michael began to stammer his thanks. He felt behind his eyes the threat of tears that would shame him if they came.

Spenton held up his hand. 'It is agreed then. A forty-year lease. Would you like the agreement to be made directly with your father?'

'No, sir, thank you, a would like to surprise him with it.'

'Well, it amounts to the same thing. I shall have the notary brought over from Hartlepool. If you will return here, let us say the day after tomorrow, towards eleven o'clock in the morning, we can have the deed of sale drawn up and signed in proper form.'

32

Michael had to find explanations for the summons to Wingfield and for this second visit and the absence from work it would entail. Lord Spenton was thinking of having sidewalls built on the handball court, he told his father, and this would mean converting to the English game, which was more complicated, as the ball could be bounced from the sidewalls as well as the frontwall, and four players could take part. As this year's colliery champion, he had been asked to enquire into general opinion on the matter and make a report to His Lordship. He was not used to lying and went too much into detail, but his father showed no sign of doubting the matter. In mid-morning on the appointed day he set off to walk the two miles or so of rising ground to Wingfield.

Spenton himself was not present at the meeting. He had left instructions with Roland Bourne, who dictated the terms to the notary. Then, while the copy was being made, the steward quitted the room on other business, leaving Michael and the notary alone together.

For a while there was no sound but the scratching of the pen. Michael sat and waited, still in a state of only half-belief that this was really happening. He had said nothing to anybody about the agreement reached with Lord Spenton, wanting it to come to his father as a complete surprise.

His copying still not quite finished, Bathgate laid down his pen, glanced up, met Michael's eye, glanced away again, cleared his throat with a rasping sound. 'Young man,' he said, 'you have been fortunate, but it is within my power to make you more fortunate yet.'

Taken by surprise at this announcement, Michael made no immediate reply. He saw the notary take up his pen again and heard him say, in the same solemn and measured tones, 'I am one who believes in helping a young person to fulfil his promise. I am prepared to buy this piece of land from you, as a private transaction between us, you understand. I can offer you double the price you have paid. That is to say, double the price recorded here, which is stated as received, but which in fact has not been paid, since no sum of money has actually passed out of your possession. I will give you one hundred guineas, cash in hand.'

'A want to give the land to my father,' Michael said, and once more encountered the gaze of the notary, which had grown steadier and sharper in the making of the offer.

'He will not get much of a living from such a small plot.' Bathgate glanced down at the paper before him. 'Less than three acres. Nothing prevents you from selling. It is leasehold, the period of ownership is stated, the date of reversion is stated, but the document contains no restriction on your right to dispose of the property as you see fit. With a hundred guineas you could quit the mine for good, no more toiling in the dark, sweating your life away. You are a likely fellow, I can see that. You could set up in some business, manufacturing say – there are excellent opportunities in the pottery trade. Or you could set up a shop or buy a share in a slaving venture, that is the thing nowadays, you acquire a share in a cargo of Africans, you buy sugar and rum with the proceeds of the sale, and you make a handsome profit on the London Exchange when your ship returns. You increase your investment on each voyage and in a few years you find yourself a rich man. I have seen it happen to others.'

'A canna sell the land, sir, it is not truly mine.'

'How, not truly yours? We are presently engaged in drawing up a deed that will convey it to you.'

'No, a mean . . . if a had thowt to make a profit from the first, that would be different. Sellin' it now would be like sellin' my own father, it is him that wants it.' He could see no sign of understanding on the notary's face. 'Tha could offer me double again an' a wouldna sell it,' he said more loudly, and in a tone more emphatic.

'I see.' Bathgate lowered his head and resumed his copying, and for some minutes there was again only the scratching of the pen to be heard. Michael had not really believed that the notary was concerned to give him a helping hand. But what came now made him less sure of this. Bathgate finished his task, laid the documents side by side on the desk and said, 'Mr Bourne will take these to Lord Spenton for his signature, then he will return to see you make your mark and to witness the signature. I shall sign as second witness. You will not sell to me, well and good. I made you an offer in the line of business. Let me give you a piece of advice. Sell to nobody, nobody at all. I have reason to think, between you and me, that there is interest in that land, and who has a piece of it, however small, will be likely to profit very considerably.'

'A dinna see what tha means, sir.'

The notary paused again, remembering the arrogant manner of the man who had come to question him. Close questions about rights of access, the title to the line of the shore. Only thoughts of making a way through could lead a man to visit a notary with questions of that kind . . .

'They may be purposing to take the coal that way,' he said. 'Here in the County of Durham who owns the land where the wagons pass can prosper greatly on the wayleave.'

'What is it, a wayleave? Tha means a charge for the passin' of the coal?'

'When it is over private ground, yes. And when it is a question of saving costs for the owner of the mine or the lessees, the charge can be high. I have a client, I do not mention his name, who receives two thousand five hundred pounds a year, without lifting a finger, for a wayleave over Wickley Moor, a pittance of ground scarcely above two hundred yards in extent. Say nothing of this to anyone, if you know what is in your interest. Of course, I may be wrong, time will tell. But if there is benefit, I would rather see it go to a local man than some interloper from London who puts on airs and thinks he is superior.'

Michael uttered his thanks for the information, which he saw was well meant, and promised to keep it in mind. But nothing in the notary's words, whose significance in any case he had not yet fully grasped, caused the slightest wavering in his determination to make a gift of the land to his father. When, some time later, he issued from Wingfield with the deed in his hands, this determination was as strong as ever.

His father had left for work that day at the usual hour. These summer mornings the world was alive with birdsong; there were clumps of meadowsweet in the fields, growing tall where the hedges gave protection.

It was in this season that Bordon experienced the bitterness of servitude most keenly. The promise of the day, the sense of strengthening light, the openness of the countryside around him, everything he saw and felt brought home to him the knowledge of his subjection, the knowledge that he would soon be thrust down into darkness. He minded less in the winter, going from the dark to the dark. But at this time of the year the light was clear as he reached the mine, as he bound his limbs in the loops of rope and took a grip on David and heard the banksman shout that all was clear for the descent. It was the world of light he was leaving; it would be a different light he was drawn up to at the end of his stint, a light that had spent its promise, as he had spent his strength in the hours of hacking out the coal in the cramped space of the seam, with no light but the candle flame for guide.

At the time that his eldest son was listening to the scratch of the notary's pen, about halfway through the shift – though he did not go by any measurement of time, only by the amount of coal he had hewed out – he was on his knees, striking with a short-handled pick at the glinting face of the coal. The putter and his mate were working at his back; they were at a distance from him, dragging the loaded corves along the gallery towards the pit bottom.

He was striking with short, rapid strokes to free the coal from its bedding of slate. The cracking sounds of impact prevented him from hearing the first signals of strain from the timbers overhead, strangely like a man bringing up phlegm from his throat, preparatory to spitting. Had he heard them he would have known what they meant, he would have downed tools and crawled away from the face and might perhaps have saved himself.

By the time he heard the roar of collapse it was too late. The pillar of coal that had been left to support the roof buckled sideways towards him, the heavy timbers and the mass of stone they had held back fell down on him and crushed his back and legs and covered his body.

He was face down, powerless to make the smallest movement. He felt no pain at first, only a paralysing constriction of the chest and a sense of terrible harm done to him. The weight of the rock pinned his body down and kept his face pressed close to the ground, but some chance shift in the fall had spared his head and left a space below his mouth and chin, and so granted him the cruel respite of some minutes more of consciousness and growing pain. Into this bowl his blood dripped heavily. He could hear the splash of it. He could see the shine of the beck. Someone was throwing pebbles into the water, trying to prevent his boat from winning.

33

'There is much to be done,' Erasmus Kemp said, 'but I knew before I set out that would be the case.'

He was where he had so much looked forward to being, the drawing room of Ashton's house, talking to Jane Ashton, telling her about his plans for the mine. Ashton himself was not present, a happy circumstance. 'Time is being wasted there through faulty planning,' he said. 'And money with it – the two things go together.'

He was swept by the wish to lay everything at her feet, all that he had seen and learned during his visit, all his intentions for improvement and profit. She was intensely present as she sat there before him, her eyes, her voice, the form of her body in the loose gown. As always now, whether he was with her or not, thoughts of his mining enterprise and the desire to have her in his arms were inextricably mingled – it was like embracing the future. And she saw the desire for her expressed in his eyes and in the postures of his body and felt a response to it, an excited wish to be joined with him in giving and receiving. He was so fine, with his certainty, his passionate directness of speech, his fiery looks, his mouth so firm and determined. His plans for the mine were homage to her, she knew herself to be necessary to him, powerful in granting and withholding.

He told her about his plans to make more shafts and sink them deeper. A thousand feet you could go down if you got the right people to do the boring. It was easier – and cheaper – to sink shafts than to construct long galleries from the pit bottom, galleries that got longer as more coal was conveyed away from the face. Besides, you saved money on labour, because the carriage of the coal took more time if the galleries were long. The putters were paid by the amount of coal they shifted, but this was not an efficient way of doing things, as they varied in their capacities and much time was lost in dragging the corves along the galleries. He thought it better to pay a fixed daily wage for shifting the hewer's stint, this wage to be reduced if they fell short of their task or left without completing it.

'But won't that mean they will lose money, these putters?' Jane said.

'No, no, nothing of the sort,' Erasmus said smiling. 'No, it means that more coal will be produced at less cost. The putters will still get their wage.'

Jane felt some shadow of uncertainty at this, as it seemed to her that there was a degree of confusion in his words between the amount of coal produced and the welfare of the working people, which was to put things in the wrong order. But he was so eager and so sure, his face was so full of ardour, such doubts seemed grudging and cold. And of course there was so much about it all that she did not yet understand . . .

'I suppose it will make their work less hard,' she said, 'I mean, if the galleries are shorter they won't have so far to drag those heavy sledges with the loaded baskets on them.'

'Exactly.' Erasmus looked at her with a brilliant air of approval for her sagacity. 'You have put your finger on it,' he said. 'Beautiful fingers you have got, and beautiful hands – all of you is beautiful.'

These last words had come out in a rush, totally unpremeditated. Her judgement and her person were closely, intimately blended in his mind, he was increasingly given to plunges of impulse in his talking with her. He saw the colour rise in her face, though she did not look away. He had gone too far, he had embarrassed her, insinuating a knowledge of her beauties that still lay beyond his experience. There was need to retreat . . .

'I have discovered,' he said, 'that in some collieries, but not at present in Durham, they lay metal tracks along the carriageways so that the loaded sledges may pass more easily along. I am intending to introduce this system at Thorpe. It would have great advantages. Metal tracks of that kind would lighten the task of the putters, enabling them to start the work at a younger age, with a great saving in wages.'

Jane's confusion at the compliment, abating now but still present, prevented her from giving these last words the attention she might otherwise have paid them. Later she was to remember them and puzzle over how the task of the putters would thereby be lightened. 'At what age do they begin this labour?' she asked.

'At seven, or such is the practice in Durham.'

'What, they would start dragging those baskets along the tracks at the age of seven?'

'No, no, at first their work is with the trapdoors, opening and closing the doors to keep the workings of the mine properly ventilated. No, they will not have the strength for the corves until they get to nine or ten.'

He paused now for some pleasurable moments; he had been keeping the best of the news for the end. 'Spenton will be back in London the day after tomorrow,' he said. 'I am intending to visit him at his house. There is a proposition I wish to make to him, something that came to me during my visit up there.' He waited for the simple question from her that would authorise him to confide his plans, bestow a blessing on them.

'What is that, is it something new?'

He told her then about his idea of building a road through the Dene, a road straight through to the sea, only three miles – four if you counted the distance from the pithead. The sides of the ravine were steep and wooded, he told her, but below, where the stream ran, the ground was level, there was space enough. Straight through to the sea without impediment. The land where the Dene opened out was marshy, but the roadway could be raised. He would have a harbour built. 'At present,' he said, 'a good deal of the coal is sold locally, there at the pit, to save the cost of transport. The road once made, we can abandon that practice, we can have all of it shipped south to the foundries, where the prices are much higher.'

'So the road would pass over where the stream is now?'

'Yes, the water will have to be dammed up somehow, or

diverted, otherwise it would wear away the foundations of the road. We will have to fell some of the trees so as to give space for the wagons.'

Erasmus paused for a moment, aware of the face before him, the look of serious enquiry on it, so sweet to him. Love gathered in his throat. 'If only you could come and see for yourself,' he said. 'If only we could go together. I want you to see it as I see it, and understand what it will mean to the work of the colliery.'

'How could I?' She smiled at his eagerness. 'We could not travel together or stay together when we arrived there. I suppose you do not see us as fellow guests of Lord Spenton.'

With a sudden movement Erasmus set down the teacup he had been holding. 'Say you will marry me,' he said. He would have knelt before her but the table lay between them. Instead he rose to his feet and stood glowering down at her. 'Say you will marry me,' he said again. 'If you will marry me you will make me live again. Everything I have and everything I am I lay at your feet. I will give up the bank's holdings in the West Indies, if it will please you and your brother. Anything you ask of me I will do, only say you will marry me, say you will be my wife.'

Her smile had faded with his words. In the surprise of it – not the question itself, she had entertained the possibility of his proposing to her, but the haste and violence of the pleading in it – she felt the colour leave her face. She had never thought to be wanted in such a way. Even some pity for him came to her, for the terrible nakedness of his declaration and his promises, some apprehension too, as if, on his feet as he was and with looks so burning, he might move to her, take hold of her, before she could find resolution or words to stay him.

'I cannot decide so quickly,' she said. 'You must give me time, Erasmus. You must give me some days. There is my brother . . .'

'I will speak to him. I will undertake to sever all my connections with the Africa trade. I will declare my support for the abolition of slavery. I will announce it in a form that he and I can agree on together, a form he can use for his purposes, for his cause . . . When can I have your answer?'

'I must think . . . You must give me some days.'

'May I hope, at least?'

The look she gave him was an answer sufficiently eloquent and it was this look, and this hope, that he carried away with him.

34

Ashton returned home early in the evening after a long consultation with his new lawyer, Harvey, the young barrister recommended by Stanton, a convinced abolitionist who had offered his services free in the Evans case. It was Ashton's view now that Horace Stanton's withdrawal from the case – felt at the time as failure of nerve and betrayal on his friend's part – had been on the whole a good thing. This new man was still on the right side of thirty, full of fire and energy, just what was needed. He had entirely supported the decision to prosecute Bolton and Lyons on the original charges of criminal assault and abduction carried out in the attempt to return Evans by force to Jamaica. And he shared Ashton's hope that such an action – never brought before on behalf of a former slave – might result in a judgement that set an absolute prohibition on all private attempts in future to transport anyone without consent out of the Kingdom, which Harvey hoped to show was tantamount to saying that no person, having once set foot in England, could any longer be regarded as the property of another. The date for the hearing had finally been set, and Ashton was intending to inform his sister of this, but she was before him with the news of Kemp's proposal, eager to confront, as soon as she could, what she felt likely to be an unfavourable reception.

Her brother's looks confirmed this suspicion now. He was silent for some moments, then said, 'Well, it has hardly been a protracted courtship. I had no idea that things had reached so far between you.'

It was as if he were accusing her of a haste that was unbecoming. 'He spoke on the spur of the moment,' she said. 'He will be leaving for Durham again before very long. He wanted to have some hope of a favourable reply while he is still here in London.' Did Frederick really think she would keep him informed from day to day of the attraction that had grown, the looks, the tones? She was not herself conscious of any precipitation in the relations between them. It had all begun the evening of her visit to her friend, Anne Sykes, a good while before Frederick had so much as set eyes on Erasmus . . .

'You did not give him an answer then?'

'No, I told him I needed time to consider.'

'Well, my dear Jane, you must consider it well and carefully. Mr Kemp represents many things that you and I dislike and find deplorable, the wrong use he makes of capital invested through his bank, the fortune he has made in the sugar trade – the slave trade, in other words.' He paused a moment, then said sombrely, 'At least, I have always supposed that we share these feelings.'

'He is much more than that,' she said with sudden warmth, recalling the pity she had felt for him, the terrible singleness of purpose that made him undefended. What Frederick said was like comparing a creature with a beating heart to a bloodless abstraction, a bank, an economic system. 'He is changing,' she said. 'He could be guided by someone who understood him and appreciated his talents. He wants to introduce new methods of production, new ways of doing things, he wants to create more wealth so that everyone will benefit. He never wanted to go into the sugar trade, he was forced into it in order to pay his father's debts. He always wanted to build things, to make roads and canals, to construct a better society.'

She broke off, aware of having gone too far in these praises, revealed too much of what she hoped, rather than what she knew. Frederick would not understand in any case; he could not envisage progress except through changes in the law. But improvements could be made by acting directly, fighting abuses where you found them. She had always believed this, it was what had first attracted her to Erasmus, his combativeness, his readiness to enter the lists and charge at things and make them better. She would be able to help him in this, if she so chose . . . 'He is ready to do anything,' she said. 'He will withdraw completely from the Africa trade, he will dissociate himself entirely from it, cut off all the ties of business that unite him to it.'

'What, he has said this?'

'Yes, he said so to me.'

'Would he be willing to make a public statement to that effect, declare a change of heart, come out as an opponent of the slave trade?'

'Yes,' Jane said, and felt a familiar dismay at this new tone, this alerted, sharp-eyed face that was her brother's now. 'Yes, so he declared to me,' she said.

'Well, that makes all the difference,' Ashton said. 'It would be an earnest of his good faith.'

She could not see that it made any difference at all, not to the desirability of the marriage, not to her prospects of happiness. But she knew, with a hurt that had also grown familiar, that these were matters of secondary importance to him. 'It would be an earnest of his desire to marry me, so much is true,' she said. 'And of his desire to disarm your enmity,' she added after a moment.

But he was too much taken up with thoughts of the use that could be made of such a declaration to pay much heed to this. 'It is exactly what I wanted from him.'

'Yes, you wanted me to ask it as a favour. You will remember that we disagreed about it.'

'Well, for all practical purposes it comes to the same thing. What did you say to him? Did you accept this offer of his?'

'I said nothing at the time, I was in some confusion. But if I had replied it would have been to say that I think he should only make such a statement if he really means it, if it is truly a change of heart and not just a form of words designed to please me.' Or worse still, she thought, an offer of exchange, a form of bargaining such as one might use in the marketplace. But would there be, for Erasmus, any discernible difference? She had been pleased by the offer, by the air of sacrifice he gave it, pleased and flattered. But was it so great a sacrifice? All his interest now lay in the coal industry . . . She felt a sudden lurch of uncertainty, a fraying of safe moorings.

'You and I are very different in the way we look at things,' Ashton said, 'and it has taken the advent of Mr Kemp to make this difference clearer – I think to both of us. I see it matters to you what his motives are but it has no importance for me. Motives are a labyrinth we need not enter. All that matters is the use that can be made of his words. Every year ships leave our ports and ports all over Europe, bound for the West Coast of Africa. Hundreds of ships. Every year scores of thousands of innocent human beings are taken by violence from their homes to be worked to death on the plantations. If Kemp's words can make any contribution, however slight, to the movement to end this infamous traffic, what can it matter whether they are uttered to please you, or because he means them, or for some other reason?'

'It is not the same thing,' Jane said. 'Abolition is a noble cause, I do not deny it, but the numbers are very great, you are not involved in close relations with anyone in particular, whereas it is very necessary for any couple who think of marrying to have respect for each other, and that must include a regard for the truth of the other person and the honesty of his motives.'

But he scarcely listened, his own words had impassioned him. 'We have a date set now,' he said, 'a date for the hearing concerning the condition of Jeremy Evans, whether slave or free. We may get a verdict that will change the face of the law, abolish for ever the right of property in another person, in England at least. That is the purpose, we believe it is noble. We may have ulterior motives but what end would it serve for us to examine into them?'

'But there would be no need to do so. Your motive and your purpose are one and the same thing.'

'And so it is, I suppose, with Mr Kemp.'

With a sense of falling back on to safe ground, Jane strove to infuse her voice with firmness, and said, 'If Erasmus, or anyone, makes a declaration in order to serve his ends rather than serve the truth, that is wrong and will always be so, no matter what use is made of the words or how noble the cause.' But suppose Erasmus thought that serving his ends *was* serving the truth, suppose he saw no difference. It seemed possible from her knowledge of him . . .

35

When Kemp thought afterwards about his conversation with Lord Spenton, and went over in his mind the words exchanged between them, what struck him as least supportable was the way in which he was allowed to go on at such length and enter into such detail about his idea for a road through the Dene, before Spenton raised a hand in languid fashion – rather in the manner of one requesting less volume of sound – to announce that a piece of the Dene was no longer in his ownership.

'Not for the next forty years at least,' he said, and Kemp, in the midst of his consternation, saw that he looked quite unperturbed as he spoke – there was even a slight smile on his face.

'How can that be?'

He listened, staring straight ahead, while Spenton explained how it had come to pass that Michael Bordon was now the owner of a piece of land adjoining the stream, about halfway through the Dene. It was a saga, as he related it: the offer of reward, the young man's very affecting wish to acquire the land for his father with the money, and then, following hard upon this, the father's death in an accident at the pit. 'He was dead when they got to him,' he said. 'It seems that he was killed outright by the fall. Even if they had reached him sooner it would have been to no avail.'

But Kemp had no thought to spare for this obscure and irrelevant death. 'You sold the land without so much as consulting me, the lessee?' There was fury in his face and his voice. The agreements for the lease had been drawn up and signed, he was no longer Spenton's guest, there was no need now to countenance the man's follies. 'You have done a most ill-considered thing, sir,' he said. 'And for the idlest of reasons.'

Spenton's face did not change, but his voice was colder when he answered. 'I suppose you do not think I should refer to you for my reasons? They seemed sufficient to me. The Dene does not form part of the mine. You are not thinking clearly, Kemp. How on earth was I to know that you had this plan in mind? You chose not to broach the subject while you were staying with me. Do you think I am a mind-reader?'

There was justice in this, he was compelled to recognise; the caution that had kept him silent had been needless, due only to inveterate habit. But the knowledge did nothing to lessen the rage he was labouring under. Spenton's smile had deepened with this last question; it seemed that in some outrageous and incomprehensible way he was finding the situation humorous. And not only that: it was clear that his sympathies lay with this miserable pitman, rather than his partner in business. 'There is no great harm done,' he said now.

'What can you mean? There is no other route than the bed of the stream. The land ends in cliffs on either side. The slopes of the ravine are too steep, we could not build a road that would be safe from slipping under such heavy loads.'

'The young man is far from stupid. No doubt you will be able to reach some settlement with him. It will involve you in expenses of course, but that is no great objection, as far as I can see.'

There had been a note of contempt in this, quite undisguised, and Kemp knew as he got up to leave that Spenton too saw no further need for conciliation between them, knew that just as he resented the nobleman for the privilege that surrounded him, for his air of immunity to the common struggle, so Spenton disliked him for the fact that he had been through that struggle and acquired wealth from it – wealth in the form of capital, not land. The nonchalance of manner was a form of hostility, expressing disdain for the mercantile class Kemp knew himself to represent, which grew always richer, always more threatening to the power and influence of the landed gentry. 'At least you will have no great objection, as far as I can see,' he said, repeating the other's words with deliberate sarcasm, 'to the road being built, provided of course that the costs are met by the lessee.'

'None at all, my dear sir, good heavens, no,' Spenton said, and Kemp detected in his voice and look the complacent knowledge that profits deriving from the road would continue to accrue long after the lease had run out. He had considered the matter after all, without appearing to. He was far from indifferent to his own interests, despite the assumption of vagueness. This was the knowledge that Kemp bore away from the interview, a certain sense of duplicity on Spenton's part, together with the conviction that the dislike thus revealed between them would prove to be lasting.

He would have to return to Durham sooner than he had intended, more or less immediately in fact, and endeavour to come to terms with this Michael Bordon, if possible buy him out. He would stay at an inn somewhere within a few miles, he would go nowhere near Wingfield. But he had to see Jane before leaving. The need for her to know at once of this new development was urgent with him; without this, without her blessing on the enterprise, he would be weaker. On arriving home again he at once sent Hudson with a note asking if he might be allowed some minutes of her company, and obtained an appointment for that afternoon. She had paid – as always when she knew she was to see him – particular attention to the details of her appearance, and Kemp was smitten anew by the radiant pallor of her face, the beauty of her eyes and brows, the alluring grace of her movements in the lilac-coloured taffeta gown, close-fitting at the waist and hips, as was then becoming fashionable.

'He has never shown any real interest in the running of the mine,' he said. 'In all the time I have known him he has never shown much interest in anything but sopranos and waterworks and clockwork toys and handball.'

It smarted still that Spenton should have waited so long, sported with him, before coming out with the fact that a piece of the Dene had been bought. Kemp had begun with this news, wanting her to know at once the blow to his plans. 'Buffooneries of that sort,' he said with contempt. 'I shall have to return to Durham as soon as possible. This Michael Bordon is young and illiterate, he has never known anything but labouring in a pit.

He may not realise the value of the land he has bought. If I can get to him in time I may be able to prevail upon him to sell at a reasonable price.'

'But I understand that he bought the land as a gift for his father, to free him from the mine. This being so, he is not likely to sell it, surely – it would be like a kind of betrayal, wouldn't it, changing his mind like that and taking money instead?'

'No, I forgot to tell you, the father is dead. I thought at first that the deed was in his name and that it might be possible to have it annulled with his death, but unfortunately it is made out to the son.'

'Forgot to tell me?' Jane looked closely at him as if there might be something in his expression, some quality of sympathy or regret not evident in his words. But she could see nothing of the sort there, only the look she had always found so compelling, the dark, level brows, the eyes brilliant, full of light, the mouth firm-set as if there was something to be resisted or endured, but not mean or ungenerous. It was the look that came to her mind when she thought of being with him, sharing his life. 'But it is the most important thing of all,' she said. 'He will want to keep the pact, keep faith with his father. He will want to fulfil his father's wishes for the land by cultivating it himself, growing the things his father wanted to grow. He would be right to do that, surely?'

Her face was alight with approval for such a course, the love and duty it would show. 'How fine it would be,' she said, and saw a smile appear on his face of the kind she had seen on other men's faces when she had gone so far as to express enthusiasm for some cause or idea thought to be eccentric, a smile of indulgence for sentiments that only ignorance of the world could account for.

'Do you really think that will weigh so strongly with him? He has never seen more than a few shillings at any one time. I know these people, the immediate gain is everything to them. I will make him a good offer, be assured that he will not resist for long.'

Despite the smile with which he accompanied these words, he felt disappointed at the way the conversation was going. She was not seeing things in a way that accorded with the realities of the situation; she was failing to put his interests first when they were so much more important, so much larger in scale. 'No,' he said, 'a lump of money in the pocket will always count for more with them. He will not choose to spend the rest of his life labouring on two or three acres of ground if he is offered a capital sum that would rescue him from the mine for good.'

'So if you were in his place you would sell out?'

'If I were in his place?' The question was misguided. How could he be in the place of someone who toiled his life away underground for a mere pittance? 'I would weigh up the alternatives and choose the one most reasonable,' he said. It might be that Bordon still did not know that this was to hold on to the land and wait for the road to be built, so as to levy charges for the passage of the coal. He might have time enough yet to persuade Bordon to sell before the potential income from the wayleave became known to him. But he said nothing of this to Jane, who might think it was unfair – she was completely unversed in matters of business. It was the first time he had held something back from her regarding his plans for the mine, and he felt a certain desolation at it.

'After all,' he said, 'the father is no more, why should his wishes matter so much? Compared with the building of the road, I mean. We have to try to improve the world in the way that seems best to us. The road will change the whole working of the pit; in the end the whole community will benefit from it.'

He had thought to regain her sympathy with these words, knowing her belief in direct action – a belief he shared. But she was still regarding him more narrowly than he liked, with a look in her eyes he had never seen there before, a look not so much of disagreeing as of adversely judging, which was worse. She had allowed herself to get caught up in this sentimental notion of honouring the father's wishes, against all rational arguments of self-interest . . . 'You have a tender heart,' he said. 'I am aware of it. I know the value of it.'

'Erasmus,' she said, and there was suddenly a note of patience in her voice, almost as if she were talking to someone of less than ready understanding, 'you have told me of your feelings when your father died, and how you gave years and sacrificed your ambitions in order to pay the debts he left and clear his name. Was not this due to the love you bore him, the sense you had of a pact, of a vow? Did his motives and purposes not matter any longer to you because he had died?' Again she scanned his face. Surely he must see the similarity, the closeness of the connection . . .

'The debts were real,' he said. 'Debts are not motives, they are not wishes. I did not build a shrine to my father, which is what Bordon would be doing if he made that piece of land into a garden.'

As he spoke, and during the silence that followed his words, there came to his mind a memory like a throb of pain. So many years ago now, kneeling at his bedside in the loneliness of his room, in the immediate aftermath of his father's death, he had made his vow to God and to his most cherished possession, the brace of duelling pistols hanging on the wall. He had wanted to say the words aloud, but his mouth and throat were too dry for more than a whisper. *Every penny* . . .

'It is true that I made a promise to him,' he said, and Jane saw his eyes lose their fixity of expression, and the line of his mouth slacken and grow softer. 'I made a vow to restore his good name. But it wasn't only the money . . .' He hesitated a moment then plunged into words never before uttered to a living soul. 'My father took his own life, though we managed to get it brought in as a death due to natural causes. He hanged himself because of his losses, the disgrace of it.'

He had come to a position of attention, hands by his sides, as if only thus braced could he bring out the words. 'He hanged himself in the dark,' he said. 'It was I that found him hanging there. I should have known it, I should have seen it. We were together a great deal. I was not a child, I was twenty-one years of age. Someone else would have seen it. I was too much occupied with myself. We might have talked together, shared the burden. But I left him to die alone. It has always been in my mind that I left him to die alone, in the dark. I understand now, as I did not then, that it was this that I was promising to make up for, this that I was vowing to put right. I have never put it right. I paid the debts, I made money in the sugar trade and then through the bank, but I have not kept my vow.'

For some moments, deeply moved by these words and

distressed at his visible suffering in pronouncing them, Jane remained silent, not sure she could trust to her voice. Then, with a conscious effort of control, she said, 'You have kept it, in the only way it could be kept.' Hardly a failure at all, she thought. Only someone so dedicated to success as Erasmus could have thought it so, kept the wound open for so long. He had been young, two years younger than she herself was now, and probably not much accustomed to looking for feelings and thoughts that lay below the surface. His father would have taken care to conceal the signs of his despair; no one would advertise such an intention unless wishing to be prevented from carrying it out. 'You have kept your vow,' she said again. 'In what you have just said to me, in what it cost you to say it.'

He saw a look on her face that seemed like pity for him – intolerable in anyone else, sweet in her, like a balm to him, a sort of forgiveness. He could not know, as he stood there and felt the love for her gather in him, how far his confession – made to no one else – had been to ease his heart with a truth finally acknowledged, finally released from the prison of his need to think well of himself, and how far it had been to regain Jane's good graces, which he had feared he might be losing through her failure to understand the importance of this road through the Dene as against a few cartloads of cabbages and turnips and potatoes . . .

The compassion, however, the softening of her feelings, was plain to see. It was in her face and in her voice. It might be propitious for him. 'Have you thought more about my proposal?' he said. 'I shall have to leave for Durham again very soon. Can I hope for an answer before I go?'

'I will write to you. You will find my letter on your return.'

'Think kindly of me. You are at the centre of everything I wish for. You are my guiding star.'

36

The barrister for the plaintiff in the Evans case, Harvey, had been joined now by a serjeant-at-law named Compton, who, while not active in the abolitionist movement, was convinced of the evils of slavery and indignant at the mistreatment of Evans. Like Harvey, he was at an early stage in his career and eager to prosecute a case that might set an important precedent. He was a tall, bony man with a prominent jaw and narrow eyes, tenacious in argument, not easily daunted.

After various delays and postponements the Lord Chief Justice had finally decided to refer the case of Jeremy Evans to the Court of King's Bench, a decision which had surprised Ashton and given him renewed hope of a favourable outcome. A formal hearing before the King's Bench obliged the presiding judge to give a decisive opinion. Soon after receiving news of it he and the two lawyers came together at Compton's chambers at Gray's Inn to discuss matters and plan a strategy.

'He has committed himself to a definite judgement, he cannot escape it now,' Ashton said. 'Perhaps he has had a change of heart.'

'That I greatly doubt,' Compton said. 'Unless we are entering upon a new age of miracles. He has more than once expressed the hope that the issue of whether blacks can lawfully be returned by force to the plantations will never finally be settled. It is an ugly matter for him. A good deal of his acquaintance benefits by the trade and will not enjoy any threat to what they regard as their rights, either in the West Indies or here in England.'

Harvey nodded. He was portly for so young a man and

high-coloured, with a habit of lowering his head at hostile witnesses in court and glancing up threateningly, as if about to charge them. 'All the same,' he said, 'I think Ashton is right, he cannot avoid a judgement. Strictly speaking, the condition of Evans is still that of a slave. He ran away from his master, he has not been manumitted. So the issue is very clear.'

'He might try to evade the issue by declaring Evans to be free,' Ashton said. 'On the grounds that the condition of slavery has been interrupted, and so broken and annulled by his three years as a free man.'

'Too dangerous a precedent, considering the number of runaways in London,' Compton said. 'It will suit our case better if there is no doubt of his condition. We will have him declared free by the ruling of the court, not by some convenient argument beforehand.'

'If we have any doubts as to where His Lordship's sympathies lie,' Harvey said, 'we only need look at the costs he has laid on Evans.' Like the others, he had been taken aback and angered by this mark of the judge's bias, the placing of Evans under heavy financial penalties should he fail to appear, a manifest wrong, since Evans was the plaintiff in the case, the one seeking redress for injury. 'It is the defendants, this precious couple Bolton and Lyons, who should have had sureties laid upon them, but there is nothing of the sort, they have been excused all obligation. If things go against them they can have the case withdrawn merely by relinquishing their claim to the ownership of Evans's person.'

'They will not do so, however,' Ashton said.

'What makes you so sure? In this way they suffer no consequences. They can withdraw their claim with impunity at any time they choose. I suspect that this is what the Lord Chief Justice hopes will be the outcome, leaving the issue comfortably unsettled.'

'You may be right in that. But I am sure they will not withdraw. They will go through with it to the end. To withdraw would be to relinquish right of ownership in Evans, and by extension all right of ownership in former slaves brought to this country who have severed the relation by taking flight. This case has been dragging on for months now and in that time it has become a vital issue of rights. For them it is a question of fundamental principle. Evans has been purchased; to deny their right in him seems to them like a violation of the laws relating to property, an aggravated form of robbery.'

This confidence was still unshaken when the day of the hearing arrived. He was confident too in the strength of their case. They had the affidavits of two persons who had witnessed the seizure of Evans, and that of the officer who had presented the writ and obtained his release from the ship, where he had been chained to the mast.

Harvey opened the case for the plaintiff before the Lord Chief Justice, who was assisted by Justices Lewis and Stewart, one on either side. He pointed out that the feudal system of serfdom, where people were attached to property, was the only precedent that could be thought applicable to slavery on British soil, though the connection was extremely remote and the practice had been extinct for several centuries.

'Where are the serfs, My Lord?' he said. 'Where are the inhabitants of this country who are to be regarded as chattels? Is it not the case that everyone residing in this country becomes de facto a subject of His Royal Majesty, King George? Subject to the King, My Lord, not to any other person dwelling in this dear land of ours. As subject to the King, is he not therefore subject to the laws that obtain in the King's realm? British laws, time-honoured, refined by a long course of previous judgements. Not the trumped-up laws of Virginia or Jamaica. Where in our law do we find any sanctioning of the institution of slavery? Will the defence claim that colonial legislation regarding slavery can have any force or relevance here? If they will maintain this, let them stand to the question: why should not *all* such legislation be valid here, will they tell us where we are to draw the line?'

He was followed by Compton, who reasserted these arguments and expanded on the danger to public order if attempts were made to apply colonial practice to the laws governing land title and voting rights and matrimony and the relation between servant and master in England. 'To enlarge upon this by means of example,' he said, 'and to give it a more general, I venture to say universal application, let us suppose that a gentleman from Zululand were to settle here in our midst. He is a Zulu, My Lord; in his country the law permits polygamy. Would we countenance this man parading here and there and round about with a number of wives in tow, perhaps among them some of our own country-women reduced to concubines, on the patently absurd grounds that such is the law in Zululand?'

At this point the Chief Justice, irritated by this reference to Zulus and wearied already by what he felt to be the undue prolixity of the advocates, announced that, since the case promised to be protracted, and the energy and acumen of the court would certainly be needed in high measure, he proposed to adjourn the hearing until the following Monday.

37

Erasmus Kemp arrived in Durham on the day after the adjournment of the Evans hearing. He found accommodation in a small town named Sedgeton some three miles from the right bank of the River Wear. The inn was not particularly comfortable, but it was conveniently close to the colliery village of Thorpe.

On the day of his arrival, in the evening, he rode over, accompanied by a stable boy from the inn, with whom he left his horse. He found the Bordon cottage and enquired for Michael. He was told by a woman he supposed to be the mother that Michael was keeping company with Elsie Foster, who lived six doors away on the same street.

It was Elsie who opened the door to him. She and Michael had been sitting together in the small parlour. Alone together, Kemp noted. This must mean that they were affianced, intending to marry. Perhaps there was an advantage to be gained from this.

He had not seen Michael Bordon since the day of the handball game, and they had exchanged no words then, as Michael had been carried off in triumph by the Thorpe men. Now he was surprised by the frankness of the young man's regard. The blue eyes that met his own held more of curiosity than friendliness, but there was no hint of constraint, no sign of being flustered at such a visit. It was a look that made Kemp suspect that difficulties might lie ahead. Of course, he thought, the fellow is on his home ground. The first thing was to get him detached from this, on his own, without any comforting sense of being supported or reinforced . . .

'I am eager to have a few words with you,' he said. 'Is there somewhere we can talk alone?'

This at first proved something of a problem. Kemp did not want to conduct the conversation in Elsie's home or in Michael's. The houses were small, there would be people coming and going, perhaps even some who would be ready with opinion or advice, unasked for but vouchsafed nevertheless. He did not want to walk and talk in the open, because he again had the sense that the young man might find some stiffening of resolution in surroundings he knew well. The same objection applied to the alehouse, and besides he did not want to set eyes again on Sullivan, in whom he felt he had confided too much already. He wanted Michael Bordon within four walls, on his own, with no possibility of interruption and no prospect of an alliance.

The solution was found by Michael himself. He had a key to the small shed behind the handball court, where the players kept their shoes and spare clothes for the practice games. There was no one there now, to the best of his knowledge. Together the two men made their way there.

The roof was low, there was just room enough to stand upright, and both men were tall. Less accustomed than the other to physical restriction, Kemp felt the oppression of this, inclining him to fear collision, duck his head. But there was a narrow wooden bench against one wall and they sat on this, no more than a yard apart, only able to look each other in the face by a deliberate turning to the side, which Kemp felt at first to be something of a snag, as it would allow the young man to face away from him, find relief from the stresses of doubt and temptation that he was sure the offer of money would cause. But in the event Bordon proved in no way reluctant to meet his gaze, even eager and ready to do so, with the same open and lively regard he had shown earlier.

'I have come to make you an offer for the piece of land you have acquired in the Dene,' Kemp said. 'I am ready to pay you two hundred and fifty pounds for it.'

'That is much more than the land is worth, takin' it by the acre. Tha must have good reason for wantin' it.'

The frankness and immediacy of this took Kemp by surprise. There had not been much room for sporting activities in his life and he could not know that this swiftness of response was in the nature of taking the ball on a rising bounce, nor that this shed, so carefully chosen as neutral ground, would turn out to be a meeting place of considerable disadvantage to him.

'Two hundred and fifty pounds is a lot of money,' he said. 'I wonder if you realise how much. It is easily enough to establish you in some independent business on your own, or if you thought of investing it I could arrange through my bank for you to realise a good return on the money. Two hundred and fifty pounds, invested wisely, could bring you seven shillings a week. When you marry and start a family that would be a great resource to you, coming in addition to your wages.'

'There must be more to it than that. Tha canna be only wantin' to do me a favour.'

'The Dene is a place of great natural beauty,' Kemp said. Things were not going as he had expected. The offer of money had brought no change in the young man's face or manner. 'It should be kept as a whole, not divided up into small holdings. All the character would be gone.'

Michael looked for some moments in silence at the stranger sitting so close to him, who had been a guest of Lord Spenton's, who had been seen riding round the place, asking questions, looking at everything. Since he had first started playing handball, eight years ago now, he had waited quite often in this shed with the one who was shortly to be his opponent on the court, and some strain of antagonism had developed in these moments of waiting, a period of mutual assessment, of firm intention to win, to prevail. He recognised the feeling now, it was the same; they had come to the shed to meet as opponents, one to win and one to lose . . .

'Tha's off'rin' me two hunnerd an' fifty pound so the Dene can keep its character?' he said.

'Well, there is more to it than that. I have learned that you bought the land out of care for your father. I was sorry indeed to hear of the accident that befell him, you have my deepest condolences. Obviously, he cannot now fulfil the ambition of making a garden there. Not to be able to make him this gift must have been a great blow to you and aggravated the loss, and this consideration has influenced me in making the offer, which I feel to be not excessive at all but just and appropriate under the circumstances.'

'How does tha know so much? Tha must be him that wants to make the road through. He said there was someone.'

'Who was it said that?'

'The notary, Mr Bathgate, when he came to make out the deed of sale.'

'I see, yes.' He had been too high-handed with Bathgate, he had realised it at the time, but too late; aided by enmity and no doubt by native shrewdness, the rogue had sniffed him out . . . 'I had formed such an idea, yes,' he said. 'I will make it three hundred and fifty pounds, immediate cash.'

The two regarded each other closely for some moments. The words of condolence, rendered meaningless – as it seemed to him – by the swift jumping-up of the price, had gone down badly with Michael, who was in grief for his father, not long since buried. A faint smell of hyacinths came from the other's person, scent of some kind. He was in riding clothes, obviously expensive, high-collared frock coat, jackboots and spurs; a tall hat rested on his knees as he sat there; the cravat looked like silk, the pin in it looked like silver. His clothes, Michael estimated, would have cost more than he himself could earn in a year's work down the mine. He owned a bank, as it seemed, he would have a grand house. And yet he sits there, Michael thought, offering sums that are nothing to him, trying to whittle away my chances. He belongs among those who killed my father and others besides, out of greed, whittling away at the pillars of coal until they are not strong enough to hold up the roof.

'He told me I should sell to naybody,' he said.

'He gave you bad advice. How long will you have to work on that bit of land, and plant and sow and cart your produce to where you can sell it, how long before you have three hundred and fifty pounds in your pocket?'

'Tha talks as if them was the only choices,' Michael said, and there was a note of anger now in his voice though he still spoke quietly. 'But tha knows full well there is another way.'

He paused on this, thinking of his wealth of choices, knowing already which choice would be his. Choice was wealth. He remembered the sitting room at Wingfield, where he had waited for Lord Spenton to see him. The furniture came back to his mind, the objects in the room, the lions' heads on the drawers, the several chairs, the divan that fitted into a corner, the numerous pictures on the walls. Choice was having things you didn't need but wanted to have, the silk cravat, the silver pin; choice gave you freedom from need. His father had laboured all his life to escape from this cage of need, he himself had been imprisoned in it from the age of seven. And now this man was striving to keep him caged.

'Tha was hopin' a didna know,' he said. 'Tha was thinkin' to take me for a fool. A will not work on the land an' a will not sell it, not to you, not to naybody. Them that use the road will pay for passage as long as they gan on bringin' out the coal. Me an' my fam'ly will have a share in the money that's made from it. Why should you have it all? That's what my father would have wanted for us, that's what he would have said if he'd been standin' here today.'

In the face of these words and the look that accompanied them, Kemp found little to say. He was intending to point out, as he got to his feet, that there could in the nature of things be no certainty as to what the father would have wanted or what he would have said; there was only one certainty in the matter, which was that those interpreting the wishes of the dead would study their own advantage and convenience.

These sage remarks, delivered with the authority of his greater age and wider experience, might have gone some way to lessen the sting of his defeat, the bitter knowledge that this miner he had thought so ignorant had proved him wrong, worsted him, shown him up, and all without even raising his voice. But as he hesitated on the brink of speech, some delayed and changed reaction to Bordon's last words came to him. He looked again, more closely now, at the young man's face, and as he did so, as he met the other's clear and determined gaze, he was pierced suddenly and unexpectedly by a feeling of fellowship completely new to him, an emotion like an ambush, something lying in wait for just such an unwary moment. He had resisted the comparison when Jane made it. Debts are not wishes, he had said. But they were, they were – he had been wrong.

It was himself that he was looking at, not an adversary, not someone to be outwitted, but the young man he had been fourteen years before, when he had lost his own father at much the same age. The ambitions were his own, the need to repair things, to refashion the world after such loss. But the man before him did not see debts to pay; he sought to make his father the giver of blessings, the giver of freedom from drudgery and want. Of course, there was self-interest in it – no human motive was free from this in Kemp's view – but there was much more besides, so much more . . . He felt a tightness in his throat as he held out a hand to the other and felt it, after some hesitation, grasped and held, though briefly. 'Good luck to you, Michael Bordon,' he said. 'You have been in the right today.' And as he spoke it was strangely as if, in spite of the reluctance to take his hand, in spite of his own lingering sense of defeat, the congratulation was for them both.

There was no other form of farewell between them. As Kemp rode back to the inn, the sense of kinship faded, the sting of the defeat returned and with it the knowledge of financial loss. In the light of what he knew now about Michael Bordon it was highly unlikely that the young man could be beguiled into accepting anything less than the standard rate for a wayleave of such a kind. Jane too had been wrong about the young man, he thought, but somehow she had come closer to the truth of things than he had. It was the kind of distinction he was not used to making, and he puzzled over it for a while without coming to any definite conclusion. But when they met he would tell her how things had gone, he would not conceal anything, he would confess the sympathy that had taken him so unawares. Sympathy for an opponent, and one, moreover, who had defeated him, an emotion deep enough almost to bring tears. She would be pleased to hear of this rush of feeling on his part. In fact, he was already feeling slightly ashamed of the display; it could not be regarded as anything but weakness to allow feeling to obscure your objectives; there might have been further arguments that could never now be put forward. He would say nothing of this to Jane, however . . . He had not so far told her of his interview with Sullivan, but he would do so when he saw her, he would tell her how he had been compelled by that runaway into a sense of sharing, still not fully accepted or understood . . .

Should he mention the brass button? To do so would cast him in the role of beneficiary; he had been left in possession of the token and the gifts of fortune it had brought. It was as the granter of pardon, the dispenser of mercy, that he wanted her to see him. He had forgiven Sullivan, or so he felt now; it was in this light that he would relate the matter. She would approve, she would think it high-minded, he would gain merit in her eyes. Sullivan had not forgiven *him*, in the slightest degree, any more than Michael Bordon had, but there was no need to dwell on this. Instead, he would tell her of the words overheard as he approached the open door of the alehouse, the only ones he could afterwards recall. *It is the power of imagining that makes a man stand out.*

She had that power in full measure. She had said something not much different when they had last talked together and he had seen the compassion for him on her face. Probably a faculty more common among women than among men, he thought – they had more leisure. He saw it as a sort of task, an effort of the will, requiring concentration. A man with important aims in life would be too much occupied for it. Pike too had spoken of the power of imagination, he suddenly remembered. Disapproval of the lawyer had prevented him from giving much weight to the words . . . By reporting that vagabond's remark and giving it some stamp of his own assent and sympathy, he would please Jane, he felt sure of that. And he wanted, before all else, to please her. All the same, it was odd, he thought, extremely so, that an itinerant fiddler, a person of no substance and no standing, a fugitive from the gallows, should have the last word.

38

In the silence of her apartment, seated at the small writing desk, Jane Ashton strove to compose the promised letter, the main labour of which lay in the effort to understand herself.

There were things about Erasmus Kemp that she could not admire. The way he set the achievement of his aims on the same, unqualified, identical plane of success, whatever their nature, the way he neglected to consider the cost to others. However, she felt that she understood these things better now, after their last talk together. Something of the compassion she had felt for him on that occasion returned to her mind. He was endlessly seeking to fulfil the vow he had made to his father, as if in the end his successes would leave no room for any sense of inadequacy or guilt. Like trying to fill a pit with gold, not knowing that the pit was bottomless . . . Or was she simply trying to find excuses for this lack of care he showed, this overriding devotion to his own purposes? Finding excuses for him was easy, he was attractive to her in a way no other man had ever been; she was stirred by the thought of lovemaking between them, his imagined touch upon her. His desire was so strong, so evident in his looks and behaviour. Sometimes she had found it hard to meet his eyes, fierce with need in that dark-complexioned face. He was relentless . . .

It came to her, in this room where she had thought so much about him from the very first, where from girlhood she had tried to understand life and the world and her place in things, where she had thrilled to Gray's Pindaric odes and wrestled with Hume and Voltaire, that perhaps it was this, the relentlessness, something merciless in him, that attracted her so. She reviewed all she knew of him, what she had sensed and what he had told her, the wishes, the ambitions. His life had been a series of aims imposed on himself. Was she no more than this, something to achieve and possess and then lay indifferently aside among the other trophies? Like the mission of justice that had taken him in pursuit of the survivors of the *Liverpool Merchant*, like this Durham coalmine that he would take over and then perhaps lose interest in and relinquish.

No, she did not believe he would let the mine go; he had found something to devote himself to. He wanted to improve things, bring more efficiency, reduce the harshness of the labour. Was not this a desire to improve the lot of his fellow men? Even if he himself did not altogether regard it in this light, or at least refer to it in this; way, was not this perhaps what underlay his ambitions, the desire to be a benefactor? Profit, efficiency, material improvement, was not this the way forward? She had always believed in measures that would bring more independence, more well-being to those that were deprived, whose lives were all toil, who were ignorant and kept in ignorance and helpless because of it, always at the mercy of those richer and more powerful.

She could help him in this; it was something she had always dreamed of, practical measures, practical solutions, looking to see what could be done. The boys went to work in the mine at seven years of age! It was appalling, they were children still, they were not grown, their bones were not properly formed. For children to be racked with toil and have no remedy, it cried out for betterment. She could speak of it to Erasmus if they were married, she could prevail upon him to see things with more tenderness. For love of her – and she could not doubt the love – he would be prepared to change. For her sake, for what he would see as the sake of her happiness . . . Guided by her, he would come to see what was due, what was just – not the justice of the courts, but the justice of human dealings, where the quality of mercy entered more closely and decisively. She could press for the setting up of a school; it was an ambition close to her heart to teach people to read and write – the children, anyone else who wanted to attend and learn. A kind of Sunday school. The working people would benefit, they would be able to understand what was happening in the world, discuss things, form opinions. But what leisure would they have for reading, what energy left over from their work? She had been assuming a way of life not far different from her own. The answer of course was to reduce the hours of labour, but she could not imagine Erasmus agreeing to this. However, he had other ideas for making things better. The men worked by candlelight at present, but he had spoken of a kind of lamp that might be devised, that they could attach to their caps in some way, no, not caps, they would wear a sort of metal helmet, a modified version of what soldiers sometimes wore. It would be safer, he had said, but the main thing was that better light would save time and so increase production. He sometimes put things in what seemed to her the wrong order . . .

These things might not come soon, but all manner of more immediate reforms could be introduced. She and Erasmus together would make this colliery village a happier place. Other collieries would imitate them, follow suit.

He would listen to her. She had been struck from the first by the way he listened to her, hung on her words. She had been flattered by this attention, the way he confided his plans and designs to her, made her a partner in them.

It was now, thinking this, that a shadow of fear came to her. What he had always sought was her accord, her complete approval and endorsement. Not once had he consulted her on the grounds of opinion, not truly. She remembered his face as it had been when she had taken the pitman's part and defended his choice – and his right – to keep the land and cultivate it for his father's sake, as a memorial to his father's memory. He had not seemed to see the similarity with his own case. He had assumed an air of amusement, which she had not much liked, but he had been surprised and displeased – it had shown in his expression – because she had not seen things exactly as he did. Unendurable to be trapped for ever in his expectations of her, his need for her blessing. Like an imprisonment . . . Her only role, the invariable one of support and assent. But he could be supported in a deeper, more meaningful way; he would come to recognise the value of her independent judgement, which would be exercised for his good. Even disagreeing, always for his sake. He would know she had his interests at heart, his true interests.

The fear, however, persisted. In the toils of guilt and debt and obligation that had long lost all reason, possessed by the need for successes that might silence the voices but never did, he had made a cage for himself and now he wanted to draw her into it. But to draw her in he would have to open the cage door and take the risk of freedom . . .

She looked around the room, the objects in it so familiar, accompanying her through all the stages of her life so far. It was time for a new stage, it was time for her to marry. With this recognition, a kind of partial yielding, Erasmus's face and figure invaded her mind, as if they had been waiting only for that, endowed with an extraordinary vividness and immediacy. She was enveloped in thoughts of him, there was no closing them off. The sense of him – what she knew and what she surmised – was too potent, there was no door that could be closed on it. She knew herself to be strong, not easily daunted or browbeaten; she would not consent to be imprisoned in his judgements; she would give battle if need be. In the fear that she felt there was love and a sense of rising to challenge, a sense that such a moment, such a desire, would never come to her again. She drew the sheet of paper towards her and wrote the first words of the letter: *My Dearest Erasmus* . . .

39

The case of Jeremy Evans had aroused very considerable public interest, and this increased during the period of the adjournment; letters and articles on the topics of Evans in particular and the institution of slavery in general filled the columns of the newspapers. There was a letter from a white man born in the West Indies who maintained that whites could only keep control of the slaves on the sugar plantations if black people were prevented from coming to Britain. Once arriving here, they would see the weaknesses of the whites and learn to despise them, and as a consequence the use of terror that had kept them in subjection on the plantations would be of no avail when they returned, in the face of this new-found contempt for their masters. One letter expressed the fear that white criminals, in order to get rid of their enemies, would organise blacks into gangs of assassins, something that could be done with total impunity, as the confession of a slave could not be offered in court, and he could not give evidence against his master. A man who signed himself 'Humanist' argued that black people living in Britain were unhappy because alien, and therefore constituted a pernicious and dangerous element of society. If unwilling to leave of their own accord they should be shipped back at public expense and the costs recovered by selling them. If they remained in the country they should have no claim to any rights under English law.

When the case was resumed, counsel for Evans continued to argue the irrelevance of colonial laws regarding persons living in Britain, whatever their condition or the colour of their skin.

When Jeremy Evans set foot in England, from that very moment, he had become possessed for the first time since being sold into slavery of rights that were common to all mankind. In England, where liberty was so highly valued, was regarded in fact as a precious birthright, how could it be permitted that he, or any man, should be seized and bound and carried away out of the realm?

Ashton had conferred with Harvey and Compton as to whether Evans should be called on to speak for himself, but it was thought that he might be too assertive, or even combative, to gain the sympathy of the court. Once brought to England he had not accepted his lot, he had run away, sought his own freedom. He had resisted to the best of his strength the attempts to take him by force – it had needed three hireling slave-takers to subdue him. He was not meek in his bearing, he stood up straight and met the eyes of those who questioned him. All of this, it was feared, might go against him. He was useful as a presence in court, a victim of injustice, unoffending, ill-used and helpless. But in the end they decided against calling on him to speak on his own behalf. Harvey even went so far as to advise him to keep his eyes lowered, and his head hanging down a little while he was in the courtroom.

The counsel for Bolton and Lyons, finding no convincing argument for the subordination of British law to the laws of slave-owning communities in America and the West Indies, sought to claim that this lack favoured their case. Since there was no law in England prohibiting slavery, it should be clear to any view not obscured by bigotry or prejudice that the practice was legal. Moreover, if once the slaves learned that in England they were free, they would come flocking in vast numbers and overrun the whole country, to the grave detriment of the economy and the ruin of the sugar trade, as there would be no one left to work on the plantations. This frightening prospect caused some stir in the court, which Compton endeavoured to allay by requiring his learned friends of the defence to enlighten him as to the means by which the slaves, captive and destitute as they were, would be able to undertake such a journey – a question to which no coherent answer was forthcoming.

The Lord Chief Justice made few interventions in this debate.

He was still very much hoping, even at this late stage, that Messrs Bolton and Lyons, seeing that things were going against them – and it was clear that they were – would relinquish their claims of ownership in Evans and withdraw from the case, or that something else might occur that would deliver him from the looming duty of a verdict. Further delays would do nothing to help matters. During the adjournment he had sent people to one of the witnesses of the assault, a widow of some means named Mary Dunning, in an attempt to persuade her to purchase Evans and free him, but she had indignantly refused on the grounds that it abetted the practice of slavery, of which she was a convinced opponent.

As the time passed and the proceedings drew to a close it became clear that a verdict would have to be delivered, that he would have to commit himself to a judgement. He worried that his words, if not extremely well chosen, would set at liberty what had been computed at fifteen thousand blacks at present in condition of slavery in Britain, at a cost to the owners of more than £700,000, his clerks had estimated. A flood of actions would follow, disputes over settlements and wages, claims of coercion against the masters. It was a nightmare. A number of these same owners were members of his club, with whom he took coffee or played faro . . .

Westminster Hall was packed with spectators when the day appointed for the judgement arrived. The public galleries were crowded with black people, awaiting words which they knew would affect them closely. Reporters from most of the major newspapers waited in the body of the court to take down the words of judgement verbatim. Slave owners too were there in good number. To this audience, silent with expectation and tense with conflict, the Chief Justice uttered his ruling in the case of Jeremy Evans.

He had thought long and carefully in preparing the terms of his decision. The only way he could see out of the dilemma was to confine his remarks strictly to the particular situation of the plaintiff, avoiding all reference to the wider issue of slavery as an institution, and restricting his judgement to the specific issue of whether it was legal to take a slave by force out of the country.

The only laws to be enforced, he told the court, were those

of the country where the cause of the action occurred. No justification for the seizure of Jeremy Evans could be established by a negative, by the absence of a law forbidding it, as the defendants had attempted to do. Only positive law could be brought to bear in such a case, and there existed no law that could confer the power claimed by the defendants. It was a power never in use in England that a master should be allowed to take a slave by force to be sold abroad, whether the slave had deserted his service or for any other reason.

He sat up taller in his high-backed chair and raised his voice for the final words of the judgement:

'The cause set forth by the defendants cannot be said to be allowed or approved by the laws of this Kingdom. Therefore the man must be discharged.'

There was an outburst of applause at these words from the crowded galleries, and this had to be hushed by the court attendants, and silence restored, while the judges descended from the bench. Ashton had been disappointed by the narrowness of the Chief Justice's wording, though in some part of his mind he had been prepared for it. All the same, the victory was there, Evans walked free, no longer would it be allowed to return black people by force to the plantations. It would continue to be done, he knew that, but no one could ever again claim that it was lawful. As he rose to shake hands with Evans and his lawyers – both of whom were beaming with delight – and with the various friends and well-wishers who had attended the trial from the first day, he allowed himself to be swept along in the tide of congratulations, moved by the rejoicing he saw on many faces, though by no means all.

That evening he dined out with friends, fellow abolitionists. Toasts were drunk to liberty, to the final end of this iniquitous traffic in human beings, an end just round the corner now – they would see it in their lifetime. There were even toasts to the Lord Chief Justice for this historic ruling, which, someone declared in the euphoria of the occasion, had abolished slavery in England. There was a speech of thanks to Ashton for his selfless efforts on behalf of Evans and his long campaign in the anti-slavery cause.

He arrived home late and made his way to bed, light-headed with the praises and the bumpers of wine. He slept deeply in the first part of the night, but woke at dawn with something of a headache and a strong feeling of thirst. When he had drunk a glass of water he realised with remorse that he had lain down to sleep without saying his prayers, without any word of thanks to the Divine Author for the outcome of the trial. He knelt at his bedside and prayed aloud, asking forgiveness for his neglect, the failure to show gratitude, thanking God for guiding the judge's mind to a right decision. True, it had been narrowly worded, true it had been restricted in scope, doing no more than deny the master's right to compel a slave aboard ship and transport him back to the plantations. But a step had been taken, a decisive step in the struggle he had given his life to.

Then it came to him suddenly, as he still knelt there, that the narrowness of the wording did not matter after all, that it had no significance. He remembered the remarks of his fellow diner, that the judgement had abolished slavery in England at a stroke. An error he had thought it at the time, but he saw now that it might by general belief be converted to truth. This was the line to take, these were the words to promulgate and repeat. As many people as possible must be brought to think that the ruling had abolished slavery in England. If it were said often enough and emphatically enough it would come to be generally accepted as fact, and so it would become true . . . By these means the tide of opinion would swell, it would submerge the quibbles of the law. All slaves setting foot in England would be regarded from that very moment as free. Spurred on by this, they would follow the example of Jeremy Evans, they would repudiate their bondage, smash the yoke. England would truly become the home of freedom, admired and envied among the nations. Ashton felt his heart swell with this tide of liberty, and his eyes filled with tears.

Soon after this dawn and these tears, Percy Bordon and Billy Scotland walked for the first time with the others, across the fields to the mine. Both were possessed by a sense of great occasion, though Percy still laboured with the fear of something monstrous dwelling below, some presence known only by rattlings and thuds and loud puffs of steam.

In spite of this fear, walking with his two brothers and hastening his steps to keep up with them, he felt proud to be entering the world of men. The light was strong enough for them to see the pale radiance of the sun as it rose through faint clouds before them, to the east. There was a sense of waning summer in the air. In the fields beyond the mine, towards the Dene, the wheat stood straight and tall, and there was a luminous gilding on the stalks and ears. From the edges of the wheat fields they could hear the trailing song of the yellowhammers, whether joyous or sad no one could tell.

At the pithead they waited for the banksman's call that the shaft was clear. One by one the men found a space in the swinging rope, made a loop, thrust their limbs through and bound them tightly. This David Bordon did now for the first time – a step forward for him too, to be among the grown men. Michael Bordon took Percy astraddle across his knees, told him to hold tight, grasped the rope with one hand, keeping the other free to guard against collisions with the walls of the shaft during the descent.

Four men, two youths and two children bound and clutched together, strung out along the rope, began the descent into the darkness of the pit. One of the children would spend his life toiling below ground, would never know anything else, would scarcely know anything else existed. The other in the course of time would come up into the light of the world, would move with his family away from the colliery village to a place where the air was more wholesome and the houses more spacious. He would learn to read and keep account books and he would help his two older brothers in the management of the textile factory the family came to own, which gave increased opportunities of employment and brought prosperity to some, and where many small children toiled for long hours. And this difference in the destiny of the two boys was entirely due to a dead miner's dream of freedom.